PENGUIN BOOKS

VOICES IN THE GARDEN

Since 1947 Dirk Bogarde has starred in more than sixty films. His popularity as a teenage idol brought him vast amounts of fan mail and enormous box-office success, which was to continue through the fifties and sixties. Later he achieved a different kind of success with such films as *The Servant, King and Country, Accident, Death in Venice, The Night Porter, Providence, Despair* and *These Foolish Things (Daddy Nostalgie)*.

In recent years he has become well known as a writer with the publication of four volumes of autobiography, *A Postillion Struck by Lightning, Snakes and Ladders, An Orderly Man* and *Backcloth,* and four novels, *A Gentle Occupation, Voices in the Garden, West of Sunset* and *Jericho,* all of which reached the bestseller lists and have been translated into a number of languages. *A Particular Friendship,* a collection of letters written between 1967 and 1970 to an unknown American woman, has also been published.

Dirk Bogarde lived in France for many years and was made a Commandeur de l'Ordre des Arts et des Lettres by the French Government in 1990. In 1985 he was made an Honorary Doctor of Letters at the University of St Andrews. He received a knighthood in 1992.

DIRK BOGARDE

———

VOICES IN THE GARDEN

PENGUIN BOOKS

PENGUIN BOOKS

Published by the Penguin Group
Penguin Books Ltd, 27 Wrights Lane, London W8 5TZ, England
Penguin Books USA Inc., 375 Hudson Street, New York, New York 10014, USA
Penguin Books Australia Ltd, Ringwood, Victoria, Australia
Penguin Books Canada Ltd, 10 Alcorn Avenue, Toronto, Ontario, Canada M4V 3B2
Penguin Books (NZ) Ltd, 182–190 Wairau Road, Auckland 10, New Zealand

Penguin Books Ltd, Registered Offices: Harmondsworth, Middlesex, England

First published in Great Britain by Chatto & Windus Ltd 1981
Published in Penguin Books 1992
3 5 7 9 10 8 6 4 2

Penguin Film and TV Tie-in edition published 1993

For
Charlotte and Jean-Michel Jarre
with my love

Author's Note

The Villa Triton, its owners and their guests, have never existed anywhere other than in my imagination: therefore any resemblance to anyone living or dead is quite coincidental. The same goes for 'Moviedecor Ltd', 'Aesthetic Art Models' and 'The Mayerling Hütte'. To the best of my knowledge no such enterprises ever existed.

I am grateful to Hamish Hamilton Ltd and Harper & Row Inc for permission to quote from André Castelot's excellent book on L'Aiglon, published in England as *Napoleon's Son* and in America as *The King of Rome*; to Mrs Joanna Hart for tracing the song 'Just Once for all Time' (lyrics by Rowland Leigh, from the German 'Das gibt's nur einmal', music by Werner Richard Heymann, lyrics by Robert Gilbert, © 1931 Ufaton Verlagsgesellschaft, reproduced by permission of the copyright owners and of Campbell Connelly & Co Ltd, London), and, as always, to Mrs Sally Betts for her patience in deciphering my original typescript.

D.v.d.B.

When the fire-fly hides its spot,
When the garden voices fail
In the darkness thick and hot, –
Shall another voice avail,
That shape be where those are not?

Robert Browning
From 'A Serenade at the Villa'

Chapter One

The lawn, green and smooth as a length of baize, sloped gently down through tall pines to the far end of the point where it ended in a neat curve, a crumbling stone urn of geraniums, a low stone wall and the end of the land. Beyond the wall, jagged rocks and boulders; shaggy myrtle bushes and a golden broom hung high above the sea.

She walked slowly and deliberately down the middle of the lawn only half aware that her heels were leaving deep holes in the sodden turf and that she had received the full force of one of the sprinklers across the front of her thin silk shirt. It would dry out in a second once she had reached the sunlight at the end of the point, and Archie could grumble as much as he liked about the heel marks. This wasn't a time to be fussy. They'd disappear in a day or two. Anyway, she didn't care. Such a minor thing. Minor things faded into the shadows of major things.

Normally she would have walked down the raked gravel path at the side; that was the rule when wearing heels. But this was not a normal day. Her first essential was to get as far away from the house, from the windows, as possible. Just so that she could have a few minutes quiet to herself. A pulling-together time. Air travel always made her feel displaced and odd, almost unsteady. That could be the wine, wine on an empty stomach. Should have had breakfast before leaving. Simply couldn't eat anything. But it would all be better now that she was home. The last four days would start to fade out in the warmth and peace of the villa.

Wouldn't they?

She had reached the end of the pine-shaded lawn and the

sun almost blinded her as she continued towards the point, screwing up her eyes against the glittering light which bounced off the sea far below. A perfect example of leaving darkness for the light; but only physically. One couldn't do that mentally. Not yet anyway. Mentally it was all dark.

She reached the crumbling urn, automatically dead-headed some geraniums only half looking at them, half looking down at the sea and the ragged line of rocks which ran along the side of the Cap winding away to her left. She threw the faded blooms vaguely over the wall, a listless gesture which scattered them among the myrtle below. On her right, across the bay, the scabby heights of Mont Boron and the old Fort on top, at this time of day soft with blue shadow. That's the trouble with the other side of the bay, no sun in the late afternoon: it was one of the very first things which Archie's father had fussed about from the beginning, when he had first seen the site in the Twenties. Where did the sun rise, where did it set? No point, he had said, in building a house in the South of France which didn't receive the sun at every moment of the day. A senseless thing to do. Since the whole ten acres was, at that time, just one large pine-wood set among great rocks it was difficult to tell immediately, but with maps and compass and carefully planned visits at all times of the day from dawn to dusk over a period of weeks, he had determined that though they would not get the first morning sun, because of the bulk of the Cap behind them, they would have it from about 10 a.m. right through until the last moments of the day.

And I the child-bride. I really didn't give a damn where the sun rose or where it set just as long as it shone and I was in it. I left all the fussing to the others. Fussing is fatiguing. Archie and his father liked fussing: a family trait. So I left it to them. Always have. Did. I'm not a fusser. Not even now.

10

She turned slowly, looking back the way she had come, Wide shaded lawns running up towards the house through a tunnel of tall pines; the few which had remained after the weeks of wrenching, hauling and carting which had gone on for many months in order to secure a level site for the house and its gardens.

Dottie Wrotham said it was like a tiny Blenheim when she saw it first, which was as absurd a remark as Benjie Westlake's when he said that it reminded him of Alcatraz; to which, as far as she knew, he had never been.

Today, embowered in wistaria, plumbago and bougain-villaea, it sat pleasantly among its trees with the comfort and security of constancy. Which was nonsense, of course. There was no real comfort or security now. No constancy. It was a mirage perhaps? A vision shimmering in the air; a reflection of some other time and place. But perhaps that is only me. Others would see it all differently of course. Supposing I said, suddenly to Tonnino, 'Tonnino, stop mulching your hideous Super Stars which I know are the pride and joy of your dreary life, and tell me just what you see up there among the trees?'

He'd take off his straw hat and hold it against his chest and he'd say, 'Nothing, Madame.'

'Nothing, Tonnino? Are you certain? Not a house?'

'Ah yes! A house. The house. Of course, the house. It has been there always.'

'You do not think it a mirage then?'

He would look at me curiously. 'I see the house, Madame,' Thinking I was a bit tipsy again.

And Archie. Archie would be very grotty. He could be at times. 'What are you talking about, Cuckoo? What can I see? The *house*, of course. Arches, windows, terraces, towers and so on. I know every stick and stone and door knob. Should do after fifty years. Are you all right?'

Oh yes. I'm all right. I would have irritated him, of course, because ten to one I'd have interrupted some tremendously involved chain of inner thought. I so often do. The trouble is that I am never perfectly certain if he is just sitting; or just sitting thinking.

Externally there has always seemed to me so little difference. He has a face which conceals thought. Sometimes, looking at him across the terrace in the evenings, it is quite impossible to know if he is re-grouping Poniatowski's troops at Borodino or simply deciding to replace the blue spruce with a willow. Either way it is a matter of complete withdrawal.

She turned her face up towards the sun, closing her eyes; bars of light drifted across her retina slowly. She opened them quickly. My mind's eye. In my mind's eye.

Archie sitting uneasily on the corner of her bed in his Liberty silk dressing-gown, feet in red leather slippers, hair brushed neatly. A brightly wrapped package on his knees.

She replaced the mascara brush in its box and carefully closed the lid. 'There. My eyes are "on". Such a bore, fair eyelashes. I should have them dyed: someone said that you could.' She reached across the cluttered dressing-table for a powder puff. 'You haven't opened your present!'

She saw him in the gilt-swagged oval mirror finger the package thoughtfully. 'I found it in that shop in rue d'Antibes. I don't think it's one you've got, but if it is you can change it. He said so.'

Archie looked up at her over her shoulder into the looking-glass. 'I do rather hate birthdays. Being reminded.'

'Nonsense!' she said briskly and shook the powder puff gently. 'I love them.'

'You aren't sixty. I am. Today.'

'And what's so awful about that? Prime of your life, I'd say.'

'A definite landmark, sixty; we're given three score years and ten, remember.'

'Tosh.' She patted her fine-boned cheeks busily.

'Not tosh to me. I have just seen myself in the bathroom mirrors.'

'Not for the first time, darling, surely!' A light laugh, dismissing.

'For the first time as sixty.'

She turned to face him slowly. 'Archie. What ever is it? You can't have *suddenly* aged overnight! You were fifty-nine yesterday. What awful physical metamorphosis has taken place since last night?'

'My backside is flabby, wrinkled. I'm sort of shrinking. Oh . . .' He waved his hand vaguely over the package on his knee. 'Oh, not since last night, no. It's been taking place for a time now. I have watched the lines. The general,' he looked about him worriedly, 'the general sagging. Sagging. Drooping, age . . . I think it is quite obscene.'

She looked at him with startled eyes, her arms folded, hands in her lap. 'Darling Archie. So dreadfully serious. You have a beautiful figure, perfect skin . . . you always did have. You were always so vain about them.'

'And have no longer. I don't like the way things are going; I'm setting in for the winter, you might say, and I can see what it is going to be like. I dislike it all intensely. Don't care for the way things are settling down. For old age.'

She stared at him helplessly. 'You've *never* spoken like this before: I'm shattered.'

'So am I. Shattered too. Vain men are when faced with reality. Quite simply, I hate what is happening to my body: hate it.' He got up from the bed suddenly, and taking his package with him walked over to the windows and looked out into the golden morning. 'The idea of performing a sexual act repels me.'

Cuckoo let out a little cry of anguish and turned swiftly on her dressing-stool, hand to her mouth with amazement. 'What a terrible thing to say! Archie! You've gone mad. You can't be well.'

'I'm perfectly well. Merely withering. Withering.'

'Stop! Stop!' she cried and covered her ears with her hands.

'I am a fastidious man, as you know . . . don't try not to listen, I shan't say all this again, you know. In any case the "urges", or whatever they call them, are fading. You must have been aware of that for some time now: I no longer have the energy, or the desire . . . the stimulus has died. Dried up, I fear; the juices have gone along with the muscle. I detest it, and I hate to make you sad . . . but there it is. I've said it, and it is fact. It is not your fault, not at all, you are as delightful, maddening, ravishing as you always were but I feel I can no longer be a husband to you in the accepted sense of fulfilling all my duties: I am no longer capable.'

Cuckoo sat stunned with shock. Then very slowly turned back to the dressing-table, automatically found her rings and twisted them on to shaking fingers.

'This is the most dreadful morning of my life,' she said and burst into tears which caused the mascara to run down her cheeks in long ragged lines, and sting her eyes cruelly.

'I think it is a dreadful morning too,' said Archie still at the window with his back to her, 'but I realize that it is easier for me than for you. All passion spent for me.'

She was wiping her eyes desperately with a paper tissue. 'And what about me? What am I to do? You make me feel like a leper!'

'That is unforgivable of me. I intended no such thing. It is I who feel the leper, not you. But you know I have come very seldom to you in the last few years; it has not been a passionate relationship, has it, my dear? For many years now.'

'That has not been my fault, Archie! Not mine! You have grown away from me more and more and gone into your beastly books, your researching, all those damned toy soldiers and bits and pieces of someone's old battles!' She had cleaned her eyes and surveyed the wreckage of a

14

morning's intensive work on her haggard face.

'It's nothing to do at all with toy soldiers or old pieces of somebody's battles, as you call them. But it *had* to do with the war. Our war.' He moved away from the window and sat down on the corner of the bed again.

'Five years of separation. A long time. We were strangers when we met again. Nothing worked after that. Nothing. Oh . . .' He looked hopelessly into some middle distance of his own. 'Oh, there was the old affection, familiarity, habit. But the fires had died. You knew that too. It had all been too long: too far away, too exhausting and we'd changed for ever. It happened to so many people.'

'Don't!' she wailed. 'Don't say another word. You make it too cruel.'

He shrugged and smoothed his hand over the package which he still held. 'It was cruel. The end of physical love, attraction if you like, is always cruel.'

She jammed her fingers into a jar of face cream and started to cover her face with it in angry, desperate, movements. 'You left me first. It was you, Archie. I was always physically in love with you, just remember that.'

He laughed sadly, shook his head. 'You left far before me, my dear, you've been physically in love with every man who ever looked at you: so long as he was younger. What you called "scrumptious", remember? A "scrumptious" young man on a beach, on a yacht, across a dining-table; any young man with a good figure and a modicum of wit and you were an easy lay.'

She gave a little scream of rage as one of her rings, slippery from the cold cream, slipped from her fingers and rolled away across the parquet floor. 'A despicable, filthy thing to say. How can you say such vile things?'

'Easily, sadly. It doesn't matter now. Hasn't. Never did, I suppose. For I knew from the very start that I'd never change you. All I'd done was marry you. And that didn't stop you, did it? Marriage only gave you a licence to "kill", if you can follow what I mean?'

She wiped her face clean, threw the greasy tissues at her feet. 'I can't. I don't know what you mean. You are being utterly deranged and foul.'

He got up again and wandered across to the window, leaning against the folded shutter. 'My dear Cuckoo. If I had cut a notch in that big parasol pine down there for every time you had made a "killing" there would be a damned fine totem-pole standing at the edge of the lawn.'

She turned towards him unsteadily, smoothing her hands carefully. 'What a perfectly ghastly time of day to play the Truth Game. I presume that's what it is? And you've waited forty years to play it. On the morning of your sixtieth birthday. Quite marvellous timing, I suppose. And what, after this quite astonishing confession from you, am I supposed to do? Admit that I was always over-sexed and that you were, shall we say, less demanding? Do you care for that better?'

'I don't like any of it. At all. Stop please, let us stop!'

'No we shall not stop, Archie. You started it and we continue. You come into this room with the most appalling, idiotic, remarks and hurt me quite dreadfully. And now, when I am a ruin – look at me! you want to stop. Typical Archie! Typical. Well, I won't stop. I loved you madly: I thought you were the most god-like thing I had ever seen and I longed to be your wife. And I was. But I didn't know then, how could I?, that the only way you could really make love to me was dressed in full regalia as if you had just arrived from the Richmond's ball before Waterloo!'

'Cuckoo! Stop! Stop this instant!'

'I will not. It is true. Epaulettes, buttons and those damned tassled boots! This obsession with Napoleon and dressing up. How was I to know?'

'As far as I am aware you appeared to enjoy it all very

16

much as well.'

'Of course I did! It was a game. You looked wildly glamorous and dashing. I didn't mind playing your idiotic game if it pleased you, and it was fun at first.' She twisted her rings slowly, looking at her hands intently. 'But in time I realised that there was precious little love about it all. There was no tenderness really, you liked it that way because it hid you; made you feel strong and brave and masculine. It gave you a sense of power, you felt that you were irresistible. To yourself. You were really making love to yourself, Archie, not to me. I sometimes felt that perhaps you were really punishing me: for being barren.'

Archie gave a low cry, muffling it with his fist. She looked up wanly.

'That was a little below the belt. I know. But you are a vain man, you have just admitted that, a vain and selfish man. But the strange thing is that I loved you in my way, and I still do. In spite of all these cruel and idiotic things we are saying to each other after so many years. It was never the kind of marriage either of us hoped for, I know. But we managed. No one knew, I think. A perfectly acceptable marriage until the war. Until then we played your little game when, as you crudely put it, the urge came upon you. And when it did not, then I skipped off with the gypsies in the woods. I admit that. I had a simply marvellous time. But no one was really hurt, Archie? Were they?' She reached out a hand towards his bowed back. 'And I came back. I never threw my bonnet over any windmill to that extent. We tried after . . . and we failed. But we stayed together, didn't we?'

He raised his head and stared out across the gardens below. She folded her hands together on her knee.

'What an odd conversation. After so long.' She shrugged and laughed softly to herself. 'Oh, my dear! You knew very well what I was when we married all those years ago. The giddy, golden gel. Cuckoo. In and out of

17

everyone's nest. That was the saying, wasn't it? I was one of the good times had by everyone.'

He had lowered his head and rested it against the cool glass of the window. 'Oh, dear God,' he said.

She briskly addressed herself to her own reflection in the looking-glass. 'What a mess. Me. Not us really. Me at this moment. I think we have managed pretty well, frankly.' She smoothed her face and throat with slender hands. 'And here we still are. You say that your backside is sagging and your body withering, and I know that I'm really too old for much more cuckooing and in any case you are now about to take the veil, God knows why! I should have thought that a uniform would cover any undesirable signs . . . if you can find someone to play the game.'

He cleared his throat. 'It would make me feel obscene. Doing that. At sixty.'

'Oh, the vanity of it! The sheer vanity! All passion spent, you said. What utter nonsense when there really never was any: on your part, at least.' She reached out and found a jar of foundation cream and unscrewed the lid angrily. 'Well, I'm vain too. And a little younger than you. I'm not going into a convent just because you've discovered wrinkles on your bottom or anywhere else for that matter.' She started spreading the pale cream across the gentle contours of her face. 'I'm not dead yet, my dear. Not yet. Not by a long chalk.'

Not yet.

But that was ten years ago. She pushed herself away from the stone wall, saw that the sun had dried her shirt, ran long fingers through her still fair hair and started to walk slowly back towards the house. What an absurd morning that had been. What a peculiar morning. Archie going through his change of life with a vengeance.

And what a very strange time to remember it all now.

18

Life had gone on, after all. She trod carefully along the gravel path. On her left through the trees the wide bay glittered in the afternoon sun; the American frigate, she saw, was still there where it had been the day she left, lying like a grey plastic toy in a washbowl, a liberty boat leaving in a curving creamy wake for the harbour. Tonnino had replanted the long-walk bed in her absence with ugly little pink and red begonias. It looked like a municipal park in Stockport. Oh for phlox, lupins, canterbury bells and pretty-maids-all-in-a-row! The tumbled splendour of English gardens she had known. But we have begonias. To thrive in half-shade. Like me. I must try to thrive in half-shade. Only it is just possible that I shall find it not something that I can do. Easily.

She saw Archie standing at the top of the slope ahead of her as she left the shade of the trees and went up towards the terrace. Blue blazer, buttons winking, flannels crisp: neat, trim, elegant as befitted a military historian. A seventy-year-old historian who looked, from this distance and in the glowing sun, a very good fifty-six. She felt, for the first time in some days, a little charge of pleasure at the familiar, comforting sight of him. The shade thinned a little. Shadows slipped away. Almost. A nightlight in the nursery. That is Archie now. My nightlight, dispelling a little the bogies, admitting the gentle forms of safe, familiar things. She was comforted as he raised a hand in careful greeting, and waved back, hurrying up the last few steps of the slope to take both his offered hands in hers, smiling.

He shook his head wryly. 'Capricious creature. Took us all by surprise as usual: a day early and no real warning.' He bent to kiss her cheek, his lemony scent refreshing and cool, his hands firm, secure, holding.

'I just couldn't take another day in London. Drizzle and grey, and hundreds of Arabs flopping along to Harrods as if it were Mecca.'

'Probably is to some of them.'

'So I just decided to get an earlier flight. Ducked a frightful dinner for some Chinese diplomat at the Harper-Gore's tonight. That really settled it. I'd done all I had to do . . . so I just came home.'

Little lies, she thought, have always come easily to me. How fortunate.

'I would have met you, darling. But I'd fixed luncheon with Willie and Gogie.'

She patted his hand and started up the terrace steps. 'No point. Angelo was there with the car. One small suitcase. All so simple.'

He fussed her gently into a chair. 'You must be dead.'

'Not quite.'

'Eat on the 'plane?'

'Never do. Half a bottle of Krug, and Bruna's getting me a sandwich.'

The terrace was dappled with shade from the wistaria. Fat cane chair with cushions, low tables, great pots spilling with ferns and rustling palms, rather like an Edwardian conservatory. Which had been the idea originally. At the far end a small fountain bubbled softly, dribbling from the mossy mouth of a marble frog. She lay back with relief.

'Four days in London and I'm a wreck. Isn't it odd? One loved it so once upon a time . . . but now. Ugly, harrassed people. Not English at all. Traffic, awful smells, it's all gone. The elegance, the fun, the Capital City feeling. It's like one enormous suburb. Everywhere one looked there were chatters of little Japanese, black men, ladies in cheap saris and cheaper sandals, and the Arabs . . . I'm very glad to be home.'

Bruna came out on to the terrace with a tray which she set before her.

'Dear Bruna! You spoil me. So good.'

Bruna shrugged indifferently. 'You want a glass of wine? It's there. Smoked salmon sandwiches, but only

Norwegian. If I'd known earlier . . .' She went back into the house, straightened something on a table, went away.

'Thoroughly spoiled I am. I do like it.'

Archie smiled vaguely. 'How did it go then? Everything all right?'

For a second her eyes widened with alarm. Then she recovered her wits and took a small triangle of brown bread. 'Wonderfully well . . .' She poured herself a glass of wine quickly.

Archie crossed his legs, carefully adjusting his creases. 'Harriet has always been an arranger. Arranged everyone in your unfortunate family as far as I can see. Poor Richard! And those wretched girls. A frightful bully.'

'Not a bully. An arranger is better. Takes after Mamma. I was never like that, as you well know; she's always been good at weddings and picnics and Christmas and she really did this splendidly. That house in Pavilion Road, Constance Spryery in every corner, bridesmaids in Kate Greenaway dresses, all as plain as pikestaffs, of course, but there you are, poor little things. Even a couple of Royals to add lustre to the wedding photographs and a trendy Lord to take them.' She finished the sandwich. 'You'd have hated it.'

She took a long sip of her wine and reached for another sandwich.

Archie patted one pocket for his cigarette case, another for his lighter, found both and carefully started his routine. Choose the cigarette, close the case, back in pocket, close pocket flap, cigarette to lips, lighter to cigarette, cupping one hand against a non-existent flame, one deep breath, lighter back in pocket, pocket flap closed. Cigarette examined thoughtfully. He relaxed.

She watched him as if from a long distance.

'Hated it,' he said finally. 'Can't think what on earth you went for. Trailing all that way to London, middle of June. Not like you at all.'

21

'I suppose that I have a sort of rarity value. Aunt Cuckoo from her villa in the South of France. Raffish old girl who once knew the Murphys, the Fitzgeralds and danced a tango in a restaurant with Isadora Duncan . . . faded glamour.'

Archie puffed his cigarette slowly. 'Shouldn't have thought that Harriet or one member of her family knew who any of those people were. Far too solid and dim, no sense of fantasy at all.'

Unlike you, she thought, can you really believe that cigarette is alight and that you are enjoying it? That's fantasy all right. Ever since the very first scare about tobacco you've been 'pretending' to have your cigarette.

'Harriet absolutely begged me. I simply couldn't have not gone,' she said.

Harriet had written, in her poky handwriting, across the Cartier invitation: 'Know not a chance you'll come. It'll be a frightful scrum too, and couldn't put you up, but wizard if you did, so just treat this as info.'

Harriet had never forgotten that she had risen to giddy heights in the WAAF in the war, and had secretly hoped that there would be another before she was too old to join up again. The hopes had long faded. So she 'arranged' instead.

'Such a frightful expense,' said Archie tapping invisible ash off his cigarette.

'I didn't cost you a penny! Stayed with Dottie, as you know, in the greatest discomfort, went "economy" and never entered a shop.' She finished the wine, refilled her glass. Aware of his awareness. Not caring.

'No. I didn't mean you, my dear. The wedding. Nonsense. That girl will never stay the course. She'll be off again after a long week-end. Not steady.'

'She may. He's attractive; in an Estate Agents or something. He's quite grand and so are the Estate Agents. They both like horses, tennis and sheep-dog trials. And

Caroline is twenty-seven, no chicken. Time she stayed put.'

'Well, as long as it amused you.'

The only thing that amused me was Harriet's face of blank astonishment when I arrived. Everything else bored me witless. But it was a heaven sent excuse to go, so I had to take it. 'I like people, Archie dear, I like the gaiety and the fun and all that nonsense. I know you hate it, but I don't. Just once in a while it does one good to get away; to keep in touch.'

'You do plenty of that, I should have thought, here . . . all summer. The place is like an hotel.'

'And no one bothers you, dear. You hide away in your museum . . . so don't fuss about that.'

'I do wish you wouldn't call it a museum. Quite wrong. Study. My office if you like, but not a museum.'

She took another sandwich, sipped her wine. 'Whatever you like. Have you done very much while I've been away?'

He flicked imaginary ash from his cigarette, trod it carefully into the marble at his feet. 'Not much. Not really. Don't work frightfully well if you aren't somewhere about.' He smiled bleakly. 'Habit, I suppose. I feel uneasy, can't seem to settle down to things properly. Finished off the Schönbrunn chapter: made some notes for the next part. Nothing much.'

'Well, I'm here for the summer.' She ate the sandwich quickly, smothering a sudden rising fear. 'Cross fingers anyway. So you can work away happily.'

He looked up suddenly. 'Why cross fingers? Slipping off again somewhere?'

'No. No. Of course not. Just a saying. After all, one can never be sure of anything these days, it's all so fragile. Life, I mean.'

'Well. We all get older. Inevitable process. I do hate it so.'

'There is no need to embrace it in headlong flight,

Archie dear. Ten years ago you literally ran towards it, I remember. Hurried yourself: made your vows. So silly.'

He shifted uncomfortably, stubbed out the cigarette carefully, got to his feet. 'We won't go into that again. I'm glad you're back safe and sound.'

She finished the wine, held the empty glass between slender fingers, swinging it lightly by the bowl. 'Yes, safe and sound. And we won't have a busy summer this year. It's all a bit too much, you know, for Bruna. She gets awfully fussed now. It is a lot to do – guests, changing sheets, extra meals. She's getting older too, and no help really now that Maria has left. So you can settle down to work and have a long, happy summer with your Duc de Reichstadt and all his neurotic worries.'

He was standing, hands in his pockets, looking out across the bay towards Villefranche glowing in its concrete sprawl. 'What will you do, my dear?' A long quiet summer is something you'd hate. I reckon you've asked half the wedding party to stay if I know you.' He turned towards her with a mild smile. 'No Cuckoo's picnic? Impossible!'

She set the glass gently on the little tray, ate the last of the small sandwiches, brushed her lips with a slim finger. 'No. No picnic. I don't really feel up to picnics, they do get boring in the end. And anyway everyone is off to Greece now; less spoiled, they say. All the Young, that is . . . and I don't really want Harriet and Richard and the family: so I didn't say a word.' She got up and joined him, taking his hand, smiling, head on one side. 'We'll Darby-and-Joan it, shall we? Glide towards the sunset?'

He laughed softly. 'You are wicked. I bet you've got something up your sleeve. I know you far too well.'

She folded her arm in his, pressed it firmly. 'You don't know me at all. After all these many years you still don't know me, I'm deep as a well . . . and you have never lowered your bucket down very far.'

He kissed her cheek. 'Oh, I don't know. I don't know

about that. Fact is that the water at the top, so to speak, was so delicious, I didn't really need to. Will that do?'

'Thank you. Prettily put, but I expect that you fear the water at the bottom of a well might be rather . . .' she looked up into his clear blue eyes '. . . muddy?'

He laughed, and disengaged nimself. 'You are a dotty one. No. I never cared for mud.' He wandered up to the fountain as Bruna came on to the terrace and started to clear the tray.

'Enough?' she said.

'Quite enough, Bruna dear, delicious. If there is one glass of wine left I'll take it up to my room, I'm going to have a little rest.'

'And for supper? Just the two of you?' She poured the last of the wine, and offered the glass. 'Here you are. Lamb with new peas, a salad. If that will do.'

'It will do admirably.' She took the glass and followed Bruna into the house. 'It all looks so pretty and fresh. Flowers. You are good, Bruna.'

Bruna shrugged her shoulders. 'It is always the same. I don't alter things, it is routine. There is some mail for you. In your room, and three messages, none are important, they will call back. I wrote the names.'

The drawing-room was cool, lofty. White on white, which had been so fashionable when it was first designed, and still was, she thought. White walls, white chintzes, a great white rug on the honey-coloured parquet floor, polished like an ice rink. Bowls of flowers, photographs in silver frames, her John portrait over the fireplace, the Sickerts, the Magrittes which had seemed so daring, the little Bonnard of lilac in a jug. A catholic collection, someone had said; all of it rather 'lapsed', but far better than the family-portraits and the Dutch still-lifes which Archie's father had hammered to the walls and which she had removed almost as soon as his coffin had been trundled aboard the train for Calais and the family

25

mausoleum outside Marlborough. Archie had fussed, of course, but what the eye can't see the heart won't grieve for, and his father's corpse, rattling along through the English countryside, in which he had not set a foot for many years, was just that, and could no longer raise objections. Could no longer raise. For death, she thought, turning away from the cool white room and crossing the marble-floored hall to the wide stairs, was dauntingly final. As she reached the gallery Archie's voice came echoing up under the vaulted ceiling.

'You off then?'

'A little rest . . . look at my letters. I suddenly feel quite weary.'

'You do that. Good idea. I may get Angelo to run me into Beaulieu, I'm short of very large envelopes.'

His voice faded slightly as she walked along to her room at the end of the long corridor. She called back over her shoulder. 'I'll see you later, darling', and opened the polished walnut door into her room.

Tiredness fell away from her like an old, heavy coat once she had locked the door and moved across the familiar room, among cherished, personal things. Bruna had unpacked and put everything away. The shutters were closed; her bed, under its yellow silk canopy, made down; a crystal jar of cornflowers glowing on the swagged dressing-table among pots, bottles and silver-backed brushes.

She put her wine glass down, sat heavily on the little stool, eased her feet from her shoes, stared at her face in the oval mirror.

Weary, yes. Lines at the eyes, at the side of her mouth, across her brow. She ran her fingers through her hair, pulled it roughly back from her forehead, turned into profile and saw the slight sag under her chin, the tendon in her neck running from shoulder to ear, the freckles scattered lightly on her hand. She shrugged and reached for her glass, draining it in one. Age. Age creeping on. The inevitable process, Archie had said, and at sixty-eight what else could one expect? A general wearing down. One was not indestructible like the Bonnard in the drawing-room, or even this dressing-table, the chaise-longue on gilded legs, the great pine outside the window, the shadowy blue hills across the bay. None of these would fade or suddenly disintegrate. Unless someone took an axe to them, or burned them with fire, they would last for centuries still, and silently mock human frailty. She put out her hand, thrust it gently among the tight blue heads of the cornflowers. Frailty. You have only days. I, months. Perhaps.

Abruptly she rose and crossed on stockinged feet to her little day-room; boudoir it had once been called, but that had connotations of the courtesan and she really couldn't have ever been called that, however cruel the tongues had been. On her desk a small pile of letters, none of which, from the handwriting, interested her enough to open immediately, and three messages, in Bruna's tumbling scribble, which were local and could wait. Or be ignored. The room was circular, with high windows overlooking the bay and out towards the sea. She pushed the shutters open and felt the late sun fold her in comforting warmth, smelled the resin of the trees and the damp, green scent of the watered lawns rising up in the still afternoon. Leaning over the iron balcony she looked down over the trees to the still diamond-sparkling sea and the white triangular sails of little yachts tacking idly to and fro; a man on water-skis described a graceful arc, swung out, and was lost to her sight below the rocky cliff which fell away steeply through the trees beyond the path which bordered the emerald lawns, as Tonnino came slowly tramping up towards the house, a hoe over his shoulder and basket of bright pea-pods on his arm.

'Bonjour, Tonnino,' she called.

He stopped, looked up, shading his eyes, saw her,

removed his straw hat. 'Bonjour, Madame.' He raised the basket. 'Two kilos. The second picking.'

'Splendid!'

'But not enough rain to swell them. I water them from the well. But we need rain.'

He crunched past the house towards the kitchens. She remained at the rail, looking across the garden, smiling gently. 'I'm as deep as a well,' she had said, 'and you fear the water at the bottom might be muddy.' Archie had moved away. 'Never cared for mud,' he had said.

She laughed aloud, a small, caught sound, and turning from the balcony started to undo the buttons of her silk shirt as she went back into her room. On a small Sheraton card-table, under a Beardsley drawing of a black page-boy dressed only in a turban and earrings, three bottles on a silver tray. She opened the vodka and poured herself a half glass, and shrugging one arm out of her shirt carried the drink into her bedroom, where she drank half of it straight down and then sat on the edge of her bed, catching her breath, letting a solitary tear spill down her cheek and run slowly into the corner of her mouth. For moments she sat staring blankly ahead, seeing nothing but the ugliness of the waiting-room. The black marble fireplace, the grey net curtains at the windows, a table in the middle of the room stacked with tidy piles of thumbed, out-of-date magazines, *Punch*, *Woman's Journal*, *Country Life*. Matched chairs in maroon leatherette standing round the oatmeal walls, the uneasy silence broken by the whispering tick-tock of a tarnished brass clock on the veined marble mantelshelf standing between a copper jug of dried honesty and a signed, sepia photograph of the Princess Royal.

An odour of dust and methylated spirits. The sudden crack of the door hinges, and the soft rustle of the receptionist's overall.

A sharp nose. pink-rimmed glasses, hair in a net. 'Would you care to come along now, Lady Peverill? Haven't we

28

had a lovely day today.'

The best day of my life, I'd say. The best bloody day of my life. That was the best.

She swallowed the rest of the vodka, turned the glass upside down, let it fall to the smooth sheets and roll softly to the end of the bed.

All done. All finished. She pulled her arm from the other sleeve and let the silk shirt spill to the floor at her feet. No picnic this summer. We won't have any picnic this year. All done. All finished. Oh shit! Oh shit! Slowly she lay down on her side, pressed her face deep into the pillow, hands tight to her mouth, and allowed herself the extreme indulgence of weeping in hopeless despair, for the first time.

The sun was still high when she awoke from an exhausted sleep over an hour later, the lawns below were deep in shade on the cliff side of the garden, but the point at the far end was bathed in golden light and far out to sea a slim white ship moved smoothly to the west, probably bound for Marseilles or Barcelona. A cruise ship; she didn't know where it was going. She knew where she was going, that was the main thing. She buttoned the deep pockets of the safari jacket, buckled the belt tightly round her still slender waist, pushed her feet into a pair of worn espadrilles, and crossing to her dressing-table carefully removed her rings and the one bracelet which she had worn all day, and tumbled them into a drawer. In the mirror her face looked drawn without make-up, her eyes still puffed from sleep and the idiot tears of self-pity which she was ashamed to have shed. Her mouth tasted stale, bitter, even though she had cleaned her teeth, and her hair, roughly pulled back and tied with a bit of ribbon, made her look quite ordinary, just an ordinary woman with rather good bones. Those she had, and ran a hand down her cheek, in a light caress. Drab, my dear, just a drab. Like someone's maid.

No one has seen you look like this for years and years; and no one will.

She closed the bedroom door softly behind her and went quickly down the wide staircase on silent feet. The hall was still, empty. From the kitchens a clattering of china and Bruna's scolding voice raised and as suddenly cut off as a door slammed. She crossed the hall swiftly, the terrace, with the soft sound of bubbling water from the fountain; she hurried down the steps, across the lawn to the little path which led to the cliff through the trees. She hadn't been this way for ages – it was steep and zig-zagging, overgrown with broom, spiked with tall agave – but she was soon out of sight of the house. At the end of the path, she knew, there was a tiny cove of almost flat rocks from which, in other days long past, they had swum in the deep water before they had built the swimming pool on top, to save the long clamber up to the house. This had been one of the best picnic sites on the land, secret, silent, shaded by one great wind-writhen pine, and they had all humped baskets, towels, ice buckets, and hampers of white wine to the rocks, sometimes even a portable gramophone with Layton and Johnston or Yvonne Printemps, for Archie. So long ago. It was more fun than the great new pool up at the point. But things change, fashions alter; legs grew less limber and the track up became tiresome.

She stood at the edge of the flat rock and looked across the wide bay to the Darse behind its long jetty. A little yacht with a red and white sail slid gently into the harbour; the American frigate, down to her left, had swung round and presented only its broad stern, the flag hanging like a rag in the still air. There was no one about. No sound save the gentle flap and slap of the sea sliding along the rocks in little curls of white frilly foam, crickets, sawing in the dry grasses, bees among the blazing yellow broom. She idly kicked a fallen pinecone, watched it roll down the smooth rock and bob into the water, swirl steadily away in the current, and then unbuttoning the pockets of the safari jacket she looked about for the stones which she would need. There was a good selection and she chose prudently, weighing them carefully in her hand as if she was choosing lobsters. She pushed two medium ones into her right pocket and one larger one of about the same weight into the left one. Stood upright feeling the pull of her shoulders, rebuttoned the flaps, and pushed a couple more, for good measure, and to make perfectly sure, into her two breast pockets. She buttoned them up as she walked slowly down the steeply shelving rock which thrust out into the sea like a narrow causeway for some distance, its colour gradually changing from crystal clear, turquoise, deep emerald until it was suddenly dark, sapphire blue where it fell away into the depths. Cupping the two bulging pockets with her hands she moved slowly and carefully through the water, feeling it rise above her ankles, swirl about her shins, the rock becoming slippery, under her feet, the jacket pulling as she released her hands and spread her arms wide to keep her balance until she reached the edge. A quiet voice behind her jerked her to a stop: she almost fell, arms swinging to keep upright, the water dragging at the hem of her skirt.

'That's a fucking silly thing to do.'

She stood frozen, then lowered her arms slowly, bowed her head. 'Don't, don't, don't,' she said and started to shuffle on but felt a hand grab her arm and pull her back. She swung her free arm up to strike it away, but the grip was too tight and as she tried to wrench herself loose she slipped and fell heavily backwards pulling a naked body down with her into a flurry of foam and seething water on to the rock, struggling violently against the restraining arms and the weight of the stone-filled pockets of her jacket. A vicious blow across her face stilled her suddenly, and choking and retching from the water which she had swallowed she allowed herself to be dragged slowly up the shelving rock until her head and shoulders were clear of

31

the swirling sea, and she lay, half in, half out, gasping, sobbing, snorting; mucus, tears and salt water streaming down her ashen face. The hands were pulling at the pockets, the stones dragged out and rolled away, and then they were under her shoulders and she was inched up out of the water, rolled on to her face and pummelled violently so that she retched, gulped, spluttered. And lay still.

'You're all right. Didn't swallow much. What the bloody hell were you up to?'

The arms dragged her to a slumped sitting position; she rested against a wet body, her eyes closed tightly; a hand, smoothed hair away from her face, brushed it gently back over her ears. I suppose I lost the ribbon, she thought, and tried to open her eyes. A blur of stinging water. The hand wiped her face with strong, careful fingers. She regained focus; the flat, shining sea, the shadowy blue across the bay, a gull wheeling idly. She looked slowly up into the face of a young man, blue eyes narrowed, firm mouth, good brow creased with anxiety, fair hair sea-sleek to his head. She regarded him through half-closed eyes: he appeared to be completely naked.

'You've cut your knee,' she said, and started to cough. He pushed her forward and thumped her on the back a couple of times. She waved a weak hand to stop him.

'I'm all right. It hurts to do that.' She lay back against his raised leg, catching her breath.

'All right? Got your wind?'

'You interfered.'

'Got any more of those?'

'What?' She closed her eyes against the glare of the sun.

'Clichés. What was I supposed to do? Just sit on my arse and watch you walk on the waters?'

'It's my business. This is private land, you know.'

'I didn't know. You could have broken your neck.'

'You interfered, pushed me over on the rock. My arm hurts.'

32

He suddenly moved away from her, and she flopped heavily on to her back, staring up at him.

'Come on,' he said. 'Try and get to your feet, see if you can move anything.'

'I wish I was dead.'

'You bloody would have been. Give me your good arm, come on, you can't stay here all evening.'

'I can if I want to. It's my land.'

He reached down and took her hand firmly, eased her upwards, until he could take her in both arms and pull her lightly to her feet. For a moment they stood together locked in a close embrace.

'Now. Try and stand by yourself, can you? Nothing broken?' He let her go slowly.

She stood swaying, stretched both her arms outward, flexed her fingers, straightened her back. 'Nothing broken. My arm hurts, my elbow. I fell on it.' He's not naked. A little blue slip with a silver buckle. He's very beautiful, and very cross. 'A scrumptious'. She smiled a wavering smile. 'But I'm all right. I'm all right really. If you could help me . . . to the side there; in the sun. Sit down for a moment.'

He helped her over the rock, on to a tussock of springy grass and thyme. She sat gingerly, taking her weight with her good arm. He squatted beside her.

'You ought to get out of those things, soaking wet.'

'I will, in a minute. I'm not quite pulled together yet.'

'Where do you live?'

'Up there. The house is up there, at the top of the path.'

'Can't see anything.' He was squinting up through thick lashes lightly rimmed with dried salt.

'No. No. You can't from here. This is a secret place. Was.'

'It's very steep.'

'I'll manage, in a minute. Would you help me?'

'Of course.'

33

'There will be people. My husband, the servants, you won't say anything?'

'No. But you'd better get rid of the stones in your top pockets.'

Nervously she fumbled with her hand at the buttons, he watched her in silence making no further effort to help. She undid one pocket, tugged at the large round stone, dropped it into the grass and started on the second flap.

'You could say you were collecting them. For a rockery,' he said.

She threw the second, larger, stone down towards the rock below. It skittered across the smooth surface, plopped heavily into the sea.

'I am a keen gardener, and I detest rockeries.' She scraped the hair from her face. 'I just fell . . . you'll say that? I just fell, caught my ankle and you pulled me out. You'll say that?'

'If that's what you want.'

'Yes. Say that.' She rebuttoned the two pockets deliberately. 'They won't be very surprised, you'll see. I am always in some kind of . . . trouble. My name is Cuckoo, so that explains things, doesn't it? Do admit?'

'If you say it does, fine.'

'Well, it does. To me. What's your name?'

'Pollock, Marcus.'

'How did you get here, it's all private.'

'You've said that before. I didn't know; came along the rocks, through a broken fence along there. I've walked.'

'From Villefranche?'

He smiled suddenly and looked very young, twenty; not that. 'There. Via Shepherd's Bush.'

'Shepherd's Bush? London. You walked?'

'No. Hitched a lift in a furniture van. Two days it's taken. Come on, I'll help you up. You'll catch your death.'

They started slowly towards the zig-zag track. He stopped.

34

'I've got some jeans.'

'It doesn't matter, it's the seaside. Besides, it looks more . . . convincing in those, we are both wet. I'm all right if you'll just give me your arm: it's the *moral* support I'll need at the top, if you wouldn't mind.'

'I don't mind. Take it easy though; don't sprint.'

'Not likely to do that.'

For a few moments they walked in silence.

'Where are you staying? In the town?'

'No. Got a sleeping bag. Travelling light. I've also got a Camembert, a loaf, a six-pack of beer. I was going to doss down there, on your private land, until tomorrow.'

'Well, you still can, of course.'

'Deeply grateful, Mam.'

She ignored the sarcasm, held his arm firmly, clambered on up, her skirt heavy with water, dragging, rasping her shins, the safari jacket clammy and suddenly cold as they moved up into the shade of the pines at the top.

'There's the house. You see? It's not far now. I can manage this part on my own, I mean without your arm. It's quite level.' She disengaged herself, smoothed her hair again, patted her skirt. 'God. I must look frightful.' She was shivering.

'Well, if you can cope all right, I'll just clear off.'

She turned in anxiety towards him. 'Oh no! No, don't go, please, you must help me out . . . about it all. You're my witness. I just fell.'

He looked at her steadily with unsmiling blue eyes. 'You just fell. Caught your ankle or something. I pulled you out?'

She nodded slowly. 'Yes. You did too. Didn't you?' She turned and started ahead. 'But it won't change anything.'

'Not my business.'

'No. Not at all,' she said.

As they reached the edge of the lawns Archie and Bruna came hurrying down the terrace steps, colliding together at the sight of the two figures coming slowly towards them.

'Cuckoo!' His voice was high with anxiety. 'We've been looking for you. What on earth happened?'

Bruna ran towards her, arms outstretched. 'You are wet! You've been in the sea!'

'I'm so sorry. So sorry. I'm quite all right, Archie dear, quite all right really. I fell, so silly, down at the old picnic place.'

Bruna hurriedly put her arms around her sodden shoulders and started to move her towards the house.

'Bruna, dear Bruna, don't drag me. I'm rather stiff, my arm hurts. This kind young man is Mr Pollock. You pulled me out, didn't you? So lucky, he was . . . you were swimming there, weren't you?'

'Yes. Swimming.'

'Wasn't that lucky, Archie?'

'You shouldn't go down there alone, it's frightfully dangerous. Come along, let's get you to bed. I'll call Poteau.'

'I don't need a doctor, Archie. Just stiff, and wet. Don't fuss.' She turned at the first step and raised her hand towards Marcus. 'It was so good of you. I'm most terribly grateful . . . terribly grateful. I'll just get out of these things. You won't go away, will you? Archie, give him a drink.'

'Get upstairs, Cuckoo. Bruna, take her to bed. I'll call Dr Poteau.'

He watched the two women cross the terrace and into the house.

Marcus was standing at the foot of the steps, barefoot on the gravel path; he pushed his hand through almost dry hair. 'I'll be off then,' he said.

Archie turned quickly. 'Oh no, don't go. Do have a drink, something. Beer? I'll just call the doctor, I think I'd better. Come up into the drawing-room, drinks are all there. Do help yourself. Come along, I'll show you the way, just must get Poteau.' He hurried up the steps leaving the boy to follow slowly, stand awkwardly at the terrace doors.

'Over there, on that little table,' said Archie, waving vaguely across the drawing-room. 'Help yourself. Please do, anything you like.' He hurried out into the hall and Marcus, crossing the thick white carpet uncomfortably, heard him start to dial a number.

The decanters on the table sparkled in the last of the sun. He looked round the big white room, feeling uneasy, barefoot and practically naked among the deep white chairs, bowls of flowers, shining wood, silver frames. Abruptly he walked back on to the terrace, leant against one of the marble pillars, cold on his back. Archie came hurrying out, worried, aged and thin, as if he had been pressed for a long time between the pages of a book.

'Ah, there you are. He's coming right away . . . lucky I caught him. I don't know your name, do I? Did my wife mention it. Such a worry.'

'Yes, she did. Pollock.'

'It was so good of you. What on earth did she do?'

'Slipped. On a flat rock. It wasn't anything much. Just a little fall.'

'Bit of a shock, of course. At her age. She's tired, just come back from London.' He was twisting one of the brass buttons on his blazer. 'I say, no drink? Won't you have something?'

'No thanks. All my gear is down there. Haversack, wallet, so on. I'd better go back.'

'You were down there, were you? By the rock?'

'She said it was private land, I didn't know. I'm sorry.'

Archie stopped twisting his button and threw up his hand. 'Oh no! It's quite all right – I think the fence fell down years ago, never go down that way – most welcome, thank God you were, I'm really so deeply grateful.'

'That's all right. It wasn't anything. Well,' he put out his hand. 'I'll clear off, don't want everything pinched.'

Archie took his hand, shook it vaguely. 'No. Well, off you go. I can't thank you enough, anything you need . . .'

It's all right if I stay there? For tonight?'

'Of course! Of course, long as you like. Do. Please. Got a tent thing, have you?'

'Yes.'

'Splendid.' He suddenly looked at Marcus for the first time, and smiled apologetically. 'What *am* I thinking about? You must come up here. Masses of rooms, the place is like an hotel . . . you can't sleep on the beach.'

'No, really, I'm fine.'

'I insist! Come back here. We'll fix you up for the night. My wife would never forgive me. Of course, you come up here. Go and get your things at once, we'd be delighted, so grateful.'

'I'm fine, really thanks.'

'Mr Pollock, you have done us the greatest service, the least we can do is give you a bed for the night. Now I'm going up to see my wife; see you down here, in what?, twenty minutes or so? You know where the drinks are. Off you go.'

Marcus stood for a moment uncertainly. 'Jeans and a sweat shirt. That's all.'

'Absolutely perfect. I shan't be in tails.'

'Okay. Thanks. Twenty minutes.' He turned and crossed the lawns towards the trees.

Archie stood perfectly still watching his retreating figure. The blond head, broad shoulders, long legs. Six foot something. Must be. I know I've seen him before. I know I have. I know the *face*. He bit the side of his thumb thoughtfully. Where? Don't know the name. Speaks well. Somebody's son we know? No. No one I've *met*. Just seen him somewhere. In the town perhaps. Was he at the Russells' last week? Lot of young people there . . . could have been. He walked slowly across the drawing-room and into the hall as Bruna came down the stairs with Cuckoo's wet clothing in her hands.

'She's in bed. I made her. She's cold and shocked and very tired.'

'I'm going up. Poteau's on his way, tell him to come straight up, will you.'

'What a thing to do. Down on the rocks; she's not a girl any longer.'

'Nothing broken?'

'She can move everything. She'll be bruised, you see. She's so foolish.'

'She's a worry,' he said and started up the stairs. At the first landing he stopped, his eyes wide with surprise. He struck the stone bannister with his fist. *That's* who he is! Of course! I knew, I knew! He stared unseeingly along the wide corridor ahead. Of course he is. He's l'Aiglon!

Chapter Two

She had the widest blue eyes he had ever seen. Startled; a surprised child propped up among pillows in the enormous canopied bed, wrapped in a frilly bed-jacket, a black velvet bow in her hair, two gold bracelets on the arm which was not in a sling.

'I have told Bruna to put you in the "bachelor's room"; it's rather small, but I do think you'll be happier there. The others are so large. It has a divine view right down to the sea. Rather more comfortable than the picnic place.' She had tilted her head to look up at him, smiling. 'You really are quite amazingly tall. Six foot something?'

'One. About.'

'Tremendous. So fortunate. I always wanted to be tall. But tall girls are not really awfully popular; or at least they weren't in my day. So I settled for being a bantam. Would you call it . . . pint-size?'

'I'd call it absolutely the right size.'

'Lud!' she cried throwing up her good hand lightly. 'He flatters me! Isn't it too maddening that I have to stay here, in this boring old bed? Nothing broken. Bruised and frightfully stiff and I bashed this elbow, it throbs like billy-o. I'll be up and about tomorrow, you'll see.'

Bruna, who had been standing silently in the wide bay of the window with clasped hands before her, now started to draw the long lace curtains with slow deliberation. They whispered along the brass rail.

'My chaperone appears to think that it is time you went. Poor darling won't speak a single word of English, but she understands it well enough, eh, Bruna dear? Do *you* speak French?'

'School stuff: savez-vous planter les choux?'

40

'Madly advanced. Most of my guests can't manage "Bonjour". Well, anything you need, just ask Bruna here. Eh, Bruna? Anything the young gentleman needs. She's just pretending not to listen, take no notice, she only *looks* disagreeable because she has been tied to me for forty-five years, a life sentence, poor angel. I'll see you in the morning. You won't dash off somewhere, will you?'

'No. I'll wait. If that's all right?'

'It's perfect. I'd be furious.'

'Sir Charles asked me to look in and have a night-cap in the study; perhaps I'd better go.'

'Yes. Do. You'll find your way all right? Down to the hall, the long corridor on the right, door at the far end beside a bust of Marie Louise looking dreadfully sulky.'

'I know.' He had moved to the door and Bruna joined him, to show him out.

'Do you know anything at *all* about Napoleon?'

'Waterloo.'

'Excellent. You'll know a great deal more by the time you've had your night-cap. It's Archie's passion. Or does one say, "*He* is Archie's passion"? In any case you'll be trapped, I fear.'

'Archie?'

'Ah yes. Most people call him Charles. I call him Archie.'

Bruna opened the door with a discreet rattle of the handle, and went on to the gallery.

'You'd better go. You're being thrown out.' She raised a fragile hand towards him, the bracelets clicking and winking on her slender wrist. 'And thank you. Not for the sea-part. Not for that at all. But for the . . . conspiracy. You follow me?'

'I do.'

'Splendid fellow.' She lowered the hand and lay deeply into the pillows. 'Too idiotic, wasn't it? At my age. To go shrimping. Without a net?'

'Wasn't it though? Good night.'

She nodded, silently dismissing him, her eyes closing in tiredness.

He went out on to the gallery alone. Bruna shut the door behind him. For a moment he stood looking along the empty length. In the high-vaulted ceiling a Venetian-glass chandelier cast soft light through a myriad of coloured flowers. He leant over the marble rail; below, the black and white tiled floor of the hall, an immense glass table, a giant fern in a fat Tuscan pot; Archie standing at one side, half in the shadows, a bottle of wine and a corkscrew in his hands. He raised them.

'Wine? Do you prefer to stay with your wine? Or a whisky? Perhaps a brandy? Whatever you like . . . I have everything in the study. Except wine, that is.'

He was smiling anxiously, curiously, in the filtered light from the glass flowers.

'I'd like a Scotch, if that's all right?'

'Splendid. I never take wine *after* my meal . . . but some people do, you see. Scotch it shall be. Coming down?'

He closed the door of the 'bachelor's room', leaned his back against it, crossed one leg over the other, hands clasped behind him, rolled his head slowly from side to side against the polished wood. 'Well,' he said aloud. 'Well I never did.' He grinned, shook his head. Crazy! The whole set-up, the whole day, crazy. God knows, I've been around in my short life but I have never come across a lot like this one before: I really didn't know they existed. They are all nuts. Nutty as a Fuller's walnut. Archie Charlie with his pretend cigarettes, his collection, brasses, belts, buckles, maps, battle scenes on every wall, books spilling from shelves and chairs, the wax-figure in full uniform staring glassily into space. I mean, if that isn't freaky, then what the hell is? And his wife, Cuckoo. Still pretty, I have to admit that; even wet, shivering, pale and tired. Still

42

smashing looking. Must have been a knock-out once; almost is still. Almost. But what about her? Dragging herself about with pockets full of bloody great rocks. What was that all about, I'd very much like to know. But probably never will. A conspiracy, she said. Thanks for the conspiracy! She's welcome. Freaks. Really freaky. Out of this world, practically lost and forgotten: a wiped tape. The dinosaurs in the V & A or stuffed birds in dusty glass cases: better really, because you don't have to imagine them. There are still faded signs of splendour. But dusty. Locked away, sealed up, colours dimmed. Christ! I'm bright.

He lifted the edge of the large Persian rug with his toe, pressed it flat again, smoothed it carefully. And how the hell did I get involved?

By interfering, she said. 'You interfered!' Really pissed off. Almost disappointed. But what the hell else do you do when an elderly woman chucks herself into the sea three feet from your nose? Wave goodbye?

'Bonkers,' he said, and went across to his rucksack standing neatly on a chair by the high wooden bed and fished about for a packet of cigarettes which he remembered he had put there earlier in the day, before all this had started, when he was walking along the coast road from Villefranche and thinking that that little cove across the bay might be the best place to shack up for the night.

But instead I have the 'bachelor's room'. Very masculine. Heavy wood, military chests, gleaming brasses; brass everywhere. Lamps with green glass shades, a fat, buttoned leather chair, small club-fender before the fireplace, pictures covering the white-washed walls. Engravings in maple-wood frames. Seen enough of those in my time.

Drove truck-loads of this sort of stuff down to the studios to 'dress the sets'. The whole house looks like one great big set. A multi-million production. All very elegant and upper class: like a sherry commercial. It's all from some other time, it's all on a different plane. I got on the wrong escalator somewhere during today; it's going backwards.

The bed was so high that he had to climb two leather-covered steps to reach the mattress and, laughing, rolled across crisp linen sheets. If you fall out of this having a nightmare you'll break your neck.

'It's only a scratch supper, I'm afraid,' Archie Charlie had apologized worriedly. 'We weren't expecting my wife back from London until tomorrow, you see. Caught us quite by surprise. I normally only have a boiled egg or something when I'm on my own; saves fuss.'

A scratch supper. Four ruddy courses, if you count the cheese, two kinds of wine and the pissed-off French woman waiting at table. He's never had a scratch supper in his life, I'd say. Tinned spaghetti on wet toast? Soggy schnitzels? 'Country-style' pork pies sagging in limp chips? If you were lucky. He'd seen me look a bit doubtful, I suppose. Came to, what he thought was, the rescue.

'Use your hand-irons from the outside inwards. That was my father's advice always. Bruna is still very formal, even in these careless days. In my father's time, of course, we used only one set. Knife and fork: cleaned them on a piece of bread between courses . . . except if we had soup, of course, but we seldom did. "Can't found a meal on a lake!" my father used to say.' Chattering away nervously. Probably worried about his wife. 'Can't think what she was doing down there by the rocks. She never goes there as far as I know. So dangerous, one can slip so easily. As she did. Obviously?' He had looked up with clear eyes, a worried frown. I didn't say anything. A conspiracy. That seemed to fuss him more. Fiddled with his finger-bowl. Spilled it. I know all about the cutlery. Been there before, although he's not to know, I suppose. Decca saw to all that. Good old Decca, bringing me up to be a little gentle-

44

man. In the early days. The *very* early days. When she had hopes. High hopes. Silly bitch. Silly, silly 'Mummy'. But it was never 'Mummy', or 'Mother', 'Mum' or even just 'Ma'. Decca. Her choice, God knew why. 'Looks better on the canopy,' she said. ' "Decca York" throbbing in crimson neon outside all the theatres.'

Great. Well. I'll buy that. Except that it never did. The nearest she ever got to Shaftesbury Avenue was the De La Warr Pavilion, Bexhill-on-sea, and the Male Comic got the billing. For all the audiences knew, she might just as well have used the name on her passport. Jessie Pollock.

'We won't call anyone Mummy or Daddy in this household: it's out of date. Cissy. I'm Decca to you as I am to my friends. It's friendlier. Less ageing.'

So that was that. I didn't give a bugger anyway. Called her Mum behind her back. Couldn't call her 'Decca' at school, for Christ's sake; they'd have thought I was talking about a gramophone record.

He sat upright, lit a cigarette, swung off the bed, stepped lightly down the little steps, stood for a moment in the middle of the room, hands thrust into the front pockets of his jeans. High hopes.But they didn't work after all: they hardly ever do for actors, far too many of them tarting about for too few jobs. You've got to be extra special to break through. And she wasn't. Wasn't extra special enough. Or Dad. Poor Dad. God's gift to womanhood without the 'spark'. James Pollock changed to 'Jeremy Steerforth' overnight; and there they were, the golden pair, Jeremy Steerforth and Decca York on the threshold of the Sixties, with glamour, fame and glory ahead: hell-bent on tipping the Oliviers from their golden throne. At least she was, when the time came.

Except it never did. It was a paper-fire, giving a bright blaze for a short time and then just floating, drifting, ashes in a cool grate. As if nothing had ever been there. 'The cold

45

ashes of old dreams.' I'll be a fucking poet yet! And the running tape of woe!

'We *could* have done it, we *could* have been there, right at the top of the bloody heap, only Jeremy hadn't got the balls. He wouldn't fight, like me: I was the leader, I went ahead, I pushed, I shoved, I sold. He didn't want to work hard enough; and it's all bloody work, striving, climbing, shoving, elbowing, clambering, kicking, stamping on the clawing little fingers on that ladder coming up behind you. But he didn't want that way; thought he'd done it all after one bloody season at Stratford.

' "I've done it!" he said. Silly bugger. It was only the start, the first floor up. He got off there; but I went on up without him. All he really wanted was a blasted Aston Martin and a recommendation to Wentworth and the Garrick. A social actor. But there is more to it than that. I knew. I went up on the ride alone. He started the slide; I wanted highest! I pushed, I bloody pushed, I want you to know!' Endless tape. And she did. Pushed herself into a poor contract with a poor film company who swore to make her a star if she did what they wanted. And she did, only that didn't do much good after all. A pretty, empty, shadow, that's all she was; they always had to pad her tits, and even that gave her no dimension.

He wandered across the room, cigarette hanging from his lips, a sour taste in his mouth from just remembering: bitterness becomes physical. He stopped before the tall wooden wardrobe, ran an exploring finger round the carved panels, leant his forehead on the shiny surface. Face to face, on the wall beside it, with an engraving of a pudgy child in a shift, little red slippers, a feathered hat clutched in one hand, the finger of the other coyly placed to pouting lips. He squinted through cigarette smoke. 'The Mother's Hope'. Engraved by Holland, 1807.

The mother's hope. Me. Except that I was never that; her hopes went far beyond me. I was just a respectable part

46

of her plans. The rising star at nineteen with a 'bonny' baby to dandle for the *Sunday Express* or the *Mirror*. Unwanted, as it happened, but quickly turned to her advantage.

'Motherhood and Decca York!' 'Nappies and Stardom'. I was a useful 'prop', that's all, and as quickly set aside when the scene was played. Hardly ever saw her at first. Studio calls at 5.30 a.m., then back exhausted to dress for a première or a party. 'Don't, Marcus, you'll smudge my face.'

And the 'Uncles' started almost as soon as Jeremy went off on his tours. Ten weeks, sometimes more. They'd take her out to supper at Hurley or for the weekend to Le Touquet. I knew them better than I knew him. Kind, sometimes, some tall and thin, some short and fat, all with too much white cuff and brown suède shoes. I handed round the cigarettes and peanuts which they accepted to make me feel happy and 'wanted'. The only thing I ever felt was hatred for those little bow ties, frilly shirts and god-awful velvet knickers I had to wear. Christ!

Remembered irritation moved him from his wardrobe support; he flicked his cigarette clumsily over a bowl of daisies. Reproved by the grey ash, he blew it off. A tidy mind.

And then the studios started folding. Telly and Bingo came in along with bitterness, disillusion and finally panic. The 'Uncles' listened to her endless cries of distress uncomfortably, the drinks got stronger and longer; after the drinks the Seconal, to sleep. And then the big, slow slide down. Jeremy still capering away in cheap farces which never made the West End but had them in fits from Bournemouth to Bradford. The dolls' house at Hurlingham went first, then the prep school at Virginia Water, the Tunnicliffes, the Regency chairs, the satin loveseat and finally the hasty move to a dank cottage outside Dorking. That was the final crash. The end of the line. The buffers.

'It'll be all lovely, you'll see,' she had said distractedly. 'Healthier, lots of fresh vegetables, our own eggs perhaps. And a dog. Wouldn't you just *adore* a dog?' I didn't give a sod about a dog. I didn't give a sod about anything. I didn't know who, or where, I was. Dorking would do. And if she wanted Dorking, she'd have it. So there we were. But the 'Uncles' grew fewer in time, and with the thinning out, there were less 'goodies'; bottles of vodka, sides of smoked salmon, hit records for the player. And then Jeremy met an 'Auntie' who wrote poetry, read it aloud, played a tambourine and shivered in her sari in the rising damp of the Surrey Hills, was called 'Bangladesh' by Decca, who hated her and caused constant scenes, so that finally she cleared off back to her flat in Muswell Hill. Taking Jeremy with her. For good. A divorce. The dream crumbled away with the end of the Sixties. Fade out.

He crushed his cigarette into a small shell, pulled his T-shirt over his head, crossed to the open windows, the night air warm on his naked chest. Through the trees a half moon turned the sea to steel. Along the coast road the rear lights of motor cars glimmered silently like trailing embers round the dark bulk of Mont Boron. It was still. The only sound, the sibilant, rustling swirl of the sea in the dark, caressing and nuzzling among the tumbled rocks far below like a blind thing.

Where were they all now, he wondered. Where on earth? Last of Jeremy, months ago, was a postcard from Cape Town to say that he was the hit of the season in yet another revival of 'Private Lives' and 'why not come on out and get a super tan?'

How? By swimming?

And Decca? Swimming all right. Floundering about with one foot desperately on the bottom. Bitterness, anger, failure and frustration had rotted her like old silk. Crumbling, faded and frayed, protesting noisily at the failure of her life and her career; against the killing of seals, racial discrimination, nuclear power, the use of the birch on the Isle of Man and anything else which caught her avid fancy during the dreary discussions round the long kitchen table in the Dorking cottage with all her hairy, granny-glassed, spotty companions in dirty jeans and Afghan coats drinking cheap Spanish rosé and pounding out their theories on Truth, Love, Freedom, and the Individual's Right to Exist.

That's where they were; and here is where I am. Standing in the night in a strange house with strange, freaky people. But, if you think of it, are they really any stranger than my lot with all their lost dreams and ambitions, their constant search for identity, for belonging, for background? Jeremy still on the social climb in Cape Town. Can there *be* anything to climb, I wonder? And Decca decaying in Dorking. Hey! That's quite good. You'll be a poet yet. Who are the freaks? The couple in this bloody great house, rattling about in a lost-time slot, jumping into the sea and banging on about Napoleon, or my tacky group still searching, still looking, still trying to catch on. To hold something. At least the people here know who they are. No question about that. And they've known all their lives. Secure and sure. Belonging. They know all about it even if they are at the end of the trip. But Decca with the Afghan coats and Jeremy and his diamond-tycoons, still trying, still looking, still hoping. For what, for God's sake? Even if they got it they wouldn't know what to do with it: all the poor sods ever had was a rotten ten years. That's a decade. A single decade and then snuff. Reached their only peak in the Sixties and can't manage the Seventies. Ten tacky years. Tough. I'm going to have longer than that. They are all old tape. Mine is just beginning to run.

He kicked off his boots, pulled off his jeans. In the white-tiled bathroom, thick blue towels, an immense bath on ball and claw feet, brass taps, a clam shell full of

49

wrapped soap, he saw himself reflected from head to foot in four wide mirrors. The Body Beautiful. There I am. Available in black and white or colour: matt or glossy. Sets of six to twenty-six, postcard size or ten-by-eights, larger prints by request at extra cost according to size. You can have 'The Greek Captive', 'Lonely Sailor', 'St Sebastian', 'The Gay Hussar', 'Cowboy Capers'. By courtesy of Aesthetic Art Models Ltd. In plain brown envelopes by return post. He turned on both bath taps full, water roared, steam billowed. I'm pretty bloody tacky myself. He sat on a cork-topped stool. Well: family characteristics will out, they say. He took up a bottle of bath oil, poured it into the water, stirred it into foam. A bubble bath for the Body Beautiful. He watched himself with pleasure in the mirrors. Narrow-flanked, flat-bellied, long-legged. Among the freaks. I *like* how I look! What had Archie Charlie said down there in the spook-room not long ago?

'It is an astonishingly true resemblance. Same height, hair, same . . . how can I put it? "Look"? I *do* find it quite amazing. You know, of course, who I mean by l'Aiglon?'

'Well, very vaguely. Terribly sorry, I was badly educated. I don't really.' Didn't. Do now though. God! Got it chapter and bloody verse.

'He was the only child of Napoleon Bonaparte. On the wall behind you, there, in the astrakhan collar, you see? And over there, the full length portrait. Splendid, don't you think? And there, on the figure, is the same white uniform, a colonel in the Austrian Infantry. So fine. But look at the face. You can see what I mean?' And in a way I could; give or take a bit here and there. 'A rather weaker jaw, you might note, than your own: the mouth is, what shall I say? Petulant? Spoiled, perhaps? Faults inherited from his frightful mother, Marie Louise. And the hair, of course, very Germanic. But the width of his eyes, the brow, the length of the nose . . . you see? Perfect Boneparte. Has no one ever pointed this out to you before? But surely?'

No one. Ever. Or if they thought so they never said so. The people I know aren't bothered about the width of my eyes; or the length of my nose. They don't go back as far as Napoleon Bonaparte. They hardly go back to last Sunday. But he was so damned pleased. Pushed the decanter across the desk. 'Oh, do have another glass, won't you? The evening is still so young, and it's been a very fraught day, quite horrid. Well, it would have been had it not been for you, thank God!'

He slowed the taps to a trickle. And then we had Napoleon and son non-stop. He tested the water with his hand, took a cake of soap, sniffed it, unwrapped it, stepped into the bath and lowered himself into the water. But quite funny; interesting too. He knows what he's talking about; should do, I suppose. Poor bloody l'Aiglon's Mum had a run with the 'Uncles' too, it seems, while Dad was off on tour carving up Europe and having a very nasty time of it; one way and another. He lay back slowly, sliding the soap about between his hands. Then Dad got carved up himself and carted off to his island, Mum pissed off with the 'Uncles' and poor little l'Aiglon got himself stuffed into a bloody great palace all on his own, and snuffed it at twenty-one with a hacking cough. That's *his* story. You wait until I tell him mine. That'll put a curl in his hair.

He laughed aloud suddenly, and dropped the soap. I'll bet l'Aiglon didn't have an 'Uncle' Desmond.

'Look, my dear, if he doesn't want to go back to school next year, what's the good of forcing him?'

'Now Desmond! Don't interfere in family matters, remember? That's out. You're not his father. Two spoonfuls of sprouts left: anyone?' She shrugged, scraped round the saucepan. 'Lucky hens: again. Or maybe bubble-and-squeak?'

51

'I'm not interfering, Decca, you know that. Your affair entirely. But if he had set his heart on leaving, what's the point of pushing him?'

She reached across for his plate, scraped some bits off into the saucepan. 'Hens. I'm not pushing him. He's going, that's all. Everything else in my life has fallen apart, it seems, but he's going to get a decent education if it kills me.'

'Or him?'

'Tough as old boots. Knows when my mind is set on something.' She stacked the plate, gathered the knives and forks in her hand. 'And it's set on school.' She went to the kitchen door, turned suddenly. 'If things had gone the way I hoped, the way they should have, he'd have been at Stowe two years ago.' She pushed the kitchen door open with her foot and they heard her clatter everything into the sink and start whistling.

Desmond refilled his glass, stretched across for the cheese dish, cut a large chunk, spread it with mustard. 'Sorry, Marcus, I tried. But you know Decca.'

'I know. Thanks all the same. I'll be sixteen next year. Buggered if I'm going to sweat away at bloody school at sixteen.'

'If she's made up her mind . . .'

'She can unmake it. I'll just piss off. Walk out. That's all. London. I'll get a job, something. She can't stop me and she won't find me. I'll see to that.'

She came back into the room, caftan billowing, ethnic earrings swinging, a large glass bowl held high. 'Now! Everybody guess! Goodies! Desmond's favourite. Trifle. There!' She set it on the table like a chalice, stood back smiling, head on one side.

Desmond shifted in his chair. 'Decca! How good of you, super.'

Her eyes narrowed like a cat's. 'Desmond! *Des!* You're on the cheese already. I did this especially for you. You

52

might have waited a minute. We usually have a pudding, don't we? Usually? For God's sake! All damned morning I've been . . .'

'I'll have a bit later perhaps. Eh? For tea, why not? You really gave me such a whacking great helping of beef and things.'

'Nearly half a bottle of sherry in this. It's so disheartening. You *know* how I try. And it won't keep, it'll be all soggy and foul. You could have waited, couldn't you? What's the rush? It's Sunday, isn't it? Stuffing yourself with the cheddar . . .'

After they had helped with the washing-up and she had gone up to her bed with a script of some telly thing she was rehearsing, they went out into the sodden October garden.

'I rather fucked that up, I'm afraid.' Desmond kicked a rotten apple across the uncut grass.

'Doesn't take much to do it.'

'Just a trifle. Eh! Quite funny that.'

'She's not funny. She's getting worse. All this education. I don't need it.'

'Oh, come on now! We all need a bit of learning, especially nowadays. You're pretty bright, she says. Good reports, that sort of thing.'

'I'm all right. I quite like it. Gets me out of this place. Cooped up all day, just the two of us. Gets on my wick.'

'And when she's in London? Rehearsals and so on?'

'Look after myself, boil an egg. Tinned spaghetti. I can do that. I'm fine. I like it alone.'

'Got Rags for company, what?'

'The dog? He's dead.'

'Oh. Sorry. Yes, I wondered a bit, didn't see him about.'

'Someone shot him. a two-bore. Full of bloody pellets.'

'Who'd do a thing like that? Poor old Rags . . . he was so friendly.'

'She said it was the gamekeepers, or something.'

'Could be.' They were crossing the little orchard. Ducked under unpruned branches. An apple fell with a soft thump into the grass.

'I think she did it herself.'

'Marcus! Christ, what a thing to say, come on . . .'

'No. She gets funny sometimes. You must have seen it. Keeps Jeremy's old two-bore up in her room; says it's not safe, a woman alone up here. Hippies, drop-outs, Hell's Angels, you know . . . and the rats in the chicken-run.'

But that's a terrible thing to say. Why would she? She couldn't.'

'Ah, she could. Another row. School again. I was offered a job by Dick Griffin up at the garage. I'm handy with cars. He lets me muck about. Help out at week-ends with the pumps, minor repairs . . . five quid a week cash. She hit the roof, I wouldn't fight. Just kept quiet. Took Rags off for a walk, sort things out, let her simmer down. She yelled that I thought more of the damned dog than I did of her.' He pushed his hands into his pockets. 'I said I did.'

They walked on in silence; a pheasant scratching in the hedge looked up startled, blundered clumsily out into the field, whirred across misty grasses.

'If you did clear off . . . to London, I mean, know anyone?'

'A few. Mostly her friends though. Tacky theatre, you know.'

'I'm her friend.'

'No. Not like that. I didn't mean you.' He looked up quickly into the older man's face. 'Sorry. Not you. Known you all my life.'

'A long time anyway.'

'No, not you. What she calls the "thinking" set. The Young. She wants to be with thinking people. Her "thinking" people are all into jeans, pot, politics, the Workers' Revolutionary Party and fuck the Queen. Know

54

what I mean? This is a quiet Sunday, because she's learning her lines. But most Sundays, Christ! It's like a bloody pub in the Fulham Road. Of course she pays for it all. The booze, food, ciggies all that . . . they wouldn't come otherwise: it's all free hand-outs. She can't bear to be alone, see?'

'Yes, I see.' Desmond laughed wryly. 'A bit different from the old days, eh? Do you remember them? Too young, I suppose.'

'Oh no. I remember them all right. The Hurlingham days. Handing round the peanuts. The caterers carting round the food, plus a ruddy butler for the evening. Rented flowers, and all those dud scripts stacked neatly on the coffee table; so everyone could see them.'

Desmond smiled through the drifting mist. 'Didn't miss much did you?'

'Not a bloody thing. All I had to do was watch. And listen. Little boys should be seen but not heard. Sat there. Or handed round the peanuts: then off to beddy-byes with that hag Sheila from Dublin's fair city where the girls aren't all pretty, and a ten minute read from "Winnie the Pissy Pooh". God! I remember.'

'Was it really that bad then? Seemed all right.'

'That bad. Okay for you; she's never been able to boss you around. She used to give poor old Jeremy a rough time. "Wet! Spineless! You with your mighty three inch cock!" It wasn't a big house, I heard all I wanted to.'

'Yes . . . she was a bit bossy. Still is.'

'She's got to be boss. Can't take it any other way, wants to be on top all the time. You can't boss successes so easily. So she gets hold of the failures, like the lot who come down here. She can boss the shit out of them, they can't answer back.'

They reached a gap in the hedge, Desmond stopped. 'Not going down there; all plough, and I've got my London shoes on . . . forgot my wellies in the hurry.' He fumbled about in his jacket pocket. 'If things get, well, you know . . . if you decide to clear off, and I don't think you should, mind you, I agree with Decca that education is bloody important and all that, a good speaking voice and so on, but if you do want to skip off, to think things over, so to speak, this is where I am.' He handed him a business card. 'Moviedecor Ltd. That's me. Goldhurst Road, Shepherd's Bush . . . just off the Green.'

Marcus took the card, slid it into his pocket; they turned and walked back up the hill towards the orchard.

'But not unless you really feel you must; it would have to be pretty serious, you know. Not just a fit of sulks, know what I mean?'

Marcus nodded. 'Yeah. I know what you mean. Don't worry, but thanks very much all the same . . . it will be serious. Something's got to give, one day.'

Six months later, sitting at a greasy table in the Café Positano in Goldhurst Road, Desmond dropped a lump of sugar into his espresso, and looked across at his exhausted guest who was eating his second egg-and-bacon sandwich.

'You'll feel a lot better after that,' he said.

'I feel a hell of a lot better already.'

'You look swacked, old man.'

'Walked all bloody night. It's a long way, Dorking.'

'There are trains.'

'Not without lolly. End of the week, I was skint. She kept me pretty tight, you know. I had to ask.'

'So you're broke, I take it, too. As well as on the run, that it?'

'That's it. I've got ten pence, a change of jeans, and this anorak. A couple of shirts. I had to get out quickly and light.' He wiped his mouth with the back of his hand, smiled across at Desmond. 'Sorry, Des. But you did say. And it *was* serious. Not a fit of the sulks.'

56

'No. No. I can see that. The, umm, the LSD business. How long?'

'Oh, I don't know when she started. It's been gradual: sobbing her heart out one minute and then suddenly all bright and gay and airy-fairy. I though it was just "bennies" at first – she was on them for ages – or Valium with the vodka. But it was more, I don't know, sort of weird . . . freaky. She was banging about like Peter Pan all over the place. Floating. When she came down it was pretty grim.' He picked up his coffee, held the hot cup tight against his cheek. 'Sick, everywhere. I was cleaning up; scrubbing rush matting and vomit isn't such a big deal. Then the tears; oh-what-will-you-think-of-me-I'm-ill, Marcus. All that shit.'

He drank his coffee, shrugged, set the cup into its saucer. 'Then yesterday, another Sunday . . . the same crowd. In the evening she lost her head over something, I don't know what . . . some argument about Vietnam being backed by Russia or something; nothing I listened to really . . . I was up in my room, reading.' He took a dusty bread-stick from the glass on the table, snapped it into three pieces. 'Harold Pinter. *The Caretaker*, do you know it?'

'No . . . know what you mean. Never saw it.'

'Bloody marvellous. Anyway, she was taking care of everyone downstairs. I heard her shouting at them, telling them all to piss off. "Get out of my house!" she yelled. "You've brought blood into my house . . . there's blood everywhere . . . your hands are dripping with it. Get out, go away." I don't know what all else. Then I heard her coming up, go to her room, slamming about there. I knew she was looking for the gun, only I'd hidden it that morning. I know about Sundays, and she had been pretty funny for a day or two. So I shoved it under my mattress. Then she went down again, started chucking everything about. They all cleared off pretty fast, three car loads. It was pretty funny really, all scuttling off like rabbits. She was so "gone" by the time I had finished clearing up, that she forgot about the gun for a bit. She knew I'd taken it . . . said so. But she went back to her room and pulled that about and then there was silence. I just packed this bag and cleared off: about one o'clock, I think. Walked along the railway . . . seemed the straightest line and she might have just sobered up and come after me in the car, you know? At Epsom I got on to the main road and hitched a truck.'

'And here you are.'

'And here I am and not going back. I'm not, you know? Ever.'

'I know. Understand. Now . . .' Desmond smoothed his thinning hair. 'Got to get you sorted out, haven't we. You sixteen yet?'

'Two weeks ago. March.'

'That's a help. Only got another two years to go before the age of consent.'

'Screw that. I'm consenting now.'

'Can you drive?'

'Yes . . . anything. But Des, I don't want to be trouble. If you can think of something, somewhere I could go . . . get a job, anything . . . till I get things . . .'

'No, no, we'll sort things out. Lots of odd jobs about. You can muck about here in the warehouse . . . I think Georgie can give you a bed for a while. He's the night-watchman, got a little flat, couple of rooms. You'd better have a bit of pocket money right away, toothpaste, soap, that sort of thing.' He took some notes from his wallet and pushed them across the table. 'That do for now?'

Marcus stared at them in silence, his head down. Nodded.

'Oh, come on! Don't look so miserable. Marcus, it's all right.'

'Thanks.' The voice gruff, uneven. When he looked up his eyes were bleak with tears. 'Thanks, Des. I'm sorry . . .'

'Look, old boy, I was very fond of your mother. She

58

was very good to me years ago, a lot of fun, pretty, laughing, brave then; but there you are. No looking back . . . just start looking forward. There's a lot of life ahead, you go and take it . . .'

'You bet. From now on it's my turn. I'm going to take it all, with both hands open.'

'That's it. But you'd better let me telephone her. She'll have the police out after you, or do something silly, you know . . .'

'But not where I am? For God's sake. She'll be here in a flash.'

'I'll handle it my way, leave it to me. She won't. And I won't tell her where you are. Just that you are all right, so on . . . that you'll write: one day. Eh?'

'One day, maybe. I'll see.'

'Finish your coffee and we'll go over to the warehouse; see Georgie.'

Desmond had inherited Moviedecor Ltd from his father on demobilization from the RAF in 1946. Then just a second-hand furniture shop and junk dealer's called simply 'Bennett's Bargains', which under his careful and shrewd eye prospered into 'Bennett's Antiques and Second-hand Furniture', then 'Antiques'.

When he realized that he could make more out of renting his stock to film studios and commercial photographers as 'props' he enlarged his premises, changed to 'Moviedecor Ltd', and was justifiably proud to have it known in the business that he could supply, at short notice, anything from a stuffed hedgehog to a fully furnished Georgian pine-panelled room, a Persian lacquer pen-box, or the entire staircase from a long demolished Wyatt mansion. He travelled the country securing his 'bits and pieces', as he called them, and the warehouses which he acquired were jammed from floor to rafters with the products of his journeys.

Into this strange world of wood, glass, porcelain, stone and stuffed animals of every sort, Marcus settled very easily. He liked the feel of the things, the fabrics, the plaster, the smell of beeswax, the sudden calls for anything from a bed-pan to a wine glass; he loaded and unloaded the many vans, polished and dusted, washed and burnished, was shortly put on the payroll by an impressed Desmond, rented a couple of rooms which he shared with a bright youth who was an expert French-polisher, went to night school in Hammersmith, and, by the time that he was eighteen, was driving the vans himself and checking the long inventories nightly with Georgie. He had seized the odd chances offered by Desmond and had, as he had promised, taken all that was on offer 'with both hands open'. He had never looked back and never returned to the dank Dorking cottage or set eyes on Decca who, after three or four half-hearted efforts to force him to come back, which had run the gamut from fury to grovelling, had given up and drifted completely out of his life, except when she inadvertently appeared on his television screen, at which time he calmly switched channels.

One morning he found Georgie sitting hunched over his ledgers in the cluttered cubby hole at the end of Shed Three which he called his Office.

'The Pinewood stuff loaded then?' said Georgie. Marcus nodded.

'I think we've hit a bit of a snag here,' said Georgie, prodding his ledger with a thumb. 'You know if we've got a stuffed 'orse, chestnut or black, rearing, and a pair of vultures? One's got to be circling, wings open? Do you know if we have?'

'Got a couple of horses. The piebald from "Death at Beechers Brook" . . . and a white, the one the whisky people had a couple of times.'

'They want a chestnut or a black. Rearing.'

'Who do?'

'Bender's Studios, Covent Garden. And a circling vulture. Last time they wanted a Moorish fountain, practicable, and a set of village stocks, ditto. They don't make it easy.'

'When for?'

'Tomorrow. The seventh. By two o'clock. But I don't know about the vultures, I'm sure.'

'We do quite a bit with them, don't we? Theatrical photographers?'

Georgie looked up glumly. 'Yes. Theatrical. And something called "Aesthetic Art Models" on the side. Rum lot. Still, they pay, if we've got what they want.'

'I'll have a look,' said Marcus. 'I know we've got the piebald and the white.'

'It's the bloody vultures, mate. Bugger the 'orses. 'Orses is easy. Except for the rearing.'

'Well,' said Gus Bender pushing the grey hair off his bony forehead. 'There's three little things wrong with this horse, laddie. It's not a black, it's not rearing, and it's on wheels.'

Marcus followed him across the big studio, stepping over cables and junction-boxes, a record-player thudding Streisand. 'It's all we've got. We're Moviedecor not Newmarket.'

'Don't want no lip,' said Gus Bender turning at his office door. 'You bring me a white horse when I said black, and a dead-looking vulture.'

'It is dead. Stuffed.'

'And stuffed for bloody years by the looks of it: I can't get no movement from that thing . . . all hunched up. No sense of *horror* . . . I want horror. It looks as if it had the croup. *That's* what I have to reproduce, that there.' He jabbed a finger towards a dark engraving pinned to the wall. A crumpled figure among jagged rocks, eyes rolled heavenwards, lightning flashing, vultures wheeling: wings outspread. 'Got it? "Icarus" . . . And that one there is

''Mazeppa'' . . . full of *horror*, see?' Another figure, eyes to heaven, sprawled across the back of a galloping horse, more lightning, billowing clouds, whirling dust.

'That's a white horse!' said Marcus.

'Yeah. Maybe the artist saw it white all those years ago. *I* see it black . . . more horrifying. And besides, it'll show up the model better, white on white is tricky. You can lose detail.' He went back into the studio and stared at the wheeled-horse, rubbing his chin in worried thought. 'Suppose I could jack the forelegs up on a couple of boxes; come in close to miss the full shape, a wind-machine blowing the mane. Might work. Try and give it some movement.'

'Someone is going to sit on it?'

Gus Bender looked up slowly. 'No. Not sit. Lie. You've seen the engraving in there?'

'He'll fall off.'

'Not Dieter, he won't. And not for eighty quid a session. Anyway he'll be tied on.'

'You got it wrong, boss. Sorry to tell you, he won't.' A deep voice made them turn suddenly. Standing at the office door, a black man of immense height: at his side, barely reaching his waist, a slight pale-faced girl wearing a green tartan skirt, silver shoes, a mouldering rabbit-skin jacket.

'What do you mean, he won't?' Gus Bender pushed his hair from his forehead.

The black man nodded at Marcus, smiled. 'You want to come in the office, boss? I got some dandy news.'

Gus hurried after him, pushing past the girl without a look and closed the door, leaving her outside. She dropped a cigarette butt to the floor, screwed it into the boards with a silver foot.

'I'm so sorry. We have bad news, I disturb you.' Her voice was husky, low, almost a whisper with a strong German accent.

'It's okay. I was just delivering some stuff.' He indicated the horse with a jerk of his head. 'That thing . . .'

She looked at the horse with indifference. 'You don't work here? An actor?'

'No.'

'I think you don't. I haven't seen you before.'

She looked in need of care and protection, he thought. The waif type, small white face, intensified by an ill-applied ashy make-up, green eyes, drab fair hair cut like a boy's, a shaky side-parting marked by a plastic airplane pinned, it would seem, to her scalp. Without the rabbit coat and tartan skirt she'd look like a plucked starling.

'What's happened to the Dieter character then?'

She looked over her shoulder to the office where Gus was jamming the telephone into the side of his head and waving a hand in helpless, silent, anger.

'The ''fuzz'' picked him up. At Harwich. He's in, I don't know the word, not prison . . . but he's locked up, they say.'

'Custody?'

'Like that, I think. He came this morning from Hamburg, and they searched the car.'

'What was he doing?'

The rabbit coat moved up to her ears, the green eyes widened with innocence. 'I don't know. With Fritzie and Bennie. Mr Seeger is his boss and Mr Seeger made me this telephone call to say what happened. From London Airport two hours ago.' She rummaged in her coat pocket, found a packet of Gauloises, shook out a cigarette and held it between worn, stubby fingers. 'Mr Seeger has quickly gone to Paris for a few days. Have you got some fire for me?'

She inhaled deeply, blew smoke down her nostrils with professional skill. 'It is trouble for Dieter, trouble also for Mr Gus . . . it is a pity.'

'Trouble for me. I'll have to cart this lot back again.'

She nodded sadly. 'It is a big pity, Dieter was the most popular with all the Arab clients. He was so German, you know? Blond, blue eyes, they like that. And is also big trouble for me too. I stay in his flat for no money, just cook for him; good German food he likes; I clean and make it nice . . .' She hugged herself with thin arms. 'But now . . . if he is away, or if they send him back to Hamburg, something terrible. What will I do? Mr Seeger said I must clear out right away. Take everything and "get lost", he said, before they come to search the rooms. So I came here to tell Mr Gus. I don't know where else to go. Maybe . . .' She laughed uncertainly. 'Maybe he will give me a little bit of moneys. He is liking Dieter, and I think he is also liking me. I make Dieter happy and be on time for the sessions, you see.'

'Sessions?'

'He is a most popular model. He poses very well. I suggested him to Mr Gus. We are working at "The Mayerling Hütte" restaurant. You know this place, in the Kings Road? Is all German specialities, and Mr Gus gives me twenty-five pounds for finding him. So maybe . . .' She flicked her cigarette ash over the board floor. 'So maybe he will give me something to find a room.' Her green eyes narrowed, her boy's head tilted into the moulting collar of her jacket. 'You don't work here; for the photographs?' She appraised him through a haze of smoke from her nostrils.

'No. I told you. I just brought some stuff.'

'You should, you know. I can tell. You are . . .' her voice was soft and whispery like a soft wind stirring dead leaves '. . . very fine, you know. A fine fellow. You would be very good. Fantastic, I think.'

Gus came out of the office followed by the black man. He stood for a moment in silence pushing his lank grey hair out of his eyes.

'No joy. No joy at all. Had a word with Sergeant Mason up at the station. Of course he doesn't know anything . . .

64

not his area. Says he'll try and find out and let me know; but it'll be too late by then. Custody could mean anything.' He turned to the pale girl crossly. 'What the hell was he up to, Leni? You know? Did he tell you? Must have,' he added, 'but you won't tell, I know you.'

The girl shook her head. Dropped the cigarette, trod on it. 'I don't know. He is always going to have a little journey . . . it is not for me to ask. He went with Fritzie and Bennie. To be back today, he said. Certain.'

'Well, he's not and won't be and that's final. You'll have to cart that ruddy horse back to where it came from; we'll have to scrub the session and that's farewell to a hefty lump of lolly. A very good client . . . knows what he wants. If he'd liked them, he wanted them blown up nine foot by four, panels for his bathroom. Huge. It's a bloody shame.'

The black man was picking his teeth with a matchstick, leaning against the office door. He spat out a splinter of wood, wiped his mouth with his hand. 'I could give Terry a call? Or Allan? If they're free they'd do it, boss.'

Gus Bender thrust his hands into his cardigan pocket. 'They aren't *blond*. Terry is too thin anyway, and Alan's too butch: he's all right for military stuff, torture chambers and that; but he doesn't look romantic. This stuff has to be classical, Nig, I keep telling you. It's four classical poses he wants. And he wants Dieter. And where am I going to find another Dieter in ten minutes? I got all the props, got the rocks, the dead tree. Even got the bloody horse and the vulture, even got the stick-on arrows for the Sebastian pose; and no bloody Sebastian. Great! I'm getting out of this business – you get let down every time. I'll stick to portraits and wedding groups.' He stabbed an angry finger at the pale girl. 'Leni, you're bad luck, my girl. You and your bloody discoveries.'

'I got another,' said Leni with a wide smile. 'Fantastic!' She pointed a thin arm at Marcus leaning against the horse's rump. 'There.'

Gus Bender turned slowly on his heel. 'Him?'

'Not me,' said Marcus.

'Fantastic,' said Leni.

'Hey! How about that, boss?' said Nig with a deep laugh. 'That's an idea!'

Gus Bender was looking at Marcus through cupped hands, screening him from the clutter of the studio. 'It's an idea. Same height. Blond. Ever modelled?'

'No,' said Marcus. 'And I'm not about to try.'

'For forty quid? Three sessions at forty quid. Hundred and twenty. Cash?'

'Fifty,' said the pale girl.

'Fifty? Christ, I paid Dieter eighty and he was the fucking Star.'

'So this boy you pay fifty. He is new. Also you need him.'

'What is this! Leni? You his bloody agent?'

'Yes. Now I am. He is my idea, so it is forty for him, and ten for me, and that is fantastic.' She reached for the Gauloises packet and took another cigarette.

'If you think I'm going to lie around stark naked on a stuffed horse you've got another thought coming.'

Gus Bender raised a worried hand. 'Not naked! No! This is not a pornographic studio, I'll have you know, it's all very tasteful and above board. Aesthetic. I don't hold with that filth. Good God! I'd be locked up in a week if I did that sort of thing.'

'Could you give me some fire?' The pale girl put her blunt fingers on Marcus's arm. 'Why don't you try? Forty pounds, you see?'

'Wouldn't know what the hell to do; come on now . . .'

'The boss is very clever, he will help. And Nig will help you also, he arranges the lights and things. Everyone will help. And it is only in the night, when the Studio is closed up . . . so you can do your daily job and then this one and have some pleasant time . . .' Her voice was rough and

66

low, as if she was speaking through a tube of sandpaper, her eyes half closed. 'And forty pounds cash.'

'You are all bloody mad,' said Marcus.

'Tell you what,' said Gus Bender suddenly. 'Why don't you pop up here this evening, have a shot at a couple of poses? If it's no go, then no go: you'll get twenty quid from me, and the hire of the horse and things and you can do what you like about Joseph Goebbels here, that's up to you. But I don't see what you stand to lose. It's all good clean fun, and you would make a useful bit of money. What about it?'

Before Marcus could reply the pale girl pressed his arm. 'If I come back with you now to your place, where you work, then I can tell you all about it, many things. That would be wise? I have nothing to do. I have nowhere to go . . . I have plenty of time . . .'

'Where's the receipt then? For the horse?' said Gus Bender briskly. 'I'll sign it and you can leave the things; if you come back this evening. Otherwise you'll have to take them back now. No use to me without the body, is it? Hardly my fault if the silly bugger gets copped at the docks, is it? And I'm not paying good money for a ruddy stuffed horse I can't use and only clutters up the place.' He ran his hand through his grey hair with irritation. 'Now: look here, all this mucking about, all you have to do is straddle the blasted thing, drape yourself over a couple of paper rocks in a pair of wings, and lean against a tree stump looking holy with a few plastic arrows stuck here and there. That's all. Nothing to it' *Forty* quid.'

'That's only *three* poses, boss,' said Nig, a matchstick stuck between his teeth.

'Well, the Greek Slave is a column instead of the tree, and no arrows, it doesn't make any difference to him. A little bit of oil for the highlights and a posing-pouch. Nothing to it. You game?'

'You're weird, the lot of you.'

'You got it on you then? The receipt, delivery receipt?'

Marcus looked down at the pale, earnest face, and the wide, anxious green eyes, the stubby little hands, the nicotined fingers, the airplane slide in the short shaggy hair. He suddenly laughed at her, nodded. She laughed back, her eyes dancing.

'Fantastic!' she said, and clapped her hands.

He found the receipt and handed it wordlessly to Gus Bender.

He pressed his face gently into the warm angle of her neck and shoulder: she smelled of fresh apples.

'God! My wrists and ankles, they are practically severed, look where the cords were.' He raised an arm towards her face, she took it and pressed her lips to the wrist tenderly.

'I have some stuff in my bag, very soothing. I will find it for you.' She made a sudden move from the bed, he grabbed her, pulled her back to him, holding her very tightly.

'No. Don't move. Stay where you are. This is very nice. They're getting better already.'

She moved his head gently on to her shoulder and nodded contentedly. 'I think it is very nice also. You must be very, very tired. So energetic . . .'

'Almost dead. I don't usually spend half the night tied to a stuffed horse, stuck all over with plastic arrows and buckled into a pair of paper wings stark naked.'

'Not so. Not stark.'

'As near as makes no difference.'

'You were very beautiful. Classic. Mr Gus said so. I thought so.' She laughed suddenly.

'What?'

'*You* thought so. I saw you looking at yourself in the mirrors, very pleased.'

'Shut up. Spy.'

Her hand caressed his cheek lightly, ran along his chin, pressed against his mouth, a finger slid against his lips, he bit her.

'You bite me. You have a terrible hard beard. I think you are a sadist.'

'With you I am. I could eat you all up.'

'You have already. And you will have indigestion because I am nothing but skin and bone.'

'I love your skin and bone. Smooth and warm. Soft.'

Her finger ran round the inside of his ear. 'Perhaps then I can stay a little while, here with you?'

'Where else would you go?'

'I don't know. I have a friend in Holland Park.'

'But you are my agent now: you said so.'

'Yes: I am. But you don't have to love your agent, you know.'

'I haven't said I did, have I?'

The finger stopped tracing his ear and was still. 'No.'

'But I am new to the job. I will need advice all the time.'

'And what will your friend in the next room say?'

'Martin? Across the passage? Nothing. He likes German food.'

'He does? Fantastic.'

'He'll have to.'

She eased herself away and leant up on one elbow looking down at him. 'But you must not get fat.' She placed her hand flat on his stomach. 'This must not have a little bump on it. German food is heavy, you know, the clients will say, "No thank you, we do not want photographs of Buddha, we are Arabs." So I must give you salads and fruit.'

'Why don't you shut up and come back.'

'I am not far away. Here only, watching you.'

'I want to watch you.' He dragged her down and wrapped her tightly in his arms.

'I don't want to go away,' she said after a moment.

'I don't want you to go either. What about this Dieter? I seem to have moved him out.'

'Oh, Dieter. Oh well, I don't know. It was not like you with him, I just was like a friend, is it? Cooking . . . I make the flat pretty, so on. Fantastic. He was good to me, but you know he smokes too much, and "stuff". He is not always quite all right.'

'Was that what he was in Hamburg for. Ciggies?'

She suddenly thrust her head hard against his chest. He felt her shoulders shrug.

'Was it, Leni? Ciggies and "stuff"?'

'I don't know.' Her voice was blurred. 'Perhaps more than that.'

'That's bad.'

'I know. I have seen. In Berlin I had two friends; they died. Amin was sixteen. He just went to lie down on a seat in the zoo, and piff! Just like that, he was dead. Also my friend Hannah, she is dead . . .'

'Leni. You don't handle "stuff", do you? Swear?'

'I swear.' She pushed the bend of her arm close to his face.

'You can see. No marks. None anywhere. Never, never, never.'

'Because it is the worst thing,' he said, 'the very worst.'

'I know.'

'Is that what Dieter did? Bring it over to the Mayerling place, smuggle it in?'

She struggled out of his arms suddenly, put her own round him. 'Don't ask me these things. I don't know. Please let me stay with you. I will be no trouble, you will see, I am very neat . . .'

'All right.'

'I can?'

'If you like.'

'But do you like?'

'I do.'

'I could only stay if you said so.'

'I have said so. Just now. Saying it.'

'Not the important thing. You haven't said that.'

'Oh Christ! What's the code word? What do I have to say?'

'I could only stay if I was . . . loved.'

'How can I tell? I've only known you for twelve hours, for God's sake.'

'You do not have to swear at me all the time. I just asked. It is so simple.'

'Saying a thing like that isn't simple.'

'It is very simple if you feel it.'

'How do I know what I feel? It's never happened to me before.'

Her eyes grew wide with astonished delight; she pressed the stubby fingers hard to her lips, whistled softly.

'I am the first lady? Not possible.'

'No. Not the first lady. But the first, well, it hasn't happened like this before.'

'Then you must love me! That is the *sign*. If it is the first time for you this way, then of course you do not know, but I can tell, women always can, and I can tell you that you love me. Now. Fantastic!'

'I'm very glad to hear it. Doctor Goebbels. What do I do for it?'

'You say it aloud. You will like the sound it makes.'

'And will that make me all better?'

'All better. You will see. It is simple: but perhaps if I put on my clothes you will find it easier, I am less like a whore perhaps.' She slid lightly off the bed and stood for a moment in the middle of the room not perfectly certain where she had left her belongings. He watched her, smiling with amusement. A boy with his first pet mouse. She pulled on the tartan dress and the rabbit jacket, buttoned the two mangy buttons. Stood to attention, hands primly clasped before her.

'It won't do,' he said shaking his head.

'What is it?' Alarm in her eyes.

'No airplane. In your hair.'

'Oh my goodness! My slide!' Hands flew to her cropped hair, patted the sagging rabbit pockets, scrabbled about pulling out bits of paper, a crushed packet of cigarettes, the airplane. With trembling fingers she opened it and fixed it firmly to a spike of hair, stood erect, folded her hands, tilting her head a little to prevent it sliding down her face. 'There I am,' she said.

'You said it was simple to say, didn't you?'

She nodded and the airplane fell to the floor' If you feel it.'

'Well, I do,' he said grinning across the tumbled bed. 'I love you.'

'Fantastic!' she said.

He stood watching the water swirl away at the end of the bath in a minor whirlpool, removed the towel from his hips, rubbed his hair, looked at his reflection in the mirrors, stuck out his tongue, punched lightly into the air and went back into the bedroom. Somewhere in the pines a nightingale was singing. He draped the towel over a chairback, climbed up on to the bed, stretched out long and wide, folded his arms behind his head and stared up into the shadowy ceiling. Smiling.

And that's it. All of it so far. My story, all nineteen years long. Took longer to live than to remember. What would you make of it, Archie Charlie? How would it grab you, hey? Put a curl in your unruffled donnish hair? Open a little wider your backward-looking eyes? I wonder. Rummaging about in your attic full of yesterdays: second-hand yesterdays at that. If I told you you'd probably smile politely and push the decanter across the table. 'Do have another drink. The night is so young . . .' You wouldn't believe it, or pretend you hadn't heard, or it didn't happen, like your wife's little 'slip' this afternoon. The silence of discretion, good manners, incomprehension. Breeding. That it? I mean, look at it this way, if Decca had tossed herself off the rocks with her pockets full of boulders they'd have called the *Daily Mirror* long before the ruddy doctor. Front page, two columns; 'happy snap', too. Great 'space'. Something you wouldn't understand in a life as serene and still as a summer pond: perhaps you're scared of pushing in a stick and stirring up the mud. Is that it? I'll never know anyhow.

Did you love that funny woman I hauled out of the sea today? Did she ever love you? Did you touch? Kiss? Lie together under those pines, in this great echoing house; were you ever young once? I can't imagine it. Like the Queen going to the lavatory. Mind-blowing. Impossible. I suppose it was passionless love twice a year and then back to your history books; no wonder she went shrimping. Without the net.

One thing is certain though, it would send a well aimed ball right down the alley to the bowling-pins of your l'Aiglon image. Kerplonk! Rumble, rumble, rumble, rumble, ting, tang, tong, tung! Kerrasssh! Exploded! All fall down. I may look a bit like him, I'll give you that, but that's where it ends. And I'll bet he never fell in love with a German tart in a rabbit-skin jacket who couldn't cook. I know what she'll say. He said the word aloud to savour the sound.

'Fantastic!'

Chapter Three

Adolph Seeger and his brother Carl, who were chefs, left
Vienna two weeks after the Russians pulled out and headed
for the brighter lights, at that time, of London. They
worked hard and diligently and in the early Sixties secured
a failing greengrocer's shop in the then exploding Kings
Road and turned it into a thriving and fashionable
restaurant, serving Viennese and German specialities,
which they called 'The Mayerling Hütte'. Everything from
the Sacher Torte to the gherkins, the waiters and the
waitresses, was imported from their home city. For a
reasonable sum you could drink your steins of beer, sup
your bohnensuppe, and savour your smoked eel beneath
vast murals of Rudolph and Maria entwined in amorous
delight, or rocky peaks staccato with dark fir trees, laced
with racing torrents. There was zither music and candles,
stags' heads and pine benches carved all about with broken
hearts. The waiters were blond and personable, flapping
about in lederhosen, the waitresses comely, smiling, with
plaited hair, swirling about in dirndls with foaming jugs of
beer. The Seegers made a modest fortune. But by the end
of the Seventies knew that a change was needed. The
folksy-zither had become a deathly cliché, the lederhosen
shiny with sweat and wear, the dirndls definitely dated. To
this end they stripped out the murals, stags' heads, and
pine-cone candlesticks, dressed the staff in black satin and
white shirts, covered the walls in plastic tortoise-shell,
illuminated the room with coloured spotlights and built a
minute glass podium, lit from below, at the far end of the
room on which from midnight until one, every night, a
small figure in a shabby black dress, hair cropped short

and held in place by a cheap plastic slide in the shape of an airplane, sang old Zarah Leander songs from a Berlin long since pounded to dust.

Leni Minx was an instant success. The small, husky, bitter little voice, often uneven and unsure, commanded strange attention, and produced a deep nostalgia even in the breasts of those who had never been further East in their lives than Felixstowe. No one ate while Leni sang, and indeed some silently wept and carved small swastikas into the soft wood of the bar. The Mayerling Hütte swung back to popularity, and Adolph Seeger blessed the night that he went into a cheap bar off the Kurfürstendamm for a late bowl of soup and found his 'star' singing, literally, for her supper to a noisy and inattentive audience who had heard this kind of thing long before; and done better. But the Kings Road, he reckoned, hadn't yet become over-familiar with the world of Isherwood and Grosz; she was an amateur, and the English liked amateurs far more than professionals; she was also cheap. Three days later, in the same black dress, she arrived with him in London where he gave her a small advance, which she considered a fortune, and bought her a rabbit-skin jacket at a C & A sale, covered her face with a thick white make-up worn by the No dancers of Japan, and carted her off to Bender's Studios in Covent Garden for a photographic session, buying every known recording of songs from pre-war Berlin and a record-player which he insisted she listen to day and night.

Bewildered, exhausted, and with only a modest amount of English which she said she had picked up 'from the American Forces' Network on the radio', she gratefully accepted the use of a bed in a small cupboard in the flat of Dieter Muller, the head waiter at the Mayerling Hütte, who charged her no rent on condition that she did a little house-work about the place and washed out his white shirts. He required no other service, as he considered her too skinny

75

and far too boyish for his lustier tastes, which, at that time, were being sternly suppressed owing to the fact that his training routine (he was making his third attempt at Mr Body Beautiful of West Paddington) was so severe that he frequently found it an effort to move among the tables at night, let alone smile at a customer.

After the first flush of success, which lasted all of four weeks and then levelled out into a pleasant routine, the 'Piaf of the Kurfürstendamm', as she was originally billed, settled down comfortably, enlarging her repertoire and her English vocabulary at the same time, for she was quick to discover that it was not just her voice which attracted many of the customers; and being a willing and industrious girl she seized every opportunity for advancement and very soon found that she spend less and less time washing Dieter's shirts or listening to his agonized sobs and groans as he raised and lowered his bar-bells, but more and more time extending her range of talents.

Herr Seeger had offered her a number of useful contacts here and there, and she was delighted, if astonished, to discover that underneath the thick layer of white No make-up her appealing innocence and childishness were still apparent to those who wished to discover it; and a lucrative number of gentlemen did. To this end Herr Seeger sent her back to Bender's Studios, removed the make-up and the black dress, scrubbed her face, gave her a lacrosse stick, a gym-slip and a Shirley Temple wig, in which disguise Mr Bender took a series of poses which he said, himself, were 'Saucy, but impish. And in the best of bad taste.' She didn't know exactly what he meant, but found that she quite enjoyed the work and the extra money which 'posing' brought her, for Herr Seeger gave her a very small 'cut' on every still sold at the restaurant and they sold well. Briskly in fact. So that in time, the gym-slip alternated with little gingham aprons, poke bonnets, dancing pumps, and modest hand-smocked pinafores,

76

worn with wrinkled white socks. But although she enjoyed the dressing up and make-believe in an appropriately childish way, she was always secretly relieved to pull on the shabby black dress for the Dietrich-Lenya-Leander numbers which she croaked out in the evenings accompanied by an elderly, weary Jew who had once played Schubert and Bach in Prague.

But the 'Sessions', as she learned to call them, in the hustle and warmth of Bender's Studios, delighted her, for the people with whom she worked were above all things kind, and she responded to kindness like a cat to an open fire.

In the motley assortment of people who made up the Staff, Gus Bender was without doubt the Boss. A warm, intelligent man, well into his sixties, he knew all there was to know about his craft, and practised it with care and devotion. He was a calm, down-to-earth creature who brooded no kind of 'nonsense'.

'I always call a spade a spade, don't I, Nig?' he said one day to the tall, gentle Jamaican who trundled the lamps and cables about the studio. And Nig agreed with a happy smile, rolling himself his eternal 'ciggie'.

'You know just where you are with the Boss,' said Nellie Boot, the re-toucher, who had spent twenty-eight of her sixty years wielding paint and air-brushes in her little room littered with prints and negatives. 'He's a good man, like the three brass monkeys, you know? See, hear and speak no evil. And that's rare in a firm like this.' She made endless cups of tea for everyone and fed them with buns and biscuits from a battered tin box.

And there was Stanley Plum, the Boss's younger assistant who was particularly good at 'women', priding himself, not without reason, that he could turn a Medusa into a Monroe with a little bit of 'diffusion' (a tiny smear of Vaseline on the lens) and a high key-light. He taught Leni, who wanted to know, all she needed about key-spots, highlights, shadow, flares, focus and profiles and often gave her a lift back to Chelsea on the back of his Honda. All in all they were a family to her, and as, she told Gus Bender one evening, she had never had a proper family of her own as far as she could remember, for her mother had distractedly handed her over to her grandmother almost as soon as she was born and faded out of her life, while her unknown Marine Sergeant father had returned routinely to Texas and was never heard of again, she held on to the Studio Group tightly, and spent a good deal of her time among them.

Quite apart from everything else, she enjoyed the rush and bustle that went on in the dusty studio, the strange people who hurried in and out for 'portraits' and 'groups', the constant blare of the Hi Fi with its endless tapes of everything from Rock and Roll to Stravinski for 'mood setting', the smell of paint, make-up, dust and hot lamps, the glitter of sequins and silver paper, the coloured lights, cables and junction boxes and walls covered with photographs of smiling soubrettes in organza frills, clowns with bubble noses, conjurors with budgerigars, dancers in lamé on roller skates, and anguished-faced youths in open-necked shirts yearning to play 'Hamlet'.

'A theatrical factory,' Gus Bender called it. 'A factory for dreams, hopes, fantasy and illusions. Nothing more and nothing less.' It was the main function of his work and had been ever since he had started out with a plate camera and a couple of lamps to supply these commodities for the hundreds of determined young people who had set their sights on fame and success in the world of the theatre. And who very seldom succeeded. However, *his* business thrived from the start, as his prices were modest, his skill undoubted, and his premises fortunately central to the activities of that world. He also did his best to keep ahead of fashions and was always willing to experiment as long as everything was kept within the limits of what he personally considered to be good taste: being a sensible man he made these limits reasonably flexible.

At some time in his career, and he always blessed the day, an elderly actor of some fame and distinction visited the studio to arrange a private sitting for a nephew who was just about to embark on his road to the Theatre. He stressed that his nephew was quite unused to the ways of the profession as yet, having only recently left the Army, and that he himself would be present at the sitting in order to assure that everything possible was done to relax the sitter and bring out the very best in his personality. He hoped that Mr Bender would not be annoyed by this suggestion, and that he would keep the appointment as private as possible since the whole thing was to be 'a delicious surprise' for the young man's unsuspecting family. He added that he was fully prepared to pay extra for any trouble he might put Mr Bender to, and suggested that a very plain and simple backing would be all that was required, perhaps a grey velvet curtain or something?, as the subject was exceptionally good looking and needed no embellishments. Which was perfectly true, and clear for everyone to see, for all he wore that day was a pair of thigh boots, a lifeguard's helmet and a three-foot sword.

The 'Special Sessions' had started. For clients with particular interests and very particular pockets. Mr Bender never looked back and his reputation for tact, delicacy, firmness, and splendid results spread quietly about London like couch-grass in a lawn. Sometimes the clients provided their own models and 'story-lines', and at others just the story, leaving Bender's Studios to supply the personnel, which was not at all a difficult task as the vast majority of his usual clientele were out of work anyway and he was always happy that he could find a 'little job' for his boys and girls from time to time, and they in turn always hoped that 'it would lead to better things' with the stubborn optimism of their profession. Which it never did. But for Gus Bender, 'Aesthetic Art Models' was born.

In this manner Leni Minx had joined her 'family' and she it was who, seeing Gus more than usually troubled one day, suggested Dieter Muller as a perfect example of a 'Siegfried', a suitable specimen being difficult, at that moment, to obtain. Dieter accepted the offer with pleasure at the idea of the fee suggested, and at the thought of having his months of strain and struggle put to good use. He had an instant and resounding success as Siegfried and went on to pose as an 'Atlas' in plastic chains, the central figure in the 'Laocoön' (without a beard). Hercules, Ulysses, and a varied collection of Greek Slaves, Captives, Storm Troopers and Roman Centurions. The fact that he had lost, for the third time, his West Paddington title didn't worry him in the least: he was making extremely good money, his splendid muscles were being preserved, for all time, on film and he blossomed under the adoring eye of Stanley Plum's Rolleiflex. In a very short time he became the star of the 'Special Sessions' and his classical extravaganzas were avidly collected by a wide variety of clients, ranging from a Liberal Peer, a bank manager in Willesden, to a Lebanese plastics manufacturer with an unlimited pocket, and a broad imagination. Sadly, Dieter was a simple-minded young man and sudden success went almost instantly to his head with the money and fame his plastic-chained, heavily oiled, classical body brought him. His work, both at the Mayerling Hütte and at the studio, began to suffer, he was often late, always exhausted, and sometimes not always 'quite there', as Leni noted with growing alarm.

Although it was strictly forbidden by the Studio to give any information on their models, from names to telephone numbers, somehow Dieter had managed to make contacts and broken the golden rule, and his appearance in the company of a sturdy girl from Sweden called Ursula, was greeted with delighted expectation at many a private party from Weybridge to Highgate Hill. His trips home to his doting parents in Hamburg seemed to become more and more frequent and just as Herr Seeger had made up his mind reluctantly to a change in his Staff, Dieter Muller's car was stopped and searched at Harwich and he, two companions and fifty pounds of cannabis were taken into custody.

'Uncle' Desmond's stuffed horse might very well have been the wooden horse of Troy, such was the surprise, astonishment and disarray it caused in Marcus's hitherto moderately routine and orderly life. Not only had its delivery brought him an unexpected, if curious, way of extending his finances, it had also brought him face to face with the wan, slender, wide green-eyed creature who came out of Gus Bender's office that afternoon. He had, instantly and irrevocably, and for the first time in his life, fallen in love. Driving it back to his rooms in Shepherd's Bush in the van he had hardly dared touch it for fear it might shatter into fragments; he was so in awe of it that all he could do was smile inanely all the way while it chattered happily on in a husky, whispering voice, and counted again and again the ten one pound notes which Gus Bender had reluctantly handed over on the firm promise that he would have a 'Mazeppa' at least, by nine o'clock that evening.

Over chipped mugs of coffee in his shabby room the advice he was offered on how to perform his duties that evening for the Session was detailed, knowledgeable, and finally almost reassuring; she knew every trick in the book and had introduced a few more to him from her own which was extensive. Later, lying with her apparently fragile body in his arms, as smooth and pale as alabaster, as soft and pliable as silk, he realized that he was holding everything which he had lacked throughout his life so far: enchantment, need, love and beauty. For there was beauty in the small snub nose, the delicate bones of cheek and wrist, the slender thighs and budding breasts and in the strange green eyes which, looking at him suddenly, brimmed with tears which she let slip slowly down the sides of her face like melting ice. He made no move to dry them, nor did he ask her why they had come: he thought he knew, and bent to kiss her in gratitude.

Leni moved in; and the French-polisher in the room opposite moved out very soon afterwards. A combination of margarine smoke meandering about the tin cooker on the landing outside his room all day, the steady diet of soggy schnitzels, cabbage and caraway, watery gruel and grey dumplings, heavy as curling-stones, finally proved too much for him and he left to find accommodation elsewhere and returned to his normal diet of eggs, chips and ketchup in another part of town.

Leni sprang into action and her cooking became marginally better: at least rather more varied and out of tins, but edible. Marcus, in a haze of love, wondered occasionally if her strategy had been deliberate, but hearing the little voice whispering in crow-like song about her possessions, dismissed the idea almost as soon as it arrived. Which was unwise.

The rooms, plus the dark landing, became 'her' pad. She scrubbed and polished daily. The cooker gleamed like a surgeon's knife, the place had the sparkle and light of a Dutch Interior, a green plant trailed from a hanging pot, and 'Uncle' Desmond, a willing, if bemused, assistant, supplied them with a brass bed from his stock, and a chest of drawers for Leni's meagre possessions.

Marcus supplemented his job at Moviedecor Ltd with a 'Session' at the Studio from time to time, for they were delighted with his work and with the response from their Special Clients who had been greatly impressed by the modest portfolio of his 'poses' which Mr Bender circulated, tactfully, among them. Within a short time he had settled down into the routine, and although he found it exceptionally childish, he didn't find it tiring or arduous, always just within the bounds of taste, and as time went on, profitable. For he speedily replaced Dieter in the Catalogues as he was able to do contemporary poses as well as merely Classical, and as Leni's job at the Mayerling Hütte had come to an abrupt end with the departure of Herr Seeger the extra money was both essential and comforting.

Herr Seeger's brother, Herr Carl, had decided to play very carefully after the arrest of Dieter. The 'fuzz' had been extremely curious for a week or two, and a number of regular clients faded quietly away to other haunts. A low profile was considered advisable at the Hütte, and, as he pointed out, Leni's act, such as it was, had run its course. They were weary of the same songs nightly; something new and young was needed to go with the beer and wurst, so he had engaged a new, exciting group of three young men called The Rape Hunger Trio. He gave her four nights' salary and she left with a high heart for she had grown bored with the job herself, with the thick No make-up and the mournful songs which now, she discovered, people paid scant attention to, so that she whispered away to a constant barrage of knives and forks and the clatter of glasses. Enough was enough. She applied herself to sewing on buttons, washing shirts, preparing her hideous menus and travelling about the countryside occasionally with Marcus in his vans delivering the 'props' or helping him in or out of the varied costumes required for his evening work. A life, one would think, of almost immoderate domestic bliss.

One evening in early summer, driving back to London with a van load of junk which Desmond had purchased at an auction in an ugly house outside Hove, Leni suggested that perhaps they might stop for a drink and a sandwich at 'some dear little inn in the fields, the air is so fine, the light

83

so pretty, we will listen to the birds perhaps, and smell the grass and the leaves'.

The inn wasn't in the fields, and there weren't any birds, but the air was sweet and the silence comforting, and Marcus was tired and felt a rest would be wise before the assault on London's traffic. They had their drinks and a toasted sandwich at a tin table in the yard, so that he could keep an eye on the van. Leni sat in the last of the fading sun, her eyes filled with light, her lips curved in a soft smile of contentment under a thin moustache of beer foam.

'You know? I am very happy here. I like the country, it is so still. We couldn't come to the country, to live?'

'No,' said Marcus. 'I've had all I want of the country, thanks.'

She nodded thoughtfully. 'Ah yes. With your mother, and the dog. But you were only a little boy then: perhaps now that you are grown up you would like it better?'

'I wouldn't. And I couldn't afford to; be sensible.'

'So masterful! Snap, snap! I will forget the suggestion, therefore. I like it so when you are severe, you know? Like the other night at the Studio when you were in that costume. So strong! So masculine! Do you know I thought it would be very wonderful if we made love together, just like that. You could carry me off to your tent, or wherever it would be, and we would make love all the night long.'

'In a tent! In a suit of lights? Christ, I'd be half dead. I can't move in it.'

'So beautiful. All women like things like that, you know? They have secret dreams about handsome Sheiks in the sands . . . like Rudolph Valentino, remember?'

'No, I don't. And neither do you.'

'But I have seen pictures. Fantastic.'

'You are a slut, that's all. A servant girl slut.'

She shook her head slowly. 'No. I *am*; but not really. I am very romantic, you see. Also I am German, you must 'not forget this.'

'Difficult to. All the uniform-kick. I know you like it when I am dressed up as soldiers. Jack boots and swastikas . . .'

A sudden stab of anger in the green, luminous eyes. 'I did not know that time. In 1958 I was born. It was finished then.'

'But I expect you saw the pictures?'

The anger left as swiftly as it had arrived; she placed a small hand on his on the tin table top. 'We are breaking our own rules, remember? We don't speak of that time, it is not our time and nothing to do with us. You make me sadder than I am already.'

He was instantly contrite, held the hand tightly. 'But why? What are you sad about? You didn't say anything.'

'No, not today because it was a busy day for you with the Sale and everything. But yesterday a girl from the Mayerling Hütte brought me a letter. From Germany. I have to go back, you see . . . which is why I am sad and so . . .'

'Why didn't you tell me? What's happened? Why must you go back?'

'For my Granny, you know. It is nearly one year since I have seen her and she is missing me and is ill. Very, very ill, they ask me just to come back, for a little time, to see her, to hold her hand, to perhaps make her be better, but this they do not really believe . . . it is serious.'

'Who is "they"?'

'Oh . . .' She shrugged and pulled down her shirt sleeves. 'It gets cold, no? My auntie, she has written. So I think that I must go, it is not for so long, a few days only. Just to see her.'

'But when?'

'Oh, in a day or two. Monday perhaps. Soon.'

'What about money. The fare?'

'I have some. I saved all the time because you have been

85

so kind, and Dieter was so kind and also Mr Bender. I will get a cheap flight to Hamburg . . . it's not so hard.'

Marcus finished his beer, put the pint glass on the table. 'Well, that's buggered up my Super Idea. I had something to suggest.'

'Oh, what? What? You must say to me, what did you have?'

'Desmond has a truck going down to the South of France at the end of next week. He said we could hitch a lift, free; keep an eye on the stuff, then go off on our own for a few days. I thought we could take a tent, sleeping bags . . . just wander about there. I've never been.'

Leni looked at him in stricken silence. 'A *tent*! It would be *awful*, a tent. All the animals, the walking, the rain and things creeping about at night. I would have to cook like a Girl Guide person, on sticks.'

'You'd like it.'

'I would hate it. And you would hate me for not liking. So it would be terrible.'

'Well, anyway, if you must go to Germany . . .'

Leni suddenly had a brilliant idea. 'I know! I know what we will do. I will go to my Granny, you will go on the van and I will come to join you when you are there . . . and we will come home together in the tent thing. Is a good idea? Where would you go?'

'I don't know. Near Nice, I think.'

'And that is the airport, and you could meet me and maybe by then you will have found a sweet little place that we can stay. Very cheap. In the sun. By the sea.'

'I don't like the idea of you going off on your own; without me.'

'I am very capable,' said Leni swiftly. 'I have done this many times before, you know. I shall be quite well in Hamburg. I will be with the family.' She cupped her chin in her hands and looked wanly across the table. 'Oh, Marcus! Lucky Marcus, you do not have a Granny.' She smiled, ran her hand through the spiky hair, the airplane slide clattered to the table top. 'And I am all she has left . . . I must go to her. And we must go to London now, I think. Look! The sun is dying and I must have a little pee-pee. It is just up the path there, I think. By the big tree, you will wait for me?'

The path sloped down through the cornfield to a brook and a clump of pale willows standing in circular pools of heavy shadow. The sun was high. She walked through the greening heads of barley, brushing them with the palm of her hand, her bare feet scurrying the fine dust of the track over nodding drifts of poppies, her skirt rustling through the dense green thickets of stalk. She stopped, shading her eyes from the glare: down by the brook, moving with cautious, angular gait, a stork on thin vermillion legs prodding here and there in the sedge. Larks singing, insects, a bee droned away, giddy with pollen. Beyond the brook the land rose steeply from the valley, unkempt, neglected, rusty with fronds of many seasons of bracken, springing cables of bramble; the stumps of the orchard that had once been there buried in thistle and ragwort, the twiggy tops lying as they had fallen, like long discarded kitchen brooms. Beyond the destruction, striding the hill top for as far as she could see from north to south, the grey steel mesh of the Wall, wire looped tightly along the top, a watchtower, black as a witch's hat. A uniformed figure tight against one of the supports, the sunlight winking on the lenses of his binoculars like silver pennies.

She turned and walked back. The cobbles of the farm yard spilled with water; long sparkling streams, clanking of buckets, clatter of metal on stone. Horst in the seat of the big, red tractor, Frieda scouring a gleaming churn with a fast-running hose, geese wobbling along with high-raised heads, scurrying, suddenly outstretched wings as the tractor roared into life and shuddered down the yard.

Frieda called out something but she couldn't hear; she waved and turned down the brick path between the dairy and the Dutch barn, where she sat on a tumbled bale of hay and pulled on her shoes. Not silver, she thought, not for this place or this time or this life. Perfectly respectable tennis shoes. White. A perfectly respectable white silk dress, a pale blue cashmere slung over my shoulders, no hat against the sun, no airplane slide in my burnished blond hair. Marcus's face . . . dear Marcus, what would you say if you saw me now?

Then is then: and now is now, by courtesy of a Lufthansa jet. My native soil. The heritage which I have willingly renounced. She walked into the lime avenue from the yard; ahead, the house pink-faced in the sun, high-pitched red-tiled roof, the two pavilions, East and West, tall sashed windows, grey lichened steps to the shallow terrace, bay trees in white tubs, sparrows; Dalmatians dozing in the sun. Schloss Lamsfeld, an absurd name for a modest dwelling. In England, what? A Manor, a Place, just a House? Too small to open to the public, too large to maintain, but here in Schleswig Holstein a 'Schloss'; secure, proud, smug in its acres, half its acres, with the Russians 300 metres across the brook. Fantasy land. Here they live out fantasies too, just as I do in England, but mine are safer. In the cool drawing-room, glowing with polished-wood tapestried chairs, a great white porcelain stove in the corner, the lingering scents of wood-ash and beeswax, my mother predictably arranging flowers. Sweet peas in low crystal bowls. Elisabeth von Lamsfeld, tall and slender, high-boned, high-browed, trim little mouth, tapering fingers, a Dürer Madonna with cool green eyes.

'How far did you go?' she said.

'Not far. To the Schwarzbrücke, that's all.'

'Ah yes. One can't go very far there. Only east.'

'I brought these.' She laid a bunch of cornflowers on the table.

'Oh, those things. Pretty but a bore. Horst has put the whole place down to barley this year and he simply can't get rid of them. They poison the cattle. Find a bowl and have them in your room, I'm doing these for tonight, I hate big things of flowers on a dining-table, they get in the way of the conversation dreadfully.'

'How many of us will there be?'

'Ten. Horst and Isobel, of course, you and me, Helmut and Annie, the two lawyers, and Klaus has asked a pretty child he met last season at Kitzbühel, Agnes Gollrad. You haven't met her? A comfortable table. The Family. I'm so happy that you came, Luise, you know how much it means to me . . . it's an important event.'

'Me being twenty-one, and you being sixty? A double celebration?'

Elisabeth smiled, lifted a bowl of flowers and carried them to a tray. 'Not being *sixty*. Handing over to Horst. Losing the reins. That's important.'

'And Horst wants the responsibility? And Isobel, does she?'

'Horst is the eldest son, it's his duty and his responsibility. He's always known that ever since your father died. He has no option, and in any case, the answer is yes. Not everyone runs away.'

'Point made, Mamma.'

'Give me the scissors, will you? By your hand there. Isobel is a splendid girl, I am immensely happy for Horst, she is the perfect wife. I have no fears for the future at all. I can hand over the baton, so to speak, to a pair of "splendid runners". My part of the race is run.'

'Such optimism! You will retire happily to the West Pavilion to sew and tend your roses, with half the estates divided and just across the Schwarzbrücke the Russians polishing their rifles? The enemy is not at the gates, Mamma, they are in the orchards.'

'You always exaggerate! You always did. You speak so

loosely. Not *half* the estates, Luise dear, a *third* only. And how do we know it is the enemy beyond the wall? Are you certain? Germans, I am told. The same blood as ourselves, and in time, you will see, we shall be united once more. This is a temporary thing. We survive. We have suffered two atrocious defeats in this house practically within my life time – *and* a brutal occupation; I feel perfectly confident that we shall survive a wire and concrete wall.'

'Would you say, perhaps, three defeats in this house?'

Her mother's eyebrows arched slightly; she turned, the scissors in her hand. 'Three?'

'Me. I fought you. I won. I left.' Her voice low, firm.

'I never considered that a defeat. Not for me, or for this house, or for the family. For you perhaps, yes . . . I do not know; but *I* have never thought of it as a defeat that you left to do as you chose. Madness, wilfulness, headstrong stupidity, whatever you like to call it. But not defeat. And in any case, Luise dear, defeat can make one very strong, did you know that? One is not always destroyed by defeat but often strengthened, as this family has been. We fight harder; and we survive.'

'Making myself feel more important than I was; I can see that. Oh, dear!'

'Ah yes. But you always did! Always did! Perfectly natural for an only girl in a male family I understand, but tiresome: and you lost. Secret and aloof, dreaming in a world of books and diaries . . . or on the other hand determined to be the centre of everything, to dazzle, amuse, astonish. You have never been a sensible young creature, never balanced. One only hopes that this strange time away has made some improvements. We shall see.'

'I shall be very sensible and calm this evening, you will be greatly pleased.'

'I am sure that you will.' The scissors snipped briskly, stalks scattered, she fluffed up petals. 'You have something to wear, upstairs? Not that awful tartan thing

90

you arrived in . . .' She laughed, but there was a tremor of anxiety.

'No. Not that. I found something suitable. If I can still get into it.'

'You should do. Thin as a rail. God knows what they give you to eat there.'

'I eat well. They run a restaurant after all.'

'Jews, you said.'

'From Vienna.'

'Ah. The worst kind. Next to Armenian. Orthodox?'

'No. Quite ordinary. Like you and me.'

'Thank you. An au pair to Austrian refugees in England! One would hardly call that ordinary, and before that a Berlin bar or something. Surely unusual?'

'Thousands of us are doing it.'

'Us? And why did you change to that absurd name, what was it? "Leni Minx". It was quite like writing to a stranger, Leni Minx at the something Hütte.'

'A stage name, if you like. I could hardly use von Lamsfeld in Berlin. Supposing someone had recognized me, you'd have had a fit! Such a shock for the family.'

'How loosely you talk. A "shock", and "fit". Luise, what you do to the German language is monstrous, really! No. I shouldn't have been happy, of course. But I imagine few of our friends venture into the Berlin cellars. However, it was careful, and that shows some kind of consideration at least.' She picked up the last bowl of flowers. 'But "Leni Minx"! Really . . . and that awful hair. It is so sad.'

'I'll wear a hat, if you like.'

Elisabeth turned sharply at the doors, the bowl steady in her hands. 'A ribbon would do. Perfectly. Dr Langerdorf and his partner and Klaus's friend, the Gollrad child, have all been informed that you are studying in England. English. That's quite suitable, isn't it? A ribbon would be perfect.'

'So. A ribbon will make me appear respectable? But

nothing is ever quite what it seems, Mamma, is it? You have your fantasies just as much as I do, and you live them also. There is no Wall beyond the Schwarzbrücke, defeat will make you strong, I didn't escape from you and leave this house, you are handing on the "baton" to two "splendid runners", and you have no fear of the future. My God! How strong!'

Elisabeth was perfectly still in the doorway. 'Quite so,' she said. 'The truth is often much too harsh to face. Sometimes the only way to live one's life is to live in fantasy, in order to survive at all. I am certain that this is something which you have discovered for yourself, isn't it? Probably you have known it all the time. However, you have omitted one particular fantasy of mine which perhaps, since you are now of age so to speak, you should be told. I even pretend to myself that I am *not* a widow.' She smiled a clear unshadowed smile. 'The difficult thing, of course, is to remain believing in your fantasies . . . as such. It is exceptionally hard to do because quite often, you see, they turn into nightmares.' She nodded lightly. 'Yes. *Do* . . . wear a ribbon.'

Horst came into the room quietly, a bottle under his arm, two glasses bulging the pocket of his velvet smoking-jacket.

'Here we are. As promised. A secret night-cap.'

'Dear Horst. The "splendid runner".'

'What does that mean exactly? You always bewilder one.'

'Mamma said that you and Isobel were "splendid runners" to whom she would hand over her baton. Whip, more like it.'

He laughed, settled into a fat wicker chair. 'That tongue of yours! You really are unforgiving.'

'I am so stimulated by the conversation of this evening,

such wit! Such originality, I reel with pleasure at the sophistication of it all. Particularly Dr Langerdorf.'

He handed her a glass, pressed back the cork with the heel of his hand, took up his own glass and smiled across the lamp-lit room. 'You can hardly expect Berlin or London at Lamsfeld. We are simple people with simple things to discuss. But you *can* expect the best schnapps in Germany.' He raised his glass. 'To you, dear Luise. The little sister now a woman.' Horst was tall, thick-thighed, thick-necked, with strong hands. 'This is your celebration as well as mine.'

'Is yours such a celebration? Such responsibility . . . poor Isobel. Prisoners here for the rest of your lives.'

'No, not so. Isobel is happy. I am happy. It is what I expected, what I wanted. We have Klaus and Helmut to help us, we are a united family still. I am also, as I have told you, a country boy, I have no love for cities and so on, and I love my land.'

She sipped her glass carefully, he had filled it very full. 'What is left of it.'

'Yes. But enough.'

She looked about her room, familiar, unloved. The high wooden bed, blue porcelain stove, a lithograph of The Crucifixion, the cuckoo clock, a worn plush teddy bear. 'The relics of my youth,' she laughed and raised her glass. 'Adieu! Goodbye youth, goodbye relics, goodbye past! My celebration.'

'You gave Mamma great pleasure in coming.'

'I hadn't much option. She wrote and said, "Come!" and sent the fare. I came for you, the new "Squire" of Lamsfeld.'

'I knew. Thank you.'

'I shall not return, you know.'

'Perhaps? One day? Later?'

'No . . . no, I have a new life. I invented a new person to be, I like her best, I like her life, she amuses me, I know her well now, she's not very original, and she doesn't belong here. But then, even I never really did.'

Horst crossed his thick farmer's legs. 'Oh come now. What nonsense. You were born here, you are our blood. Of course you belong.'

She pulled the ribbon from her hair and rolled it into a ball. 'I came fourteen years too late to enjoy you all. Fourteen years, Horst! The unlucky surprise. The gravest mistake Mamma ever made was thinking that she was safe because she had reached thirty-nine! Poor Papa! One last burst of passion and, lo and behold, me! The ewe lamb, the outsider, the changeling, the only girl child . . . what to do with her? But not you, my dearest Horst, my saviour. my safety valve. You were so good and sweet to me, always; and for that reason I am here today, and for that reason I will never forget you. But the rest . . .' she threw the ball of twisted ribbon into the shadows '. . . I obliterate. Tonight, you know, it was just as if I had never left. An endless strip of film, continually running, like the thing in the Reichstag Museum, you know? A continuous loop; as soon as it finishes it starts all over again, endless, endless. The history of the German people, repeated every fifteen minutes, lest you forget. The same this evening; the Land, the Wall, the perfidy of Eisenhower for allowing the Russians to take Berlin, the squalor of the Vulgarian and his SS, the nostalgia, the looking back. And after dinner, Horst, the *same* music on the gramophone! The same as when I was knee high . . . as when Mamma and Papa used to have their evening concerts. Wagner, eternal Wagner . . . Schumann; Papa reading from Schiller, and then, before we went to bed, lighter things, Willi Fritsch, Lilian Harvey, Leander, Hans Albers . . . those voices are still in my head. I sing the songs to this day! That is all the dead, Horst, the *time* has gone. But this evening the same thing again. Not the Schiller, to be sure, but Fritsch, Leander . . . operetta, nostalgia! God! The continuous belt of film . . .

as if nothing had happened, as if the Wall through the orchard was not really there.'

'Oh, it is there.' He was smiling. 'It is there. We see it, feel it every moment of the day. Perhaps, you know, that is why we look back all the time? The present is not so beautiful. But we *are* aware, have no fear of that. We have been here on this land long before Charlemagne, before the Danes, before the Prussians. We are the Wends! The warrior race, true Mecklenburgers, you cannot forget that. And we have stayed, whatever came, whoever came. We are not little grey mice. We shall stay.'

She shook her head. 'I shall not.'

'One day you will come back, of that I am certain. When you have done all that you want to in the world beyond these fields, you will come home; because it is your heritage, and your blood. We hold fast, you see? Your place is here for always, remember that, and remember, too, that I love you.'

She knelt on the pine boards between his thick legs, one hand on his knee. 'You have so much courage, Horst. I pray for you and Isobel, and I don't pray very much; do you think I will be listened to?'

'If you mean it very strongly.'

'Oh, I shall! I do. Everything I do, I do with strength, you know? Even this new life I am living, I do it with all my heart.'

'Mamma said something about being an au pair girl. Is it true?'

'No. For her it is true. I do all kinds of things. I manage.'

'Even to sing! But you can't?'

'No! Awful. But I speak them mostly. My voice is so strained that I think I have nodules on the chords or something, you know? Very German, very nostalgic. When I left here that was the only part of my "heritage" that I took with me, you see? Those terrible "concerts", all those songs. I knew them by heart. So some good has come out of them, I suppose.'

He cupped her face in his broad hand. 'You are mad, you know: completely mad.'

'Oh, I know! And it is so marvellous!'

'You chide us for being dull and unoriginal, of conforming, of living in the past, and yet there you go, trotting down the path of predictability as happy as an untethered goat!'

'But that is the whole point, don't you see? I *am* happy, and I *am* untethered!'

'You are also a goat; a dear goat, but nevertheless a goat. What is so unusual and original about your life! What is so extraordinary? Working in cheap bars and managing, as you call it. I can make a pretty shrewd guess what that means, can't I?'

She shrugged, rubbed a foot. 'If you like.'

'All people of your age today are the same. All chasing after some ill-defined form of freedom. You don't even know what it is! You think that *we* are the dull conformers, but you are exactly the same. You conform all the time. The pattern is the same, although our standards are different, but it all comes down to the same thing in the end, conforming. You break the rules, we hold to them for sense and stability; you hate the past, we cling to it for strength; you dress in the same manner as the rest of your tribe, so that you will be easily recognized, so do we; you have a private language, as we do also. Your generation has made its rules, just as we have, but our rules are founded on experience, whereas yours are founded on hearsay. We have one thing equally in common, an uncertain future; *we* know it is uncertain, but you don't even know if it is there at all, neither do you care. That is the only thing which sets you apart. We believe. You do not.'

'I care! I do care! I care for my future. Mine!'

'And what is it? Yours?'

'To be free. To do as I wish, to make my own life for myself.'

'An emancipated woman, sleeping where you like. Is that it? Singing in bars?'

'Well, I exist, I exist, Horst. I am not some vegetable as I would be here, sitting shelling peas. Yes Mamma! No Mamma! Crops and cattle, politics and parties with the elite of Lübeck! A well-bred German cabbage! Ah no: I exist.'

'And who exists? You or the person you pretend to be.'

'Both. We are indivisible, you see. I am the same person inside, all I have changed is my shell: like a hermit crab. All I am doing is escaping.'

'All that you are doing is denying your heritage and your blood.'

'All I am doing is denying the guilt of being German. I will not be responsible for the heritage and the blood which I have been forced, forced, Horst, you see, to inherit. It has nothing to do with me. *Nothing.* I came into this world as a hideous surprise to everyone, myself included. I had no choice. No one asked me if I wanted to be born. I *was.* Twenty-one years ago today. But it is not my fault and I will not be held responsible for the terrible things our people did more than thirty years ago. Why should I? Why? To spend my life in shame? Apologizing?'

Horst made small circles with the base of his glass on the chair arm. 'I was not responsible either, Luise. Not my generation either.'

'Your generation is linked more closely, you cannot escape it. Mine can, and I did. Mamma calls it "running away". And so I have; I have started my new life, far away, and I am happier than I can tell you. I will not live with guilt, and I have no proud memories of the past . . . I am only starting to make mine now.'

'In bars?'

'Oh that. No! That is over, it was a joke only, finished, done. I wasn't any good anyway, but it was a start. It was the only thing I knew a very little about, those bloody songs . . . they got me started. Now I move on, but not alone. There is someone in England.'

'Ah.'

'I love him very much.'

'And he?'

'I suppose so. He says so. I hope so. I love him with all my heart.'

'Of your generation, I would think?'

'Of my generation, you are right.'

'And does he know about this? Lamsfeld?'

She laughed suddenly, hugged her knees. 'God no! Not ever, I hope. Perhaps one day I will have to tell him, how do I know? But for the moment, he thinks I am just an abandoned German-American bastard with an ailing grandmother in Hamburg.'

'Dear God! Why . . . I mean, why Hamburg?'

'Because Hamburg is near to here, that's why. I had to have an excuse to come and so I said that my Granny was ill and alone, and asking for me. I cannot dazzle you with originality, Horst my dear, that I can see! But that is the sort of girl he thinks I am, and there are a great many of them about in this brave Germany of today. Relics of the Great Fraternization Period, you remember? After the Cold War time. It all fits in well for Leni Minx. I have been very thorough.'

'That awful name. Why?'

'I think it is so good. Simple.'

'It is unbelievable.'

'Not when you hear my English accent. Fantastic!'

'And this boy, this man, whoever he is, is quite happy with the cliché creature which you have invented?'

'Yes, quite. What you don't understand is that I have only invented the background, not the creature. She is just

98

as I always have been underneath my correct Mecklen-
burger surface, only none of you ever knew that . . . not
even you who were the closest.'

Horst lay back in the wicker chair, ran his hands over his
face, and when he looked down at her again he was
smiling. 'I don't suppose that I shall ever understand you.
Or what you are doing, or even why, properly. The
guilt . . . that, yes, I suppose that I can understand that, but
so many people of your generation have overcome that
perfectly comfortably without going to such extremes. I
can't believe that your life here was so restricted, so
Victorian, so unhappy . . . perhaps it was. I cannot tell.
But one thing does reassure me and that is your determination to succeed in whatever idiotic life you have
selected for yourself. That determination is in your blood,
the despised heritage, it is the family strength. You
will survive at all costs, and one day, as I have said, I am
certain that you will come back to us. Certain. But as you
said, my generation is closer to the last and we believe still
in a future, however obscure.'

He leant forward and took her hand between his large
ones. 'But don't lose me altogether. Sometimes just a
postcard, a note . . . nothing too demanding. I shall not
pry. I love you too well for that; only keep in touch now
and again. That's fair, isn't it?'

She nodded. 'That's fair.' She bent and kissed his
hands, holding them against her cheek for a moment.

'Just one thing more,' he said. 'Promise me that you are
truly happy?'

She nodded firmly. 'I am truly happy. Thank you.'

He rose, pushed the glasses in his pocket, took the bottle
by the neck. 'And when, or if, you are unhappy, you will
tell me here? I am the "patron" now, I will ask no
questions and if you call I shall hear.' He flipped a modest
packet of Deutschmarks on to the bed. 'It is quite
possible of course that you will not call; but just decide to

come home. That's your air fare if you do; and no questions, of course.'

She watched him going along the corridor, pause at the end, raise the bottle high above his head in a salute, and disappear down the creaking staircase. She closed the door, leant against it, and found that she was crying. She wiped her cheek briskly. To cry so easily! Sentimentality. Such a romantic creature. Of course, I don't cry for myself but for his courage; courage is always wonderfully moving in the face of adversity. And he faces that all right. And that heavy Isobel, God what a dumpy bore she is. Kind, sure, but a bore. A child-breeder. But that's just what he wanted for his tribe.

She pulled off her too-tight shoes, and dropped them in the hearth of the blue-tiled stove, traced her finger round the cool tiles. A swan, a mill house, a well, a leaping stag. I remember you. Lying here in bed on cold winter nights, Frau Schmoller creeping in to see if I was asleep, a bundle of clothing in her arms. 'Not asleep yet! Here are your things for tomorrow, we'll put them round the stove to air, to take off the chill. There, like that and that and that. All warm for the morning.' And hid you with woollen vests and stockings. So long ago. So far away and yet, tonight suddenly, terrifyingly near. Mamma at one end of the table, Horst at the other; candles, Frieda with the soup tureen, the house-wine in tall glass jugs, sweet peas, the high-boned face of Agnes Gollrad from Kitzbühel: 'I *long* for the snow, I am not a summer-woman.' And by God she was not. Dr Langerdorf smiling through thick glasses. 'And where in England are you studying? In London or perhaps in the country? It is so gentle, the English countryside, very much like this . . . of course we are also very much like the English here, don't you find? We are, after all, *not* Bavarians!' A great laugh of windy pleasure, he had wiped his lips. 'I know very well that English people think of all Germans as fat and beery and wearing hats with feathers and badger brushes! But we are not like that up here . . . I am sure you make that very clear where you are? A good ambassadress, for this State, eh?' He talked so much about his bloody State that I had no chance to answer, which was a relief to Mamma, I could see.

And the Toast to Horst. Touching, idiotic, solemn, as it should be: with the searchlight sweeping beyond the hill. And after, on the terrace, coffee and cognac, midges spiralling upwards, the air soft, bats swooping, soft rustle of silk, Agnes, Isobel and Annie laughing together, the wavering blue flame under the coffee pot. Mamma's strong arm, pouring. The scent of cigars from the men still talking in the saloon, the rumble of their conversation blurring the wistfulness of 'Ich bin von Kopf bis Fuss,' from the record-player as Horst started the 'Concert'. Sentimentality, nostalgia, sticky sweetness seeping out into the stillness of the evening. Time coming in like a tide, and I trapped in their cave of harmony. The searchlight flicking rhythmically across the far skyline, the diffused beam of a lighthouse, the water of hated-familiarity lapping at my feet, swirling about my ankles, mounting to my shins, higher and higher, colder and colder, to my waist, my chest. Panic growing. I would suffocate there, I would drown.

'Luise!' Elisabeth's voice, crisp as a rip through calico. 'You look so *bored*. Or tired? Tired perhaps after yesterday. A long trip. London–Hamburg . . .' she turned to the women '. . . and then that frightful drive on to Lübeck. It takes hours. Agnes dear? More coffee? Sugar? The brown or the little coloured kind?'

And walking away from them to the far end of the terrace under the lime trees, leaving the relics of the Last Supper. A Judas. Above me, a moth in the trembling leaves, the music far away, diffused. Breathing again, the tide ebbing but the red glimmer of a cigar and Dr Langerdorf coming towards me, a glass in his hand.

101

'Luise? Hiding away? Elisabeth says that you are tired from the journey yesterday. Flying is most distasteful, I find. One travels steerage now.'

'No. Not tired really. Too much to eat. I forget how much we Germans eat.'

'And in England they do not eat well?'

'Yes, well . . . lighter.'

'Roast beef, I think?'

'I think that I am not quite adjusted; my stomach is not adjusted. Is that brandy you have there? May I?'

'Please!' He offered her the balloon. 'The flying does that, of course. It upsets one's balance: I try to avoid it when I can, but . . .'A helpless spread of thick fingers. 'In business one must be quick, isn't that so? And when I was a young man, oh so many years ago now alas, when I was young I loved it. It was my passion. But that was *then*, a different time, of course: now it is like a trip on a filthy bus, nothing more.'

'You were a pilot? In the war? Horst said . . .'

'So long ago. Yes. With your Papa indeed. He was very brave, very daring, we all admired him greatly.'

'He never spoke of it. Mamma does, sometimes.'

'No.' The cigar glowed brightly as he drew on it. 'He was a very modest man. I would imagine that you know London quite well now?'

'Quite. Not so well . . . it is large.'

'Ah yes . . . Before the war I was there often, '37, '38. The Café de Paris! Ah what happy times one had there. Very "snob", most chic. Do you know this place, it is not so far from Leicester Square, I remember?'

'I don't know; it is possible.'

'Such elegance, I recall. You know,' he lowered his voice confidentially, 'there is a strange thing I can tell you. We bombed it, did you know that? Very terrible indeed. But they rebuilt it after the war, I am told, which made me feel not so unhappy, because you see, and this is most extra-

102

ordinary, *I* was over London that very night! Can you imagine such a coincidence? When we all heard the news that it had been hit we were most deeply shocked. It had a glass roof and no one knew about that.'

'I don't know if it is still there, I'm sorry.' She handed him back the balloon.

'Yes, it is still there. I have been assured. But a different class of people go there now, working people, the middle class, the people who jumped up after the war everywhere, even here I am sad to say. But everything has changed now, nothing is as it was before, is it? But how could you remember? A lucky girl . . . so young and so much time ahead. But it was a wonderful time. *Then* was really fine.'

'And it worries you that perhaps you dropped your bombs on that place?'

'It worries me, I confess. But it could have been any one of us. The Squadron was up, we were very busy indeed, we had severe losses, of course. But you can just imagine my feelings! To have been responsible for such a thing; as you must know, when you are young you take things to heart so much. Oh that war! What foolishness it all was. We should never have fought each other, the English and the Germans; we are practically brothers, you know. And the Royal Family has a good deal of German blood in its veins; some from this very state of Holstein. Now then! What better proof do you need than that?' He drained his glass. 'No. A tragedy, a grave error. Together we could have ruled Europe, we Saxons, but the Vulgarian, Hitler. What a terrible mistake he made over those Jews. My God! To expel them to the East, where they belong, *yes*: but to burn them, if it is really true, was the wildest folly. The English are sentimental, the Americans are financed by their Jews, and, of course, as we know, Eisenhower wished to punish us, so they let the hordes of the East cross the Oder. But for that one idiotic mistake we could have joined forces and pushed the Russians back far, far beyond the Vistula.'

He stubbed his cigar butt deliberately into the base of a stone urn beside him, lifted the soggy stump towards her between thumb and forefinger. 'But as it is, if this were a javelin and I had the strength of my youth, could throw it as once I did, they would catch it just over there, in open hands.' He dropped it instead into the flower-bed below.

'A sobering thought: the Americans are a devious race. They wanted to divide Europe, bring her to her knees, and then dictate their own terms. But they have made a dreadful political blunder, as they usually do. For they have spread the cancer of Communism far and wide and now they cannot contain it.'

'Please!' she said. 'Not on this evening! All that was long before I was even born, it is history, and I have never been very good at that. Shall we go back?'

He offered a ringed hand. 'Disgraceful of me! On such an occasion too! I must blame too much wine at dinner . . . and the music, you hear it? So *reminding*, the old songs. Of course not to you, I know. I apologize, but this one is charming, no? "Ein Lied geht um die Welt", such memories. I was a little younger than you are now. Come! They will think that I am flirting.' He took her cold hand and they walked together towards the candle-lit group which was laughing at one of the dogs begging elegantly for a sugar crystal.

She moved away from the tiled stove against which she had been leaning and stood in the centre of her childhood room. 'Adieu,' she said aloud and pulled the suitable dress over her head, threw it across a chair, rummaged in the battered hold-all, stuffed the packet of Deutschmarks at the bottom, found her airplane slide, pinned it in her hair.

A whirring of wheels and weights behind her; the little bird sprang from his rustic house. 'Cuckoo!' The door snapped shut behind him. She hunted about in her bag for the Gauloises, lit one, took the packet to the high wooden bed and sat down staring at her feet swinging above the polished boards of the floor. Barley-fields and the prodding stork; sweet peas and Mamma's pale eyes, the music loitering behind the visions, candlelight on the still terrace, Horst's quiet kindness; 'We are not little grey mice'; the red glow of a cigar coming towards her, the Café de Paris. Guilt. Her eyes started to brim with tears, she checked them, cleared her throat, took a long expert pull at her cigarette, patted the plastic airplane.

'Fantastic!' she said. 'Fantastic!'

Chapter Four

At half past five Cuckoo awoke and snapped open her eyes like a china-doll. An instant wakening: no gentle drift from blessed sleep to comfortable awareness, but a sudden arrival into the morning. She lay perfectly still in the shadowy room, the early light glimmering through the cracks in the shutters, fanning above the gathered head of the curtains.

She had, it appeared, not moved at all during the night and lay now as calm and straight as a Crusader's lady on her tomb; save that her eyes were open and her arm in a sling and she felt altogether far too comfortable, cosseted, warm and alive for such an analogy. Alive being, without doubt, the operative word. One arm relaxed at her side, the other lightly across her breast, two feet neat white cones beneath the unruffled sheet. Refreshed, relaxed, aware.

And no dread. Absolutely no dread at all. For the first time in weeks the sudden clutch of fear did not strike at her heart; no suffusing terror mounting in her throat to dry her mouth and cause her fingernails to press even white brackets into the palms of her hands. Dread had suddenly flown. How strange, she thought, it has *quite* gone away. As suddenly as that. I have awakened from a thousand years' sleep like that dotty creature Sleeping Beauty. Perhaps if I look out from the window I shall find that I am embowered in giant brambles, nettles and forest trees, and all my courtiers are rubbing their eyes and yawning in the halls and kitchens below and the Prince's horse, richly caparisoned, stands tethered in the courtyard. But where is the Prince?

On the other hand, perhaps I am dead? Is this what

death is like after all? So sweet, so calm, so gentle. That's it. I have very likely 'passed away' or whatever the proletariat call it to soften the blow of total extinction. And if it is so, I really can't say that I mind it very much. It is exactly how I hoped it would be. In my own bed, my own room; I rather expected clinkers, ashes, roaring fire and people writhing about prodded by toasting-forks. I was pretty sure I'd land up in Hell, if the truth must be told. Convinced of it. But then perhaps Hell *is*, after all, the life you make for yourself on Earth? Like the last few months. Suspicion growing to doubt, turning to anguish, becoming hideous fact – that was Hell – and so perhaps this is simply the 'after care' department or something. And of course, there were other Hells before that . . . not to be remembered and none as terrible. So here I am, safely through the trial, purified. Golly! What nonsense you talk, Cuckoo dear.

She moved, for the first time, her arm in the sling. Cautiously, but there was no pain, a dull ache only, stiffness; the bruising after the fall. She flexed it, slid it from the silk scarf, stretched it high above her head. My dear! It works! What a bit of luck. I could have broken it falling like that: what an idiotic, thoughtless thing to do, do admit? Grabbing me suddenly on a frightfully slippery piece of rock, I could have cracked my skull open; really. It is simply madness to awaken a sleepwalker, everyone knows that. It's the most awful shock to the system, people have become quite peculiar after a sudden jolt of that kind. What you have to do is gently guide the walker back to bed, urge them along with gentleness and care; not grab them like a falling tree. Witless youth. Sea slip-slapping along the rock, swirling caressingly at my ankles, pulling at my skirt.

I might have been drowned.

With infinite caution she slid her legs over the side of the bed and stood up. A little wobbly. This is neither Death nor Hell. I can smell coffee brewing. The courtiers are awake. Just a blissful sleep. She opened the shutters and stepped out on to the balcony. The garden was hazed in blue shadow. Across the bay the rising sun tipped the ragged hills with gold and scarlet; gulls wheeled and spun like a scatter of torn papers across the stern of the sleeping American ship; halfway down the lawns under the pines a hoopoe, with flicking crest, probed the grass with a beak like a scimitar. The air was soft, scented, the iron rail cool against her thighs. In the brilliant sky, a vapour trail scored through the incandescent blue like a chalk mark. She ran hands roughly through her hair, shook her head, pressed fingers to her lips as if to stifle joy. And then she saw him. At the end of the lawns, coming up towards her from the point, heedless, half naked, tall, shining in the shadow, lithe, arms wide, head thrown back, laughing to himself. As the hoopoe swung in startled flight above the trees, he jumped high into the air, danced a little jig, spun round on one leg and with neat high skips, hopped up the gentle slope of the grass to throw his arms tightly about the trunk of a pine, pressing his head hard against its scaly bark, his back towards her.

The Prince, of course.

She leaned over the railing and called down quietly, 'Good morning.'

He did not move immediately, neck bent against the trunk, legs astride, shoulders hunched in his embrace, but she saw the slight tremor in his back and then he turned slowly, eyes searching.

'Up here.' She made a half gesture with hand and wrist.

He saw her, dropped his arms, stood away from the tree.

'Mrs Lazarus. Remember?'

He nodded and started to walk towards her barefoot across the dew-pearled grass, hair wet to his head, sleek like a seal, eyes holding hers steadily. He's *too* much, she thought, too beautiful.

108

He stopped beneath the balcony, looking up at her, hands on hips. A certain smile on his lips. And bold too, she thought.

'You better then?'

'Much. Much, much better, thank you. I've slept for a thousand years, you see.'

'That's a long time.'

'It is, isn't it? Anyway something like that. As a matter of fact I've been waiting for you.'

'Me?'

'Yes. There's supposed to be a Prince, did you know? After such a long sleep.'

'Ah ha . . . yes, I remember. With a kiss or something.'

'With a kiss. Not something.'

'So . . .'

'So?'

He pressed a hand over his mouth, balled it into a fist, made a quick throwing gesture up towards her. 'Catch then.'

'Caught! Perfect! It is quite wonderfully kind. What a glorious morning you have given me.'

'One of my better efforts. Glad you stayed then?'

She placed both hands on the railing, looking over his head, beyond the trees, past the point, to the line of the sea. 'Very glad indeed.'

'You were all for pushing off. Been a pity to miss this.'

'Madness. That's all it was. A little mental aberration, I get them sometimes. Not quite as dramatically, it must be said; that was the very first time . . .'

'And the last?'

'Oh yes! It gave me the most frightful shock, I shan't try that again.'

'Said that I was interfering. Very pissed off you were.'

'Was I? Was I really? It was the shock, you see; do forgive me, I'm really very grateful.'

He stretched his arms out wide. 'That's all right then.

109

God! Look at the sky! What colours would you say it was . . . all that?'

'Pomegranate fading to turquoise, to opal blue.'

'I see. Ask a silly question and you'll get a silly answer.'

'Well, that's how it looks to me. You asked.'

'I did too. It's so still. Listen. Do you think that we are the only people alive in the world?'

'Wouldn't that be fun! No. Someone's making coffee. I smelled it.'

'That's a good idea. I've been swimming.'

'So I imagine.'

'Best time of the day . . . to smell brewing coffee.'

She reached up and pulled down a rope of white wistaria, draped it round her shoulders and throat.

> '. . . when Dawn's Left Hand was in the Sky
>   I heard a Voice within the Tavern cry,
>   "Awake my Little ones, and fill the Cup
>   Before Life's Liquor in its Cup be dry . . ." '

He grinned up at her. 'What am I to make of that?'

'What you like. But it's what I'm going to do from now on; I think it's rather good. I'm going to heed the voice.'

'You mean coffee?'

'No. Not *just* coffee . . . but what you could do is trot along to the Tavern, or the kitchen, and tell Bruna that we'd both adore a brimming cup of her brew.'

'And that you are awake, alive . . . and well?'

'Yes. All those things. Break it to her very gently, I'm perfectly sure she has one hand on the telephone directory looking up Undertakers.'

'I will.'

'You may find it rather hard to believe yourself, of course.'

'Why? I can see it all, can't I?'

'In a way. But I haven't put on "my face" yet. It does make such a vast difference . . . takes simply hours to do

110

but at the end of it I'll look a little more like Snow White than the Witch, if you follow me. Did you tell me your name? I think that you did, but I've forgotten.'

'A thousand years sleep is a long time.'

'I know, what is it?'

'Pollock.'

'The other part.'

'Marcus.'

'And you can speak French; you said so. *That* I do remember, and you knew about Napoleon too. See, I can remember some things perfectly well.'

'I know a good deal more about him now than I did yesterday.'

'Oh, poor you. Yes, Archie does bang on a bit, I'm afraid. Was it frightfully dull?'

'No. Curious.'

'You're going to get a terrible crick in your neck if we stay here talking like this. Go and tell Bruna, will you? You know *my* name, don't you? I did tell you.'

'You said "Cuckoo". I can't go and say "Cuckoo wants coffee", now can I?'

'No. You say "Madame wants coffee", that's all. 'Voudrait" not "veut", it's politer.'

'Yes, but what's the other part?'

'Peverill. But Cuckoo is quite enough.'

'Just that?'

'Just that. There is no formality between conspirators, is there?'

'No.'

She unwound the wistaria from about her shoulders, pulled her hair behind her neck into a bunch. 'Marcus dear, coffee, before I faint away.'

'All right to go looking like this?'

'Perfectly all right. You look simply . . . scrumptious.'

'You don't look so bad yourself. "Face" or not.'

'I was what they call a "knock-out" once, I'm quite

111

immodest. More like a lizard now. Wait until the sun hits me.'

'I quite like lizards.'

'You seemed very happy just now. Laughing.'

'I am very happy. I can't quite believe it all: it's my first time here ever.'

'France?'

'First time abroad. I feel a bit drunk. It's all wild!'

'There is so much to see. We'll have to show you everything . . . how lovely for you! We'll talk about it at breakfast, when I'm presentable . . . eight o'clock, but do go and tell Bruna . . .'

She watched him cross to the gravel path and wave as he turned the corner of the house; she spread her hands across her cheeks, smoothing the soft skin. At the end of the point the sun lanced the sea like a surgeon's knife. 'I'm going to heed the voice,' she said. 'Before life's liquor in its cup be dry.'

Face on, rings on, a light cotton print; hair a bit of a ruin, but rolled and teased and back-combed it would pass for breakfast, and there hadn't really been much time. Archie, awakened by the voices, had fussed in, concerned, tousled, apprehensive.

'My dear! I heard talking . . . are you all right?'

'Look at me! Simply splendid. What a tiresome creature I am to you.'

'That doesn't matter. As long as you are fit . . . you're sure, you are quite sure?'

'Slept like a child. A bruise as big as a plate on my bum . . . . arm's a bit stiff . . . but otherwise quite intact. I'm terribly sorry, about it all. So idiotic, poor Archie.'

'You were tired.'

'Too much to drink on the 'plane, dear . . . on an empty stomach. That's all. Self-indulgence, made me a bit woozy. I couldn't be sorrier, say you forgive me?'

112

'Of course I forgive you. What nonsense. Sure you don't want to see Poteau again?'

'Don't fuss, quite sure. I was talking to the boy, Marcus . . . he had been swimming.'

'I said I'd go with him. But not at dawn . . . before breakfast, I said.' He kissed her on the top of her head, sat on the edge of her bed. 'We sat up quite late talking. He's an interesting chap. Can't quite put him together: schooling, background, that sort of thing. But one can't really with the young today, can one? All so amazingly classless, egalitarian. I suppose it's all this Socialist stuff, you know what I mean? Speaks perfectly well, knows the drill socially: no gaffes at table, that sort of thing. But not Public School, pretty certain of that; not gauche, quite collected, sure of himself . . . not unpleasantly, a perfectly acceptable young man. Didn't really talk about himself.' Subconscious unease had made him garrulous.

'Probably didn't have much chance, if I know you. I bet you battered the poor creature with French history. Did you show him your museum?'

'Museum! I *keep* asking you. Yes. Naturally. Something to talk about, you know. After all, a perfect stranger at one's table. It is a bit difficult. He seemed very interested. Quite astonished, I do admit, about l'Aiglon.

She turned on the low dressing-stool, an open letter in her hand. 'L'Aiglon?'

'Yes. Extraordinary. The resemblance. He looks exactly like him. A pea in a pod. It's perfectly amazing. Didn't you notice yourself?'

'I've only seen him practically naked and soaking wet, dear . . .'

'Course. Of course. I'm sorry. I suddenly realized it last evening. Couldn't think who he reminded me of and then I got it. Like that. He was pretty surprised himself. Showed him the portraits and so on, told him the whole story. Well . . . once I'd made the remark I had to follow through.

113

He was frightfully intrigued, I could see that . . . never heard of him of course; I suppose that's not on the School Curriculum, his school anyway, wherever that was. Such a coincidence, you do see?'

Cuckoo folded the letter carefully, slid it back into its envelope. 'Oh, I do see. How lovely for you! And here's beloved Bruna with coffee.'

And Bruna, anxious and surprised; to be reassured from purse-lipped worry to a grudging smile. 'A naked man in the kitchen at six o'clock and me in a shift.'

And arranging breakfast and lunch, and sending Archie off to his bath and then a few moments' peace with coffee and the other letters which had come while she was away, and the telephone messages which brought her swiftly back to the pleasant trivia of a life she had nearly managed to destroy.

Later she wandered into the circular day room, replaced the letters on her desk, slid just one into the pocket of her skirt, replaced the top on the bottle of vodka which she had opened in such despair and grief only hours before. Or was it really one thousand years ago? Tears of self-pity running; futility, fear. Now banished by self-will.

The sun had risen higher. Across the bay the roofs of the old town glowed poppy red among the white concrete blocks which wreathed them; a fishing boat idled towards the long jetty, its engine put-putting across the still water. A new day. A new beginning. A new adventure. She patted the letter in her pocket. Coincidences, Archie, my dear, are the very facts of life. You can forget about Darby-and-Joaning it into the sunset, as I suggested, a long quiet summer. I'm back in harness and I'm just starting to plan a picnic.

There were palm trees, roses, geraniums and a cactus plant which looked like a large toy rabbit; but the air was heavy with paraffin, plastic and airport music. Not wine, as she had secretly supposed. Perhaps that would come later on the way to wherever Marcus had found: of course, if he hadn't found anywhere it would be a night in the tent, which she dreaded rather. But one night, then she'd see what she could do to persuade him that a bed was wiser and far more comfortable.

It had been a full flight and there was a big crowd waiting beyond the barrier. People in bright shirts and coloured trousers, brown faces, yachting caps, plastic sandals, everyone laughing, some waving newspapers, calling names loudly; a woman lifted up a screaming child and shook it. And then she saw him, straight as a staff, folded arms, unsmiling, golden in a shaft of filtered sun. He hadn't seen her, was looking over her head beyond the crowd. She walked slowly towards him, criss-crossed by laughing people and when she was at his side she touched his arm.

'Here I am.'

'I was looking for you.'

'I know. I saw. Under your nose I am.'

He kissed her lightly on the lips, eyes smiling now, bright.

'Have you been waiting long?'

'Half an hour, I was early.'

'I'm not late?'

'No. On time.' He reached for the battered hold-all. 'This all? You've no luggage, have you?'

'No, just that and this.' She hitched an old army-surplus bag over her shoulder.

'A good flight?'

'Yes. Except we had to change in Paris. I got lost. It's awful there, circular. All electric stairs and things.' She followed him across the mall and lost him for a moment in an anxiety of nuns. We meet like strangers, she thought. How strange it is. The automatic small-talk of arrivals.

Catching him up, she said: 'The exit is over there. It says so. Taxis.'

'We're going to the bar, that all right?'

'Very. Some tea or a beer. Are you pleased to see me?'

He stopped immediately, pulled her towards him with one arm and kissed her hard. 'I'm very pleased. Very pleased. It has seemed years ago . . .'

'I know. Years. I feel quite shy.'

'It's the crowds: come on.' He led her across to the elevator which arrived as they reached it, delivering two elderly women with Yorkshire terriers. He pushed her inside and pressed the button; they rode up alone in each other's arms for thirty seconds.

'You said a bar.' She settled uncertainly into a deep leather couch.

'It is a bar. A grand bar.'

'Can we afford it?'

'I've only ordered beer.'

'You're wearing your best jeans. And your new T-shirt.'

'A celebration, seeing you again.'

'Only four days.'

'Eternity. You look nice, that new?'

'Yes.' She pulled the sleeves of her blouse down to her wrists. 'It's Hungarian, all hand-embroidered, I thought it would be cool.'

'Everything all right. In Hamburg then?'

'Yes. Everything very well. My Granny is much better now.' I must keep the lies to a minimum, she thought, lies catch you out. 'But I'm not happy there.' That's true. 'It is so . . . so very German there. They live all in the past.' True. 'I felt quite homesick and strange. I have to be a different person with them, you would be very surprised.' Absolutely true. 'My Granny was so happy to see me, she is really my "mother", you see.' And that's true too.

The beer arrived on a silver salver with dishes of nuts and olives.

He raised his glass. 'I love you.'

'I love you. Oh, I'm so happy, so happy, to be back. It's very exciting! And you, when did you get here, are you already French? Was it a good ride?'

'Yesterday afternoon . . . a good ride, no problems: it's a bit nice here.'

'I'm sure. I saw from the 'plane, all the hills, the sea so blue . . . palm trees and things. And it's hot!'

He pushed the dish of nuts towards her. 'Are you hungry . . . would you like something to eat?'

'No. No. A very nice Arab man bought me a sandwich, in Paris. It was huge, like a whole loaf, you know . . . with pink ham. He was most shocked! And I must get some sandal things here, can I do that? Today, because I can't walk in these, you see. Oh yes . . .' She looked vaguely round the elegant room. 'Marcus? the tent and things? And you are in your best jeans. You can't walk in those.'

He had half finished his beer, topped up the glass carefully with the bottle. 'We aren't walking, not today. I've got a surprise for you.'

She listened to him with growing astonishment and without interruption. He kept the story neat, tidy, brief and deliberately undetailed. An elderly English woman had slipped off a rock, he had saved her, taken her to her house, was offered a bed for the night in gratitude by her husband and pressed to stay by them both, with his 'friend from Hamburg' for as long as they cared. As far as it went, and he went no further, those were the facts, and they were perfectly true. What he omitted, he omitted deliberately. There was no point, he knew, in frightening the wits out of Leni with the size of the house, the grandeur of his hosts, the splendour of the household, and the strangeness of the whole set-up itself. Had he told her all the facts, from attempted suicide to Napoleon and the general 'freakiness' which, he thought, existed up at the villa, Leni would have crumbled into panic and settled for the tent, which was fast

117

fading from his thoughts. In the same way he had gracefully, and gratefully, accepted the rather astonishing offer to stay 'as long as you care to . . . we'd be simply thrilled unless you'd think it would be frightfully dull here?' without saying anything more about his partner from Hamburg except that he lived with her, which did not phase them, that she was German, which was perfectly reasonable, but nothing at all about their life together or what they did for a living. Neat and tidy. Salient *facts*. In a conspiracy, naturally, you all kept your mouths shut.

Something which Bruna, hovering about the breakfast table with coffee, kedgeree and a keen ear, also knew very well. She was perfectly certain that her beloved mistress's fall had not been an accident. She was equally aware that the present mood was one of almost desperate delight and brilliance and it could fade and dim almost as quickly as it had sparked into radiance. She had seen it happening fairly often over the last few months, and noted it with growing concern; the sudden fall from high to low, the swift fatigue, the drawn face and worried eyes. But nothing was said and at times, indeed, she thought it might simply be a question of age, boredom; and tried to comfort herself with that thought. But the sudden trip to London, and the very uncharacteristic amount of vodka drunk followed by a 'slip' on a dangerous rock so far from the house distressed her greatly. The young man from the sea could very well be the lynch-pin to her anxieties and as such he would be treated with all due deference: which is why she had gone from room to room that morning throwing open shutters, pointing out bells, switches, cupboards and drawers and smiling agreeably when he had chosen the Harbour Room, for each had a name, with a splendid view across the bay to Villefranche. He was good looking, well mannered, polite and made a brave effort to speak French, with an appalling accent, but at least making the attempt. At some time, she could not be certain when, she would try

118

to trap him into giving away, very subtly, exactly what had occurred down on the rocks.

For his part, Marcus was perfectly aware that he was being given preferential treatment by this suddenly charming Frenchwoman, who was almost over-eager to make him comfortable, and spoke slowly and clearly, so that he should well understand, of her intense love and loyalty to Madame Peverill whom she had known all her life as her father had been the Head Gardener there in the great days when he had four men under him and the staff in the house amounted to six, all of them from her family. These were quite unnecessary details offered to a guest who would probably stay for just a couple of nights, and he had a shrewd feeling that the bright eyes before him and the pleasantly chattering tongue would slip through the guard of his reserve unless he was extremely careful. So far the two or three well-placed references, among all the other little observations, about Madame's 'tiresome accident' were easily ignored. But there *might* come a time . . . For the moment he concentrated on choosing the pleasantest surroundings he could find for Leni, remembering her anxious admonishment to try and find 'a sweet little place that we can stay; very cheap, in the sun, by the sea'.

Sitting opposite her astonished face in the 'Ciel d'Azur' bar he knew that he had done exactly that. Only the word 'little' was at variance with her request, and she'd soon become accustomed to that, as indeed he had himself, just as long as she was not scared witless before she set eyes on the place. Let the surprises come gradually, he thought, like the sight of the Bentley and Angelo in the car park below. For all her apparent toughness and strength, she was really a very timid and shy little creature, and the contrast between the glittering villa ahead of her and the certainly crummy flat she had just left in Hamburg that morning, not to mention their two rooms in Shepherd's Bush of four days ago, would be a devastating one which could easily be too much for her. She might plead to leave before they even got there, which would be a disaster, for the twenty-four hours of life which he had enjoyed with his generous, if unusual, hosts had completely seduced him, and the added excitement of a yacht full of Counts, Princesses and film stars, due to arrive at almost any moment, as Cuckoo had announced from a letter which she had read to them all at the breakfast table, had made firm his resolve to accept the invitation to stay, no matter what happened. He was aware, deep down, that he was easily corruptible, which didn't bother him much. All he really wanted was to see Leni's eyes when she saw the 'sweet little place' which he had found for her, and to hear her say, once again, that particular word of hers which turned his heart to liquid honey. 'Fantastic!'

Which presently she did, her green eyes bright with light. 'Fantastic! But do they really mean it? Is there room?'

'Oh yes. There's room.'

'But they don't know us?'

'We don't know them . . . except for yesterday, that is.'

'I can't believe it! How brave you were.'

'She only fell over, you know. It wasn't much . . . not even deep.'

'But she's old, you said.'

'Elderly. Yes: old. They both are. And very British, you know what I mean?'

'Oh dear. I think so.'

'But nice with it. And I think pretty bored. Alone there together all year round, they want a bit of cheering up, I imagine. He's a historian or something.'

'Leni's eyes glazed very slightly. 'Well. I think it was very clever of you to do what you did. And we don't have to stay there very long, do we . . . not if we don't like it, I mean?'

'No. Of course not.'

'You see, it is our first holiday together. I would like to

be with *you*, not just have afternoon tea and play games
. . . you know? Cards. Bridge. So on.'

'I think they'll understand that, and we can go, if you really don't like it there.'

'We mustn't be rude.'

'No, we won't be. And it is a smashing offer. A free room, free food. It'll be a big saving . . . just for a day or so, you'll try?'

'I'll try. Really anything for a bed tonight and not a tent. I'm quite tired, you see. I had to get up at dawn to drive to Hamburg, it's miles and miles away . . .' She let the truth dry on her lips, her heart missed a beat, she fiddled with the iced bottle before her.

'Hamburg? But you were . . .'

'No . . . no . . . I mean the *airport*, at Fuhlsbüttel. That is miles: and the traffic and changing in Paris. I'm so weary, I thought maybe we would be starting to walk now, with a pack and things, hitching. No . . .' The moment neatly saved. 'No, I am very happy.'

'Well. What about making a start? It's getting on, you're tired and they are a bit sort of punctual.'

'Punctual?'

'Tea at four-thirty. Cucumber sandwiches.'

'Cucumber sandwiches. Why?'

'An English tradition. Especially for you, I think.' He signalled to the bar for his bill.

Leni collected her hold-all, eased her foot into the too-tight shoe which she had pulled off under the table. In the forefront of her mind she had started a mosaic, slipping in the little pieces to form a slightly depressing picture. An aged English couple, white-haired, rather infirm, tweeds, stout shoes, a neat bungalow set in a trim garden stuffed with red and yellow roses, which they would all admire once or twice, a croquet lawn on which they would have to play, bread and cheese for supper, a game of whist and cocoa in mugs. She hoped that they would not discuss

121

Their Finest Hour, Churchill, The Labour Government and the loss of the British Empire with deprecating little smiles which would suggest with exquisite English tact that though it couldn't be helped, it was, as a German, all her fault. Cucumber sandwiches, she thought glumly, and sweet sherry. Oh well! Better a bed than a tent and wandering about in a strange country looking for a field in which to put it up. She wasn't altogether sure that she could manage the tent part. But hoped that Marcus would. He was very clever with his hands. And seeing his broad shoulders just ahead of her as they crossed the wide mall to the exit doors she felt a surge of love and comfort again. How clever he had been, and really, when all was said and done, a very good way to start a holiday. A day or two at least; it would save a bit of money, as he said, and give them time to settle down, look at maps, find their way about; and alternative accommodation. Between games of whist or croquet. The mosaic completed, she followed him cheerfully into the blazing sun, the army-surplus bag slung over one shoulder, her shoes hurting, but her heart high.

'We take a bus, is it?' she asked, catching him up in the car park.

'No. Not a bus,' he said, well prepared for the moment. 'That, over there.'

Distractedly she followed his pointing arm. A pale grey Bentley, a slight figure beside it, standing easily in dark blue, the shiny peak of his cockaded cap sparkling like tin. The mosaic trembled.

The interior smelled of leather and a woman's scent which she recognized but could not immediately place; she was silent and only when the car swung into the main stream of traffic heading towards Nice did she dare to open her mouth, and then her voice was low and almost a whisper.

'Are you sure?'

'Perfectly sure.' Marcus was calm, eyes sparkling,

122

sitting back in the corner, arms folded, relaxed and confident, with a smug upturned smile as if he had always ridden in this manner.

So bewildered was she that she almost didn't see the enormous curving sweep of the Promenade des Anglais, the masts and ships cluttering the old port, the tall umber, pink and yellow houses, arched and galleried, the sun splashing through giant plane-trees, the palms and roses, the dust and drifting crowds.

The mosaic started to shatter as they swept through two immense stone pillars crowned with swagged urns down the long curving drive between brilliant beds of flowers, blossoming trees, orange, fig and palms, under a high arch into a cool, cloistered courtyard, an emerald lawn, banana trees, a mossy Triton spouting water in a marbled pool among darting fish. It splintered into fragments as she crossed the echoing galleried hall and came face to face with the slender woman hurrying across the terrace towards them. Hands outstretched in greeting, thick with earth and damp peat, bracelets gleaming, a wide straw hat shading the vivid oval face, thin blue shirt knotted at her waist, cotton shorts, brown legs thrust into red rubber boots.

'I heard the car! Oh my dear! How divine of you to come.' She threw her arms about Leni's shoulders, hands spread wide, and kissed her lightly on each cheek. 'My hands! Filthy on your pretty blouse. I'm battling with the dreaded begonias, don't you simply loathe them? Wrenching them out in hundreds, planted behind my back: so out they go. Marcus dear! Take her bag, sit her down. I'll just rinse this off.' She hurried to the end of the terrace, plunged her hands into the dribbling frog's mouth, came back shaking them in the warm air. 'Oh, do sit down, children. Leni dear, it's going to be Leni if that's all right with you, you must be exhausted . . . all that flying. I did it yesterday and I was a total wreck, wasn't I, Marcus? Sit, do. Marcus!' She pulled off the straw hat, a tumble of soft fair hair about her high brow, fumbled in her shirt pocket, found a black velvet bow, pinned it firmly in place. 'I'm like a sheep-dog. So sensible to have it short: like yours. Marcus, I was going to say; a blackbird! Saw him this afternoon down towards the point, got a nest in a big bay tree . . . isn't that marvellous? A real blackbird, first time in years.' She turned to Leni, pushed her bracelets up her arm. 'The French are simply monstrous, you know: they massacre everything in feathers and chumble them up for a deeply overrated pâté. Thrushes, blackbirds, everything on wings, so I'm going to treasure this one. Oh! It is *so* good of you to come, what a brave thing to do! Hurled into a house of strangers.'

Leni discovered that she could speak. 'Well. I'm a stranger too. I mean for you.'

'Oh no! You don't really feel like one. And you're so pretty! Marcus. Really! You never told me she was a beauty. You are, you know? I expect you do anyway, now what you must do is go up to your room, have a wash or whatever you want, come down for tea, and then just relax. Relax . . . you must be dead and I'm nannying away. Just come down and sit in a heap in the sun, or swim if you'd rather. Is this all your luggage?'

'Yes. All. We were going to be in a tent, and Marcus said to travel light.'

'Well, the thing is that I'd have to carry it, on my back,' said Marcus.

Cuckoo clapped her hands. 'My dear! Have you seen his pack-thing? Vast, bright red and covered in bags and straps and a frying pan. He looks like a Sherpa. Now off you both go. Take her, Marcus dear, and then we'll have tea.' She got up and went over to the drawing-room doors. 'Unless you'd rather have a lovely, cool, voddie-tonnie?'

'Tea,' said Leni in a whisper, not understanding anyway. 'Tea would be fantastic.'

As they crosed the hall and started up the wide stairs

124

they heard her singing in a light, sweet voice:

> 'Over my shoulder goes one care,
> Over my shoulder go two cares . . .'

'I don't know what a voddie-tonnie is.'

'Vodka-tonic.'

'Oh.'

'She talks a bit like that. Very Art Deco.'

'It's quite hard.'

He pushed open the big walnut door into their room, bars of sunlight slatting through the shutters which he pushed open, flooding the room with light.

'Look here,' he said.

She stood just behind him, her hands on his arm. Through the branches of a great pine lay the whole bay, dazzling in the sun, bounded by high craggy hills, blazing with yellow broom. The air was so still that the town beyond, climbing up the rocky slopes, reflected itself a thousand times in the sea in bars of white, red and gold until they faded into the gently swelling blue frilling creamily against the tumbled boulders at the foot of the cliff below. A lone gull, like a paper dart, swooped, sailed, and spun silently out of sight. Leni turned from the window, her face in her hands.

'Crying? But why? You don't have to . . .'

'I do have to. Yes, I do.'

'But why, darling? Why?'

'It's so beautiful. That's why.'

'Not what you expected?' He put his arms around her.

'No. Nothing is. You didn't say.'

'I didn't want to say too much . . .'

'That she was so kind . . . all that.' She made a little gesture with her head towards the windows. 'And all this . . . look, it's so beautiful, all the roses, bowls and bowls.'

'They must have put them here while we were at the

125

airport. When I said "yes, we'd like to stay", she sent everyone off to the market.'

'But what do I call her? And I haven't any clothes, you know. You know that.'

'You call her "Cuckoo", she said so; it's really Lady Peverill, but she likes to be called just "Cuckoo". But he's Sir Charles . . .'

'Lady? Oh my God! Marcus! It's too grand for us.'

'No it isn't. You'll see; and it doesn't matter about clothes, they won't mind.'

'But I do! I can't wear just this thing all the time. And only one kimono in my bag, all squashed, and old jeans.'

We'll go to town and get you a couple of things. Now come on, stop snivelling, go and have a wash or whatever you want to do, here's the bathroom, look.'

Marble, mirrors, piles of towels, a bath on lion's feet, a crystal bowl of sweet peas. She dumped her army-surplus bag on a white cane chair and sat on the edge of the bath. Sweet peas on the long table at Lamsfeld. The snip snip of her mother's brisk scissors. 'You have something to wear, upstairs? Not that awful tartan thing you arrived in . . .' Her face, reflected in the looking-glass above the marble wash-basin across the room, was pinched and plain with anxiety. 'The difficult thing, of course, is to remain believing in your fantasies . . . as such. It is exceptionally hard to do because quite often, you see, they turn into nightmares.' Snip, snip, snip. She started to wash her hands automatically. Now. Just remember. You are Leni here. Always at all times. You see everything as she sees things, you are astonished, delighted, at ease. Otherwise you'll trap yourself. Innocent, adoring, unaware of what to wear and what not to wear. You are yourself. Leni Minx. No one else. You left Luise behind in Lamsfeld this morning. You are Leni Minx from the Mayerling Hütte, Shepherd's Bush, and Aesthetic Art Models, and if your shoes are too tight, then take them off and go barefoot. Leni would. Leni does. So do it. She kicked off her shoes and washed her feet in the bidet. You made her, you live her.

Archie looked up and closed his book at the very moment that Cuckoo shut the study door quietly and came towards him in a haze of scent and a sigh of thin silk bearing two glasses on a tray.

'Interrupting?'

'No.' He pushed the book across the desk, closed a fat file, put the top on his fountain pen. 'No. All finished for the moment. Just checking, re-checking . . .'

She set the tray beside him carefully.

'Not a drop spilled. Clever old me. Seven almost. Martini time.'

'How kind. How very kind.'

She took her glass, sipped it, and lowered herself into a fat leather chair. 'Buried away in here all afternoon. You are dotty. It's been a heavenly day.'

'Well, I'm not frightfully good at heat, now . . . at my age. It's cooler in here.'

She looked about the dim room; shelves of books, crossed swords, plumed helmets, glass-fronted cupboards of jackets, belts, pouches, brasses, a worn saddle, faded banners. On one wall a gigantic painting of tumbling horsemen, billowing smoke, and shattered trees; in a corner the white-uniformed dummy standing stiffly to attention, one wax arm draped with a sash. Archie behind his desk, searching for his cigarette case; behind his head a huge map of St. Helena.

He opened the case, chose a cigarette, felt for his lighter. She watched him through half-closed eyes, sipped her drink. Cigarette to lips, lighter to cigarette, cupping his hand against the non-existent flame, one deep breath of satisfaction inhaled, lighter back into pocket, flap closed, cigarette thoughtfully examined. He relaxed, reached for his glass. She thought that one day she might very likely strike him; instead she said, 'Feel better?'

'Much. But I'll really have to give it up. Lack of character. But then you've always said that. Can't quite break the habit: been a bit rattled, you know. I don't mean your fault at all, but all these people suddenly arriving. You know? And to see me! Got to have my facts absolutely ready; when people want facts you simply can't waffle about . . . know what I mean?'

'Absolutely. But I do think it is frightfully complimentary, coming all this way to pick your brains, don't you?'

'Not particularly. Pick my brains? Why should they?'

'Well, if someone is going to make a tremendous film about your favourite period, and something you know all about, then it's sensible for them to get the facts absolutely right, don't you think?'

'Damn waste of time, I think. That's what I think. They always make a botch of history in the flicks.'

'Well, you must help them not to.'

'What do they pay, eh? Do I have to have my brains picked without payment.'

'My dear, I don't know. Minna didn't say in her letter: it was just a quick note saying they were on their way and that Grottorosso was absolutely dying to meet you.'

'To pick my bloody brains.'

'She didn't say so. Oh don't be tiresome, be sweet . . .' She leant across and put her hand on his fist. 'Darling? Smile? Be kind; it's really not my fault. I was away when she wrote. I only read it this morning before breakfast, there's nothing I can do. On this huge yacht somewhere on the high seas between here and Elba. I should have thought that the very mention of the name would have brought a thrill to your heart. Elba!'

'Bloody awful place. Been there. You got stuck all over with sea urchin things.'

'Yes,' she said vaguely, and remembering. 'I'm not very good at the sea, it seems to me.'

He was immediately contrite. 'Oh my dear! I'm sorry. It wasn't your fault. Anyone can tread on a sea urchin, hundreds do.'

'They don't sit on them.'

'No. No, they don't. That was a bit silly.'

They laughed together, she raised her glass and drank. 'Anyway, I'm sorry that I rattled you at breakfast. I did say no picnic this summer . . . we'd just do a Darby and Joan thing. And I meant to: but what can one do? Anyway the picnic has already started, I'm afraid.'

He flicked a bit of imaginary ash into the ashtray, brushed imaginary scatters from his sleeve. 'Ah yes. Of course. That why you've spiffed yourself up? You look very pretty.'

'Thought I'd better. Have I overdone it?'

'No . . . no . . . charming. Quite lovely, really. The girl has arrived, I take it?'

'She's arrived. Marcus is delighted.'

'What's she like? All right?'

'Enchanting. Odd perhaps, I don't mean "fey", not that, she's no Gretchen by any standards, or a Brünnhilde, thank God. She's tiny; hair like a bottle brush, voice like dried leaves, sweet and rustly, the dress sense of a rag-picker.'

'Oh Lor'.'

'No, no, you'll like her, really. Dreadfully shy, of course; all this was a bit overwhelming, I imagine. She's apparently got a grandmother in Hamburg or somewhere . . . so you can imagine. An orphan, of course; they so often are, these footloose children, but she was immensely sweet at tea. Very poised. You'd have thought it was an everyday thing, lace cloth, silver, cucumber sandwiches.'

'Good heavens! You haven't done that for years.'

'No. I thought I would, Bruna was livid.'

'Speak English? Or do we have to wallow along in gutturals?'

'No, English. Very pleasantly, when she speaks at all. She's busy taking stock at the moment.'

'As long as she doesn't take the silver.'

'You really are odious. She's not that sort, I can tell. Eyes you could drown in, they are so wide and so deep, ravishing skin, hands like a skivvy and feet like a Botticelli angel. She arrived in a pair of simply frightful silver shoes, took them off, thank heaven. Much wiser.'

'Silver shoes?'

'Well, you know the young today . . . anything goes. They are a bit like we were. Perfectly free, uninhibited, accepting, unsurprised to an extent, unquestioning, gay, life for the living. I find it wonderfully refreshing: no fuss about Class, position, so completely unlike Harriet's lot who were brought up with all the old standards and are as stuffy and dull as cotton stockings.'

Archie finished his drink, placed the glass carefully on the tray.

'And no sense of tradition either.'

'No. They've chucked that away too. No bad thing.'

'Egalitarian. I detest it.'

'Wasn't Napoleon a bit for that?'

'Different thing.'

She sighed, got up and walked across to the white dummy figure. 'This creature really gives me the shivers. What did Marcus think of it?'

Archie swivelled round in his chair. 'Ah Marcus. Yes. Last night. Fascinated, I think. Said the eyes were dusty, washed them with spit. They were too. Funny. I explained it was not a portrait, so to speak, of l'Aiglon. Just a shop-dummy.'

'He'd look rather fabulous dressed in that. Wouldn't he? Marcus?'

'Yes. Extraordinary.'

'And show him to Grottorosso!'

'This bloody Grottorosso. Who is he anyway?'

'An Italian director. You know perfectly well, remember we went to see "Donna Infernale" in Paris with the Maltbys.'

'Oh God! That. A lot of Lesbians in a factory making wireless sets. Arty farty stuff.' He reached for the ashtray, stubbed out the virgin cigarette. 'Talking away like this, nearly burned my fingers. Down to the butt. Look?' He offered the glass dish full of squashed cigarettes. 'Seven this afternoon. I really must give it up.'

'You must go and have your bath,' she collected the tray, 'and I must go and see the children, they're down at the pool.'

He looked up blankly. 'Children?'

'Oh, you know. Come along now, it's after seven.'

He got up reluctantly, took out his keys, locked the desk drawers methodically. 'I really must make a stand. Seven in an afternoon. No will-power. You were right, I'm afraid. No will-power. Water weak. When is this frightful cargo of peacocks arriving, did she say? I can't remember.'

'No. She didn't say: just that they were leaving Elba that day, a week ago, on to Livorno, then La Spezia, Genoa and here . . . drifting along.'

'What an exhausting thing to do.'

'Well, he lives on his yacht, he's terrified of being kidnapped by the Red Brigade or something, so he keeps on moving about.'

'They could nab him at sea.'

'Probably hasn't occurred to him. Do come and bathe.'

'Where's he going to make this ruddy film then?'

She set the tray on a pile of books. 'Vienna . . . Schönbrunn . . . it's all about l'Aiglon, darling, that's why he's coming to see you, I do wish you'd listen.'

'I do listen, that's why I've been stuck in this room all

afternoon, getting things sorted out. I won't have to go to Vienna, will I?'

'No, of course not, he's coming here to get all his facts right, that's all. For the script.'

'They never do, so it's a waste of time. It's always rubbish. Bend history all the time; history isn't romantic enough as it stands, they have to tart it up.'

'Much better idea if we always did that. History is very dull, life *should* be tarted up . . . more romantic: it doesn't last very long.'

He suddenly took her hands, bent his head, and kissed them lightly. 'You really are very sweet. Pretty too,' he said.

'Do I look all right, really?'

'Really. Lovely. I was being very disagreeable . . . got fussed. You're looking forward to all this, aren't you? You've always loved a lot of people about you, I know that . . . I'm an awful stick in the mud.'

She withdrew her hands, kissed his lips. 'You're not disagreeable at all. You are very dear and you *can* be wonderfully charming.'

'It'll cheer you up, I think. You've been a little . . . sad, haven't you? Recently?'

'Have I? I didn't feel sad.'

'Looked it sometimes, when you thought I didn't notice.'

'Did I? Oh it's just age . . . one gets weary.'

'I notice things, you know. An eye for detail, after all; my job really . . . sifting through the things other people have overlooked. But I *see*. Come along . . . I'll just take a quick shower while you mix me another Martini.'

She watched his straight back going up the stairs, elegant, spare. 'Come to the pool when you are ready, darling. Drinks down there. You must meet the child before we dine; she's made up her mind that you'll terrify her.'

He raised a hand in agreement and went into the gallery. For a moment she stood by the table in the hall, snapped a yellowing frond from the fern in the Tuscan pot, crushed it in her hand. Sifting through the things which other people overlook. What an odd remark to make. I must watch my step. She went out into the late sun and walked slowly down the gravel path towards the point and the pool, past a sullen Tonnino replacing begonias with nicotianas.

She lay tightly curled up, completely covered by the thin, white sheet like one of the dead in Pompeii, of whom he had seen pictures. A tiny figure overtaken by the events of a hot summer morning. Only Leni wasn't dead, thank God, even though she was hardly breathing. Just knocked out, that's all. Overcome by the events of another summer day; out like a light. He kissed a spike of hair which was all that showed of her, slid into his own bed and put out the light between them. Stared up into the sudden dark, arms behind his head, too bemused to seek sleep. Amazed, serene. Peter Gabriel low on the pocket-transistor. A magic kind of day, you could say. Well, say it. Magic. They don't come often. And a different night from last night up in the Bachelor's Room sorting out the facts of a flash-back life. But I was different then.

The darkness faded in the light of the rising moon through the open windows. Across the bay the ragged hills were soft against the pale sky, lights sparkled, the sea lay silent, black oil marbled through with silver.

Wiped out tapes, I said. Stuffed birds in dusty cases, dinosaurs rattling about in a lost-time machine. What the hell was I thinking? I had no comparisons. It was a new world for me. It still is. But I was right about one thing. They know who they are, no confusion there. Not the very least particle of doubt. Secure, sure, belonging. That's the whole crunch to life, I can see. And in knowing who they are they make you feel that you know who *you* are, confident, brave, alive and daring. It's a bit like it must be when you do your first solo on the High Wire, flying through the air without a safety net, your heart in your mouth because you dared, and might not make it, and then you are caught on the other side in steady hands. The catchers. That's Cuckoo and Archie Charlie, I'd say; the 'steadies', the 'know-how-to-do-its'. I mean, this afternoon, Leni scared half to death, overcome by the car, the house, the whole bit: Cuckoo giving her a kiss, right off, thanking her for coming! As if *she* was doing *them* the favour and not the other way around. Now, I mean to say, honestly . . . that is something, that's amazing! Could you see Decca doing that? Christ! You see? And because of that moment Leni was 'secured'. She'd have gone right back and tried a bloody *double* somersault just to feel the safety in those hands again.

And Archie Charlie, down by the pool this evening, tall and slender, all in white, smelling of lemons, his hands outstretched shyly in welcome. 'Don't move! Don't move! How pretty you look sitting there. Oh, if only Matisse could have seen you like that. They are his colours, you have his line. What a great pity.' I don't suppose that she knew what he meant but she laughed, and that was that; ice shattered. But he was right, absolutely right; she did look fantastic suddenly, bare feet, that old kimono Gus Bender gave her ages ago, a big red scarf round her waist, the collar of silver spoons she had made herself, a jug of anemones on the table beside her. I could see just what he meant, but I'd never have been able to express it . . . and she'd been so panicked before, nothing to wear, all that. And knew he meant it, wasn't sending her up.

'Oh, please!' she had said. 'I'm not pretty, you know.'

'Better than that. Arresting, unusual, interesting, much better than being merely "pretty". I find that pretty people are usually quite dreadfully dull, don't you? My wife here is the only exception to the rule, as far as I am concerned, and she was simply staggeringly pretty; still is, I think. But then, of course, I *would* because she was my choice. But there was one other exception to the rule, it is very slightly possible that you may even know her, or know who I mean rather. Lilian Harvey, do you? Or is it too long ago for you?'

'Oh yes, of course! She was also German, like me.'

'English born as a matter of fact, so we can both lay claim to her; ravishing creature.'

'I have seen her only once, "Congress Dances". We say "Der Kongress tanz". Do you know this film?'

'Time and time again, I was deeply in love. That marvellous song.'

'Das gibts nur einmal,' said Leni and started to hum it under her breath, and he joined in singing it, in English, she in German, as if they had known each other for fifty years. Now that's what I call bloody manners. Just the kind that Decca didn't know about. Oh, she knew about giving your seat to a woman on a bus, don't pick your nose, 'please' and 'thank you', leave a little on your plate, elbows off the table, but not this kind of behaviour.

And in the laughter, with that song, Cuckoo sitting in the dying sun, so pretty, so alive, laughing. But then, when she caught my eye, the laughter died in her huge blue ones; she raised her eyebrows very slightly, still smiling, but with the light gone; and when I shook my head, so that you really couldn't see the movement, the light came back again. A look between conspirators. What happened to make her do that yesterday down at the beach? Not my affair. Secrets. All right by me; we've all got a few of those tucked away in our luggage.

He slid from the bed and went out on to the balcony, leaning his back against the folded shutters, looking down the path of the moon across the water. Orion's belt tilted above the hills.

That's how we got here. Ask no questions, you'll hear no lies; what the eye doesn't see the heart won't grieve over. Like Aesthetic Art Models and me strutting my stuff for a bunch of tired old closet poufs, and Leni dancing about in her gym-slips and knickers at twenty quid a set of six. Christ Almighty! There has to be something better than that. A couple of tacky little cock-teasers: that's us. But I don't think it shows, we're behaving all right, all the social graces. So far. And Leni! Dead cool. She was amazing at dinner tonight, really amazing, carrying on as if she had done that kind of thing all her life. Asparagus tongs! Well: I didn't know what the hell they were for, she did. And all that fiddling about with the fish things; didn't turn a hair, to the manner born, extraordinary. You'd never guess she'd just picked it all up from a few suppers with her geriatric 'fans' at the Inn on the Park. I think we passed muster, but we won't push our luck, a day more, if we're asked, and then clear off, otherwise I'll really be corrupted.

He pulled the shutters together carefully and felt his way across the dim room to bed. A magic day. Really magic. The Peverills. Funny pair, pretty deep, pretty odd; they've got their own problems, that's for sure, something's rumbling about, but you never know about people, do you? Can't really tell. And *he* said, not everyone born in a stable is a horse. He switched off the transistor.

And that's a fact.

Chapter Five

The 'day or two' for which Leni had stipulated that they should remain, and to which Marcus had readily agreed, extended gently into three or four and then she very soon discovered, like Millament before her, that she had allowed herself to be 'dwindled' into remaining at the villa for the duration of their holiday. It was almost inevitable, because Cuckoo had taken the greatest pains, from the first moment of their arrival, to make it perfectly clear that they were free to use the house as an hotel, that they could come and go as they chose, that they must have no feelings of obligation or gratitude, must go out and discover the joys and horrors of the Coast for themselves and only give, if possible, advance warning about which meal they would be there to enjoy, for the sake of Bruna who must cook it. Beyond that, and the fact that they must under no circumstances 'fuss' Archie while he was working, there were to be no rules, utter freedom; otherwise she knew that she would lose them, and that was the very last thing she wanted. Their presence in the house, even after only twenty-four hours, quite enchanted her: their life, laughter, and dazzled delight in everything which they ate, saw, touched or drank filled her with tremendous pleasure and the villa with vibrancy and light. It was as if shutters had been thrown open and awnings raised. She needed them desperately, and to that end worked with the greatest tact and wisdom to keep them there.

Maps were marked with places they had to see, where they could eat reasonably, what they could safely avoid, where to cash a travellers' cheque, catch a bus or the train, plus all the holiday minutiae of where to get the best espadrilles, sun lotion, swimming costumes, sandwiches and postcards.

The scarlet tent remained unstrapped and unrolled on a corner of their balcony while they set off, with towels and guide book crammed into Leni's Army Surplus, and hearts filled high with anticipation, to discover the varied delights of the Riviera.

For some strange reason, which she was quite unable to explain, Leni had got it firmly fixed in her mind that this golden length of coastline was a paradise of hidden coves, wine-scented air, deserted beaches, and what the travel writers call 'sleepy little fishing villages' buried in sighing palms or blazing with bougainvillaea. She was deeply shocked to find, almost instantly, that this was not so, and that the whole agglomeration stretching from Nice to Cannes was really nothing but a gaudy hot-Watford. The traffic terrified her, the beaches were jammed with bloated red bodies and crushed paper cups, the air heavy with the rancid stink of fried chips, sun oil and petrol; and the sleepy fishing villages, if they had ever existed in the first place, were long since demolished and smothered in concrete blocks twelve storeys high with rubber plants on every balcony and television aerials on every roof. That was the first shock. There were others, inevitably, to follow, such as the price of a glass of beer, a sandwich in a cheap bar, and the fact that whenever she most needed its comfort there was absolutely no sign, to the naked eye at any rate, of a Public Lavatory anywhere to be seen. She suspected miserably that everyone just hurried into the sea to seek relief, and on closer examination of that deceptively blue expanse discovered that she was correct.

To be sure, in this hot, overcrowded property dealers' paradise and ruin, there were some things which could be assumed to pass for glamour and sophistication: but they were few and far between and most of them prohibitive on the modest allowance which Marcus had carefully put

138

together. There were the private beaches of the Croisette, neat with serried rows of coloured mattresses and giant parasols, the cool public gardens shaded by palms, pines and oleanders, the frilly bulks of the Majestic and Carlton hotels tinselled with Rolls-Royces, Cadillacs and Mercedes, the flying flags, the brilliant sky, the jagged mountains of the Estérel hazed across the immensity of the bay adrift with little yachts and countless pleasure boats: all these were there to be seen if one cared to look, but, apart from the gardens and the view, they were not for them, and they quickly concealed their dismay from each other, and strove hard to show no signs whatsoever of disillusion or deprivation. Bravely they explored the sights of Nice, Antibes and Cannes, from fish markets to Prisunic's, at one of which Leni bought a swimsuit, sandals, sun oil, and postcards to send to 'Uncle' Desmond, Gus Bender and Nig, which they dutifully wrote on a filthy beach eating cold, sand-covered pizzas, drinking warm beer from cans.

'I think,' said Marcus, folding the map and putting it away with the empty cans in the Army Surplus, 'that perhaps we ought to move further down the coast. It's rocky there, it says so on the map. Perhaps there won't be such a scrum at that end.'

'Today?' said Leni faintly.

'No. Not today. It's miles, but perhaps we could take the train beyond La Napoule.'

'It's very slow, the train, it stops at every station.'

'Or into the hills up at the back. Only there isn't a railway line marked.'

'Then how could we get there?'

'A bus maybe? Must be a bus. We can look one up. Or hitch a lift.'

Leni ducked suddenly to avoid a large plastic ball which thudded between them, desperately pursued by a hairy man in a cod-piece, and a frantic Alsatian. She brushed the

139

scatter of sand and bottle tops from her legs and readjusted her straw hat.

'It's terribly hot, Marcus . . . to walk all that way, you know this?'

'Well, that's what we had *planned* to do, remember. And with a tent. We haven't got the tent at least.'

'No. No, we haven't got that.'

'I mean, that was the whole idea, hitching . . . to be independent.'

'And a dear little hotel, very quiet, by the sea, in the sun . . .'

'Not much chance of that. Coming in then?'

'In?'

'For a swim. Come on.'

'But our things. Someone might steal everything, you know.'

'They won't . . . Come on, nothing to steal anyway.'

'But your money, our clothes, the Army Surplus, and things. You go in and I'll stay here and keep guard, and when you come out I'll go in.'

'But that's not the *idea*. It's not the idea at all! I want to go with you.'

'Well, we can't, you see. If everything is stolen we would have to walk all the way back to the villa naked and that's miles and miles from here. You go.'

'But what's the *point* in being here if we can't go for a bloody swim together?'

'I don't know. And don't shout, you go red in the face.'

'Well. There's *no* bloody point, that's all.'

'There is a point. I want to make a pee-pee, you see it's the beer, so I'll go in first, and you wait here and when I come out you can go in.'

He lay back and covered his face with his hands.

Leni adjusted a shoulder strap, took off her straw hat. 'You may not believe it,' she said, 'but I love you with all my heart.'

He made no reply, so she walked through the crowds, tripped over the Alsatian, and moved cautiously into the water.

Later, in the cool of the late afternoon, walking down the long curving drive to the shaded courtyard with its green lawn, the pool, the Triton blowing water, a soft breeze frilling the heavy banana leaves, the heat and irritations of the day slid from them both gracefully. He reached out and took her hand and they smiled at each other with tight new shining red faces.

'This is better, isn't it? I mean all this . . .' He waved his free hand across the brilliant grass, the darting fish, the shadowy arches, mossed stones.

'Much,' she said.

'It's rather funny along there. The coast . . . we're not used to it really. A bit of a surprise, I think. But we'll find our feet; after all, it's only two days. Perhaps tomorrow we *should* try going beyond La Napoule . . . to the rocky places.'

'Yes. Yes, we could. We could try that.'

'Or unless . . .' He kicked a pebble; skittering across the shorn grass, it plopped into the pool. 'Unless you'd just like to stay here. Be quiet. Stay put?'

'Put? What is put?'

'Well, here, by the pool. Stay here.'

She shrugged. 'If you like. I don't mind. Perhaps it would be lovely at the rocky place . . . perhaps we should go and see?'

'Whatever you say.'

'Well, it's just that I like to lie in the sun, quite alone, except for you . . . and not think or hear anything. Everywhere seems so crowdy, you know?' They were crossing the gallery towards the terrace. 'We could never put up the tent at places like those today, could we? There isn't any room. Where could we put up a tent, Marcus?'

'I don't know. I thought there would be somewhere . . .

141

a camping site, something.'

'Nothing. Well, perhaps tomorrow at the rocky bit. Shall we see?'

'Or stay here? Which? I don't mind. I mean there's the pool here, sun . . .'

'All right.'

'I mean, it does seem a bit silly, doesn't it? Perhaps just one day here, shall we? Or would you rather try along the other end of the coast, where we haven't been yet? Monte Carlo. Menton . . . go along that way for a change? Or where?'

The terrace was deserted, shaded, the fountain bubbling softly, a bowl of full blown roses, deep cane chairs, in a bucket a bottle of Laurent Perrier, a neat white cloth about its shoulders, two glasses; moisture beading.

Leni dropped the Army Surplus into a chair, shook off her sandals with a quick flip of her feet.

'Here,' she said and 'dwindled' in acceptance.

This decision was greeted by Cuckoo with undisguised delight. Her shrewd idea that her 'pretties', as she now privately called them, might possibly find the pleasures of the coast questionable on their limited means had proved correct. They were not, as she had hoped, easily satisfied with third best, nor did they appear to crave the company of people of their own age, had no desperate desire for the sound of Rock and Roll, or Disco music or moving about in a herd. They were obviously very much in love, wanted to be alone together, which was reasonable, and seemed perfectly content with what they found around them at the villa. Which, she thought wryly, they jolly well ought to be: a five-star hotel entirely at their disposal with a willing staff to attend to their every need. For as soon as they had made their decision, quietly and without fuss, she had instructed Bruna to get her sister Maria back into harness immediately and to bring her elder daughter, Fanny, to help with the washing-up. For her own part she had picked up the scattered loose change of her life and re-opened her account: spending it lavishly in time, effort and thought to give her young guests pleasure and herself the sense of security and optimism which she so desperately needed. Life was 'life', now, and no longer an apprehensive drift through the days, but one of force, determination and occupation which set the flurry of furies snapping at her heels to flight, giving her no time to consider anything beyond the immediate present.

Archie's reaction to the decision was ambivalent. His reactions often were. On the one hand he was always uneasy when there were strangers running about his house, which with Cuckoo's capricious nature there often were in the long summer months, but on the other hand their presence so obviously gave her pleasure that it would have been extremely churlish to have made any objections, and also because of that pleasure she was less on his mind; she was kept occupied doing the things she liked best, amusing, and being amused by people, while he could quietly go back 'into his head', as he called it, and escape into his own world of privacy and self-thought. He had his own quarters, his study, his books, his work. People, he had to admit, hardly bothered him at all with those defences. He could slip away whenever he wanted; and did.

For the last ten years, ever since his sixtieth-birthday announcement, a form of renunciation which had so surprised and wounded Cuckoo, he had, he knew only too well, sensed the strain between them. It had not been a totally comfortable time, but he had stuck resolutely to his decision, and she had grown to accept it; and gradually, he thought, things had eased, sorted themselves neatly into a reasonably harmonious pattern which gave him great relief and clarity of mind. Now, unencumbered by guilt or doubt, he was able to carry on with his work peacefully. However, in the last few months he had noticed the subtle

143

change in Cuckoo's behaviour. A sadness, a kind of slow withdrawal, weariness, lassitude, which had made him uneasy and disturbed the orderly tenor of his days. It fussed him a little, and that was irritating. So that the sudden arrival of two unexpected young people had come almost as a relief. If she was happier because of them, then he would be happier because of them, the stress of worrying would be eased, and he need not alter his pattern. Altering a pattern, like altering the pieces of a puzzle or the fragments in a stained-glass window, led to great confusion and disarray, and that led to the destruction of one's work, the clarity of thought, and peace of mind, and this he strove to preserve as assiduously as he preserved his elegant body. By exercising it.

Some people, he supposed, might consider it selfish. But in his eyes it was a perfect manifestation of willpower, discipline, control, all qualities which he shared with Bonaparte. If there were errors in their behaviour these could only be put down to perfectly human ones which they had not quite managed to eliminate. No one, after all, was one hundred per cent perfect. Even he, with all the strength and effort at his command had not entirely managed to eliminate smoking. But if he were selfish he was also capable of great and lasting generosity; in this he was quite unlike Bonaparte who had cruelly dismissed the wife who could not bear him children, and this he always found to be callously unfair although, of course, it did produce l'Aiglon. However, the one was attempting to found a dynasty while he had only sought, under great pressure from a desperate father, to continue the Peverill line of which he, Archie, was the last. The end of the blood. Was there ever a sadder phrase? And after six hundred years. However, there it was; a most unfortunate business. Nothing to be done about that. A matter of behaviour. And he considered that he had behaved in an exemplary manner.

So. Cuckoo was happy and occupied, and he was fully engaged in preparing whatever notes he felt might be important to Signore Grottorosso. The thought of the impending arrival of a boat-load of Italians filled him with vague unease, but the fact that he and his hoarded knowledge were the main reasons for their visit gave him a certain feeling of comfort. After all, he reasoned, it was rather pleasing to think that at last the mountain was coming to Mahomet. No one had bothered him much before.

The pool, blasted out of the living rock over the bay at the far end near the point, and approached by a steep flight of stairs, was a much scaled down version of the one at Hadrian's Villa. No vulgar blue tiles, chromium or public lavatory marble. Honey-coloured stone, tall pillars, along either side. At one end, backed by slender arches, an over-life-size figure of Mars in helmet and shield; at the other, overlooking the bay, a Piranesi tumble of pillars, blocks and crumbling capitals, in planned disarray, among which lizards scuttled or basked with half-closed eyes, and through which a blue confusion of Morning Glories thrust an orchestra of trumpets towards the sun.

Leni sat up, pulled off her straw hat, and hugged her knees to her chest. In the clear water below, Marcus drifted, on his back, spread-eagled, almost motionless, eyes closed.

'You are *so* brown.' she said.

He rolled over and swam leisurely towards her. 'It's a good life,' he said.

She pressed her chin between her knees, stared at him with narrowed green eyes. 'I think you are getting very used to it, isn't it?'

'Doesn't take long. Easily become addicted. Does it show?'

She nodded. 'Yes. You have all the signs.'

'Such as?' He folded his arms on the warm stone ledge and grinned up at her.

145

'Oh, I don't know. Well: so many baths . . .'

'*Baths?*'

'Yes. You have a bath in the morning and a bath in the evening.'

'So?'

'In London only once a week. And you grumbled.'

'Two floors down in London. Fifteen pence and take your own plug with you, that's why.'

'Yes, I know.'

'Do you mean two baths a day is a sign of corruption?'

'No . . . but you don't *need* two baths a day: people say it is bad for you, it washes off all the natural oils.'

'I like it. It's very luxurious indeed.'

'That's what I mean. And your T-shirt. Another sign, I think.'

'T-shirt?'

'I bought you; the lovely red one.'

'Oh Leni, come on. I can't crash about here with "I'm Hers Because She Appreciates Perfection" all over my tits.'

'Why not? It was lovely. You did in Canteloupe Road.'

'That's different. Well, you know: it doesn't *feel* right here somehow. Too much "glit".'

'It was a compliment to me, you see.'

'Sorry. Really. But you don't need written proof, do you?'

'No . . . it's just a pity.' She squinted into the sun.

He pulled himself out of the water and stood dripping before her, smoothing his hair over his head. The water slid like crystal beads down his skin.

'You're being a bit serious, aren't you?'

She shook her head and laughed up at him. 'Only a little, little bit, so tiny.' She measured it between forefinger and thumb. 'No. I'm glad you are happy; really. And I am happy also.'

'Well, if it'll really make you happier, I'll wear it.'

'It doesn't matter.' She pulled a toe thoughtfully. 'Cuckoo wouldn't mind.'

'No, she wouldn't mind. Of course not. But, I mean, well . . . you wouldn't see Archie Charlie wearing anything like that, would you?'

'But he's different! He's quite different.'

'He'd look really freaky.'

'But they are different from us. I think you don't remember that sometimes. We can't be like them; it's only a little holiday we are having; and then we must go back to being who we really are. You know that, don't you?'

He sat down slowly beside her, put an arm round her shoulders. 'Yah. I know that. Canteloupe Road and bring your own plug. I haven't forgotten.'

'And the van, and Mr Bender. You know . . .' She wasn't looking at him but pushing a finger worriedly between her toes.

'You think I'll get to like all this too much? Turn my head, or whatever?'

She looked up at him finally, her eyes half-smiling. 'You could. It would be so easy, and then so dreadful to go back – which we have to do.'

He hugged her tightly to him. 'You're the most awful fuss-pot, really. Look: Leni. I'm having a ball, we both are, we've never had anything like this in our lives before. All my life I've been walking past other people's gardens with bloody great "Keep Out!" signs everywhere, but this time the fence was down and they said, "Come in", and here I am. And I like it. I love it. I simply, absolutely, bang on, cross-my-heart-and-hope-to-die love it. But it won't change anything, it won't change our lives. I'll go back when the time comes, I'll go back. I know I have to; but at least I can say I've *been* there; and that's good enough for me. See?'

She nodded, took his face in her hands and kissed him on the lips. 'I see. I know. I don't mind about the T-shirt,

147

honestly, anyway I like you much better like this, bare, and wet.' She slid her hand across his chest, pinched his nipple. He cried out, and she pushed him gently backwards on to the stones, lay half across him pressing her mouth hard to his, her fists tight to his ears, her small tongue seeking. His arms reached for her and pulled her closer to him and somewhere far across the still morning a ship's siren sounded, deep and pulsing, three short blasts. Leni twisted away from his grip and buried her head in his neck.

'Oh God,' he said weakly. 'You're a slut; a dreadful girl: you've undone me.'

'I know,' she said, sliding her hand down his body. 'Fantastic.'

The siren went again, two sharp blasts shattering the stillness. Suddenly he wrenched away, stood up, adjusting himself, looking beyond the tumbled blocks and capitals towards the bay.

'Look what you've done, I'll have to go in again.' He was about to turn towards the pool, stopped, shaded his eyes with his hand. 'Hey! Leni, look! Oh! What a *beauty*!'

She knelt up following his pointing arm.

Below them in the wide bay, sliding gently past the grey ruggedness of the American frigate, a long, sleek, white ship with a fat blue funnel, a white awning at the stern, sun winking on brass and steel, dressed all over in dancing little coloured flags.

'Oh!' she said. 'How beautiful! It must be them. The film people. Can you read the name?'

'Not from here. Jeeze! Isn't it terrific.'

The ship eased gently past the frigate, idled to a halt. Marcus went to the edge of the cliff beyond the tumbled blocks and swung the long brass telescope round, fumbling for focus. A blur of figures at the stern, the frilled edge of the awning, a woman standing at the rail in white trousers, the name in black and gold letters on a gentle curve.

The *Papageno* – Panama.

148

'It's them,' he said.

Umberto Orestes Grottorosso gave himself one final spray of Mitsuko, buttoned the cuffs of his Hermes shirt, crossed the state-room to the three-way mirror with a puma's grace, and approved himself in triplicate.

Broad shoulders, narrow hips, long legs, a Caesar's head capped in close-cropped hair like a silver helmet. 'Perfezione,' he murmured and pulled in his crocodile belt one notch as his valet, in green and black-striped jacket stepped out of the bathroom with a bundle of damp towels and a chest expander.

'We are in, Signore.'

Grottorosso turned slowly and examined his back, smoothed the nape of his neck with muscular fingers.

'In *where*, Peppe?'

'In Villefranche, Signore.'

'Then you should say so. Not simply, "in". In *where*? Valparaiso, Catania, Piraeus? How am I to know where we are? Every port is exactly the same. You confuse me quite deliberately. It is slack thinking, slack speech. We are in Villefranche, say 'Villefranche''. So. And where is the Principessa? It is almost eleven.'

'I will see, Signore,' said Peppe and hurried out.

Grottorosso addressed himself once more to his reflections, bared his even white teeth in a humourless grin, peered closely at his nostrils for signs of a possible hair, and then, satisfied that there were no blemishes, and finally with what he found generally, carefully closed the triple mirrors which folded away compactly into the steel-panelled wall, and swung a David Hockney painting, a nude sailor sitting in a deck-chair, over it like a door, thus concealing three facets of his vanity and returning the state-room to its normal elegance. Burnished steel walls and ceiling, deep-pile carpet, steel and white leather chairs, a long low divan in the same materials; his bunk, spartan, sterile as an operating table, on two steel pedestals, a vast glass-topped table, crystal cylinders massed with fleshy lilies; behind the bunk a tape-deck, above that a Jackson Pollock abstraction, red bars on an intensity of black; and on the table among the lilies a silver tray of drinks and an ice bucket in which his Bernkasteler Doktor chilled.

He moved to the tape-deck, pressed a button and filled the morning with Mozart at the exact moment that Princess Volturino made her entrance from the saloon. A coral silk Russian shirt belted with a silver chain, white trousers, a head of bleached hair brushed high, fine and rounded as a dandelion clock, a tall glass of pastis clutched in one hand tipped with crimson nails, knuckle-dustered with gold. In the other a packet of Muratti's and her lighter.

Grottorosso inclined his head politely, conducting intently with outstretched arms. Eyes half-closed.

She closed the door and leant against it, glass half way to her lips.

'Bert! Lover! Can the Classics, will you? Your auntie wants off.'

He turned down the volume. 'Good morning, Minerva, carina . . . you said?'

'I want off the ark.'

'The ark? You call my *Papageno* the ark?' He poured himself his first glass of Bernkasteler, raised it to the light, sniffed it, sipped it. 'Why?'

'I just do. I'm off, honey. Like the Dove. I'll bring you back an olive leaf.'

'I am wordless. Why, my heart?'

'It's too much. Just too much.' She sat carefully in one of the steel and leather chairs. 'Bert, I love you with all my heart, but really a whole damn month on this Fun Bateau is trop beaucoup. I need terra firma for a while.'

'You want to go ashore?'

'Target! Right! The firmer the less terror.' She looked at him defiantly. 'I get better as the day goes on; I swear.' She leant forward, spiky elbows on bony thighs. 'Honey lamb of mine, no way will I go through a storm like the one we hit off Elba again. No way. I'm the gal who throws up in a calm on the Dead Sea, remember? I just want a nice old-fashioned mattress that doesn't float about like a goddamned water-bed. I haven't had a good night's sleep since we left Ischia and I'm old, honey, old, old. Look at my face this morning! Curdled milk.'

An albino giraffe, he corrected privately. A rich, albino giraffe. He took a sip of his drink, looked at her over the rim of the glass.

'But what will you do? Stay here in Villefranche? At the "Welcome"?'

'I called Cuckoo Peverill at the villa . . . she's giving me shelter; just till we set off again. A change of scene and faces will do us all good, you know that.' She lit a cigarette, prodded the ice cubes in her yellow drink with a long finger.

'I have an instinct that you are bored with us? Is that it, you are restless?'

'If you mean I haven't *had* any rest, then sure. That's what I mean. And,' she dragged hard at her cigarette and blew the smoke above his head. 'Lover, your two Movie Stars are just a teeny weeny bit dreary, I hate like hell to say it.'

He looked at her in astonishment, rearranged the crease in his trousers before he spoke.

'Dreary! Sylva and Wolf? My Princess Károlyi, my l'Aiglon! Dreary?'

'As "Parsifal", honey. What sparkles in Parioli loses its lustre in the sea air. *He* wanders about as if he were carrying the full weight of German Guilt on his shoulders, and she sits about all day painting her toe nails and sighing "Poor Sylva!" because no one throws in with the compliments. God knows, I've tried my best. They're pretty façades, I give you that, but when you knock there's just no one home.'

'Wolf is under stress, you know. He is preparing for the biggest role in his life.'

'I know he's under stress . . . you see to that, poor little brat. Down in the gym every morning, stuck into his books, sitting under a parasol because he daren't get a tan.'

'L'Aiglon was an ill man, he was always pale, it is well known. I cannot have a brown l'Aiglon, Minerva.'

'And that god-awful dyed hair.'

'He was blond, l'Aiglon.'

'But Wolf looks so *weird* with blond hair and those huge brown eyes.'

'He will wear blue contact lenses. He wears them for two hours a day when we are in the gymnasium together.'

'And afterwards he's Oedipus. Pools of blood.'

'You exaggerate as usual. Wolf is my personal choice. He was magnificent in "La Farfalla", I was stupefied: how he came off the screen!'

Minerva took a long sip of her pastis, licked her lips. Stared across at him. 'Honey, he comes off the screen like melting tar.'

'It is not so! Not so! Never! He has a very subtle charisma.'

'He has all the charisma of dandruff.'

Grottorosso swung out of his chair in anger and went to refill his glass. 'You speak with cutting cruelty. Why do you say this to me now? Why *now*? After all these weeks together.'

'Because I didn't know the kid all those weeks ago. And because I'm putting up the money.'

'And Sylva! What is wrong with Sylva? United Artists *insisted* on her. There was no fight to have her, she was their choice; she is perfect for Károlyi. Perfect.'

'Oh, she's all right, she'll do. It isn't the biggest role in the epic . . . and what she lacks in brains she makes up for in boobs. They'll love that. That night off Elba I thought, Minna, I thought, if she goes over, go with her; she'll keep afloat for a week with that pair.' She finished her drink in one swallow, rattled the melting ice cubes. 'Freshen this up, will you, Bert?'

He emptied out the melting ice, filled the glass with fresh cubes, poured in a liberal measure of Ricard, handed it back. His hand shaking with anger.

'You make my heart heavy, *you* are putting up the money! Not all, Minerva, not *all* the money.'

She stubbed out her cigarette carefully. 'No, not all. UA put up a third. Gaumont a third. I dig in for three-quarters *more*. That's what you'll need by the time it's through. I don't mind, I'm happy. It's a great subject, it's a great idea, I just think you should have left that boy exactly where you found him: in Room Service at the Four Seasons, Munich. It's not fair.'

'It is perfectly fair. He will become a star with me. I have never failed yet. It is the dream of his life, he said so. He agreed willingly to my régime, to work hard, to study . . . to train.'

She sighed wearily, took out another cigarette and lit it. 'Of course, it's the dream of every kid. Of course he'd agree.'

'I have fought for Wolf Hagel, fought hard with UA. They wanted Travolta! Or Ryan O'Neal. I *fought* for this boy and I won and he will play my l'Aiglon. I do not curtsey to the Americans.'

'Okay. Fine. Maybe he will . . . I'm sure he'll try. But don't bully him so much, Bert, he's scared shitless of you, you know that? This week, while you're sitting locked up with Charles Peverill and the script, let him go free for a while, won't you? Swim, get away on his own . . . *get* a tan. He'll lose it fast enough when you start work. Let him just be normal for a while.'

Grottorosso pursed his lips, studied the gleaming toes of his white Jourdan slippers. 'He has riding to do . . . there is a stables near Nice . . . he is not good enough. L'Aiglon rode like a madman, he was expert.'

Minerva got up, pulled the shirt down over narrow hips, drained her glass. Set it on the table. 'Just give him a break? Get it? Let him off the reins for a day or two. He can come up to the villa . . . lie about there, swim. You've got to take care, Bert . . . he'll crack. I'm warning you. And I'm off, they are meeting me at the "Welcome" at eleven-thirty.'

He sat sullenly in his chair staring at his feet.

'Oh come on! Take off the hooded look, Bert, it's all Family Business.' She stooped forward and kissed his smooth head. 'I'm your loving Aunt Minerva and I adore you and I think you're a genius and I believe in you . . . and I've fixed it so that you get to meet one of the greatest authorities in the world on the subject. Maybe he could give you a hundred little details you didn't know about . . . it'll be fun, you'll see. So let the kids have a little fun too. I'll fix it with Cuckoo, she's great at picnics and things. We'll have some fun times, and you get on with your work: you need a rest from us as much as we need a rest from you.'

She crossed to the door with the gracefulness of a tall woman well accustomed to composing her limbs. She is like a plastic mop, he thought. At the door she paused, a hand on the steel knob.

'What time will you be back from your Family Lunch at the Colombe d'Or, about four-ish?'

He examined immaculate finger nails, looked up at her slowly from under hooded lids.

Black as polished slate, she thought, and twice as hard. 'Anyway. I'll give you a call at about six . . . to see if you want to come up to the villa . . . just for a drink. They long

154

to meet you.'

'I may go into Monte Carlo . . . the Casino. I don't know. To relax. Tomorrow we start to work, that is so? Is arranged with this "Professore"?'

'Correct.' She swung open the steel door.

Grottorosso took up a thick blue script from the table beside him. 'If you go to the villa today, you will perhaps take this for me? The Scenario, so that the "expert" can read it before we have our conversation. Tell him it is only First Draft. Not Final . . . I will be happy to answer his questions.'

She took the bulky package. 'God! It weighs.'

'It's the life of a young man, of course it weighs.'

'Well . . . I like it. You think he'll have questions?'

Grottorosso examined a thumb carefully. 'They always do, the historians. They never realize that one must condense.'

She put it under her arm. 'I'm sad I won't be with you today.'

'I also. I would have liked you there. We go only so that it will amuse what you call my Dreary Stars . . .'

'I'm truly sorry. But I've *seen* the Picassos and the Braques and I just don't want to watch one more Texan drown his Salade Niçoise in ketchup. Okay? You go along and have a happy day and if you see Signoret tell her I send my love, and if she doesn't remember who I am, tell her I'm the one that drinks my pastis through a straw and calls it lemonade. Do that for me honey?'

He shrugged, buffing his nails slowly on his sleeve.

'And I'll call you around six. Be bright-eyed and bushy-tailed, now? Right?' She raised a golden fist. 'Ciao, Umberto.'

'Ciao,' he said sullenly.

Grottorosso's convoy of three gleaming black Mercedes left the harbour exactly on time and headed for the

Colombe d'Or, more like a cortège of hearses than a celebration. He travelled in the first car, sitting bolt upright in the front beside the driver, his devoted First Assistant, Nino Bucco, in the back charged with the care of his cashmere, lest he should feel chilled at some point, his box of cigarettes and gold lighters, two should one run out, and a small flagon of eau de Cologne in case he might wish to rinse his hands at some moment during the morning, also his wallet, vitamin pills and all his keys. Things which, combined together, could disarrange the sleek perfection of his Lanvin suit. The very thought of carrying a bag, or a purse, was repugnant to him: it was un-masculine.

In the second car, both silent and grimly aware of his suppressed fury but unaware of its cause, Wolf Hagel, his slender figure immaculate in white linen, his dyed blond hair rigid with lacquer, and Sylva Puglia, demure in skin-tight silk jersey from shin to chin, staring dully ahead seething with anger that she had been forced, at the last moment, to change from shorts and a halter into a dress which she considered more suitable to a cathedral than a terrace restaurant in the hills.

'You do not come to my table dressed for a public beach! Like a puttana on the autostrada! Show me, once only, some good taste. You are playing a Princess for me. Not a vulgar stripper.' He had rasped the words like a file on metal. It was the word 'vulgar' which had spiked her bitter resentment. However, she consoled herself; the silk jersey, by concealing, was far more revealing. It was not the amount of flesh one exposed but the degree of contour one displayed, and she displayed a veritable Himalayan range.

One consolation for his suppressed anger was that she and Wolf were banished to a separate car, and could now speak together in Italian, and not struggle through in English, as he insisted that they do, as the coming film was to be made in that language and he wanted them to be completely familiar with the alien tongue before work commenced. Although Wolf, as a German, found English easier than she as an Italian, they were both far more at ease in her native vernacular, and the knowledge that they were not to be under surveillance for at least half an hour so relieved her that she sank back into the soft cushions with a contented sigh, her anger fading, her hand stretching out to rest comfortingly on Wolf's hard thigh.

'Don't be so unhappy, cara. Poor Wolf! Poor Sylva! It is a lunch we go to, not the Première.'

He tried to smile, sadly shook his lacquered head. 'I don't know what is wrong. Early this morning he was happy. I let him win.'

'Win?' She looked past him at the sea as they swung round the War Memorial towards the Promenade des Anglais.

'Wrestling. In the gym. He likes to win.'

She shrugged. 'Oh that! Crazy stuff. Why do you do it? If one day he hurts you, what then? No l'Aiglon.'

'He is old. Forty-eight. I'm half his age and stronger. I could beat him every time, but it is better not to.'

'You pretend to lose?'

'Sure. To keep him happy. He likes his illusions. He must always be strong, brave, the male, the bull: the Master . . .' He stopped suddenly, patted the hand on his thigh, rubbed his nose, was silent.

'Illusions! Ah Dio! He pretends to be someone who he is not. Fantasy. He is really not so strong and so brave . . . underneath it all he is afraid of something. I know, a woman always can tell, it is a scent we get, an instinct. He knows this with me; it makes him feel uncomfortable . . . I just smile. You know something? He is terrified that he will be kidnapped. "A bullet I will take bravely," he said. "But I am afraid of torture. If they tortured me I cannot say what I would do." He said this once to me and now he

157

is ashamed. I can tell. I am not so stupid, I have known too many men.'

'Well, you know, he is very, very rich . . . they could.'

'Torture him? Why?'

'No . . . no. Kidnap him.'

'They kidnap only industrialists, politicians, so on. You know he sends them money?'

'The Red Brigade?' Wolf's brown eyes were round with disbelief. 'Not possible.'

She nodded, but said no more, regretting what she had said already. Pressed his leg firmly. 'I wish they would take him . . . then this damned film would collapse.'

'You want that?'

She stroked his thigh, looking vaguely ahead along the curving Promenade. 'Sometimes. I don't know. It is all so *serious* . . . there is no fun. Poor Sylva!'

'But you are a star. You can just go, surely? Just say "no thank you", and go.'

She looked at him with a sour smile. 'Leave Grottorosso? Quit his movie? Are you crazy? I'd never be employed again. They would think that he had sacked *me*, not that I had left *him*. He would say so anyway. He would tell the Press pronto. After Grottorosso sacks you, you can only go down. Anyway . . .' she ran her free hand through long red hair '. . . I want the dignita.'

'Dignita?'

'The rank, the distinction. A Grottorosso film gives you that. The Americans are very impressed . . . and I want to go to America. So . . . I stay. I will suffer but I will stay . . . poor Sylva! He chose me, it is a big honour; he chose you too . . . he will make you a star.'

'He says so. But I suffer too. My God! English lessons, fencing, riding, my hair . . . the gym . . . the contact lenses.'

'But what do you want? To be a movie star or not?'

'Better than a waiter, eh? The money . . .' He shrugged,

158

staring out at the crowded beaches.

'Ah, the money. You want to buy a little hotel one day, is that it? The usual dream.'

'Maybe . . . not big. Ten rooms. A little bar.'

She slid her hand into his fork. 'You are too beautiful for that. Be a movie star, come to America. You will have a Cadillac, a swimming-pool . . . many lovely dumb Californian girls. No brains, but legs like nutcrackers.'

He removed her hand gently, crossed his legs.

She laughed and shrugged. 'It's a lousy job, even for man.'

'Better than a waiter's.'

'You will find out . . .' She opened her compact, held it close to her face, licked round her lips with a pointed tongue, lowered each eyelid separately, like small roller blinds, smoothed the blue lining-shadow. 'Whatever went wrong this morning was because of Minna Volturino. She came out of the state-room and told me, "Rough weather ahead, honey . . . take your vomit bag along".' She snapped the compact shut, slipped it into her bag. 'Vulgar! Dio Mio, he thinks that *I* am vulgar, and she is a real Principessa, can you believe it?'

Wolf shook his head, the first pale smile lit his eyes like winter sunlight. 'Not a real Principessa, Sylva. She just married a Prince, that is different. Her father made a fortune out of lavatory pans, did you know? In America. Grottorosso told me.'

'Hah!' said Sylva. '*That's* vulgar!'

In the third, and last, car rode Nando Belluno, the Associate Producer, a small, fat man whose tear-ducts had been blocked ever since birth, so that he appeared to spend most of his life in a vale of depression and copious tears. An affliction useful, perhaps, to a professional mourner or an undertaker, but disastrous to a film lawyer and accountant. In consequence he was forced to wear very dark glasses at all times lest he unnerved those anxious clients whose 'projects' depended entirely on his handling of their finances. But neither dark glasses nor his corpulent body could conceal a brain as shrewd, uncluttered and financially brilliant as a Getty.

Beside him, smoking furiously through a paper holder cigarettes which she had been forbidden by her doctors for over thirty years to touch, Lilli Scarlatti, the Costume Designer, who had that morning drawn the full force of Grottorosso's wrath upon her hunched shoulders when she had arrived at the launch dressed as a Bedouin.

'He is in the pit of hell this morning,' she said gruffly. 'Was it you? What did you do to him? Say?'

Belluno spread plump hands across his bulging stomach. 'I? Nothing. I neither said nor did a thing. I haven't even mentioned the word "money" for days; not a single syllable crossed my lips. But we know his moods. They are like tropical storms, they come from nowhere, a big blaze, and then they go away. It is nothing.'

'Tropical storm! Hah! "You suppose that you will come to my table in one of your own hideous confections?" he said to me. "Shall you also bring your tent and your camel?" ' She puffed furious smoke into the already blue air of the car and coughed harshly for a few moments, eventually turning the ugly sound into a controlled, if bitter, laugh. 'To me, Scarlatti! With more credits to my name than he has movies! "You show no style," he said. No style! And how should he know what style is, I would like to know, eh? I who studied under Pabst, trained with Renoir, slaved with adoration under Visconti! *We*, the designers, set the style on his films; he takes the credit, we do the work. *We* made the famous "Grottorosso Style" as they call it, we taught him! How could he know about style? How could a mineral water merchant know what style is, hey? Tell me that? Sparkling *mineral* water, this you know.'

'Of course I know,' said Belluno cheerfully. 'I am constantly grateful for that water, my dear Lilli. Every time we run short of money, and you know as well as I do how often that is, I simply remind the backers that we have the Grottorosso Spring at our command, finally . . . and that is inexhaustible. *Inexhaustible*.' He repeated the word with deep pleasure. 'It not only assists their digestion, their livers and their punished kidneys, the progress of gluttonous meals through their alimentary tracts, but it also progresses their pens smoothly, across their cheques. And for that I am ever grateful.' He stroked his stomach affectionately. 'As you know, he has never put a single lira of his own into any production he has ever made in all the years; so I am always filled with infinite joy at the remembrance of that fortuitous little spring in Tuscana bubbling merrily away into all those millions and millions of bottles. It is a most refreshing thought, it is also a great consolation to my budgets.'

Lilli coughed again, shook a thin wristful of silver coins, untangled them. 'Money! Dio Mio! He thinks style is three Mercedes to go to a luncheon. Style was me alone: in an Hispano Suiza – going *anywhere*!'

Belluno laughed softly. 'You have used the word style nine times in less than two minutes. Can you not make it a round number?'

'Your passion is figures: mine, style.'

'Ten,' said Belluno pleasantly, and belched.

'He is a vulgarian, Grottorosso. Strip off Lanvin and Jourdan and what would you find?'

'Apollo?'

'Ah, he's a splendid figure of a man, that I agree. We have all seen that, we are *obliged* to see it, in all its guises. But beyond that, what?'

'A soul?'

'Black as a cauldron.' She removed the butt of her cigarette from the holder with bottle-green finger-nails, pressed it into an ashtray, crushed the paper holder tightly in her hand.

'After all, soul black or soul white, he has a splendid brain. It is almost that of genius. Remember, Lilli,' he touched her clenched hand lightly, 'he it was who chose his Team of brilliant Designers: he knew your worth and value, he was aware of all your varied talents. He draws all the greatest artists about him, and I have never known him yet to make a vulgar film. Daring, disturbing, provocative, but never at any time, in any way *vulgar*, or for cheap effect. Mineral water merchant or not, he is true.'

Lilli relaxed slightly at the implied compliment, dropped the crushed holder to the floor, and adjusted the chain of coins and crescents about her narrow forehead.

Her mind had suddenly veered away from Grottorosso's soul to a flash-image of his aunt, the Princess Volturino, in the launch astride a pile of battered Vuitton luggage, cradling two bottles of Pastis in a plastic bag and singing 'Swannee!' at the top of her voice as she sped across the harbour. She shuddered at the memory and searched in her draw-string sack for another cigarette.

'And Volturino. Can she be true? Can she be real?'

'Real enough to sign the contract; it is enough for me . . she is vastly rich.'

'So I am told. Sanitary ware. They are well matched, he the water, she the recipient of its efficaciousness.' She snorted with sour amusement. 'Style!'

'We have had worse backers. The man who financed almost all of 'Amphytrion'' was a pork butcher with pretensions from Bologna.'

'And now l'Aiglon is financed by water-closets. What a profession!'

'Who else but Family would finance a picture of such cost starring a completely unknown waiter from Munich! Tell me that. United Artists have only put up a third, because of Puglia's name. Thank God, therefore, for Family; water-closets notwithstanding.'

'And she really is Family . . . I am constantly amazed,

they were so elegant once.'

'Not after Mussolini . . . the elegance faded . . . you may remember? Yes, she is Family. Her husband, poor Volturino, is brother to Grottorosso's mother. Dunque! Family . . .'

'Well, let us hope it is a success. "La Farfalla" was *disaster*.' She lit the cigarette and inhaled deeply, swallowing the smoke like a devouring python.

Belluno blinked at the sight, and turned his attention to the passing scenery. Garages, caravan sites, unfinished blocks of flats, builders' yards, estates of 'provençal' villas crushed among the concrete poles of the Electricity Company of France. Here and there a mutilated tree, a used-car dump, a spillage of tumbled stone walls, abandoned vineyards, Schweppes hoardings. Progress.

'No more disasters,' he murmured. 'There are enough all about us.'

It is possible that I am heading for disaster, thought Grottorosso grimly as the car sped through the péage and out on to the semi-autoroute towards St Paul de Vence. 'I have let my personal interests intrude upon my professional ones. A fatal error. Minerva, coarse, crude, blunt as she is, has touched upon the secret fears I have found growing within me for the last three weeks. Touched, not gently, but with a red-hot sword. A hammer to the nails of my crucifix! Ayeee! What do I do? What have I done? Am I losing judgement? Can it be that? Am I growing old at forty-eight, for God's sake? Have I started to lose my touch so soon? I know "La Farfalla" was not so good, an uneasy compromise between styles, and I used Box Office Stars . . . but surely one is allowed one modest failure, and it was not a failure to me, only to the Critics who said that I was whoring to popular appeal. So, I try to repair the error of my ways, I find an unknown youth, for the role of a lifetime, and have I gone mad? Am I crazy? Is Minerva

right? Melting tar! What cruelty! The charisma of
dandruff.' He winced and turned his head away, clenched
his fists, thumped his knees. The driver flicked him a
nervous look. So vicious! But . . . but . . . is it so? Is it so?
Am I blinded by the grace, the gentleness, the innocence of
the youth? Can it be that? But these are the qualities he
needs for l'Aiglon . . . the diffidence, the sweetness, the
patience, the bearing of a young Prince. That is what I saw
those months ago in Munich that is what I *saw*.

And so I tried him out in the little role of Narcissus.
Certainly he had little to do but move like a God . . . and
he moved like a God. Of course obeying my every
command, no words to speak, himself; but the camera was
kind to him. And I was the master, I dictated every
gesture, every look, every tilt of his head, every breath he
drew, and he obeyed me completely, unquestioningly. the
clay in the potter's hand and I the potter. But . . . but! Clay
has no resistance until it is fired; it is fluid, soft, pliable, it
accepts the expert touch of a master craftsman as easily as
it accepts the coarser hand of the peasant potter. I am the
Master Craftsman, that I can say with no fear of doubt.
But have I chosen common clay to try and fashion a piece
of Meissen? Have I made the most appalling error? He will
give me the grace of my prince, but can he give me the
fury? For fury I must have. L'Aiglon was possessed of
fury. A boy who could beat a horse almost to death, who
could fight with a will of iron the slow rotting of his body,
who was blazing to rule over France, Belgium, Italy and
Poland, son of an Emperor! Can he give me this, this Wolf
Hagel? Can he suggest the force, the passion, the rage to
live? I can teach him the manners of a prince, naturally . . .
but can I teach him rage? We wrestle; he gives in, pleasing
me, he thinks, by losing. We fence; he crumbles when I
prick him. I humiliate him, he accepts, meekly. He rides
but is afraid to take a jump . . . Ah no! He is weak!
Weak! Cheap peasant clay.

He stared furiously up at the village of St Paul strapped tightly within its ramparts, a ship stranded upon a hill. But strong! Proud upon its ridge, serene, having defied centuries of invaders from Saracens to Moors and turned them back with brute force, remaining unconquered, victorious, secure. Strength! Fist jammed hard against his cheek he glared balefully at the clutter of jumbled roofs from which the square church tower rose indomitably, glowing like cornelian in the sun. It had even managed to repel the new invaders, the builders and tourists who had littered the gentle hills about it with a sea of ugly villas and sodium lamps, a tide of metropolitan mediocrity lapping at the very base of its foundations. But a masculine village, strong, brave, resolute, surviving. There is nothing weak there: but I have chosen from a frail stratum for my l'Aiglon; common clay better suited to a chamber pot than a work of art. Flawed rubbish which will explode in the furnace of my creativity or else reveal its blemishes under my master's hand. Why was I so sure at first? Why so captivated? Am I indeed losing touch? Am I completely mad?

The answer to that was, quite simply, yes.

Grottorosso's madness was not the kind for which one is locked away, it was not the kind which was ever immediately clear to even the most practised eye; it was a 'gentle madness', more eccentric than lunatic, and one which was easily, and often far too quickly, confused with genius – which, after all, is a modest sign of madness in any man.

But Grottorosso was not any man in any sense. Certainly as far as he himself was concerned, he was extraordinary; a piece of self-knowledge which suffused him with delight. From the moment of his birth his astonished parents, nurses and maids were left in no doubt as to this quality. No plump, pink gurgling baby this: a muscular, cold-eyed creature, strong and determined, who fed at the breast of his wet-nurse like a carnivore, and beat, pummelled and roared for constant attention from all about him. At one year he staggered about on legs as sturdy and straight as columns, at two he ran; at three he spoke fluently, the words 'I', 'want', 'shall', 'give', 'no', and 'take' predominating over the more usual 'Papa' or 'Mamma' which never, at any time, figured in his growing vocabulary, being replaced neatly and tidily by 'him' or 'her'. At four he could hum Rossini and read La Fontaine with ease, and at five, breaking away from a crucified governess one day in Rome, he tripped over a cat, which he had been about to kick, and crashed cruelly down the marble stairs of the Victor Emanuel memorial to land heavily on his head at the bottom, which left him with a fractured skull from which he eventually recovered, and a secret terror of marble staircases, from which he did not. For the rest of his life he ascended or descended only among a tight group of people or by firmly clasping a handrail. This was put down, to those who were aware of it, as a mere form of his brilliant eccentricity. But he knew only too well that it was a hideous flaw in his otherwise steel-like strength and masculinity. A flaw which he did all he could to conceal, even from himself. He despised, above all things, weakness and indecision, and was absolutely unforgiving of both in all their forms. The Tower of Pisa made him ill.

His supreme pleasure was seeking out, in the most rugged and virile of his fellow men, any secret thread of weakness. Once detected he would mine away carefully like some silent weevil until the hard shell had been pierced and the hidden kernel of frailty had been reached; and then, with expert timing, he would expose it to the cruel light of day and derision, and so destroy. In exposing the flaws beneath splendid façades he could expiate his own happily. He never applied this form of destruction and torture to women, whom he considered far too easily crushed, and appallingly weak in any event, but addressed himself particularly to the most masculine, strong and courageous of men. This destruction, when it came, as inevitably it did, was greatly rewarding to him, as rewarding as dynamiting skyscrapers, felling great trees, or sending a battleship to the depths with one slender torpedo. Each capitulation gave him intense physical pleasure, akin indeed to sexual release, and at the same time each one armoured him, and made him feel strong. Applying the same tactics to a woman would have given him no greater pleasure than treading on a fledgling.

The only women whom he could countenance, with any degree of comfort, near him, were those like Lilli Scarlatti or Minerva Volturino whom he considered to be half-male in any case, and un-real, living half-lives: he easily crushed the feminine side in them, and their male-side amused him. So. But women in general he detested for their passivity, passivity being as unforgivable as weakness or indecision. There could be no physical, or mental, pleasure in any operation directed against creatures such as they for they offered no challenge.

Which was why he was presently so anguished on his way to luncheon at the Colombe d'Or by the blunder which he had very probably made in choosing Wolf Hagel as his next, and most interesting, subject for vivisection.

At first sight he had appeared to be exactly the right material. Male, handsome, strong, with just a hint of grace which was so essential for the envisaged role of l'Aiglon. Clean-limbed, determined, innocent. Innocence above all. How splendid then to take this glowing creature and mould him carefully into shape, to build him, to lavish him with learning, train him, develop his quite unaware nature, give him self-pride, arrogance, ambition, make him aware of envy, avarice, greed and power. To make him, in short, a true Man, drape a cloak of brilliance and glory about him and permit him to swagger in his splendours for a time.

And then gently unpick the seams.

But what was this? The boy was passive? He was weak all through; there *was* no hidden flaw . . . he reeked of goodness! Nothing within but honesty, truth and innocence, blinding in their banality. There could be no possible excitement here, no achievement, no destruction, for he was but an empty shell and when crushed would leave only dust behind. There could be no victory. A shell is not a soul, a puddle is not a lake, a stick not a tree, a fly not an eagle and Wolf Hagel is not l'Aiglon!

As the car came softly to a halt beside the great stone archway of the Colombe, an applause of white doves clattering up before it, sunlight spilled through the heavy plane-trees of the square in which people played boule, red dust drifted through the wandering crowd, two small boys in newspaper hats fought a laughing duel: with bamboo canes. And, quite suddenly, Grottorosso smiled.

At his long table under the fig-trees he surveyed his guests with cool detachment. The pleasant atmosphere about them, the wine, his sudden change of mood from cold rage to sparkling humour, the laughter and gentle murmur of easy conversation and excellence of the food, had relaxed them into almost normal Italian conviviality.

Only Wolf Hagel, at the far end of the table, listening intently to a furiously gesticulating, laughing, Lilli Scarlatti, stayed gravely contained.

How fine he looks, thought Grottorosso slicing through his jambon de Parme and melon; such a splendid head, the smooth brow, clear skin, perfectly set eyes, firm chin, sculpted mouth, strong throat, the golden head haloed by the sun. The perfect l'Aiglon façade. A beautiful façade indeed. But there is no one at home when you knock, she had said. Bitch of hell! For me to have made such an error! A tremor of anger, slight as the whispered ripple from a distant earthquake, forced him to grip the handle of his knife so tightly that his knuckles shone like silver shillings through the bronze skin. And then, quite suddenly, it passed; he smiled, set the knife carefully across the edge of his plate, thrust his fork into a small cube of melon and raised it to his lips.

If a building is empty and there is nothing of interest within, then one might turn one's eyes to the façade instead, and this one has a great deal of architectural interest. One must look closely; why seek only the hidden flaws? A flaw is not necessarily concealed. I wonder, he thought, slipping the melon into his mouth, why I didn't think of that before?

Chapter Six

Minerva, her head bound up in a white silk turban, her long body draped in flowing chiffon, arms folded lightly across her chest, hands to shoulders, elbows tight to slender waist, a vague smile of content on her lips. A caryatid in drenching moonlight. She stood for some moments perfectly still, looking up the gentle slope of silvered lawns towards the lights of the house. Somewhere in the pines above her a nightingale; laughter from the distant pool, fireflies drifting, spiralling; in the house, light in Archie's window, the terrace shadowy as a church, sparkling with votive candles, the high bay-window of the drawing-room thrusting into the darkness, a crescent of amber.

She tapped the soft grass beneath her foot, feeling its resistance and solidity, and throwing her arms wide, as if to embrace all that lay before her, she walked slowly and deliberately towards the terrace steps, retrieved her bag from a body-indented chair, her empty glass from a table where she had left it more than half an hour before, and went into the drawing-room.

Pools of shaded light, gleam of polished wood, silver, glass, massed spikes of white delphiniums, the John portrait above the fireplace, the Sickerts, Magrittes, the Bonnard lilac glowing as if incandescent, from hidden lights. In a far corner, sitting at a bonheur du jour, pencil to her lips, Cuckoo with a thick book, her free hand idly twisting pearls at her throat.

'It's all to die! It's too much . . . all too much!'

Cuckoo turned in startled surprise, eyes wide. 'To die? My dear; what? What is?'

Minerva waved her empty glass vaguely above her head. 'The whole bit: this room, the house, the gardens, the moonlight . . . the peace, the calm of it all. If you *knew* what calm means to me after three weeks on that bloody bateau . . . nothing moves any more, nothing *lurches*.'

Cuckoo closed her book, marking the place with a slip of card.

'You gave me the most awful shock. I was utterly lost in *Larousse* . . . something quite delicious for tomorrow. Lunch. Does this monstrous creature eat *anything*? Or is he what Nanny used to call "choosy" about his food?'

'Well . . . not anything. He has fastidious tastes in all directions, as I told you. No battery hens or veal . . . because of the hormones.'

'We don't have battery hens. Archie's terrified too. And Bruna. I think in the end we'll just have a sort of picnic, pâté, cheese, crudités. Larousse is worse than Mrs Beeton; at least she was bourgeoise, but Larousse hasn't quite come to terms with the French Revolution. We'll keep it simple for tomorrow, first "working day" after all.'

'Well, for God's sake don't fuss . . . he'll be happy with a salad. I'm going to have a night cap . . . you too?'

She poured herself a generous drink.

Cuckoo joined her, put her arm round the bony shoulders, hugged her. 'I've never been very far behind you, have I? It's absolutely "deevy" having you back again . . . the years fade away. Golly! How we've laughed . . . a Scotch sur les jolies roches. Have you been down at the pool?'

'Watching your "pretties", the dolphins. They really are divine . . . and she's wild! That hair, that voice. They're coming up in a moment.'

Cuckoo raised her glass. 'He's not bad either, is he? Quite dishy.'

'Terrific! And you picked him up just like that! Trust you! The only thing I ever picked up when *I* fell down was

171

myself.' She settled comfortably in the corner of a deep settee, patted a place beside her. 'Come sit here, you look quite weary. Far too many of us, I didn't know you had a full house . . . I feel so mean.'

'Well don't,' said Cuckoo sitting beside her and putting her feet up on the low malachite table. 'I'm happy as could be. I love too many people, always have . . . but wasn't I lucky? About him? Being fished out by a "scrumptious"! I mean, he could so easily have been old and fat, or one of those bulgy Dutch tourists who gobble at one all the time. . I'd rather have drowned really. He gave me the most terrific belt across the face . . . did I tell you?'

'Good grief! Why?'

'Well . . . I was sort of snorting and choking, you know, swallowed water . . . so on. Very messy.'

'You must have been terrified.'

Cuckoo laughed gently. 'Not half as terrified as I am of meeting your odd nephew, Count Grottorosso, tomorrow. Ashen with terror I am. Ashen. He sounds too frightening for words . . . do admit?'

'Not frightening. Baroque, I'd say.'

'Well, that's bad enough, I'm really not awfully good at baroque. I like nice simple lines. All that sparkle and glitter and wedding-cakery business is fearfully exhausting.'

Minerva lit a cigarette, snapped her lighter shut, squinted at it. 'Yeah. Baroque. Brave and baroque. Very male, lots of macho, a man's-man, and of course a genius; anyway *I* think so. Nothing weak. Do you know, at age fifteen he had seven notches cut into the stock of his rifle? He's a deadly shot.'

'Friends of the family?'

'No, American GI's. Verona, June 1945. He was part of a happy band of faithful Fascist kids who swore to defend the patrie . . . until Benito got strung up at the gas-station and then they just swapped hats and joined the Commies. He was the best little sniper in the group. Swears he had a round dozen but only got around to marking up the first seven. He was still in short pants.'

Cuckoo worriedly adjusted her velvet bow. 'He sounds hellish. I'm absolutely terrified! How can you possibly like him? Your own soldiers, really Minna.'

'Oh, what the hell. It was wartime. Things are different then. All fair and so on. You know? And he was a kid. They thought they were being patriotic . . . it was really just for the kicks. But I'll tell you, he was the only member of that whole goddamned family who was really nice to me when I married Volturino. They just hated my guts, each and every one, but they needed the loot and I brought plenty in my goodie-bag. They were ruined; Fascist to the hair line and beyond, thrown out of every position they'd held; if it hadn't been for me and the Vatican who did a nifty bit of smoothing over, they'd have been destroyed. But I restored that damned great Palazzo, got the factory rebuilt for the fizzy water, got the deal through with Bloomingdale's and floated Manhattan Island in Grottorosso Water; and still they hated my guts. Except for Umberto who was dear, he really was. I made him laugh, and I was tough . . . he likes that, tough women; and I was as tough as anyone he'd ever met. I had to be, in that family; tough "Zia Minerva".' She blew a pair of smoke rings into the still air. 'It was the chapel, of course, which finally did it. They never forgave me for that. A crummy goddamned little chapel, covered in dust, peeling with damp, cracks all over, some tatty old frescoes not even finished, pigeon shit everywhere. So what do I do? Kind lady, I restore it all. Got a great team up from Rome, kids I knew; when they'd finished it looked like the Doge's Palace. Terrific! And what happened? Screams and shrieks. A bloody Greek funeral, beating of breasts, sobs and wails, rolling of eyes, you have *never*, in your vie, seen such hysteria!'

She leant over and stubbed out her cigarette. 'How the

hell did I know it was Giotto? I didn't know Giotto from Osso Bucco in those days, for God's sake!' She grinned wryly. 'I learned. But Umberto was just darling, he laughed so much he threw up. Said I should try my hand with the Foro Romano: I loved him for that.'

'Well . . . yes, I do see. But it was madness, the whole thing. Marrying into that vile family. I did warn you.'

'Yes, I know. But he was breathing, and male, and he asked me. And after thirty years of being Miss Minerva Kamm I kind of hankered after the Princess bit. I wanted a change, and got it. And really, Cuckoo, swear to God . . . I had a ball. Minerva Kamm! Ye gods! When Daddy gave my name to one of his high-class stand-up-stalls for gentlemen, black, gold and pink mosaic, Klimt colours, he said, for the Jewish Trade, I cried for a week. "They're pissing over my name!" I cried. "You should be so lucky!" he said. Right! Only I didn't get the point, not then. But, brother . . . now I do. I love it all.'

A sound of laughter from the terrace, a chair scraped across stone.

'My pretties,' said Cuckoo and went to meet them. 'Leni!' she said in astonishment. 'You're on fire! Your head . . .'

'Fireflies,' said Leni. 'Isn't he so foolish, this one? He has caught them and put them in my hair. Marcus! Take them off.'

'They won't bite, they're only flies,' said Marcus. 'Doesn't she look super all lit up?'

'Super,' said Cuckoo. 'Such a pretty thing to do.'

Leni was pulling anxiously at her spiky hair. 'I can't feel them, they'll die. Oh, it such a silly thing to do. Flies can bite . . .'

'Come here,' said Marcus and pulling her head down brushed three glowing sparks on to the terrace which Leni quickly scooped into her hand and scattered into the garden.

'Poor little things. Looking for a gentleman, and now they're all broken.'

'You won't get cold, will you?' said Cuckoo. 'All wet still.'

'Oh, it was so beautiful, you know, like swimming in silver. No, it's not cold.'

'Would you like a whisky? Or there's some wine chilling, the Sauvignon.'

'No. Thank you very much.' Leni pulled her towel round her waist. 'To bed, I think . . . and Marcus to his bath. He loves this bath more than the bed.'

'He's crazy,' said Minerva. 'With you for a Dutch wife.'

'What is this? Dutch wife?'

'A kind of bolster, honey. You have them in the East where it's terribly, terribly hot. They keep you cool in bed.'

'I'm a bolster, you see, Marcus?'

'Too skinny.' He put his arm round her shoulder and pulled her to him. 'And tomorrow, Cuckoo, we'll take off. Go up into the hills: there's a bus from Nice. To Peïra-Cava and Turini, or wherever.'

'He says there are marmots there.'

'What are they?' said Minerva, filling her glass with ice.

'Rabbits with no ears, he says. Right?'

'Right. You don't mind?'

'No,' said Cuckoo sitting down again. 'Of course I don't mind, you do as you like.'

'Only it's a pretty full day for you tomorrow. Signore Whatever and so on.'

'It's simple. A picnic lunch, that's all.'

'We'll have ours in the hills. Back about six-ish. For supper. All right?' He leant forward suddenly and kissed her cheek.

'Perfectly all right. You should see Lucéram, it's frightfully pretty.'

'That's a place?'

'Before Peïra-Cava, almost in Italy. Well: not far.'

'Great.'

'Tell Bruna in the morning, before you leave, about no lunch.'

She watched them as they crossed the wide room and went into the hall, her hand touching her cheek.

'Stunning,' said Minerva. She sat carefully beside Cuckoo, eyes light with amusement. 'He bite?'

'Bite?'

'Uhhuh. Your cheek? You're still holding it.'

Cuckoo folded her hands round her glass. 'First kiss. First time. A young kiss. Sweet.'

'I know.' Minerva sipped her drink, prodded the ice with the handle of her gold lorgnettes. 'He knows, of course? Golden Boy? The Napoleon thing?'

'L'Aiglon? Oh, of course . . . yes indeed. Archie told him right away, first evening. He couldn't resist it, naturally. It is odd. To come *here* of all places. Do admit . . .'

'Odder still for one Umberto Grottorosso. He'll flip. I think it's a good thing they're off to the hills tomorrow. He'll want him the moment he sets cold grey eyes on him . . . betcha.'

'For his cinema-thing? But he's got his l'Aiglon. You told me; anyway Marcus isn't an actor.'

'Neither is Wolf Hagel. Umberto was brought up in the Rossellini-Fellini School, you don't use actors, you have real people. Less trouble, easier to bully, cheaper, and truer to life. Hagel was a waiter.'

'Well, Leni says that Marcus is "in business" . . . I don't know what. You tell your vile nephew to stick to his waiter. He's here to see Archie, for nothing else.'

'They're bound to meet, aren't they?'

'At the picnic on Thursday, they'll all be here from the ship.'

'The two l'Aiglons! In person! Spot the fake! What

176

fun!'

'Now listen, Minna.' Cuckoo placed her glass deliberately on the table. 'No games on Thursday. It's my picnic: I don't want anything to spoil it.'

'Cuckoo, my heart . . . you have a chain of coincidences running for you, it's not my fault. I won't say a single mot. Not a petit mot. I won't need to; just watch Umberto when the penny drops, when the scales fall, when the chips are down. He's greedy.'

'Revolting and spoiled.'

'No,' said Minerva raising her glass. 'Not so much spoiled as a *spoiler*: that's the rub.'

From the hall a sudden cry of laughter, a clapping of hands, Leni's voice. 'Show Cuckoo . . . oh, show her! Cuckoo! Look . . . how fine he is, isn't it?'

In the doorway Marcus: in the white uniform, tunic and breeches, bare feet and shins. Behind him Archie smiling anxiously.

'You see! It quite fits, isn't he lovely?' Leni led him into the room by a cuff.

Cuckoo got to her feet slowly, still with surprise. 'What is it? Where from?'

'That dummy-thing. In my office.' Archie nodded his head once or twice. 'I was taking the damned thing down before the Italian fellow arrives. Looks a bit, well, silly stuck there. You know.'

'What's under your arm?' said Cuckoo.

'Oh. Yes. This. Its head,' said Archie, lifting it by the jointed neck.

'You make a great Salome, Charles dear,' said Minerva.

'Well, they rather caught me at it. I was tidying up. All this wicked girl's fault really. She dared him to try it on. Didn't you? Fits too; astonishingly. It looks quite indecent without boots.'

'But he looks very fine, doesn't he?' Leni stroked a sleeve. 'I wish that he could wear it always.'

'Too damned tight,' said Marcus. 'And hot, the collar's choking me.' He turned slowly, admiring himself in the long gilt mirror between the windows. Leni removed a jar of flowers from the console table so that he might see better. 'It is pretty good, isn't it? I mean, quite glamorous. Not bad, not bad at all . . . cuffs a bit short. But did he actually wear this?'

'Not that. Not that very one,' said Archie, placing the head carefully in the seat of a chair. 'It's a copy . . . Gieves did it. Cost a fortune, but that's what he wore. The White Uniform. A Lieutenant-Colonel, Duke of Nassau's 29th Infantry Brigade. His greatest joy, poor fellow.'

'Was there a hat . . . a helmet?'

'Yes. Exactly like his father's . . . sort of fore and aft. Not very becoming.'

'And he fought in this outfit?'

Archie shook his head sadly. 'No. No, never fought. He was too fragile, and too dangerous politically; he was, I fear, only a Toy Soldier, you see.'

'What are these, so pretty,' said Leni touching the tarnished stars on the jacket.

'The Order of St Stephen, and that one is the Parmesan Order of St George. I say, you'd better got out of it all, I could talk all night, you know. But I must get it packed away, and I still have half the script-thing to finish before tomorrow.'

'How do you find it, or shouldn't I ask?' said Minerva sitting on the arm of the settee.

Archie looked across at her as he retrieved the head from the chair, smoothed its hair. 'Interesting. Very condensed, of course. I suppose you have to. One or two things I'm not very happy about, sort them out perhaps. Come along, let's get you out of that.'

Marcus turned away from his mirror, faced the two women, hand on hip, one arm raised in a salute. 'Exit the Toy Soldier. Do you fancy me then?' He was grinning.

'Not nearly as much as you fancy yourself, honey.' Minerva finished her drink, put the long empty glass to one eye like a telescope. 'You should be in movies: you know that one?'

'We'll take a photograph, shall we,' said Leni. 'For Mr Bender?'

'Oh please!' said Archie. 'Do come along you two, it's after midnight. I've got work to do still.' He tucked the wax head under his arm and they left in a shuffle, their voices fading as they crossed the hall. A door shut on a thread of laughter.

'Well,' said Minerva, her voice as dry as scorched grass. 'You *do* see?'

Cuckoo moved for the first time, as if awakened suddenly, and went over to the bonheur du jour to collect the *Larousse*. 'Yes. Yes, I did see.'

'Spit and image,' said Minerva.

'Let's keep it a secret, shall we? Not a word.'

'Not a word. Pas un mot shall pass my lips. There's someone on the terrace . . .'

'Tonnino. Taking in the cushions. I'm going up. Coming?'

'Right behind you. You know, in the notes in the scripts Charles is reading there is a quote from some eye-witness who said that when he looked at the girls in the streets of Vienna "roses blossomed in their cheeks and their eyes sparkled like stars, sending out flashes of fire". Isn't that divine?'

'When who did?'

'L'Aiglon.'

'Shop girls and milliners. Hysterical and over-romantic. Do admit?'

'First time I knew you ever trimmed hats, Cuckoo Peverill. You could have fooled me.'

She was sitting naked, cross-legged on the bed, smoking,

179

when he came in from the bathroom, a towel in one hand, a comb in the other.

'Slut,' he said and threw the towel at her. 'Stinking up the room.'

'Gauloises. You said you loved the smell of Gauloises.' She blew a thin stream of smoke upwards.

'I do. But not in here. Can't you smell the other things? Sea, pines, roses, whatever.'

'No. And you can't either. It all smells of that green stuff you put in the water.'

He bent to see himself in the dressing-table mirror, slicked his damp hair into place.

'You are so vain,' she said.

'Piss off.'

'You have a white thing on your bottom, do you know?'

He half turned towards her, arms above his head. 'What sort of white thing? Where?'

'In the very middle. Quite small, like this . . .' She sketched a shape in the air.

'Triangle?'

'If you say. Where your slip has been.'

'Small slip.'

'Most rude. Let me see your front. There too. But very small. The white part.'

'I'm glad. The rest all right?'

'Fantastic. Did you see her face, down there just now?'

'Whose?' He put the comb on the dressing-table, smoothed the back of his head.

'Cuckoo. Cuckoo's face, when you were in the uniform.'

'No. Not really.'

'I did.' She leant across to the side table and stubbed out the cigarette. 'So did the Princess, she saw . . . she was watching her all the time.'

'What for? What was she doing?'

'She's in love with you.'

'Oh come on now! Cuckoo? You really are bonkers.'

'No. Seriously though. I think so . . . it's a special look, you know; women have.'

He crossed slowly to the bed, hands behind his neck. 'Too much sun. Gone to your head, my girl.'

'I saw very clear. Also you kissed her.'

'Well? That was ages before. Why not?'

'You never have before. You just did it.'

'So?' He sat on the edge of the bed. 'A little kiss, nothing. She looked rather, I don't know . . . a bit sad. Lost. I just felt I wanted to; I don't know why.'

'Perhaps you . . . do you think she is attractive?'

'Cuckoo?' He leant back on his elbows, looked up to the ceiling. 'Yes. Yes, I think she is . . . well, was. Was . . . still is. Yes. If you want an answer to that. Yes.'

'I wondered. Would you sleep with her? I mean if she asked you?'

'What is all this? Have you really gone dotty all of a sudden?'

'But would you?'

'I don't know. Leni! I don't know . . . never even thought about it.'

'Never?'

'No. Never. What a daft thing to say.'

'I only asked. She's old, you know.'

'I know.'

'Older than my mother even.'

'Your mother?'

'Grandmother. Older than her.' She drew her legs tightly towards her chest, wrapped her arms round her shins. Dry-lipped at the slip.

'Look, if you have any idea that I'm going to skip off and screw Cuckoo Peverill behind your back, put the thought out of your idiot mind. I wouldn't. And it's nothing to do with her age. I just wouldn't.'

'But you could fancy her? Younger men do, you know –

older women, it's quite usual.'

'I could, yes. Why not? What on earth is all this?'

'It's just the look she gave you. Standing there very still. Hardly to breathe. Her eyes were so wide, so full, light . . . as blue as you can't believe. And suddenly I knew that she was in love with you. Quick as that.' She uncurled herself and lay across towards him, her hand reaching for his. 'I'm not surprised. I'm not: *really*. But I am sad for her. Suddenly she was so very young; for an instant, I could see the woman she had been. In her eyes.'

'You know,' he said and lay flat on his back holding her hand. 'You know, you *are* unreal?'

She nodded. 'I know. That's why you love me to death, isn't it? Because I am unreal, say so?'

'I've said so.'

'That you love me because I am.'

'I love you because you are.'

'Good. I am unreal but I am real. All unreal things are real. Did you know?'

'I never know what is in your mind, do I?'

She shook her head, smiling at him. 'No.' The Wall cutting through the orchard, the apple-tree tops like old brushes, Langerdorf's cigar glowing as it came towards me on the terrace, Mamma's pale eyes, standing in the doorway. 'The truth is often much too harsh to face.' She lay back, resting her head on his chest.

'From here I can just see that funny thing in your throat, then your chin, and then right up your nose.' And Cuckoo's eyes. Wide, clear, young; an instant only.

'Gus Bender's,' he said suddenly. 'The Studio; you in your gym-slip . . . all the larking about we do . . . me lying on a cardboard rock for the Lonesome Sailor poses . . . all that stuff, that's real, isn't it?'

'Oh no! Unreal. It is all pretend. You said so. It is. It's all dreams, Gus said.'

'Seems real enough to me.'

'We don't believe it, do we, so it can't be real. Like the bananas.'

'Bananas?' He raised his head and looked down at her.

'That they put in your tight trousers, to be more suggestive. The Elastoplast I must put over my breasts, poor little things, so they don't show. It's all just pretending, that's what the people pay for, not for real. The real is more ugly, is horrible I think, that's why I believe only in the pretending part of life. It is not so ugly, not so cruel. People don't like it to be real, it is too harsh.'

'But it's cheating too. Isn't it?' He lay back, reached down and touched her hair. 'Just bloody cheating.'

'But if it makes people happy? It's all right, isn't it?'

'Cheating is never all right. It never makes people happy in the end.'

'Never?' She pushed herself up on her arms, looked down at him worriedly.

'You get found out in the end.' He laughed shortly. 'Ye gods! *Bananas*!'

She slid off the bed and wandered across to the Army Surplus, found a cigarette and lit it. At the window she leant against the shutter, blue smoke into the soft night air. 'And I am cheating, that is it? At Gus Bender's: like you.'

'In a way. Yes. I mean you *are* twenty, aren't you? Not twelve or something . . . and with no tits.'

'I haven't got many anyway.'

'No. But you have tits, you are a woman. I know that, don't I?'

'Yes.' She nodded, folded her arms across her breasts tightly. 'But they only just pretend that I am a little girl. When they take me out, to dinner or something, they know I am really not, but they like to pretend that I am. It's very confusing. They give me lots of ice-cream, jelly-things . . . trifles, just like a little girl; this they like. If I didn't pretend that I was one, then I *would* be cheating. You see?'

'Not entirely. But it is real to you, isn't it, because you

183

never were a real little girl, were you? No family . . . no brothers, sisters, no father.'

She traced a crack in the balcony floor with her toe. 'I never was. No.'

Marcus rolled himself off the bed, switched on the transistor. 'The French talk. All the time.' He found music, turned it low, crossed to her in the window. 'I lived all my life with people who did nothing else but pretend. My Mum pretended, my Dad . . . he's still pretending, the Big Star . . . all over Johannesburg and Kuwait. So I'm going to make my life as real as I can. See?'

She turned into his arms. 'People could see us over there. On the boat.'

'I don't care.'

She pushed gently away from him and went into the room. 'If I wasn't me, would you still like me?'

'Well, Christ, I don't know. Now do I? I mean, be sensible. If you weren't you, who else would you be?'

'I don't know.'

'Then how can I know if I would like you or not? Eh? You might be big and fat, or dark and thin, or have freckles or whatever.'

'I have those . . . some.'

'Anything. I can't tell.'

'But supposing . . .' She sat on the bed, hands on her knees. 'Supposing when we wake up tomorrow morning I am someone else. What then would happen? If I was someone else?'

'Are you thinking of making a change, may I ask? Is this a warning or something?'

'No. But if I was?'

He sat beside her, removed the cigarette, drew on it, handed it back. 'Now look here. I love you as you are, who you are . . . I don't want any sudden shocks or changes. You do me fine, I love everything about you . . . I'm used to you, you suit me . . . you make me laugh and you make

184

me randy. How does that grab you? Full-hearted confession. I don't want any single thing about you changed, so don't start thinking up any more pretending larks and suddenly deciding that you'll be someone else by tomorrow morning. I want you just as you are. Final. Got it? I'm randy now.'

She kissed his shoulder. 'Got it. You wouldn't want me unless I was me?'

'No. Poor Cuckoo. One kind look and you go off your rocker with fright.'

'I saw. You did not.'

'Leni . . . Cuckoo hasn't had much of a life with old Archie Charlie, do you think? He's not what you might call the Passionate Kind, is he? They never speak about kids . . . probably haven't got any . . . not our business. Maybe she is sad about that. I don't know. There's something empty about her; maybe she was just looking at me like a Mum, you know? Could be: just that.'

'Like a Mum! No. Like a woman. In that uniform . . .'

'Oh, for Christ's sake! You and your old uniform-kick! She's been seeing me half bloody naked every day for days! She hasn't gone all soppy then, has she? Doesn't lurk about the bushes with a polaroid or something. She's not a sex maniac or whatever, doesn't grope me under the table . . . doesn't take a blind bit of notice. I'm just me . . . who I am . . . she accepts, that's all.'

'You didn't look like you down there just now. In that tunic and things . . . it was different; you were different.'

'How different, for Pete's sake?'

'Different. Very male. Sexy . . . arrogant. Exciting, you see. Mysterious.'

'Well, thanks. Now we know. So; unless I'm stuffed into a bit of Archie Charlie's kinky collection I look like bloody Christopher Robin, is that it?'

She got up and squashed out the cigarette. 'I don't know this person. Ph! It's so late . . . after one o'clock.'

'All your fault. Real and unreal, Cuckoo in love with me, you going to turn into someone else in the morning. Crazy. Come here.'

'I'm not! I'm not!' She pushed herself into his arms and held him to her. 'I'm not. It's just that I am so happy, so terribly happy that I am afraid of things coming to spoil it.'

'How can they? What things?'

'That boat down there, all lit up. All those film people . . . they are all coming here, to the picnic . . . they are real. They will perhaps change things . . . we will have to be different then.'

'Why? They're just people . . . coming to a picnic . . . ordinary people. They aren't coming to stay, Leni . . . just a day.'

'They interrupt. Like this Princess, so noisy . . . all laughter and gold and talking. There is a German man down there, did you know? She told me. Very handsome. A film star.'

'Super, you can talk to him in German, can't you?'

'But I don't want to! That's the thing. I don't want to speak German. Or to see him. I don't want to talk with him. I don't want to be German again, ever.'

He rolled her slowly backwards on to the bed, lying along the length of her, his hands holding her head. He kissed her hair. 'I think he's going to be the l'Aiglon chap, in the film, isn't he?'

'Yes, I think.'

'In that beautiful white uniform, very sexy, arrogant, exciting, mysterious you said.'

'That was you. Not him. I do not know of him.'

'What else did the noisy Princess say about him, ummn? Secrets?'

'No . . . no. Just that he is German . . .'

'And blond and god-like, is that it? He is German so he *must* be.'

'I don't know. You hurt me: I do not think of him.' She twisted suddenly under him, but he held her firm.

'So. He is not in your mind, is that it?'

'Not in my mind. No.'

'A game, Leni! Pretending, umm? Let's pretend, like those fat old men who fed you ice-cream and patted your knees and took down your stockings.'

She wrenched herself about under him, trying to turn her head away, eyes closed.

'We'll pretend this golden German man, all in white, which excites you, so strong, so male. Exciting, you said. Did you? Exciting.'

'You! It was you!'

'And I'm him now. These hands are his hands, feel them? This is his body hard on yours, feel the little badges you admired, cutting into you. They hurt, don't they? Scratch . . . and the buttons on that tight tunic, feel them too?' His boots against your legs, pushing you wide for him, come on open wide, wide! Pretend. Leni! Pretend! It is unreal, all unreal things are real, you said. What is he like beneath that smooth white cloth, what do you invent him to be like? Crushing you down: your hands are on his back, I can feel them pressing him down on you, they slide lower, that's right, let them go, down, down, over the big belt, over his hard buttocks. Oh yes! Caress him, hold him tighter and tighter, grinding into you like this and this and this. He is strong, German, your blood, your heritage, push to him, push to him . . . that's it, that's right, my little whore . . . he is taking you, taking you, taking you . . .'

She tore her head away from his hands, rose high to reach his thrusting hips, cried out, beating clenched fists wildly against his back, her voice rough and harsh. 'No! No! No! Don't let him! Don't let him! Let it be you, let it be you . . . let it be you!'

Archie had no fixed idea of what a Film Producer would

look like. As far as he could remember he had never even met one, but from what he had read and from what he had heard, here and there, and without much interest for it was not a part of his world, he gathered that they must all be what his father had called 'Jew boys'. Plump, small, ringed hands, cunning eyes: like toads, from some unpronounceable place in Central Europe. Zigeuner Barons, he would venture, robbers who had fled the ghettos of Vienna, Warsaw, Budapest, or Berlin, looting and plundering on their way, stealing wantonly from the Classics and the Bible, cribbing from the Classical Composers and turning the ugly results into a messy, indigestible porridge of nonsense which, with much glitter and gloss and a shrewd, if deathly, vulgarity, they would serve up to the greedy Masses accompanied by orchestras of soaring violins. Those were Film Producers. Of course, he reasoned, not all 'Jew boys' were like that. Some could appear to be quite different; they might have fair hair and skins, even red hair. Some altered their names, renounced their faith and married into some of the very best families who had, unhappily, fallen upon hard times financially. But wherever you looked, if you looked carefully enough, you would find that the common factor which they all shared was money. So one had to be on one's guard at all times, for one could so easily be coerced or bribed, and he was determined that it should not happen to him over the heavy script that lay upon his elegant knees. For although it was surprisingly far more literate than he had imagined, it contained a grave error of fact which he would never, under any circumstances endorse, no matter what he was offered or how this Grottorosso fellow tried to persuade him to put his name on what they called 'the credits'.

Sitting there on the terrace, with his first cigarette of the day between long fingers and Bruna and Fanny clearing the wreckage of the breakfast table, he was aware that he had let his mind wander away from the essential fact, as Minerva had told him, that Grottorosso was of impeccable lineage, an aristocrat to the tip of his finger-nails and the top of his head, related, indeed, on his mother's side in some rather hazy way to Giovanni Bellini, and a Count to boot. But his imagination had snapped on the unpalatable words 'Film Producer' and his unreasoning distrust of the race from which they were normally spawned. Thus Grottorosso, whatever his background, must have inherited some of their faults, if not all.

However, he felt perfectly strong and confident; he was on his own ground, in both meanings of the phrase, and he desired nothing whatsoever from this fellow soon to be his guest. In fact the boot was quite on the other foot: he would treat him exactly as he had treated all Foreigners with whom he had come into contact during the happier days of the War, in Cairo; with cool good manners, distant politeness, firmness, leaving them with the indelible impression that he was right, they were wrong, and that in any case he knew best.

If, secretly, he was gratified that a man of Grottorosso's undoubted fame should seek his opinion on his work, for Minerva had also been at great pains to acquaint him with the rather formidable list of successes the fellow had had and the very exalted rank which he occupied in the Cinema Hierarchy, he had no intention whatever of allowing himself to show it. It was pleasing indeed to have Mahomet coming to the mountain, but there was no reason to let it go to his head, although his own work and reputation were mostly known only among students and scholars. Yes: it was pleasing but he would see to it that the fellow got his facts absolutely right first and foremost. If he refused, then it was simple. Wish him adieu and waste no time in tiresome discussions; he could take it or leave it. Even though the script was impressive in many ways, and brilliantly concise, there was one ugly fact which must be obliterated at whatever cost. History is history. You can't muck about with it for a cinema film, and if they did he would wash his hands of it. He had all his facts and figures assembled; he knew, intimately and in detail, his subject. He drew heavily on his unlit cigarette, well satisfied that he was absolutely prepared for whatever should befall.

He had not prepared himself, however, for the sight of Umberto Grottorosso as he stepped from the dark Mercedes only a very few moments later.

No black-suited toad eased itself into his courtyard, loose-lipped, button-eyed, servile. Instead a perfectly splendid figure of a man, blazingly Aryan, silver-headed, lean, bronzed, lithe and muscular, dressed all in blinding white, attended by a servant bearing a slender leather attaché case, a strapped bundle of books, and an immense sheaf of white roses, and who came towards him eagerly with a brilliant smile and the handclasp of an anaconda.

'My good Sir Charles! How graceful of you to receive me, I am so very deeply in your debt, so honoured. I am not late? The idiot driver took a wrong turning in Villefranche, an error of much gravity at such a time, for I know how greatly your days are charged, for my aunt, Minerva, has told me that you toil from sunrise to sunset with little respite.'

'No, no, no . . . not late. Absolutely on time.' Putting his crushed hand into a pocket.

'I am so relieved. Now to work . . . where shall we be? My servant Nino will carry all these things, I so dislike packages, the humble roses are for Lady Peverill, if she will be pleased to accept them.'

'Oh, well. She and your aunt are in Cannes for the day, left us completely on our own, very sensibly. Shall we go to my study? Cooler there and we can be quite undisturbed.'

'Excellent suggestion. I shall follow, please lead the way. Nino! Bring the books and remove your hat in the house.'

Once in the study, on which he had the good manners not to comment, although his quick eyes did not miss the belts and buckles, the cupboards of jackets, pouches, brasses, the worn saddle and the faded banners, and as soon as Nino and the roses had been despatched, he accepted the deep leather chair he was offered, crossed long legs, threaded muscular fingers together under a square, determined chin, and smiled encouragingly across the wide desk behind which Archie had placed himself in a position of authority; and security.

'Now,' said Grottorosso. 'I must, my dear sir, apologize for my English. In spite of the care and insistence of my English governess, a Miss Drew from Warwick, I fear that it is not all that it should be by a very long chalk, as she would have said. I know that it will irritate you greatly, for you are a scholar, but it is a language which I admire deeply, second only to my own, and I only dare to hope that you will approve of my use of it in the Scenario which I see before you. It is so? I pray you be completely honest with me, I await your cudgels.'

Archie took out his cigarette case and chose a cigarette. 'No cudgels, none whatsoever. The English is really quite remarkable. There are one or two rather ugly, if you will forgive me, Americanisms . . . here and there. You use "gotten" for "got", for example.'

'But, forgive me.' Grottorosso unthreaded his fingers and raised a manicured hand. 'I believe that the word "gotten" is correct, is it not? It was certainly used by Elizabeth the First . . . as early as that if not earlier, but has now fallen into disuse in your country. First taken to the American Colonies by the Pilgrim Fathers, even earlier, and so it has remained. That is easily rectified, I think?'

'Ah yes . . . easily. There are one or two others, offensive only to me. However . . .' Archie searched for his lighter, lit the cigarette, flipped the lighter shut, slid it back into his pocket. 'However, the language, as I have indicated, is quite acceptable; after all we are to assume, are we not, that everyone is in fact speaking in German, that is correct?'

'Correct. I think that perhaps your cigarette is not lit.'

'It never is.'

'Ah. I see.'

'No. I think that we are not here to discuss the merits or demerits of the English in the script you have written, but the facts, Signore Grottorosso, the historical facts.'

Grottorosso leant forward, hands on knees, head shining in the shadowy room like a tight silver cap. 'The historical facts! To be sure. That is why I am here today, for your full criticism or for your approbation: either will mean a great deal to me. As I have said, I am greatly honoured that you have agreed to read this thing, to see me. It was some sudden idea that my aunt had during a storm, *orribile*, which we must endure off Elba. "We must head for France", she said, "Charles Peverill will be the man to assist us!" I understand that the sad life of the young Duc de Reichstadt has become your passion . . . so what better source of advice can there be for my humble effort to portray his last bitter years. The last two years, you have already, I am sure, realized? So. I am all ears. Historical facts.'

Archie drew heavily on his cigarette, placed it in the ashtray at his side, reached for his list of notes.

To Grottorosso's great relief the list was mercifully short, and the minor errors were fairly easily explained away. He had to explain, very carefully, that to show two years of a man's complicated life over a period of only two and a half hours in the cinema necessitated a good deal of condensing and, to some extent, rearranging. The information available was all from documents, histories and letters, and, as he pointed out, one could hardly make an exciting piece of cinema from sheets of paper.

Therefore a certain licence had to be used so that the essential story line would emerge uncluttered by unnecessary minor facts which would only confuse the main pattern.

'After all, Sir Charles,' he said with a deprecating smile, 'history is not very exciting even when we are living it . . . or even, in most cases, making it. It is only really in retrospect that it appears to be thrilling, when we can see just what happened clearly and who the chief "protagonistas" were. That is the most essential thing for the cinema; we work, you see, for the average man, not for the critics as they believe! The average man covers the earth and buys his seat in the theatre for the show. He is a dull creature, unaware of his emotions, and we have to expose emotions that he will recognize; sometimes we must force them on him so that he will react. In my work I try not to patronise, I try to assist the sluggish minds by helping them to identify with what they see in my film. That is essential. I try to reach the subconscious in my audience, to pull them from apathy and indifference, to expose to them some of their own little, secret flaws, you understand?' His eyes moved very briefly to the second cigarette which Archie was lighting. 'We all have those, I would say, do we not? We are all victims of our own self-deception, is it not so? People, you know, do not like the truth, it is too real, too painful; they are not able to face it. And so in my work I give them an illusion of the truth . . . and this they will accept eventually, believing it to be the truth itself. Miss Drew, my governess from Warwick, when I was a child would force upon me a singularly unpleasant form of medicine, but she would always hide this in a big spoonful of honey . . . that is what I try to do in my work.' He leant back in his chair well satisfied with his speech, and convinced that he had overcome most of the difficulties. Perhaps, he thought to himself, I shall be able to get away very soon, and not endure a long luncheon with this dry scholar who has fortunately missed the point of the whole thing.

Archie slipped his lighter into his pocket again, blew an imaginary scatter of ash from his blotter, folded his arms. 'I suppose that I must accept what you say. I do not know enough about your work to do otherwise. It all seems to me very unreal. A form of – can I say? – cheating?'

'Ah! It is . . . we perform miracles in our work, illusions, we are magicians.'

'Well, I am a historian and I believe in facts.'

'Quite so.'

'And I can not, and will not, accept the odious suggestions which you make that l'Aiglon, or the Duke of Reichstadt, was an invert!'

Proving instantly that he had not missed the point at all.

Grottorosso's eyes widened with shock. 'But I do not comprehend! My dear sir, you have misread my work!'

'I don't think that I have. This business between l'Aiglon and Count Prokesch. Quite revolting, utterly reprehensible, absolutely untrue.'

'I cannot believe what I hear!'

'I could not believe what I read! Count Prokesch was a brave, brilliant soldier, a man of thirty-four when he met l'Aiglon who was but twenty; lonely, fatherless, abandoned by his disgusting mother, a prisoner for life in an alien land. Prokesch was his salvation, he appeared as a God of Deliverance, he gave him courage and hope, he was a man of the highest valour and the strongest morals, and in this story of yours he appears as an evil pederast, a destroyer, unclean!'

'Not so! Not so!' cried Grottorosso in a brilliant display of indignation.

'That is how I read it.' Archie was very calm in the face of the Italian hysteria.

'But my dear sir! Oh! Dio Mio!' Grottorosso covered his face with his hands, when he looked up again he appeared exhausted. 'I think that there is some *tragic* error. You have of course been reading all the *Directions*, that is so?'

'Naturally.'

'Ah . . . but those are not for you to read! They are only for the idiot American backers who cannot read anything but the Profit and Loss columns: they have to be able to see something which will attract them to finance my film, you see?'

'And this kind of disgusting innuendo will attract them?'

'Of course. It is very fashionable today.'

'I am revolted.'

'Naturally. But, my dear Sir Charles, you have not read one single word of this kind in the actual dialogue between the characters; not one word, for there is not one syllable of ugliness or suggestion there.'

Archie tapped his cigarette slowly on the ashtray. 'No . . . no. Perhaps not in the actual dialogue,' he said uncertainly.

'Of course not! That is not my way. I do not make my film from the directions! I make it from the heart, and from the soul of my people.'

'But it is *implied*. When they are fencing together and l'Aiglon collapses, he is held in Prokesch's arms . . . like, like a girl!'

'L'Aiglon, I must not remind you, is a dying boy. It is a moment of great tragedy.'

'And riding in the woods, in the storm, they lie naked together.'

'In a storm one gets wet. They remove only shirts and tunics; they rest in the barn to dry and to discuss Nandine Károlyi with whom l'Aiglon is deeply in love. Is that not reasonable?'

'Why half naked?'

'Because they are wet and l'Aiglon has tuberculosis. Is that not also reasonable?'

'I can't see why they *have* to get wet in a storm.'

'It is dramatic, it heightens the decision of Prokesch to send Károlyi away.'

'And *that* part smacks of jealousy!'

'But it is fact, Sir Charles! You know this! He disapproved deeply of the Princess because he thought that she was frivolous and vapid – which she was. Quite not right for a future Emperor's consort, or Empress. Prokesch had higher plans for his master.'

Archie scratched his head. 'But all this wrestling, fencing . . . the swimming they do together.'

'Perfectly natural, surely. Both were brilliant horsemen, both were expert fencers, both swam . . .'

'But why *naked*, for God's sake!'

'Do you swim fully dressed usually?'

'No . . . no, of course not. But whenever possible they seem to just tear off their clothes, for no good reason.'

'For a very good reason, Sir Charles. The average audience is composed of women, both young and old; it gives them great delight to see two handsome males locked together in happy pastimes. More women attend boxing matches and also wrestling bouts than men, you know. This is a fact. Of *course* it is a sexual tease! I would be deceiving you and myself if I said it was not so. But sex is very much a part of life, it is almost all the life of the cinema. If one has two splendid young men in one's film, of brave physique and golden looks, it would be folly, would it not, to smother them in cloaks! Willingly I admit to this, I am guilty of the crime of Box-Office Appeal! But of no other sin. Do you think that I would be capable of such slander, such stupidity? L'Aiglon is a national hero in France to this day! If I damaged his reputation by so much as a hair that would be the end of my work in that country. I would be hounded from pillar to post. It would cause such a scandal that I would be bankrupt both financially and in my reputation of which I am deeply proud.' He sat

196

back watching Archie through half-closed eyes which could suggest distress or caution, depending on who was watching.

Archie was not. He was nervously tapping his cigarette against his hand. 'Lesbians,' he muttered finally.

Grottorosso leant forward, eyes open. 'Lesbians? Did I hear your correctly?'

'Countess Commerata. Very savage portrait indeed.'

'She dressed as a man, rode as a man, fought as a man. We say nothing of any other disadvantage.'

'*Implied*.'

'The word is not mentioned once anywhere. Is it?'

'No . . . but . . .' He busily brushed his lapel.

Grottorosso gained courage, rose to attack. Gently. 'I think, Sir Charles that everything which worries you, distresses you perhaps, so much is only ever, in your word, *implied*? At no time in my script do l'Aiglon or Prokesch go beyond the bounds of correct behaviour, nor do they behave together in such a manner that would offend their standing as a future Emperor and his true adviser, as honourable soldiers, men at arms. Can you truthfully give me one single instance? Please, I beg you, say!'

Archie snapped his cigarette in two. 'No . . . not in the words . . . perhaps not.'

Grottorosso pushed harder. 'Are they ever seen to embrace?'

Archie winced. Looked anxiously at the windows.

'To kiss! To lie together!'

'No! No!' cried Archie in despair.

'It is *companionship*, not carnality! You have misread, alas! I am distressed beyond all reason that I should have caused you, so inadvertently, such pain. How foolish that I did not think to send you a covering note, just to explain that one must never read the Directions in a script such as this. They are totally misleading and false: they lead to the gravest misunderstandings, as they have done this day.

197

How,' he said softly, and reaching out a perfectly steady hand, 'how can I possibly make amends to your sensibilities which I have so clearly wounded deeply? You of all people, you of all. Oh! My shame . . .'

Archie briskly pulled himself together and tidied up his ashtray. 'No, don't fuss . . . no great harm done. I suppose that I have never read one of these things before, and it rather unnerved me. Quite hard to manage, you know. I can't quite say that I have "misread" it, but that is how I *did* read it . . . lack of experience, I suppose.'

'One sees things in so many different ways, of course.' Grottorosso nodded kindly. 'I remember that good Miss Drew from Warwick always used to say to me, "Beauty is in the eye of the beholder" – a very true English remark, I would think. We do not all see beauty in the sadness and squalor of life, but it is there, and I am certain that the relationship between l'Aiglon and Prokesch was one of the most intense beauty. Of course the vile Metternich saw it in quite a different light – a political light, I am certain, which is why he finally arranged to have Prokesch sent away to Italy leaving the unhappy Prince alone, helpless, and more truly a prisoner. But he may *also* have been blind, and seen only ugliness where happiness and beauty existed. But you are the expert after all! Look at all the marvels this room of yours contains! So many relics of the Emperor's past, so many books, so many papers . . . so much detail! But when all is said and done, you and I , who are so moved and fascinated by this story of the golden, dying, Prince can only conjecture, isn't that so? There are no living witnesses to that time, we can only take what we are allowed from documents.. A letter can lie, a letter can be distroyed, mislaid, conveniently overlooked; a diary can lie, history even can lie. What do we know? How can we truly tell, you and I, for we were not there to hold the candle after all.'

Archie got up and walked slowly over to the windows,

hands thrust deep into blazer pockets. 'I suppose that you have, naturally, read Count Prokesch's own accounts of this period? They seem pretty clear and comprehensive to me . . . unemotional.'

Grottorosso had been rustling softly among the papers in his slender attaché case and looked up. 'Of course! The "handsome ensign", as he was called. Yes, I have a great many notes here. The very first one is so charming, don't you think? May I read it it you?'

'Please.'

'At the dinner where he first met l'Aiglon he writes: "I had a presentiment such as takes hold of an adolescent when he happens for the first time to meet the girl to whom he is going to lose his heart." I find that infinitely moving . . . don't you?'

Archie coughed.

'And this, from l'Aiglon's own lips, so he insists: "Remain with me! Sacrifice your future to me, remain with me! We were made to understand each other . . .".' He riffled the papers, sighed, slid them carefully back into the case. 'Such a tragic destiny, to die so young, alone, abandoned, trapped in the stinking room at Schönbrunn while his disgusting mother spent her time in the streets of Vienna buying presents for her lovers! How desperately he must have needed love, don't you think?' He replaced the case beside him, threaded his fingers together, looked sadly up at Archie now behind his desk. 'Ah. How sad it all is. I come here hoping for your approbation and all I do is to raise your indignation. I am deeply shamed.'

Archie shrugged. Patted the fat script on the desk. 'Difficult to read these things. It's just . . . that implied relationship; unnecessary, ugly. Not true. But if you say it won't be like that, well, what can I say? You know it better than I, the cinema thing, I mean. Always muck up history, the cinema, take dreadful liberties . . .' He smiled grimly. 'But I can't stop you, can I, even if I wanted to?'

'No,' said Grottorosso. 'You can't, Sir Charles. I am sad that you are unhappy, but I assure you that it is entirely in your mind; nothing objectionable in the least is intended, or will be made, of that I can assure you.'

'Poor l'Aiglon,' said Archie. 'He was acted by a woman in the theatre, you know that, I suppose? Sarah Bernhardt, French woman. Wooden leg. I ask you.'

'I shall not do that.'

'No, must think of your cinema audience, what? All those women you speak of. You'll have some Yankee chap, I have no doubt, Film Star fellow . . . for the what you called it, the Box Office? Right?'

'No, not a Yankee. Wrong. I have a young German, not a Film Star. A real young man, very fine looking. But I am not so happy with him: he lacks fire, passion, the regality. I think that I will have to think again perhaps. A problem. Where to look, I ask? One does not find a true l'Aiglon just lying about on the beach, like a pebble, you know.'

Archie reached for his cigatette case. 'Oh really?' He chose a cigarette, closed the case with a little snap. 'Odd; my wife did. On our beach, just the other day.'

Chapter Seven

In the shade of the trees she stopped and looked back down the length of the lawns towards the house smouldering in the late sun.

Almost deserted; a couple of waiters wandering from table to table stacking plates and bowls into big wicker baskets, Bruna and the maids hurrying to the kitchens with boxes filled with cutlery. No one spoke. A stillness lay over the weary trodden grass, chairs tilted, a crumpled napkin in the scattered gravel of the path, Tonnino in a striped apron carefully collecting pots of white hydrangeas in his barrow; at her feet in the crushed grass an empty Marlboro packet. It was all over.

She took a deep breath, leant her full weight against a tree, hands loose at her sides. I'll be perfectly all right in a minute. Give me ten. Just a little time. The heat and all the rushing about; and age, dear. Let us not forget your age. Age creeping on, boring old age. But I still feel cold. It's the weakness really. And that's boring too. Borr-ing, borr-ing. And sudden.

She leant away from the tree, straightened her straw hat, rubbed her hands together briskly as if to warm them at a fire. Overdoing things, I suppose. That's what Archie said, but then Archie would. After things were *done*, that is to say. Then he'd notice. 'You've been overdoing things, old dear.' Old dear. God! Such a fusspot. How can one NOT overdo things giving a whacking great picnic, I'd like to know? A picnic, a jolly jolly picnic. 'Boys and girls come out to play, the sun is bright . . .' I do so hate being called 'Old dear'. Perfectly frightful how sometimes Archie falls back into that peculiar middle-class vernacular. What a tedious phrase to use. Where did he pick it up? Cairo? Aldershot? Army stuff, anyway. When did he use that phrase to me before? Darby and Joan all right.

Or was that me? I started that, I rather fear. Me. He started the 'growing old together' bit. I suppose that I caught it from him, I mean about growing old. In dignity, and so on. But it's all in the mind, isn't it? Really? When a man with a Narcissus complex falls out of love with himself and finds that he is unattractive sexually, then what can one do? I ask you. And you'll get no answer from me at this late stage of the day. Not my department: far, far too complicated that one. How about a little drink? A bucker-up for Cuckoo who has been ever so slightly overdoing things. Silly mutt.

She turned and started walking across the shaded grass towards the cliff. And get your mind off YOU. In capital letters. Far too wrapped up in yourself, that's what. Do admit? All in the mind, remember.

At the top of the steps leading steeply down to the pool, two lichened stone pillars were arched with a rampant Albertine. A long briar dragged at the edge of her hat. Clippers. Someone will get scratched. She tucked it neatly back among thorny stems. Petals fell. Such a short season, almost over. Back to yourself again! Do stop equating. Off you go, my gel.

She started down the steep steps, holding tightly to the iron rail. Below her, Marcus and the lady Film Star chopping the turquoise water into fragments, light winking and sparkling like compliments.

At the edge of the pool she stopped, leant forward, hands thrust between her knees, the coral rope swinging from her neck. Marcus had just surfaced from a wild somersault; the Film Star screamed, thrashing water, 'Be careful for my hair!'

He shook his head, water spraying from him like glass pellets. He saw her and swam across, blowing bubbles

202

through the turbulence.

'Hello.' He wiped his nose with the back of his hand.

'Is it absolutely lovely?'

'Absolutely. Coming in? Come on, be brave.'

'Not a question of courage, question of a little chilled glass of wine. Want one?'

He reached up, placed his hands on her bare sandalled feet. Held firm. 'Ten red toe nails.'

'Alarming if there were twelve. Do admit? Where's Leni?'

'Gone up to the point with the Kraut, Ach soing and Bitte schoening each other. Awful sound. Coming in then? Do.'

'And Signora Scarlatti . . . Minna? They here, no?'

'No. Gone up to the house. To have a look round.' He stroked her ankle.

The Film Star had heaved herself out of the water, sat at the far end of the pool pinning up her hair.

'I'm going to have a look round too. At the bar. For my glass of wine.'

He grinned up at her.

'For my wine. Please? Let me go.'

He pressed a toe hard. 'This little piggy went to market . . .'

She pulled her foot away swiftly. 'This little piggy's going to the bar.'

He released her, smiled, swung round, dived under the water. She waved across to the Film Star who waved back, her mouth full of hairpins.

At the bar, set up beneath the towering figure of Mars under the awning, long white cloth, glasses, bowls, dishes piled with olives, cornichons, wilting radishes, limp potato crisps, tiny tomatoes. In two silver cisterns crammed with melting ice, bottle necks sticking up like skittles. She found one half full and looked for a clean glass among the litter of drooping fern and spilled lemon rings. The barman, who had been bent over a large hamper, stacking things away, hurried to help her.

'No, don't bother, Jacques. Carry on with whatever you are doing, I'll help myself.'

'It was a good day, I think, eh? We ran out of the Sancerre at five o'clock.'

'A lovely day . . . thank you so much, so good of you. Did you manage? For yourself, I mean? Before it ran out?'

'We still had the Krug.' He grinned, offered her a glass which he had wiped on his apron. She filled it, drank it down, refilled it.

'You have a brave thirst, Madame.'

'I always have had . . . and after such a brave day.'

She carried the full glass back towards the steps. Behind her the Film Star's voice high with command. 'Yeah. *Plenty* ice; con limone!'

The sound of his bare feet on the wet stones coming towards her.

She went on up the steps, clutching both rail and glass; not looking back.

The picnic had started at exactly 7 am when the caterers from Nice arrived with assorted truck-loads of trestles, boards, boxes, table-tops, crates, spreading themselves rapidly about the silent gardens, terrace, and pool, like an invading army, with Bruna among them, behaving remarkably like a Career General. Almost instantly the place looked as if it had been struck by a tornado. Tonnino's carefully tended lawns a litter of planks and boxes, straw flying, paper whirling, ropes and poles and scattered piles of canvas, amongst which people hurried in urgent groups, sifting, sorting, pulling, lifting, calling, scolding; rescuers searching for survivors. From her balcony Leni watched the frantic proceedings with half-awake bewilderment.

'It's fantastic!' she said. 'Like a revolution starting. It's going to be so huge.'

Marcus put an arm round her neck, pulled her head on to his shoulder. 'It's a bit like the croquet game in "Alice", and Bruna's the Queen of Hearts: I wouldn't be at all surprised to see little men on ladders soon, painting the roses.'

'I don't know what that means.'

Marcus kissed her gently. 'Never mind,' he said. 'It's all for us anyway.'

'Really for the Italians, I think.'

'For them too, but really most for us. Cuckoo's picnic, traditional, and my "birthday" too.'

'That's so silly, because it isn't.'

'Not silly. Sensible.'

'It's all pretending, isn't it?'

'Yes. Pretending. You should know all about that.'

'So many people we don't even know. I'll hide, I think.'

'You'll be at the front door, as she said. Welcome everyone with her. Good manners, guests of honour, it'll be terrific.'

'Terrifying.'

'How can it be? After last night. She made it all so simple?'

'A picnic has to have a reason, I think, anyway a sort of reason,' Cuckoo had said the evening before. They were working at a long wooden table, stripping leaves from dozens and dozens of white carnations which she had massed into two large Copeland foot-baths and was spiking with tight-budded tuber-roses, 'And so what I have decided is this: it'll be Marcus's birthday, how about that?'

'Had mine already. March.'

'Well, it's your "un-birthday". A picnic for an "unbirthday". And do you awfully mind if I have you for a godson?'

'You can have me for whatever you like. At any time.'

She had not looked at him. Thrust another stalk among the white heads. 'I have simply masses of godsons, and goddaughters for that matter, all over the place, so there is no reason not to have you for another, is there? It makes it all feel a little more "in the family"? Do you know what I mean? A "belonging"?'

'I know.'

'So I'll just say, casually, here and there, "This is my godson, Marcus Pollock, and today is his birthday. It joins us somehow, do you see? And I'd rather like that. Of course, I don't really NEED an excuse for my picnics, but I do rather like to have one. Last year it was for the longest day . . . June the 21st.'

'It's that today.'

'Which is why I want a different reason, theme if you like, this year. People enjoy it so much more. Picnics really do feel better with a point d'être, otherwise they are just eating fish-paste sandwiches and hard-boiled eggs in a swarm of ants on Box Hill. Mine are different.'

'Fine. I'll be honoured to be your godson or whatever, and have an "un-birthday" . . . but no one will know before, will they? Presents and that sort of thing? It would be dreadfully embarrassing.'

Cuckoo swept up a pile of leaves and stalk ends. 'Goodness no! I simply couldn't cheat to that extent. I shan't say anything before. I mean I *haven't*. It's a frightful mistake. I did last year, told everyone why, and they all came dressed as Druids. Disaster.'

Leni put her hand on Cuckoo's arm. 'You are so wise, you know? And kind.'

'Don't tell a soul. It's a deathly secret.'

'To make us not feel shy . . . to feel not strange.'

'That would be pointless, wouldn't it?'

'It's what you call English good manners, isn't it?' said Marcus.

Cuckoo swept leaves, stalks and scattered blossoms into

a box at her feet. 'I'd call it love, frankly,' she said.

By eleven o'clock the apparent confusion and hysteria of the Flamingo Croquet Game gave way to calm, serenity, order. On the terrace a long table draped in crisp white cloth, sparkling with glass and silver, dishes and salvers awaiting the delights and delicacies which Cuckoo had taken such care to plan. It was garlanded all about with trails of fern and starred with sprays of white roses. Around the lawns and under the trees little round tables beneath plain canvas umbrellas. Down at the pool the great bronze figure of Mars gazed sightlessly across the splendid bar under a cool awning, and waiters moved silently about adjusting a plate here, a bowl of lilies there, polishing a glass, folding a napkin, elegant in blue and cream with a large 'C' on their shirts, 'So that they won't be mistaken for guests; people do get so dreadfully confused drinking in the sun, you see . . .' She took up two slender flutes of champagne, offered one to Leni, and raised her own towards her.

'You look absolutely delicious, Edible!'

'Thank you. I feel lovely. I only had my kimono . . .'

'We used to call that a camisole, I believe. Awful name. It was my mother's. She was tiny like you, adored broderie Anglaise . . . and that red silk round your waist makes it so "chic". You've tied such a pretty bow-thing.'

'And my airplane slide?'

'Divine . . . don't lose it.'

'I've fixed it tightly. And Marcus looks lovely too, don't you think?'

'Does *he* think so? He didn't mind, did he? I simply couldn't resist them.'

'Jolly glad you didn't.' He was at the top of the steps, came slowly down towards them in tight yellow dungarees with bib and braces, a white T-shirt under.

'Enter the Banana King. Do I turn you on?'

'You didn't mind? I mean, if you hate them do say. Change.'

'Mad about them, and me in them. Look all right? You haven't said yet?'

'Scrumptious! Have a glass of champagne, for courage. This is the worst part, just before it all begins. Everything's ready, calm, waiting; like a stage before the curtain goes up, you know? Will it work? Will it be a flop, a success, a non-starter? One never knows. I should be used to it by now, but I'm not. Oh! *Will* it be a happy day? A success? Better than last time? One simply can't tell, one just prays. Most of all I want you both to love it; my pretties. And you are.'

Marcus raised his glass. 'It's nearly noon. Good luck, and thank you, from us.'

'Now,' said Cuckoo, replacing her glass. 'We'll go up. Just remember what I told you: be awfully sweet to the Duc d'Auribeau, he's almost ninety, blind as a bat, was a very famous gardener, and had the most lovely house in Tangier with a heavenly water-garden and a harem of quite delicious Arab boys, and his fourth wife, Sophie, who will be with him is terribly sweet, breeds wolf-hounds and is an authority on Kakiemon porcelain. And then try and avoid, as politely as you can, the Courtneys; he's the Film Star, and his wife wears diamonds in the morning, you'll recognize them instantly. They're deeply "in" with the Monaco Set and all that Palace tra la la, "Grace" and "Rainier" – but one *has* to have them, she's British, it is tiresome . . . and then of course we have the Italians.' She looked apprehensively across the wide pool to the bay beyond and the slender white shape of the *Papageno* riding at anchor. 'One does so hope they can speak some English. Minna says they all can, but one never knows . . . it makes things awfully difficult. And Grottorosso: I'm simply terrified of meeting him. Archie says he is rather unnerving; stubborn as well.' She tucked her silk shirt into her wide belt, straightened her straw hat. 'But so is Archie. Stubborn, I mean. When he likes. I think we'll leave him to deal with Grottorosso; after all he is the main reason they've come . . . to talk about the film-thing. I should keep your distance,' she said turning to Marcus. 'You and Leni leave the elders to themselves, once they've all arrived, and go off and keep the young amused.'

Marcus drained his glass. 'Don't worry. We will, promise.'

'There's a ravishing lady film star for you, Minna says, and a handsome German gentleman, one for Leni . . .'

'I know,' said Leni.

'Well there. The briefing's over. The Auribeaus, the dreaded Reggie Courtneys, worrying Grottorosso . . . and of course fifty others, but they'll all leave by five. I don't "do" teas, you see. And then it'll just be the Italians . . . if they want to stay.' She pushed up the brim of her hat and looked down once again at the *Papageno*. 'It's all a tiny bit of a worry really: but there we are. Not a real cloud in the sky, otherwise . . . a perfect summer's day. One does so dread a sudden storm, but I think we'll be lucky. I cross fingers; they can come up so suddenly here.' She went towards the staircase. 'One year there was the most awful Mistral. It just happened without warning really . . . all the table cloths flew about the garden like demented Nuns, and one got stuck on the lighthouse down at the point.' She stretched her hands towards them.

'Come along, off we go! The curtain goes up!'

There is a halfway moment when one suddenly knows that it is all going to be quite all right: it is going as one had hoped; a picnic on a grand scale and everyone is delighted to be there and happy that they came.

The first half hour is always a little uneasy: people stand about like cattle, they laugh too loudly, admire extravagantly, cry out in sudden greeting, exclaim in over-stressed wonder, all a little strained. The herd unnerved in an unfamiliar pasture. But once they have sniffed the air, scented no danger, found the boundaries, moved cautiously about, discovered where to sit, and someone to share the seat, have accepted the first glass of champagne, seen the familiar face, been led to the bar, then they begin to relax and take advantage of the splendours all about them for which they know they will not be asked to pay. The party, the picnic, is off. And Cuckoo, sensing this moment, breathed a gentle sigh of relief as she zephyred, as she called it, from group to group, greeting, laughing, praising, introducing, mixing and arranging, leaving behind her when she left little eddies of laughter and delight. She was an old hand at the game: and did it effortlessly. Apparently. To her infinite pleasure she was aware that Marcus and Leni were following her lead with diligence. He, flashing like a golden oriole in his yellow pants among the hens, peacocks, and guinea fowl of the garden aviary; Leni modestly, elegantly, slight as an egret, and as graceful. Neither was gauche, neither shy, both assured, both confident with the sense of 'belonging' which she had bestowed upon them.

'You aren't one of Harriet's brood, are you?' someone had asked Marcus, and his reply had delighted her.

'Oh no!' he had said. 'No. I'm not a real godson, you see. I'm just part of the collection. Cuckoo collects us like some people collect stamps or paperweights or potlids. She finds us all over the place.'

'Ah yes . . . a great collector, Cuckoo.'

'But I hope that you'll agree,' said Marcus, 'that she does it with a very discerning eye?'

Ten out of ten for that, thought Cuckoo with satisfaction, and went to greet the dreaded Courtneys who were looking about for photographers with expectant smiles.

The Italians, a sparkling band of the Commedia del'Arte, had integrated smoothly and without fuss. Minerva had swooped down on Lilli Scarlatti who had chosen to appear dressed as a Chinese peasant in black silk

210

trousers and high-necked shirt with an immense bamboo hat flat on her head and a wicker basket clutched in jade-studded hands, and borne her off to the Auribeaus who had discovered, with cries of happy recognition, that they had all once shared a cure at Montecatini . . . and Sylva Puglia, shimmering in tight green silk, almost instantly collected an audience of admiring elderly males who sat around her in a giggling circle while she read their hands with many a shriek of coarse laughter and a vigorous tossing of long red hair. Archie and Nando Belluno had moved into the shade of the trees and were deeply engrossed in some discussion, while the sad-eyed Wolf Hagel, slender in trim white shorts, his brassy blond hair shining in the sun, kept a few paces behind Leni wherever she went as if afraid to lose her.

Through all this Marcus moved with obvious enjoyment, and the only cloud in Cuckoo's sky, Umberto Grottorosso, arrived very late, on his own, and instantly dispersed any possibility of cloudiness or doubt by the shimmering splendour of his appearance. She saw him quite suddenly across the crowded lawns, standing alone at the top of the terrace steps, a blinding white figure, tall, lithe, calm, looking down upon the laughter with cool detachment, a small package in his hands. She moved quickly towards him, aware that it was he, although completely unprepared, as Archie had been before her, for the elegance he presented. White patent boots, narrow glossy kid trousers, a skin-tight silk shirt, open to his waist, the patrician head capped with cropped platinum hair, a heavy silver chain around his neck. He smiled slightly as she came quickly up the steps.

'Count Grottorosso! How frightful! No one to greet you . . .'

He took her offered hand, raised it to his lips.

'My fault indeed, Lady Peverill. My fault. I am shamed, so late, so ill-mannered.'

'Oh no! Not at all. Signore Bell-whatever-his-name-is, with the dark glasses, said that you were delayed. We were warned . . .'

'A call from New York. They are always late. Six hours difference, I had to sit.' He offered the small package. 'A most modest apology. If you accept it from me I shall know that I am quite forgiven.'

'Anyone who brings me a gift is forgiven instantly. How lovely! I can open it now?'

'If you care . . .'

'Oh, I do.' She unwrapped the soft tissue paper, a spilling of tiny corals on a slender chain in her hand. 'Oh! How beautiful . . . how exquisite!'

'They were my great grandmother's. But I never wear them.'

She laughed suddenly. 'Help me with the clasp, will you? If I take off my hat you'll see that my hair is like a nest. Too awful.'

'I am forgiven?'

'I am ravished. How kind.' She took his hand. It was hard and cool as steel. 'Now come and have a delicious glass of wine. Minerva told me you prefer the German whites? Or champagne?'

They moved together through the crowd. She saw Archie coming quickly towards them and, to her relief, a sudden flash of yellow at the far end of the lawns, as Marcus disappeared out of sight between the tall pillars leading down to the pool.

The sonorous booming of a vast copper gong, struck with fiendish force by Bruna from the top of the terrace, summoned the guests to their luncheon. To the long white table on which now were displayed towering pyramids of scarlet écrevisses, lobsters in the half-shell glistening on dark green beds of watercress, platters of cold fowl, bowls of every salad imaginable, tiny amber shrimps, rosy

212

prawns, baskets piled high with brown and speckled eggs, salmon bemedalled with cucumber and truffles, and in the very centre, buried in a great block of ice, a crystal bowl brimming with raspberries and a silver dish heavy with golden cream.

'Things,' said Cuckoo, 'one can eat with a fork or fingers . . . it is a picnic after all.'

'Which has nothing to do with sandwiches on Box Hill,' said Marcus carrying a plate down the steps.

'Marcus! You aren't eating only that?' She stopped him at the edge of the lawn.

'It's not for me. For the Duc d'Auribeau. He asked me to get him just a quail and a little glass of Chablis.'

'That isn't your job. You mustn't wait on the guests. You and Leni have done your work quite marvellously, that's enough now! Simply enjoy yourselves.'

'I am enjoying myself. He's a knock-out. We're having a terrific flirt, can't keep his hands off.'

'Oh God! Has he gone wild?'

'He's great. Your fault really: these yellow pants. He said he may not be able to see very well, but he can still distinguish form. His Braille is bang on.'

'That's a terribly old joke.'

'He's a terribly old man, you said.'

'Nearly ninety, must be; you're being corrupted.'

'Pinched my bottom three times, given me a quick grope and invited me to St Tropez on his yacht for Saturday.'

'Have you accepted?'

His smile faded, he shook his head, eyes steady. 'Said you'd made me a better offer.'

She held his look. Her hand moved uncertainly to the corals at her throat.

'Oh. You didn't tell him what it was, of course?'

'Of course not. I didn't say. Conspirators, remember?'

Her eyes were wide, clear, intensely blue. She touched his hand. 'I nearly said, "That'll get cold." But it is.'

He looked down at the small bird on the white plate. 'Yes. Covered in jelly stuff.'

'Aspic. Don't forget the Chablis.'

'I'd better take it. Get his wine.' He turned and went away.

Car doors slammed, a final farewell through a rear window.

'And do remember, darling; any day next week. Supper, or lunch . . . and bring your guests. It was a divine picnic, better even than last year, *how* you do it . . .'

Bruna closed the kitchen window and turned into the room, hands on hips. 'That's the last. All over. Fanny! Maria! Come along! Into your aprons. I want to collect our things before the caterers steal them. The silver and the crystal. Don't sit there like sides of pork! There's a lot to do: ten for supper, all those Italians . . .'

Taking up a large tin tray and a wooden spoon she marched to the door into the yard and beat a sharp tattoo. 'Tonnino! Tonnino! It's all over. We're going to clear the house-things. Come and get your plants before the caterers steal them all. That man! That man! He would have slept through Agincourt!'

On a little bluff, high above the point and overlooking the pines to the bay far below, Leni and Wolf had settled themselves on a carved stone seat and sat in weary, but relaxed silence, after the steep climb up from the pool. Above, a clear sky; to their right the shadowy lawns and quietly moving waiters, the occasional clink of glass or metal as they cleared the tables. To the left beyond the rocky point, the tumbled boulders, the yellow broom, lay the sea, smudging away into the summer sky: no horizon.

Wolf lay back, legs splayed, hands behind his head. 'And over there,' he nodded towards the sea, 'in the haze, far away.'

Leni looked up. She had kicked off her sandals, pushed her feet into the prickly grass.

'Over there? Where you can't see? Corsica . . . and then, in a straight line, you would come to Africa. Tunisia. So they say.'

'I have never been there.'

She pulled the skirt of her camisole up to her thighs, closed her eyes. 'Maybe you will one day. On a film. Film stars go everywhere, don't they?'

'I'm not one. Not yet.'

'You look like one.' She half-opened her eyes, glanced at him through lashes. Sprawled back, legs apart, shining skin. From far away, as if at the end of an echo-chamber, Marcus's voice: 'Pretend, Leni! Pretend! What is he like beneath that smooth white uniform, what do you invent him to be like?' She smiled to herself, turning her head away. Wolf Hagel was real. 'Blond, god-like . . . all Germans are.' He was.

'Should you be sitting here like that? In the sun . . . bare? You said Grottorosso forbade you the sun.'

'It's a holiday. He's been okay the last few days: quite a change. I don't know why. Let me wear shorts, swim, be in the sun. Amazing. But tomorrow we start again.'

'Start what?'

'Training. Training. The gym in the morning, fencing . . . then riding in the afternoon somewhere in the hills. In riding things. Boots, jacket, breeches . . . everything.'

Leni opened her eyes wide. 'In this heat!'

'Sure. He says I have to wear heavy uniforms so I must get used to the weight. He's tough.'

Leni laughed, started to remove the airplane slide from her hair. 'And vain. Very conceited, I should think. He looks it.'

'Very Italian. Very male. He has to be best at everything. He works hard on his body. He really punishes it. All the training, you know?, he does with me. Fencing . . .

wrestling, the riding. And he is much older than I am. But he has to be best. I don't care, I'm a quiet chap, and that makes him angry. He tries to make me lose my temper, to show "rage", he says, so he hurts me purposely . . . silly things . . . to make me take risks. But I won't. Look at my back.' He leant forward suddenly. Faintly through the light tan, seven weals across the smooth skin.

'I saw them,' said Leni, putting the slide into a pocket, 'when you took off your shirt coming up the hill.'

'He did that. A whip. Riding. "You sit like a sack of shit in the saddle." he said . . . and struck me.'

'You didn't do anything?'

He shrugged. 'No. I'm a quiet man.'

'You must be mad.'

'Sometimes I think so. But if I had hit him he would have hit me back, and so on. No point.'

'You want to be in this film so much?'

'It's a lot of money. Then I'll quit.'

'It's your affair, but I think he must be mad really. And today, he left so quickly, right after lunch. His face was white too, like all the rest of him. He looked so strange, excited . . .'

'Too many people. He hates crowds, they upset him, I think. Also he doesn't like speaking English, he says it exhausts him. But we have to, because of the film.' He reached out and took her hand. 'I've enjoyed today, speaking to you, in our own tongue . . . sometimes I think I have forgotten all my German.'

She patted his hand. 'I have forgotten nearly all mine. I will be happy when I do.'

He spread her fingers across his naked thigh. 'You make me sad when you speak like that. You cannot forget completely that you are German. You must not.'

She removed her hand, slid off the seat and stretched out on her back on the grass. 'I don't want to speak about it any more. Just let us sit here in peace, shall we? You are a

216

quiet man, I am a quiet girl. After the noise today, let us
listen to the sea . . . the wind in the pines. Oh! It's so
good.'

From the moment that they had been introduced by an
ebullient Minerva, and had greeted each other in German,
he had not left her side almost all day. It has not particularly
irritated her; he was pleasing to look at, polite, eager to
help, and never for one moment had prevented her from
her duties as a surrogate hostess. He was just always there.
Diffident, shy, unsettled by the crowd of chattering and
laughing strangers, grateful for her confident presence. At
lunch he had helped her to food, carried her plate and his
own to a quiet place under the trees, and she had given in
with good grace mainly because she could see that Marcus
was enjoying himself and was fully occupied with the
ageing Duc d'Auribeau, Minerva and the strange woman
in the bamboo hat who clearly fascinated him. He was
'doing his job' perfectly, so, she reasoned, this entertaining
of the shy young German must be hers, and with all her
past experience of dealing with Mr Bender's clients, she
knew that the very best way was to let them talk about
themselves; all that she was required to do was listen; smile
from time to time, nod in agreement, pat a troubled hand
with understanding affection. It left her quite unscathed,
intact, unrevealed, but convinced the client that she was
wise, kind and brilliantly amusing. It saved a lot of
trouble. And, really, she thought, listening to the steady
murmur of his German, it was not such a chore. So she
listened sympathetically to his story which was totally
predictable from his humble birth in Cologne where his
father owned a small restaurant near the cathedral, to his
steady climb through the kitchens and bar to serving at
table, to his progress from hotel to hotel from Frankfurt to
Munich where finally, as a Floor Waiter at the Four
Seasons, he was poised to move towards greater heights
with imminent promotion to the restaurant in sight, when

he was summoned to serve a late supper in an ornate suite on the third floor where, menu and wine card in hand, he came face to face with Umberto Grottorosso and his fate.

She was perfectly content, picking through the debris of her lobster-shells, to let him meander comfortably through the trivia of his life: the problems he was having with his English, with the contact lenses; the plans he had for after the film, when the money was safely in the bank, and the small hotel, somewhere in the mountains, with just a few rooms, skiing in the winter and long hikes or fishing in the summer. It was an ordinary story, she thought, told by a charming, but perfectly ordinary young man. He had not, she was certain, got the qualities necessary for a Movie Star, and she considered his ambitions, such as they were, to be entirely suitable to his status. The only quality which he did appear to possess, which would be essential to his future career in the cinema, was an almost unhealthy preoccupation with himself. But almost as soon as she had accepted the thought she dismissed it as unkind. For who could possibly blame him, surrounded, as he undoubtedly was, by doubts and fears and the intensive, almost obsessive, attentions of the frightening Grottorosso who had him obviously completely in his power. Looking at Wolf, sitting cross-legged beside her licking his fingers clean of mayonnaise, smiling candidly at her with troubled brown eyes, she had a sudden surge of pity, and gratitude for the fact that he was so isolated in his own position that he had not once thought to ask her a single question about her own. For she had no desire to reply to any questions about her German life, or the life she presently, happily, enjoyed. The only thing he did know for certain was that she lived with Marcus, which was true, who had an 'antique shop in London', which was as near true as need be, and that she would settle in England and not return to Germany in the foreseeable future. Which was absolutely true, and which shocked him, for he was strongly patriotic, proud of his country, and homesick for it to a desperate degree. However, she went no further than that, and although there seemed little chance that he would probe any deeper, she deemed it wise to kiss him lightly on the cheek and beg him to bring her some raspberries and cream.

Foolish, foolish, she thought. He was the Real which so frightened me, but he hasn't. Real enough. God knows, with his flat Rhineland voice saying all the things a good German boy should say. We lost the war at Stalingrad, must struggle to build a strong nation, the most efficient country in Europe; lost the war but won the peace, respected and admired, the past is forgotten, East and West will be united, we are the new generation born clean, without hate or guilt, we are not responsible for the follies of the past.

And on and on and on.

Mamma. Horst. Langerdorf. The same. All the same. Why am I different? Why am I Leni Minx? Someone tell me . . . tell me. Across the lawns Marcus at his table, laughing.

A wrench of need.

He is real. The carnival all around me, the holiday, these are unreal. Real, unreal mixed together.

Oh Marcus! Marcus. Sitting there straight back towards me, small buttocks as you squat, arm sweeping wide in joyous explanation. What are you telling them? I can't share . . . Minerva laughing, hands pressed to mouth, the Bamboo Hat wagging from side to side, jade flashing; the old Duc smiling, smiling, opaline eyes dull in the light, prodding the grass with a slender ebony stick.

The stork. The stork prodding quietly in the sedge of the Schwarzbrücke, high green barley bending in the wind, apple-stumps like tossed broom-heads. The Wall.

Wolf threading his way towards me, a tray of wine and fruit balanced in his hand with the assurance of his calling. Assure *me*, assure me . . .

Luise moved into the shadows as Leni reached up to help him with his tray.

The afternoon was fully occupied by a Treasure Hunt which Cuckoo had planned, which meant that the whole picnic became wonderfully confused and mixed up, with everyone scurrying about in search of the clues which had been planted the evening before, and it was not until the end, when the prizes had been found, the signal that the splendid picnic was officially over, that she came into contact with him again and told him that after she had gone to speed the departing guests, with Marcus and Cuckoo at the front door, she would meet him by the pool where they could swim and relax and sit in the sun after the exertions of the day, for she hoped he's stay to supper?

'Well,' said Cuckoo, as the last car went up the steep curve of the drive to the road. 'That's that. All done! All over. And I think a success. Anyway it felt like one to me . . . did it to you?'

'Terrific!' and Marcus. 'Really smashing.'

'And so were you both, "really smashing"! Everybody said so. Thank you both a thousand times. Now, I must go and tell Bruna only eight for supper, because nice Signore Bell-whatever-his-name-is and Signore Grottorosso have left . . . so that makes it simpler, and it's only leftovers from today anyway, but I must go and tell her, she gets into such a fuss . . . and then I shall have a little lie down on my bed for an hour. A tiny bit weary I am. A full day. Do admit?'

'You've been overdoing things, old dear,' said Archie. 'You really shouldn't . . .'

She flashed him a spark of irritation. 'Nonsense! Never felt better. Such a happy day but a lot of chatter . . . my head's spinning with the noise.'

'At the pool. We'll be down there,' said Marcus. 'What you need is a swim, go and get your costume, be a sport. I must sober up. We'll all have a swim, Sylva is waiting.'

But she blew them both a kiss and slipping her arm into Archie's went with him into the house.

'Sylva? Is waiting for you?' said Leni as they walked slowly down the scuffed lawns among scattered chairs and littered tables.

'For us. We still have guests. Where's your Kraut? Old Seigfried?'

'I expect he's waiting too. I don't know.'

'And he was real?'

'Very real. Very dull.'

'He didn't frighten you after all?'

'No. I was just silly. He's a nice ordinary boy.'

'Poor bugger. How will he look in that smooth white uniform?'

She took his arm and placed it tightly round her waist. 'Like the figure-thing in the study, remember? Wax.'

Marcus laughed and ran her down the steps to the pool where Minerva, Wolf and Sylva were sitting in the shade by the deserted bar while Lilli Scarlatti, hands clasped before her in delight, bamboo hat discarded, cigarette hanging from her lips, swayed in ecstasy among the 'Piranesi' ruins.

'Is she all right?' said Marcus.

'Swooning with a surfeit of style,' said Minerva. 'She can't get over the "eleganza" of it all. Lilli! Do you want to come up to the house? There's lots of style in the drawing-room, Magritte and Sickert, Bonnard and big, fat, deep chairs, and I'm half dead.'

Scarlatti joined them coughing harshly, spilling ash over her silk shirt. 'Si Bella! Such style! I am wounded to my heart by the beauty . . . to the heart.' She stubbed out her cigarette, picked up her hat and bag. 'Is it possible that there would be a cup of tea in an English house? We could perhaps ask?'

'We could and we shall,' said Minerva and they started up the steps together.

Sylva reached out and took Marcus's hand. 'You come with Sylva for a swim? I have my costume here already.' She patted a small sequined purse on the counter.

'In that?' said Marcus.

She nodded. 'In that. We go?' She went across to the changing rooms, percheron buttocks swinging.

'Okay, we go.' He pulled a half-empty bottle towards him, found a dirty glass, emptied the dregs, filled it. 'Hair of the dog,' he said, and drained it in one long gulp. Leni watched him with narrowed eyes. He grinned at her, crossed his own. 'I'm a bit woozy.' He undid the buttons of the braces, slung them over his shoulder. 'A swim, umm? You both coming? Come on! Don't look so stuffy.' He pulled the T-shirt over his head and started to zip out of his trousers. 'Don't worry,' he said to Wolf. 'I'm quite decent underneath.' He stepped out of them unsteadily.

'I don't think I will swim,' said Wolf easing off the stool. 'Maybe I'll have a walk, up there on the hill . . . in the trees.'

'Off you go then,' said Marcus cheerfully. 'I'm sure old Frau Baedeker here will give you a tour . . . show you all the sights.' He folded his shirt and trousers over-carefully, threw them into a chair, kicked off his espadrilles, ran to the edge of the pool and jumped in, sending up a great spray of water.

'Come on,' said Leni. 'He's just being silly . . .'

Halfway up the steps they heard him calling, and Leni turned back; he blew her a kiss and waved. 'Don't do anything you can't do on a bicycle!'

'What did he say?' said Wolf. 'About a bicycle. But we walk, yes?'

'We walk,' said Leni. And laughed.

Sylva stood by the far side of the pool, the water on her Renoir body glistening in the sun, unpinning the heavy splendour of her hair slowly, deliberately, so that it fell tress after tress over smooth white shoulders like molten copper. From behind the tumble of 'Piranesi' blocks and columns where they had dragged their mattresses to take advantage of the late sun, Marcus watched her with admiration and a sense of vague unease. A fantastic landscape, he thought, heavy waxen breasts, narrow waist, full thighs. Not, however, a landscape which really attracted him greatly. It was almost too lush. Too Amazonian in the geographical sense, with its heavy peaks, deep valleys, dark chasms, dense vegetation. Very tropical, steamy, smothering. You could say overpowering. You could get lost in there.

He had, he realized, seeing the comparison before him, grown comfortably used to, and reassured by, the sweeter, gentler fenland landscape which Leni's body provided. Cool, apple-scented, gentle hills, soft pastures, smooth rolling fields, sweet hidden dales, all tender, submissive, yielding in a pearly light, soft as a Norfolk sky. I'll be a ruddy poet yet, see if I'm not. He rolled heavily on to his back on the canvas mattress and closed his eyes. The swim had helped; but far too much white wine throughout the day. And bloody Leni. Wandering off with the Kraut . . . grunting away at each other in their phlegmy language . . . been with him the whole day long, trailing about. Nice enough looking chap. Give him that, not exactly a ball of fire: no balls at all, in all probability. Anyway, she'd said he was 'wax'. Didn't fit the picture of the Lusty German Brute they'd invented him to be. Funny. All the right things but blank as the map of Australia. So why does she spend all day with the sod? Hardly came near me . . . wish she was near me now. As I said, I'm a simple country boy at heart, a gentle roll in the hay, not much of a Jungle Explorer. Although with what she is wearing there isn't all that much to explore. No wonder everything fitted so easily into her titchy little purse. Christ! Three scraps of green, like leaves really, the larger stuck between those terrific thighs, and the other two bits like little fingers curving round her tits and just, only just, covering her nipples, and a bit of cord round her tiny waist. I could span that with my two hands. Just. Almost. And her bum. Wow! Bare as a pig's or whatever. No tail, and twice as beautiful. Bare. Watch it . . . you'll turn yourself on. Damn Leni.

Feet pattering behind him.

'Hello. You sleep?' Her voice treacle, poured over glass.

He rolled his head slowly from side to side, eyes shut. 'Dozing. A hard day.'

'A sleeping beauty, isn't it?' She was settling on to her mattress beside him. 'You are very handsome. You know?'

'First time I've ever heard it.'

'Oh yes. *I* say. Poor Sylva . . .' A heavy sigh, clink of a bracelet. 'You like this Wolf Hagel?'

'Don't know him; can't tell.'

'I mean how he looks, this man?'

'Fine. Nice looking . . . I'm no judge.' Do go away.

'His hair is dyed, did you guess? Poor boy. Every week. For the part in the movie. I tell him it will all fall out soon.'

'Bad luck. Dear of you, though.'

A finger suddenly brushed his forehead, retreated. He lay perfectly still.

'Yours is not.'

'No. Not.'

'And your eyes are blue, I am right?'

'Red. Last time I looked.'

'His are brown. He must wear lenses, you know why?'

'Because-l'Aiglon's-eyes-were-*blue*!' Repeated like a parrot.

'Ah! So! You know. It is cruel for him, makes him molto unhappy.'

'Well, why doesn't he just piss off if he's so unhappy.'

'Grottorosso finds him. Grottorosso wants him. He will play the part. He stays.'

224

'Grottorosso is screwy.'

'I think also. You met him today. He is beautiful too, right?'

'In a creepy way.'

'I don't understand. You speak to me in a strange way. What is "piss off"? What is "creepy"?'

'Don't fret, you'll twig.'

'Oh, Ma-donna!' A cry of irritation. 'Poor Sylva! Men are all cruel to me.'

'You must be kidding.'

'Is true. Hagel is timido with me . . . he is tired all the time. I am on that boat all the day and no one is talk to, to play with, they do not speak to me, ignore me. I am *so* unhappy. Poor Sylva . . .'

Without opening his eyes he folded his arms behind his head. If I don't look at her she'll go away.

'A boat full of Italian sailors and German film stars? Joking.'

A cool hand slid along his thigh, stopped half way, moved on upwards to the buckle of his slip. Withdrew. He stopped breathing.

'So smooth, like satin. Yes, is possible. They do not like me. Grottorosso is very scared of me. I sense this.'

'Goodness me. I wonder why.'

'Shall I say something very terrible to you? A secret, about him?'

'If you must.'

'I think that he makes love to himself! In the mirror! He is in love with his own body. You are not surprised?'

'No.'

'Dio! You do not *look* at me! You too are cruel.'

He opened his eyes blearily, dazzled by the sun. 'I'm looking at you. There . . .'

She had removed the finger-like leaves from her breasts. 'You do not mind? It is comfortable not to be wet . . . we are alone, there is no one.'

'No. Fine. Great.' His throat dry. 'Go ahead.'

'And look. This is amusing, you think?' She suddenly raised her arms high above her head, pulling her breasts tautly upwards, the nipples pointing hard at the sky like tiny Howitzers. Under her arm, in the shadowy cup, a butterfly, clipped from the dark red hair.

'And in the other one, on this side, is a heart. Is pretty, no? In Palermo all society ladies used to do this . . . little butterflies, hearts, diamonds. You like?'

'Cool, man.' His lips were stuck.

'On that boat I have plenty time. And a little, baby, razor . . . it is something to do for me.'

Suddenly she lowered her arms, holding her breasts in each hand weighing them like melons. 'They are brown. You see? The sun is good for them.' She knelt upwards, her hair falling about her face and shoulders in a red torrent. Impatiently she shook her head, throwing her hair wildly about. The vigorous movement made her whole body judder and tremble. He stared transfixed with fright, then she slowly stretched towards him, her face inches from his shoulder, breasts resting on the fans of her spread fingers, an offering of ripe fruit.

'Poor Sylva,' she murmured and removed one hand from her body she placed it deliberately on his, smoothing it gently across his chest. 'Yours are pretty too. Firm . . . you see? Each one will fit my hand?'

'I really wish you wouldn't, please . . .'

'But it is nice feeling, isn't it? You have no hair, so smooth . . . I like. Grottorosso has so much hair there . . . is not attractive.' The hand slipped down his body, over his tense belly, to the top of his thin blue slip: and over.

'Don't.' His voice a whisper. 'Please don't. Now stop it it . . .'

The hand caressed him relentlessly, his eyes glazed.

'No don't, Sylva. If you don't mind.'

He unfolded his arms and tried to sit up; she pushed him

back with her free hand, leant on him firmly.

' "He" doesn't mind, this one. "He" doesn't say "don't", does he?' She said it in the hideously cloying voice of the District Nurse who had given him his first Blanket Bath at fifteen. Memory galvanized him, he struggled under her weight, but she stayed firmly in place.

'Stop. I beg you stop. Now Sylva, look here . . .'

With a sudden move which took him completely by surprise she knelt across his body and straddled him, trapping his thighs between her massive ones, crushing them together tightly.

'Oh Christ!' he gasped and tried to sit up again, but was pressed firmly backwards by the superior weight of her body which she folded over him, her lips close to his, her hair falling about his head like a heavy, fragrant, curtain. 'Oh no . . .' he moaned. 'Oh no, don't. I . . .'

She silenced him with a wet mouth, her tongue thrusting and probing between his stretched lips. It was a long and searching kiss. She broke it, kissing the tip of his nose, licking his upper lip, his chin, his throat, down to his breasts where she lightly bit his nipples, and then bit harder, so that he yelled out, throwing his arms wide, arching his body upwards with her full weight upon it, thumping the palms of his hands on the hot stones at his side.

'Not any more! No more! Stop . . . you've gone mad!'

She knelt back, her heavy buttocks crushing his knees, fingers pinching his belly and the insides of his thighs.

'Why I stop?' she said. 'Why we stop? *Now* is poor Marcus, not poor Sylva! Now you are prisoner. Slave, isn't it? Poor Sylva is happy Sylva . . . and will be happy Marcus too, I think.'

Her hands glided firmly across the taut blue cotton of his straining slip, caressing, stroking, nipping. He rolled wildly beneath her, trapped at the knees, beating his hands at his sides, crying out in little strangled gasps.

227

'No! No! No! For Christ's sake, Sylva . . . let me free.'

'I let this one free firstly,' she cried, and with a swift tug unclipped the buckle at his hip and stripped him.

He gave a helpless sob, reared upwards.

'Oh! Stupendo!' she cried happily. 'Si robusto! Si robusto!' and quickly untying the cord at her own hip, she removed with one swift, and practised, move the last shred of modesty she possessed. And raped him.

He tucked himself away tidily inside the slip, snapped the buckle right, grinned down at her. 'There we are. All neat and shipshape.'

She looked up at him, busily tying her string. 'A nice shape. I like.'

'So it seemed. Blimey! I'm almost castrated.'

She laughed happily. 'A castrato! Castroneria! You are not cross with me?'

'Good grief! Do I look cross?'

'You will not say to me "piss off"?'

'I will not say to you piss off. But you nearly broke my legs.'

She got up holding the small green cups in her hand by the string. 'Poor legs! I am so sorry. I am big girl. You will tie this for me, it is difficult.'

He assisted her to fix the slender-fingered pieces over her breasts.

'You know? You could have suckled Romulus and Remus with this pair alone,' he said.

She slapped his hand. 'You are disgusting to me. But it was a good way, eh? It was good for you, is true?'

'Great. Not much alternative.'

'It is the Women's Liberation way!'

'It sure as all hell isn't the Missionary way.'

'This I do not know.'

'I rather suspect that you wouldn't.' He looked up

suddenly towards the steps. 'And we haven't got time to try it now. Here comes a waiter or someone . . . clearing the bar. Want a drink before he does?'

'I swim first . . . I am so hot . . . then a drink. I do my hair.' She started piling it up into a heavy bun on the top of her head.

Marcus walked slowly to the edge of the pool. Leni, Leni, Leni. Well: you shouldn't have gone off with him. All day. I suppose it was my fault really. I 'pretended' him for you, in his white knickers and things. Fat hopes for you! Bet you didn't have as much fun as I did. I wish I hadn't. No I don't. Screw it all, I've fucked a Film Star. He braced himself, took a deep breath. 'Well! here I go,' he called, and dived into the water just as Cuckoo arrived at the top of the stairs under the Albertine arch.

'Mamma Mia,' murmured Sylva, slipping quietly into the water, 'it *could* have been poor Sylva . . . that's sure.'

'Welcome,' said Minerva, raising one long arm from the depths of the settee in which she lay. 'Welcome, my dear, to the Senior Citizens' Ward.' She indicated, with a vague wave of her hand, the prostrate figure of Lilli Scarlatti on the floor across the room.

Cuckoo dropped her hat into a chair, sat down. 'That remark, if you will forgive me, has the blatant sound of defiance ringing in it.'

'Not any longer,' said Minerva. 'We're bushed.'

'So it would seem. Well . . . I've had my nap, checked the picnic ruins, been down to the pool, found Marcus and the Film Star . . . can't find Leni and the German, and have had two super, duper, glasses of hot Krug. How about that?'

'Great. We've done the gardens, the pool and the house. We have seen, and we can see now, the Magrittes, Bonnard, Sickerts and the John, which she, in her ignorance . . .' indicating Scarlatti who had not moved or opened her eyes '. . . finds banal.' She turned her head towards the black figure on the floor.

'It was "banal", you said? Lilli?'

Scarlatti raised one hand, which hung like a drooping claw, crippled with jade. 'Si, si. Banal. Excuse me.'

'Quite possibly right. I never thought,' said Cuckoo.

'And we have also done the study. The Museum! Can you believe? Lili actually crossed the forbidden threshold and Charles welcomed her, if not with open arms at least without a loaded revolver. They had a very interesting time, right Lilli?'

'Si, si . . . most interesting.'

'We went through hems and lapels, button holes, badges, decorations, tissues, leather, hessian, feathers and God knows what. I think that I know just exactly what every single man in the French army was wearing on the morning of Waterloo: down to his underpants.'

'He is living history, Sir Charles,' murmured Scarlatti carefully sitting up.

'I've often thought so too,' said Cuckoo dryly. 'He was in his room; resting . . . he said he would be?'

'Well, he wasn't,' said Minerva sitting up and tucking her shirt back into her slacks. 'You want to know what? He was re-dressing that goddamned dummy. That's what. . . . that's how we found him. I told him Lilli was the designer on the movie and he said come right in and have a look round. And that's what we did. And that's what we found. Beat that?'

'I'm amazed. He had put it away? Because of Grottorosso.'

Minerva brushed her sleeve, adjusted a gold nugget on her finger. 'Who is not coming back. Finito. Goodbye. Adieu. Let Charles tell you. All I know is that he said he loathed the script, that he wouldn't put his name to it in any shape or form, and that the conversation this morning was fraught, that Grottorosso was stubborn and that

Nando Belluno said that they didn't need his name, or his permission to go ahead and so what the hell was all the fuss about? So Charles said Goodbye and that was that. He'll tell you . . . these are just the bare facts. It's sad.'

Scarlatti laughed scornfully. 'But of course he couldn't work with Grottorosso. It is like Attila the Hun being converted by Francis of Assisi. Impossible!' She managed to reach a chair, open her bag and fished about for her cigarettes. 'I am furious, you know? Furious. Sir Charles has so much wonderful information . . . so many things I could use.' She shrugged hopelessly, put a lighter to her cigarette and coughed.

'I'm certain that Charles would let you . . .' Cuckoo started to say, but Scarlatti waved a hand through the haze of smoke, thumping her chest with the other.

'No . . . no,' she said when she had gained her breath. 'No. It is kind of you. But if he does not approve, he does not approve. *I* do not approve. But it is not my job to disapprove, only to dress the actors. I am paid. So I do.'

Cuckoo got up and wandered over to the windows. 'Oh dear. I thought such a lovely day, such a success, nothing awful had happened . . . and now this.'

Minerva cracked four fingers, noisily. 'There's more,' she said.

'More?' Cuckoo turned sharply. 'What more?'

'Grottorosso wants Lilli to take all Marcus's measurements.'

Cuckoo stood as rock.

'Head, neck, waist, inside leg, etcetera.'

'Marcus? They did meet then?'

'Sure they met. Bet your ass.' Minerva leant forward, elbows on knees. 'Cuckoo my dear, I told you . . . those yellow pants. He stood out like a Bride at a Funeral.'

'How did they meet, when?'

'I don't know! I wasn't standing about like a chimney.'

'I didn't see . . . of course, they were *bound* to meet. A

231

small picnic . . . it wasn't a Royal Garden Party.' She turned anxiously to Lilli. 'But what for? I mean, the measurements?'

'A caprice, just a caprice. Nothing more. I know Grottorosso for many years.' Scarlatti smiled coldly. 'He has an idea that the boy in yellow could be a marvellous "double" for Wolf Hagel. You know what is a double? He does all the work the Film Star is not capable of. By that it seems to me that he will have to play the part himself! No, please, you look so anxious. It is a caprice, Grottorosso was struck by such an amazing resemblance to . . .'

'L'Aiglon,' finished Cuckoo. 'I know.'

'And it is amazing. When he pointed it out to me I was quite astonished, but who is this boy? What can he do? He is fine looking, strong, like l'Aiglon, certo . . . but what can he do? Grottorosso told me that you found him, like a pebble, on the beach. Is true?'

Cuckoo came away from the windows and sat tiredly beside Minerva and took her hand. 'Who told him that?' she said.

Minerva shook her head. 'Not me.' She put her hand over Cuckoo's cold one and pressed it warmly. 'You know that. He probably said it himself. Marcus . . .'

'No,' said Cuckoo. 'No. He wouldn't do that. We are conspirators.'

There was a long moment's silence. From far away in the gardens Bruna calling: 'Fanny! Fanny! Cooeee!' The sound of a barrow wheel crunching on the gravel.

'Conspirators?' said Minerva. 'What does that mean?'

'I mean . . . he's my "godson", you know. We made a plan together. It amused him. He would not have said that, about, about . . .' she tucked her little velvet bow more securely into her hair '. . . about a pebble. It's unthinkable.'

'It is only silliness,' said Scarlatti. 'Grottorosso is a man who lacks style. He seeks beauty everywhere because he has none within his soul. Forgive me, Minerva, but it *is* so. He tries to surround himself with beauty all the time. Any price he will pay. But it will pass, it will pass this idea. Anyway,' she said practically, 'we have not enough money for costumes for a double. My God! My budget is already finished; if we use a double, then he will have to wear the Hagel things.'

Minerva got up, patted Cuckoo's hand. 'I must go and take a bath. Lilli? You want to freshen up . . . a bath, shower?'

'I come! I come!' said Scarlatti, collecting her bag and hat. 'I am sorry, you know, for what I said about a "pebble on the beach". I do not wish to be offensive . . . it was just a nonsense of Grottorosso, he is like that, he has no style. I did not know it was your godson. Excuse me.'

Cuckoo went towards her quickly, hands outstretched. 'Oh no! You must not apologize, it was nonsense on *my* part. Something we invented, it is not even *true*. We were just, well, you know . . . pretending?'

'Ah!' said Scarlatti looking for an ashtray and stubbing out her cigarette as if she was pestling anchovies. 'Pretendere! They begin "Once upon a time . . ."?'

'Exactly. Fairy stories. They usually end with "And they all lived happily ever after". Do you remember?'

Scarlatti put her bamboo hat firmly on her head. 'Ah yes – but those are fantasy,' she said.

'Skin-tight white leather pants and a shirt open to his belly button. At his age!' Marcus pulled the sheet from his bed, folded it. 'Too hot for sheets.'

'But what did he say to you?' Leni was brushing her hair.

'Oh the usual stuff. You know, the l'Aiglon bit. God! I'm so bored with that old spiel. Then, could I ride? Could I swim? I said yes. Could I fence? I said a bit . . . at

233

prep school, very junior, nothing. He's going to give me lessons . . .'

She turned on the stool, brush in hand. 'But what for? Lessons?'

'Thinks I'd be a very good double for your Kraut mate. Hagel.'

'For Wolf? A double? What is?'

'To do all the bits he can't . . . I gather he isn't exactly Superman.'

'Are you?'

'No. Wants me to go to Vienna. How does that grab you?'

'Vienna . . . why, when?' A thread of panic in her voice.

'Making the film there. I don't know when. September, I think. Asked me to have lunch with him on board, so we can discuss it all. I don't know.'

'And you will?'

'Might. Mind?'

She turned back slowly to the mirror, tapped the brush in her hands. 'If you want to . . .'

'Free lunch.' He sat on the edge of the bed, switched on the radio, very low.

'But Uncle Desmond,' she said. 'The Studio . . . we have to go back soon, don't we?'

'Canteloupe Road, soggy schnitzels, one bath a week . . . two floors down?'

She dropped the brush, covered her face with her hands, started to weep.

'Leni! Leni!' He slid off the bed, knelt at her side, pulled her hands from her face. 'What's the matter? What's wrong?'

She shook her head, tears spilling, nose running. 'You'll go away.'

'Where to?'

'Vienna.'

'Who said?'

'You.'

'Lunch, I said.'

She pulled her hand from his, wiped her mouth. 'Not to Vienna?' She hiccupped, sniffed, rubbed her eyes.

'You saw him? Grottorosso? The leather pants? Know the kind? Seen them often enough at the Studio, haven't you? Eyeing "the goods", suggesting the "poses" to old Gus . . . waving the pound notes about. "Chains, Mr Bender, perhaps a whip? It's *discipline* I want . . . I am sure you understand." Know the kind? Remember?'

'And he is that kind?' Her teary eyes wide.

'*He* may not know it, but he's as bent as a tin spoon.'

'How is it possible?'

'How are all those happy company directors from Orpington, who feed you on jelly and get their jollies when you snap your knicker elastic, how are *they* possible? And you know very well they are. He was squeezing my arms, you know? Patting my arse . . . Archie Charlie twigged all right. Went rigid.' He kissed her knees.

'So?'

'So? Canteloupe Road and soggy schnitzels . . . and stop snivelling.'

Later, in his arms, staring up into the dark, she sighed.

'Poor Wolf! He's nice, honest . . . so gentle.'

'The gentle people get clobbered in life, didn't you know?'

'Yes.' She traced his lips with her fingers. 'I do know. And the Film Star, Sylva . . . how was she?'

He shifted slightly, rubbed the lobe of his ear. 'Ah. Sylva. She was a bore.'

'Really? That sexy lady? Fantastic! She bored you?'

He folded his arms round her.

'Stiff,' he said.

Chapter Eight

The buzzer on the white telephone beside the bed shattered the stillness of the morning with three sudden, sharp, blasts.

Minerva licked the honey from her fingers, reached for the receiver.

'Pronto!' she said, sucking her thumb.

'Here is Bruna, Principessa, there is a call for you from the *Papageno*, an Italian lady; shall I say "yes", or are you still asleep?'

'I'm awake . . . I'll take it, but hold it a minute, Bruna.' She cradled the receiver between neck and shoulder, scrabbled for a cigarette, lit it, for she was quite incapable of uttering into a telephone without one in her hand. 'Okay, put her through.'

A click, silence, hissing, Sylva Puglia's fretful voice. 'Principessa? It is Sylva . . .'

'Sylva!' said Minerva removing a crumb from her lip with the top of her tongue. 'You are up early.'

'I am sorry to disturb you, but it is serious. Very terrible: there has been an accident.'

Minerva sat upright carefully, steadying the tray across her thighs. 'Accident? Where? To whom?'

'Wolf Hagel. In the gymnasium. Fencing . . .'

Minerva's back was as straight as a plank. 'What happened?'

'I am not certain. But it is his face. Dio! From eye to chin.'

'There's a doctor?'

'Sure. Belluno did everything. They've taken him to Nice, to the St Roche. But can you come down, now, right away? Grottorosso is asking for you. He is shut in his cabin, he won't speak . . . he is distraught. Belluno says please will you come, they have sent a car to the villa.'

'I'll be there in half an hour.' She hung up, lifted the tray from her legs, slid out of bed and stood for a moment in the centre of the room, hands to her face, shaking her head from side to side in wonder. 'The bastard,' she said aloud. 'The shitty, shitty bastard.'

On the terrace at his solitary breakfast Archie saw her, rose in surprise. 'Minna! Good morning! So early . . . will you join me?'

She spread her fingers wide, pressed him back into his seat. 'Don't move, Charles . . . I can't stop, I'm on my way to the ship. There's been some kind of an accident, they just called.'

He folded his *Nice Matin.* 'Good Heavens! What's happened? Something very bad?'

'I don't know. But I imagine it can't be very good. It's Wolf Hagel, the blond boy, you remember, yesterday?'

'Ah yes. German fellow. I say, that's rather worrying, isn't it?'

'It isn't exactly reassuring, shall we say. Cuckoo isn't down yet?'

'No. She's staying put, rather whacked after yesterday. You know . . .'

'Sure: well, don't tell her, right? No point in fussing her, I'll call when I can. Say . . . oh! say anything if she asks where I am. I've gone to see Grottorosso, which is true anyway, but don't say why.'

'I won't. You'll call?'

'I'll do that.' She hurried out to the waiting car, waved to Tonnino who was raking the gravel by the Triton.

'Bonjour, Principessa . . . it's going to be a beautiful day, eh?'

'Just darling,' she said.

In the circular day-room Cuckoo pushed open the shutters, felt the warmth of the sun through her thin nightdress, leant against the balcony watching the hoopoe jabbing his long beak into the trodden turf. Busy thing: I should be down there too; so much to do. Haven't dead-headed for days, the aquilegia to clip down, don't suppose Tonnino's got around to that. A garden is a lovesome thing, God wot. What about God then? She leaned up, holding the rail. Go down a little later, just stay here a bit. Calm, quiet. Ought to get all those damned carnations off to the hospital . . . what on earth will they do with fifty dozen white carnations, may I ask? Wreaths? She turned into the room abruptly as Archie came through from the bedroom, letters in his hand, an anxious furrow on his brow.

'Thought you were in your bed? Bruna said . . .'

'Having a little wander. Mail come?'

'Nothing very exciting.' He handed them to her. 'Card there from a "Caroline and Auberon". In Barbados. We know them?'

She looked at the card. 'Caroline, dear, Harriet's girl. Auberon's the Estate Agent. I went to the wedding, remember?'

He sat carefully on an overstuffed chair. 'Losing my head. Can't seem to remember a thing these days. So much fuss, I suppose. Honeymoon, is it? Thought they'd be up in Cumberland, tramping the fells in a fog with a thermos flask.'

'Anything lovely for you?'

'Wine Society catalogue . . . a slip from *Country Life* regretting "Industrial Action" for the loss of four editions. Not greatly lovely. No. One for the boy.'

She looked up sharply. 'The boy? Marcus?'

'Ummm . . .'

'From England?'

'My dear, I don't know. Didn't look. English stamp . . . must be. And another. Delivered by hand. He's in luck.'

238

'By hand?'

'Yes.' He scratched his chin busily; he knew that he was about to lie, and lying made him extremely uncomfortable, since, as far as he knew, he did it very rarely. 'Minna's gone down to that damned boat. They sent a car.'

'Why, I wonder? Anything wrong?'

'No . . . no . . . she was in great form. Won't be long, she said, you know Minna . . . always in a hustle.'

'And he had a letter from the boat then?'

'Yes . . . probably that tiresome Film Star, she never took her hands off him all evening.' He crossed his legs; lying over. Relief. 'We just met in the hall . . . they've walked into St Jean, batteries for his wireless or something.'

She spread the letters out like a hand of cards. 'Isn't it boring when you know by the handwriting exactly who's sent what, and that you can't be bothered to read them. No fun.' She slapped them on to the desk, straightened the Beardsley page-boy. 'I'm sorry that yesterday was so utterly foul for you . . . with Grottorosso, I mean, and after the first meeting being so irritating. Minna didn't say much, but what did happen? Can you say? Or would you rather not?'

'No. I can say . . . no secret. It wasn't utterly foul, really. Just infuriating and, well, quite frankly insulting. He really is the most unpleasant person. I quite liked the other fellow, in the dark glasses, Bell-something, quite, civil, polite, and at least completely honest. But Grottorosso never quite hits the point, you know what I mean? Evades, slides away. I said, quite frankly, "Now look here, we have had one meeting and I'm not convinced at all; I have thought things over, re-read a good deal of the script-thing . . . had time to consider, and I see absolutely no point in discussing things any further if you still have it in your mind, whether it is in the 'dialogue' or not, to pursue this outrageous innuendo relating to Prokesch. It

239

seems to me," I said, "that it is the absolute 'nub' of your story, and it won't do. I simply couldn't, wouldn't, give my name to such a piece of infamy." I was quite calm, made myself plain as a pikestaff. Left him in no doubt. He just sat there smiling a little, shaking his head as if I was some kind of half-wit. And then this Bell-fellow said, most politely, that *he* really hadn't seen it in that light at all and was sure that I had misinterpreted the thing. Perhaps I was not used to reading film whatever-they-are. Scripts. Perhaps I was being a little over-sensitive? I pointed out, as gently as I could, that this was a subject on which I had spent a great many years in research, and about which I was considered, by quite a number of people, to be something of an authority. I didn't boast, or anything of that sort. Just the facts. And that if I was over-sensitive I probably was. And would stay so. And then Grottorosso said that it wasn't just my approbation which he had so desired for his work, he had hoped I would have been tempted to assist him with the thing in Vienna! I ask you! As a Technical Adviser! Sort of form of blackmail; I swear that I could hear the clink of coppers rattling in his begging-tin! Quite frightful! I said that I wouldn't be technical adviser, or whatever it was, to this piece of salacious distortion for anything he cared to offer. Made it plain. I was absolutely wild.'

'I do see,' Cuckoo murmured.

'And all this, my dear, in the middle of the picnic with that idiot Reggie Courtney nodding and grinning and trying to get an introduction to the man, and waiters clattering about with trays of drinks. Simply awful. And then Bell-whatever very pleasantly said why didn't we forget all about it since I was obviously unhappy about it all, which I thought most sensible and said so. He pointed out, very nicely indeed, that although my name on the Credits would have brought a great deal of distinction and veracity to the film, it was not absolutely essential, that

240

they would go ahead anyhow, because everything was far too committed, and he was quite certain that I would approve of it very much when I finally saw it. And then, my dear, Grottorosso, obviously infuriated that I had won my case, started off on another attack about beauty being in the eye of the beholder and all that nonsense, and said that I was exactly like the infamous Metternich himself! Who had misconstrued Prokesch's relationship in the same manner! He implied, in a very irritating way, that to read such an ugly innuendo into a lyrical, literate piece of work, suggested that one had an ugly mind oneself! Cuckoo! Really! I ask you. I *was* wild. He just sat there smiling that superior smile, looking sad and sympathetic as if he had heard that I'd just lost my hearing, shaking his head and tut-tutting all the time. I very nearly choked him!'

Cuckoo sat perfectly still, hands folded on her knees. 'How loathsome for you. I'm terribly, terribly sorry . . . I had no idea.'

He ran a hand briskly over neatly parted hair. 'Loathsome. And then a perfectly strange thing happened. The Bell-fellow was saying something about forgetting it all and putting it behind us, carrying no wounds, that sort of stuff, and that they really didn't need my name or permission since there was no form of copyright, all that, just that it would have been such an honour and so on, when I noticed that Grottorosso was sitting bolt upright, staring over my shoulder. His eyes were quite strange, white with light, do you know what I mean? As if he'd seen the Second Coming or something . . . extraordinary. What he *had* seen, of course, was the boy.'

Cuckoo's hand clenched lightly. 'Marcus?'

'Yes. Absolutely thunderstruck, of course. The resemblance. He turned to me and said in quite a different voice from the patronizing one he'd been using before, "Is that the pebble which your wife found on your beach?" I ask you!'

241

Cuckoo opened her hands, smoothed the nightdress over her knees, looked up at him. 'And what precisely did that mean, pray?'

Archie shifted uncomfortably, uncrossed his legs, brushed his lapel. 'Oh. The other day . . . he had said that he was looking for a chap to be this damned l'Aiglon but they weren't so easy to find, not like pebbles on the beach, and I simply said that you had found one on our beach. I think that I said it to irritate him because he had so irritated me.' He looked about the floor aimlessly. 'It was a fatuous thing to say, perfectly silly, but I was fussed . . . you know. Didn't think.'

'Apparently.'

'Perfectly odious remark, I know. Sorry. But he riled me so. Anyway he was transfixed, asked to meet him. I called Marcus over; he was charming, polite, called him Sir and so on. Seemed rather amused. I left them to it, I'm afraid – I'd had quite enough – went and got myself a drink, needed it, and got caught up with Courtney again begging for an introduction to the Great Man, as he called him. I ask you! Anyway: when I got back . . . with blasted Courtney, I mean what could I do? They both were chattering away together, and Grottorosso had the most curious expression on his face. Had his arm round the boy's shoulder, very . . . avuncular . . . very intense. He suddenly reminded me, well, the odd look did, of a chap we had in the Regiment, Hill: read Sanskrit and Greek at Cambridge, pale, aesthetic, very cold. If any of the chaps came up on a charge of some kind he used to suggest they accept *his* punishment or go on up to the Old Man. Most of them accepted his. Six of the best, across the backside with a riding-crop. Not quite right, I thought? Only suggested it to the young chaps, well built, bigger than himself. Well . . . Grottorosso had the same kind of look. I'd forgotten all about Clive "Whacker" Hill until that moment. Most unpleasant.'

'And Marcus?' Cuckoo had pleated a fold of material, pressed it between her finger and thumb.

'Oh, you know the young. Wasn't phased, stood there grinning cheerfully . . . and then Reggie Courtney butted in and bleated away about some damned film, and broke it all up. I was jolly glad when the gong went for luncheon. I excused myself as a host and hopped off . . . left them to it.'

She looks tireder than tired, he thought. Not *just* tired, I mean. Pinched. Not really listening to me, more interested in the Pollock boy: I think that everybody has rather overstayed their welcome. Enough is enough. I'd like her to rest for a bit, get Poteau up and give her a good check-up. I mean, it's silly; too many people. Time to wind things up. She's not young any longer. He got up and walked to the windows.

'Hardly know we had more than fifty pairs of feet tramping all over the place. It's all very neat and tidy down there . . . they've been frightfully good, the staff . . . worked like Trojans. They really do deserve a bit of a rest, don't you think?' He turned back; she was still sitting at her desk. 'We *all* do in my candid opinion, all go back to normal, what do you think, ummm?'

She looked up at him and smiled suddenly. 'What do you call normal?'

'Well . . . you know, the place to ourselves for a bit . . . just for a time. Minna *is* rather exhausting after a while; that voice. Fearfully monotonous. Americans have no kind of nuance, do they? No cadence. A flat nasal drone or else machine-gun bursts, rat-a-tat-tat. Minna does that. It's not that I feel I am a target particularly, but it's just the way she sort of sprays round the room, wildly at all and sundry. One can't duck.'

Cuckoo stacked the unopened letters in a neat pile with a listless hand. 'Poor Minna. I do love her, you know. Anyway, I expect now that you have shown Count

Grottorosso the way out, as it were, she'll be off pretty soon. I rather think it's St Tropez next stop. All right? We can't push her, can we?'

'Good gracious, no. Not push her.' He picked up a small silver object. 'I say, this is awfully jolly, I don't remember it, do I?'

'Had it ages, a sugar vase, Hester Bateman. I keep odd buttons in it.'

'Ah yes, so I see. And the children, young Marcus and Leni?'

'What about them?' She turned to face him directly.

'Well: almost three weeks now, you know? Don't you think, perhaps a gentle hint?'

'Hint?'

'Of course, one is extremely grateful for all he did that day . . . that goes without saying, naturally. But don't you think that, well . . .' He braced himself and thrust hands into his blazer pockets. Took a firm stand. 'Paid our dues handsomely, settled the debt?'

'I really don't consider their presence here as part of a debt, Archie. I love having them there, but if they are getting in your way, I mean fussing you . . .'

'Good gracious, no! Don't blame it on me, my dear . . . they don't fuss me. I keep out of the way. I was thinking, as a matter of fact, about you.'

'Well, I'm absolutely fine, they don't worry me a scrap. And in any case, they'll have to go back shortly; he's got a living to earn. I just want to be perfectly sure that he doesn't get mixed up with the Italians . . . that's all. It wouldn't be fair.'

'How could he get mixed up? With Grottorosso, you mean?' From somewhere at the back of his head he heard Minerva's voice. 'There's been some kind of an accident . . Wolf Hagel, the blond boy.'

He tapped his pocket and took out his cigarette case.

Don't smoke, she thought. If you smoke now I'll really

strike you.

'And if he did get mixed up, as you call it, with them, what on earth has it got to do with us? He's a grown man; he can make his own decisions, choose his own chums. Not our affair surely.' He opened the case.

'No, Archie! It's much too early for you. Not until after lunch, do remember?'

He shut the case with a snap, slid it into his pocket. 'Forgot. You see? Losing my head.'

'As soon as that wretched boat sails I just might make a tiny suggestion to them, unless they make one before . . . they aren't insensitive, you know. I begged them to stay for the picnic. It was in their honour after all, do remember.'

'Of course! I mean, my dear, I'm not suggesting you hurry them off, or anything, God forbid! Stay as long as you want them to, if they make you happy . . . but do remember that you are a frightfully kind creature, and people do rather take you for, well, for granted sometimes . . . become a little over-familiar. I notice the little things.'

Do you? Do you indeed? She got up from the desk, pushed her hair from her forehead. 'Well. Perhaps in a day or two. Just let it go for the moment. I must go and put my face on, I look like the raft of the Medusa.'

At the door he turned, one hand toying with a button on his blazer. 'A perfectly charming young couple, I do admit that. Charming. But total strangers really, aren't they? Where do they come from? What do they do? Who *are* they really when all is said and done, eh? What *are* they to one?' He cocked his head shyly to one side, smiled gently, opened the door and let himself out on to the gallery.

'My life line,' she said to the empty room.

The metal louvres were lowered over the portholes, permitting only a soft gloom to fill the cabin. It glittered here and there on the edge of a chromium table, the curve of a chair, a corner of the Hockney portrait, sparkled on the facets of a crystal jar of Agapanthus which partly obscured Grottorosso who lay sprawled, one hand across his forehead, one knee bent, on his surgical-looking bunk opposite her.

Minerva took out her cigarettes and lighter in the silence which had fallen on them for the last three minutes. Nando Belluno, sitting on her right, hands folded over his ample stomach, cleared his throat.

'Will it drive you crazy, Bert? If I smoke?'

He waved a hand in the gloom, shook his head.

'It's just that I can think better with a cigarette . . . when I am able to think at all. What I don't understand,' she said, fitting one into an ivory holder, 'is why the hell you were not wearing the masks? I mean, shouldn't you?'

He clenched a fist. 'We did, all morning. Until the last ten minutes when I told him that he would not be wearing his mask during "shooting", so I wanted to see his eyes, to see the excitement, the passion. So, we both took them off. Catastrophe!'

'But aren't there little rubber tips, button things, on the end of the foils?'

'There are. Always.'

'But not on yours?'

He covered his eyes with both hands, shook his head hopelessly; when he spoke his voice was muffled by his sleeves. 'I don't know what happened. I don't know. It was not fixed, perhaps? Suddenly this terrible cry. He fell to his knees, his hands to his face. The blood. Ayeee!'

'Bert, I'm so sorry, I'm so terribly sorry. It must have been ghastly for you.'

'Spettrale! Oh Dio! And we start shooting in eight weeks . . . what to do? What to do?'

'Can't we postpone, for a little? Go back a week or two, shoot some of the stuff which doesn't concern him . . . crowd work?'

Nando Belluno shook his head slowly, from side to side as rhythmically as a metronome. 'Impossible. Impossible. Schönbrunn is already booked, the Hofburg rooms, the gardens, it is the tourist season . . . we have to be there on the days agreed. Absolutely. It is very tight. No, impossible to postpone.'

Grottorosso swung his legs over the side of the bunk and sat, hands on knees, head bowed. He was still in his fencing outfit, white knee-breeches, stockings wrinkled, tunic open at the throat, a long smear of dark blood across his sleeve. 'I held him in my arms, you know. He wouldn't uncover his face. Whimpering like a dog. It was my fault; my fault, that I agree. I *had* tried to provoke him, to get one tiny spark of rage, of fury, of hate even . . . I would not have minded if he had shown me hate! But nothing. Fear . . . eyes like a frightened stag, red-rimmed with panic . . .' He looked suddenly directly across at Minerva. 'And *fatigue*! That stupid picnic yesterday. Too much wine, playing about with some German girl, coming home so late. Midnight when they arrived on the ship. Midnight! And he knew we had to start work again today. He had his "holiday" at your insistence, Minerva. You forced me to let him be "free", as you called it . . . get away on his own, get a "tan", you said, let him be "normal" just for a while. Well: I did. I decided that you were perhaps correct, that it would be the wisest thing to do, but what happens? My kindness brings weakness and utlimately disaster. He had lost his concentration, lost his drive, and now he has lost our film. Catastrophe!'

Minerva tapped ash from her cigarette. 'I'm really shattered, Bert, I really am. I feel just terrible.'

He crossed his legs, lay back against the crumpled pillows. 'You should perhaps feel happy, I think, now?'

'Happy!'

'Dandruff, you said! Tar! Dreary! Pretty façade but no one is at home.'

'I said all that? Me?'

'And more. Much more.'

'Oh my God! But I was just, well . . . just words, they weren't meant seriously, I was just camping about, you know me, Bert.'

'They were serious, I know. I always have listened to your advice, remember? With the Palazzo, with the contract for Bloomingdale's . . . with so many brilliant suggestions you made, all so useful, always so right. When you said, last week, that I should have left Hagel just where I found him, in the Four Seasons hotel, my heart froze . . . froze like ice. Ayeee! I said to myself, she is speaking the truth: I have been blinded by my obsession that he is right for the role . . . but she is a dispassionate woman, she has advised me all my life, she has never been wrong . . . and now! And now! My confidence that day was destroyed, completely destroyed.'

Minerva looked across at Belluno in despair. His dark glasses in the gloom two black pits where his eyes were: she found no consolation there, only a double reflection of her pale face. 'But I really wasn't giving you advice! I didn't mean you to be so literal. It was just . . . well, Bert, I was exhausted by the trip, remember? I was tired. They just came out: I agree that I suggested the kid should have a break . . .'

Grottorosso raised a steady hand. 'But that was the fatal error! I should not have taken that advice, we should have continued with the training. The boy is a peasant, you were right in that, but a peasant must be driven; you cannot let them relax into indifference, they despise kindness, and I was kind. That is my error; your error was not understanding the psychology of the peasant mind. I do.'

'So it was really all my fault in the end, is that it?'

He smiled pleasantly across the gloomy cabin. 'It was not a wise suggestion, that is all; I listened to your advice and acted upon it, that was my fault, I really must not blame you.'

He's really digging himself a hell of a pit, she thought, let me just hand him another spade.

'Are we insured against this kind of accident?' she asked.

Belluno shook his head. 'No, no . . . only during production. Not so long before. And in any case it hardly qualifies as an accident during *training*. We were all on a little holiday together . . . to get to know each other, really. No, we are not insured.'

'Dear God. And the boy. Hagel? What kind of a contract does he have? I can't remember.'

'It is with "'Orestes Productions'', just that. A personal contract between Umberto and himself. He was very happy to sign it: twenty-five thousand dollars! It was a fortune for a boy like that.'

'With an option?'

'With options for the next two pictures, if this one had worked.'

'At the same money? No. Increasing surely?'

Belluno pushed a finger under his glasses and wiped an eye. 'At the *same* figure, except higher expenses. Umberto has paid for everything so far, you know; his little flat in Rome, the car . . . even his clothes. All from Umberto. Very generous after only one modest appearance in one film.'

'And what happens to him now? Hagel? Could he sue?'

There was a silence which strangely seemed to emphasize the gentle motion of the ship beneath their feet. The jar of Agapanthus tilted slightly, a finger of thin light probed round the bulkhead springing across the Hockney sailor like a surgical torch.

Belluno found a bonbon in his pocket, started to unwrap it noisily. 'He is unable to fulfil the terms of his contract. He cannot possibly be fit and ready . . .'

'And trained properly,' Grottorosso's voice was smooth

249

as liquid fudge across the cabin, 'to perform his duties on the date stipulated.'

Minerva removed the butt from her holder, pressed it into an ashtray. 'And we can't postpone? Go back . . . no? Because of the Vienna dates . . .'

'And also because of Ludwig Bommel, who is to play Prokesch: his dates are very tight, he has a play in Berlin, we cannot juggle with the Schiller Theatre, you see.' He put the bonbon into his mouth, folded the wrapping paper into a neat ribbon, and slid it into his pocket.

'Another slight error, Minerva, if you will forgive me,' Grottorosso said. 'The Expert: Peverill. He has a very extraordinary mind. Not pleasant. He was enraged by my scenario: enraged. Especially about the character of Prokesch. He said that it was obscene, vulgar, salacious, inaccurate, cheap and God know what else! Dio Mio! I was aghast. I sat in horror at the things he had to say. This man, my dear Minerva, has a most unhealthy mind. Like a sewer. He quite lost control, you know. I could hardly believe that he was English at all! Such a stream of invective against me, against the film; I couldn't move. And I, a guest in his house! Unbelievable. If I had not had the strength of my convictions over these two days, I would have been completely undermined. Completely. Yesterday I had all that I could take. I had to leave very quickly, as soon as it was possible; I was as polite as could be . . . they are your friends, I know, but I simply had to leave. It was most embarrassing, eh Nando, embarrassing?'

Belluno shifted the bonbon across his mouth, wiped his lips, nodded silently.

'Another foul-up on my part,' said Minerva. 'Oh God. I really have bombed this time, haven't I? Not favourite aunt any longer, not "The Flavour of the Month" now, eh?'

Grottorosso stretched his legs before him, rubbed his thighs, saw the blood stain on his sleeve, touched it lightly.

'Poor Hagel. How sad. Well: everyone makes a mistake from time to time.'

Another spade coming up, she thought, open your hands, honey. 'And the hospital for Hagel? I mean the bills?'

'Belluno and I have agreed that we will pay for those, it is the least we can do. After all, he did fall on my foil, I did make him remove his mask. I must at least be honourable, that is right, isn't it?'

'Absolutely right. And plastic surgery?'

The silence again; the slow ship movement; Belluno crunched up his bonbon and swallowed it.

'Plastic surgery?' said Grottorosso, as if she had said they had discovered the body of Christ in a ditch. '*What* plastic surgery?'

'From eye to nose to chin . . . right?'

'I really didn't look . . . so much blood.'

'But it'll he a hell of a scar.'

'A duelling scar! The Prussians consider it a great mark of honour. It is very attractive to women, I am told.'

'But shouldn't we pay for that? He was, is, was, under contract to you. He's lost the job . . . we should help to patch him up, for later.'

'That is up to you. You are such a generous creature, but you must not take all the blame on your shoulders, Minerva. Tragically, I am afraid that you were wise all along: he just was not right. I was blinded to so many obvious faults; I should, as you said, have left him where he was, in Room Service. It was *my* error, my fault, I should have listened to your advice before we came to this tragic moment.'

Your pit, honey, has just become the Grand Canyon. Here's a stick of dynamite. Catch! 'I am crippled with guilt,' she said. 'Really. What was I thinking of, why couldn't I keep my big mouth shut, for God's sake? Poor Wolf, I wanted just to help you there, and the same with

251

Charles Peverill: I thought it would be so marvellous for you to meet each other. I really thought he could have given you help, encouragement. Oh God, Bert . . . how can you ever forgive me? I've screwed up your production, that's what it amounts to, doesn't it? It's a no-go? I'm destroyed . . . I shouldn't have meddled, I should have kept away from the movies . . . it's not my line, and you have managed brilliantly for years without me. Can you ever believe, from the bottom of my foolish heart, that I really only wanted to help, that's all, help you in your greatest work.'

Grottorosso rose splendidly from the bunk and came across the cabin to lay a hand on her bowed shoulder, for she had buried her face in her hands, apparently in despair. 'Minerva, my dear. Look at me. Please? Now. You see that I do not weep? On the contrary. I am alive with hope, my mind is filled with ideas and thoughts, I am filled with optimism, I breathe, the blood courses, all is not lost! Not at all. And you have only yourself to blame for that! Miss Drew of Warwick, my beloved governess of many years ago, always used to say, "Umberto! Remember! When one door closes another door opens!" and like all clichés, Minerva, it is true. Another door has opened. Opened right before my eyes at that terrible picnic yesterday. While I was suffering at the hands of the demented Peverill, when all the doors were starting to close about me and the darkness of despair and rejection seemed to smother me, what did I see? What did I see, Minerva? But there, standing only feet away from me, laughing in the sunlight, glowing, alive, vibrant, glorious, a God in blinding yellow! I saw l'Aiglon! The *real* one. A reincarnation. I almost paled with amazement, eh Belluno? You saw?'

'I saw,' said Belluno. 'You paled.'

'Perfection!'

'In yellow? Cuckoo Peverill's boy?'

'Exactly. His name is Pollock, he said. And here again,

252

this Peverill was so utterly obscene, so vile. "She picked him up on the beach, like a pebble," he said. Can you believe it? A husband about his own wife? It is not, of course, very surprising. What kind of marriage can it be? This brutal, ugly-minded creature, this English hysteric! Of course she would be attracted to a healthy, lusty young fellow like that. But to tell *me*, a complete stranger . . . I was shocked more than I can say to you. If he makes her happy, then one can only rejoice, for she appeared quite charming, still attractive; crushed of course, by this oaf in his British blazer.' He went across to one of the portholes. 'I took her a small gift, some corals I had. Nothing; very modest. She was so intensely grateful, I was moved.' He raised one of the steel louvres, sunlight flooded the cabin, dancing on the glass and chromium.

You just tripped. You're in the canyon now, honey . . . right down there, way down at the bottom.

'But we already had l'Aiglon at that moment, right? You couldn't use two, could you?'

'As a double. I thought of him as a double, of course. For the riding, the swimming, and all the things which poor Hagel was so maladroit in performing. I was flooded with relief.'

'But can he do all these things, this boy? Do you know?'

'He said all. Except this . . .' He touched the bloody sleeve of his fencing tunic.

'Oh that! But you could help him with *that*; couldn't you,' she said, taking another cigarette and fixing it into the holder with slightly shaking hands. A fact which surprised her.

'I could,' he said modestly. 'But you see, now, today, everything is suddenly quite altered; there has been, you could say, almost a Divine Intervention. Now I do not see him as merely a double, ah no.' He opened the second louvre, it slid upwards with a whisper. 'Now I can see him as the true l'Aiglon! No contact lenses, no hair to dye; he

253

has the language, the features, the grace, the maleness, the force. Of this I am certain.'

'Can he act?'

Grottorosso shrugged. 'I detest actors. You know I only ever use true and natural material, I do not like them contrived. I shall test him, of course. I am a Master Craftsman, you must remember, a potter in whose hands the clay is formed into something of breathless beauty and form. I do that. Give me pure clay; I will create.'

'And Wolf wasn't that?'

'No. Poor Hagel. He was flawed. I did not see. In spite of your warnings and your caution, I was headstrong and rejected your advice. I have been punished: so it should be. But now . . . but now, Minerva! My Miss Drew from Warwick . . . she was right: to my astonishment, to my relief, another door has opened!'

She lit her cigarette, closed the lighter deliberately with her thumb, inhaled, blew a steady stream of smoke towards the Agapanthus. 'And another one closed. Just this very minute,' she said.

Grottorosso was about to unbutton his tunic, his hands froze at the chest. 'Closed? What does that mean?'

'Didn't you hear it slam?'

'What door?'

'The Money Door. The vaults.'

He looked in puzzlement towards Belluno. 'What does it mean, the vaults?'

'In simple terms,' said Minerva, 'in baby talk that you will understand, I am pulling out. Removing the shekels.'

'Shekels?'

'You may care to recall that for the last half hour I have been very careful to use the word "we" in this conversation. I drop that as of now, it is You and I. Basta. You are on your own, Bert. I'm out.'

Grottorosso clasped his hands calmly before him. 'You are withdrawing your finance, is that it?'

254

'Exactly.'

'I am permitted to ask the reason?'

'You can ask, honey, you won't like it.'

'This is a sudden decision?'

'Came to me in a blinding flash of light, like Saul on the road to Damascus. The moment I heard Sylva Puglia say "accident" and "Wolf fencing", I knew. I don't want any part of your Divine Intervention.'

'It is incomprehensible.'

'Umberto! Sit down. Now just get your ass on a chair and keep it there, I've got a lot to say.'

He sat slowly on the edge of his bunk.

'You are a shitty bastard, Umberto. You know that? The shittiest of the shitty. I've come a hell of a long way with you over the years, through thick and through thin, and there have been a lot of very, very thin times which you may not care to recall. The ugly little business with the Issotto brothers? The Caracas fiasco? The little "misunderstanding" we all wriggled through in Beverly Hills? And many more. Right? But this time, this moment, is the thinnest and rottenest I have ever been through with you, or with anyone else, during a long, long life of Roller Coaster ups and downs. And I am revolted! You have cheated, lied and destroyed morally all along the way, but, as far as I know, you have never quite stooped to physical assault. I don't really count those wretched GI's you chiselled into the stock of your rifle. You were a kid then, there was a war, so okay . . . it wasn't very pretty but it was just about allowable, give and take the place and the time. But to go right out and carve up a kid quite deliberately just because you found someone else you thought was more suitable and liked a whole lot better is the nearest thing to premeditated murder for gain that I have ever come across in all my life.'

Grottorosso attempted to speak; she cut him short.

'I'm not through yet! Why didn't you just sack him?

Why not say, "You won't do, we've tried and you aren't coming up to scratch, I made a mistake, it is sad but I'll have to get someone else . . . you don't have the qualities we need, it's all my fault, here's a little bit of loot, you tried hard but it isn't enough for such a major role." Why didn't you say something like that? Too simple? Too straight? Instead you stage a filthy trick and run him through, deliberately! Why? What joy does that give you? What kind of warped bastard are you? What do you prove to yourself by doing that? A sign of strength? Of masculinity? You are as mad as a snake, Umberto, you always have been, ever since you were a kid. I suppose that deep down I always knew it, but I was the softie, Miss Kamm from Troy City, Wisconsin, starry-eyed in Rome, Italy. I thought you were pretty exciting. We made each other laugh, you got me through the first five years of a miserable marriage, and I stuck it and I watched you grow, I knew you weren't a saint, so that's okay . . . you were "going", you were "running" and I like that; you fought and I love a fighter; Christ knows I've had to fight every inch of my way through life for everything I ever got, and I got plenty . . . but I have never cheated, never loused anyone up for personal gain, never lied, and I've seen you do it, all along the track, and more, but I just shrugged it off and said to myself, "Well, from where I stand that's a goddamned genius, they act differently from other people, if they didn't they wouldn't be where they are." An easy way out for me, I could just avert my wooden head and look away with some kind of dignity; and so I did. Until today. You don't make me laugh any more, you make me sick to my stomach. I've got the message loud and clear and I don't care for it one little bit. You're a nut. And worse than that, a dangerous nut. There is something terribly, terribly wrong with you deep down inside, and it scares the pants off me: all this high talk about "common clay" and "potter's hands" and "flaws". Sweet God! You

256

have more flaws than a carpet has knots and one day, Umberto, someone is going to come along right out of the blue and take you to pieces; they'll slit you open from head to toe and spill you out like a sack of jelly beans and scatter you far and wide. I hope they do: I hope it hurts: I hope it happens very soon, and I hope that I am there to see it.'

Her cigarette had gone out. She removed it from the holder. Belluno sat in silence, head bowed, arms folded. Grottorosso smiled steadily into a vacuum of his own making.

Minerva reached for her bag, pushed lighter and cigarettes into it, closed the flap and buckled it firmly. 'The money for the hospital. For Hagel. I'll take care of that: and the contract, he'll get every single cent from me. As you said, Umberto, my fault, right? Brought matters to a head, no pun intended, and I don't want a disfigured German waiter hanging over my own for the remainder of my life.' She got up and brushed the seat of her trouser-suit. 'Nando? I'm off to Rome. Lawyers, right? But just so that you know, and so that we make it perfectly official and on the line, as of now I am out. You still have Gaumont and, I suppose, UA. But as for me . . . finito. I'm getting out while I still have a shred of conscience left to bind up my wounds in old age. It's not so far away.'

She slung the bag over her shoulder and went across to the door. Her hand on the steel knob, she turned back to the cabin-tableau. 'One last piece of advice, Umberto. Just watch how you tangle with the boy in the yellow pants. He may be armed.' She stepped lightly into the sun and closed the door.

Belluno raised his head: stared into space. 'You did not protest.'

Grottorosso started to unbutton his tunic. 'How do you protest to a menopause?' he said.

On the terrace of 'La Civette' looking across the little

fishing-port and the wide bay towards the distant Italian coast, Marcus and Leni sat over empty coffee cups in silence. At this time in the morning it was not very busy; a scatter of middle-aged tourists with maps or copies of *Nice Matin*, a young couple sitting holding hands, eating croissants, and at the table next to them an English couple with a small boy, murmuring diffidently to a waiter.

'Oona Coca Cola, doo coffee, compree? With lay.'

The waiter wiped the table with a flick of his cloth, hoisted his tray, and went to the bar.

The small boy stopped kicking the table leg. 'Was that French then? What he was speaking, Dad?'

'Gook,' said the man. 'Don't take no notice. Just gook.'

'Yours is coming along nicely,' said the woman, adjusting a shoulder strap of her square-necked floral print, and nodding.

'My what?'

'Your gook,' she laughed brightly, a wide display of pink and yellow plastic.

'All helps,' said the man, swinging a sandalled foot nervously. 'Otherwise they take you for a Brit. Rip you off.'

Leni looked away, picked up the card from 'Uncle' Desmond, turned it over. 'It looks so funny here. Doesn't it?'

'What does?'

'Marble Arch. Why did he put it in an envelope?'

'Safer, I suppose. When does he say he gets here, again?'

She turned it over. 'Twenty-fifth.'

'Three days.' He took the card, read it aloud. '. . . Arriving, with luck, on the twenty-fifth, Hotel Negresco, Nice. Couple of days in the sun, and then we can all drive back together: plenty of room in the brake. I'm bringing a surprise down with me . . .'

He dropped it on to the table, poured himself a cup of

coffee, reached for the sugar bowl. 'You want another cup? There is some.'

She shook her head.

He unwrapped the sugar lumps slowly. 'Well. A little cloud over the sun, isn't it? Still: It's been three weeks . . . long enough, I suppose, really . . .'

'Long enough. Yes. But what will you do about this cloud, here? Grottorosso?' She took up the crested white envelope and card, let them hang between her fingers.

'It's not a cloud, Leni. Good God! An invitation to a drink. Not even lunch. Why not?'

'But why?'

'I don't know why. If something has happened to your Kraut I suppose the film's in trouble, so he's passed up the lunch invitation and suggests a drink instead.'

'Don't keep on calling him *my* Kraut . . . it's not so. And what does it mean: ". . . has suffered a most grievous accident, which must alter all my plans, so I suggest that you come aboard for a drink tomorrow evening"? What is "grievous"?'

'Serious. Grave.'

'Oh, poor Wolf. What can have happened, how can we find out?'

'Minerva. She'll call the ship . . . soon as we get back.'

She put the card and envelope back on the table, placed her cup and saucer over them. 'I hate that man. I know this is a cloud. Wolf told me about him, everything. He is crazy, this man. And you said last night he was "that kind" . . . funny, kinky.'

'Right. I reckon he is.'

'Bent as a tin spoon, you said.'

'I did.'

'So why will you go to have drinks with him then?'

'Leni. Why not? I mean, what's wrong with a drink? Boat's full of people, I can always yell for help: hit him even. Why not go?'

She hunched her shoulders, wiped her chin with a finger. 'Well . . . last night you said, well . . . you said you wouldn't.'

'I never did.'

'Yes! Canteloupe Road, you said you wouldn't go to Vienna.'

'I'm NOT going to bloody Vienna, I'm going for a drink on his boat.'

'Why?'

He looked at her with exasperation. 'Because I've never been on a boat like that, because I want to have a look round, because I want to see how they all live on that thing, because I'm curious, that's why. Because I may never get the chance again, and because this is a holiday.'

'It doesn't say me. Only you.'

'Well, he never met you, did he? You were too shy, you said, scurried off with . . . with whatsisname. Perhaps he never even saw you but, he saw me, asked me about the doubling business, asked me to go and have lunch. That's all.' He finished his coffee, scooped the sugar out with a spoon. 'And anyway, if there has been some, whatever-accident to, what's his name?, Wolf, I reckon everything's off and he's just being polite; a drink not a meal, that's all.'

'He is an awful, awful man this. He did something very terrible to Wolf. He showed me, on his back.'

'What did he do? Bite him?'

'Oh, it's not so funny! You can laugh if you like. Hit him, with a whip thing, six, seven times, big marks. I saw.'

'On his bum? What was Wolf up to with you with his trousers down, I'd like to know?'

'Oh stupid! So silly . . . you just make a joke. It was terrible, he lost his temper.'

'Well, it wouldn't take me long to lose my temper with that bloke. Clobber him one.'

'Just because he is nice, because he is gentle and kind.'

'Minny-ninny.'

'He's not! True and good . . .'

'Jesus saves! A minny-ninny.'

'You're jealous. Stupid.'

'Jealous! You must be joking. Jealous of him? Wandering about behind you all day like something from the Battersea Dogs' Home. Jealous!'

'So jealous, that's what.'

'Bleating away together in German. "Ach soing", "Bitte schoening". Make you sick.'

'And you! With that stupid girl. Smiling, wobbling everywhere; all during dinner she was touching you, blowing kisses. Stupid, silly thing. Common.'

'Now who's jealous!'

'And so fat. Disgusting. Big fat bosoms like bags full of water.'

'Super tits, terrific.'

'Maybe you have some kind of complex . . . for a Mamma, is that it? You like to cuddle those big things, like a little boy? She is like a cow, this person, with that thing the milk comes out of. Disgusting.'

'Jealous!'

'Hummmm. Fantastic . . .' She pressed her finger on a flake of croissant, put it in her mouth.

From the next table the English woman said, 'Mrs Cushing's are just the same. Big red flowers on blue. Cheery. In her lounge.'

'And you smell of her,' said Leni. 'All over. Everywhere. I knew in bed, last night.'

'What did you know, pray?'

'Her scent. Everywhere, sicky. And marks . . .'

He replaced his spoon slowly in the saucer, folded his arms on the table. 'What marks?'

She didn't answer, leant back in her chair looking towards Italy, tilting her head high, slightly to one side, a look of complete indifference.

261

'Come on now. You started this. What marks? Leni? Where?'

She stared ahead.

'Where?'

'On your top part. On this place.' She indicated her right shoulder with a nod of her head.

'Oh that. We were swimming, that's all.'

'On your neck, your chin.'

'Yes. Swimming. Larking about. Water polo, with the big ball.'

'I know. And on your thighs.' She took her eyes from the Italian coast, looked towards the big hotel on the harbour, shading her brow. 'You play water polo with your teeth? Fantastic.'

'You've gone loopy. And when did you see all these marks, may I ask. X-ray eyes?'

'No. Quite all right eyes, thank you. I saw last night. And on your mouth, very small then.' Finding nothing of interest, apparently, at the hotel, she lowered her hand. 'This morning they show more. Quite big. And after dinner when she said, oh, I can't remember, something stupid about "Women's Liberation", and then she pinched you and you went red in the face.'

'Complete balls.'

'You did. We all saw. Everyone saw. Cuckoo too . . . and we laughed of course, so amusing, but I know, you see.'

He picked up the postcard of Marble Arch, tapped it against his lips. 'And what do you know, Miss Clever Dick?'

'That you are hiding your bites with "Uncle" Desmond's postcard. That's what I know.'

'That all? What else do you know then?'

She opened her green eyes wide and looked back across to Italy.

'Come on, Leni. Out with it. Say. What?'

'Nothing.'

'You're making a hell of a song and dance about nothing.'

'I'm not . . . I don't care.'

'Well. That's all right then, isn't it?'

'Perfectly.'

'I mean, if you don't care, it doesn't matter, does it?'

'No. It doesn't matter.'

'So it's quite all right?'

'Quite all right. Thank you.'

'Well, if it's quite all right it won't matter if I tell you, will it?'

'No. Not at all.'

'So shall I?'

'I don't care.' She shrugged, still watching the coast of Italy as if she was expecting a friend.

'Because I did then.'

She was perfectly still.

At the table beside them the English woman cried out in sudden anger, 'Roger! Take your finger out of your nose! You'll poke your eye out!'

Marcus tapped his lips gently with the card. 'Hear what I said, Leni?'

She nodded. 'Yes. Heard.'

'And you don't care.'

Her eyes were suddenly over-bright. 'Why should I?'

He folded the card in two, put it in his shirt pocket. 'I'm very sorry.'

She swallowed, tried to speak, failed, closed her mouth.

'You forced me,' he said.

She cleared her throat, remained looking ahead. Careful! Careful! You're going too far. Pull back. 'Forced? Because of Wolf, is it? Jealous?'

'Christ no! No. Forced me to tell you!'

'I don't care. It doesn't matter.'

'Well it does matter. But I couldn't help it. Honestly.'

263

'Help it?'

'No . . . I was pretty pissed, you know. All day on that white wine.'

'I know. Frau Baedeker: and something about not doing anything we couldn't do on a bicycle. Stupid.'

'I don't remember.'

'But then you did.'

'Did what?'

'Do something not on a bicycle.'

'I couldn't help it. She grabbed me. I really didn't want to.'

She looked at him for the first time directly. 'If you didn't want to, you could have said "no".'

'Said "no"! Christ, she wasn't suggesting another cup of tea! She had grabbed me. Grabbed me *there* . . . you know.'

'You could have said "no" anyway, gone away.'

'With her on top of me?'

'On top of you?'

'Squeezing me like a ruddy vice . . .'

'There?'

Yes, there. And you know me . . . what Nig and Gus Bender call me? The Studio joke?'

'Ever Ready.'

'Right. And so she just . . . well, she just jumped me. I couldn't help it, Leni. I couldn't very well shout for help, now could I?'

'Something . . .'

'I'm sorry. Honestly. But I've told you.'

She took a Gauloise from the Army Surplus, lit it with a shaking hand. 'I knew everything would go wrong . . . that boat. I hate it. The *Papageno*. It's a German name. I knew it would be unlucky. This fat woman, Grottorosso, and now this thing with Wolf. I knew it would be bad if the boat came, I told you. When the real things come in it will change everything. And it has.'

'It hasn't! That's all nonsense . . . it's fantasy land, Leni! Real and unreal, you get it all muddled, I don't know where you are. I don't think you do.'

'Yes I do. Sitting here with you, and this thing about that woman . . . it has all changed, we are different, everything is spoiled.'

He was silent for a moment, pushing his cup in circles on the table. 'Has it?' he said suddenly. 'Everything spoiled?'

She turned her head away, looked across the harbour. Elisabeth at the door with the sweet peas. 'The difficult thing of course is to remain believing in your fantasies . . .' Pull back, pull back, don't lose him, above all else don't lose him.

'Spoiled everything? Really, tell me?'

She shook her head. 'You didn't want her? It is true? Honestly true?'

'No. I didn't want her. I told you. Never. And I'm sorry, I'm ashamed, I couldn't help it, it happened, I don't like myself . . . but I just couldn't help myself. Look, Leni: I'm gravelling, grovelling . . . I can't get much lower than this. It was a five minute bang with a tart, that's all. Nothing more, it didn't mean anything, I haven't changed, got corrupted, any of that stuff. Remember what I said? I am just having a look round someone else's garden. They said, "Come on in" and I did . . . maybe I'll never have the chance again, so I'm taking it now. I know it's got to end; it is, anyway, in a few days' time. Almost over. And we'll go away together: if that's all right with you. Is it? Be as we were before? Can we?'

She twisted the cigarette in stubby fingers, head down. 'It's all right with me. If you want.' Her voice was so low it could have been slipped under a door.

'Thank you,' he said. 'I'm really sorry. I love you, you know.'

'I know. But that boat. You won't go now, will you?'

He looked at her steadily, touched her arm, she looked

265

up at him, eyes clear. 'Yes, I will go. I will, Leni. I want to go. I want to have a look. Why not? It's huge, bigger than the Greek's; there's a gymnasium, staterooms, terrific engines, a cinema . . . I want to look. He's asked me for a drink, that's all.'

'And she will be there, the woman?'

'If she is I'll be very polite, right? Cuckoo and Archie Charlie manners, that's all.'

'And if he says again about Vienna?'

'He won't. Bet you. If something has happened to your chum Wolf it can't be much good for the movie, can it? Grievous doesn't mean a cut while you're shaving, a boil, a sprained wrist . . . does it? They've probably dumped it or something . . . anyway I wouldn't; not my scene.'

'And you won't go away?'

'No. Unless you want me to . . . I mean, yesterday?'

'No. I don't want you to go away. Please.'

'Okay. We'd better be getting back.'

She collected the Army Surplus, the card and envelopes. 'You still smell of her, you know this? Even from here.'

'Oh Lor' . . .'

'It's an awful scent. Common.'

'I'll have another bath; if you won't mind.'

'No. As many as you want. Fifteen pence at Canteloupe Road, remember.' It was a half laugh.

'And bring your own plug. I know.'

'Just so that you remember.' She put the cards in her bag, closed it.

He signalled for the waiter and paid the bill; she sat looking across the gently rocking masts of yachts and dinghies in the port; beside them the English family were collecting cameras, bags, a white "woollie": the boy had a shrimping net.

'Too idiotic, wasn't it?' she had said. 'To go shrimping. Without a net?'

Marcus suddenly took Leni's hand in both his. 'I'm

266

really, truly, sorry. I love you. I do love you. There's no one else. Ever.'

She slung the Army Surplus over her shoulder, smiled, not trusting herself to speak. 'Fantastic,' she said. Coughed gently. 'We must go. Minerva maybe will be awake now.'

He followed her through the tables, colliding with the English family who were on their way out.

'. . . But you're ever so patriotic at home,' said the woman.

'Well I am! Course I am.' The man hitched khaki shorts over his paunch. 'I just don't like being taken for a Brit. Get ripped off. They've forgotten all about Dunkirk, of course.'

Leni had reached the main street as he caught her up.

Marcus stood uncertainly at the drawing-room windows looking across the terrace. Cane chairs, low tables, ferns, white hydrangeas banked at the top of the steps leading down to the lawn: at the far end, by the frog fountain, Minerva in a long Planters' Chair, feet crossed, glasses on, tugging wool through a small canvas square. She saw him, looked over her glasses, raised a hand.

'Hi! I'm here. Grandma Moses with her tapestry. Come on over, it's cooler by the water.'

He sat beside her, kicked off his espadrilles. 'Quite a day,' he said.

Minerva pulled a long thread towards her. 'Quite a day. Did you see him?'

'No. I didn't go up. Leni did. Took him some peaches.'

'Peaches! He's feeding through a tube.'

'Yes. Well. She wasn't quite prepared for that . . . nor was I.'

'He looks a mess, right?'

'She said so. "Invisible Man". All bandages.'

'Big wound.' She lifted the canvas square. 'Pretty? Don't you think?'

'Very. What is it?'

'It's to cover a brick.'

'A brick?'

'For a door-stop. Don't you think that is stunningly original? It's beginners' stuff; if I get good at it and don't throw the whole thing into the garbage tomorrow, I might just progress to a chair-back, or a cushion. It soothes me, and I need soothing right now. Where's Leni?'

'In our room. Lying down for a bit. It shook her up, seeing him.'

'I can imagine. Shook me up too. I had the morning there arranging how to get him back to Rome. The day after tomorrow we go. He'll be fine. In time. One of the few advantages of being who I am, Marcus, is that I can get people running and things get done. Money, honey, really does speak. Especially in Italy. In Italy it not only speaks, it hollers.'

Marcus leant back in the chair, hands behind his head. 'I can't think how it could happen. A swipe like that . . .'

'Deliberate.'

He looked at her in astonishment: she was threading a needle. 'Deliberate? Wolf?'

'I don't mean Wolf, I mean Umberto Orestes Grottorosso. Deliberate.'

'Cut him?'

'Cut him.'

'But Christ Almighty! He's his Star, isn't he? Why would he do that?'

Minerva looked up over her glasses, pulled the wool tightly through the needle. 'You are in the hot seat, honey. Didn't you know? Don't you love it?'

'Me?'

'You. He asked you to double for him, right? Yesterday? Told Scarlatti in the funny hat to get your measurements,

268

right? That was just the easing in. He knew what he wanted. Soon as he saw you. The l'Aiglon look, okay? Perfect reproduction, you instead of Wolf. Your eyes, my dear, look like chapel hat pegs, but I know just what I'm talking about. He'd made a mistake with Wolf Hagel, a bad choice; he knew it, and tried to fight it. Wanted him out. But no alternative eight weeks before the shooting starts; until you appeared.' She stuck the needle into the canvas with a hard jab. 'He said you were the Divine Intervention. Got it? And Wolf got it. Carved up like a Thanksgiving turkey. An accident arranged. No witness, no real proof . . . calamity, clumsy Wolf. Wolf out.'

Marcus was sitting slumped in his chair, arms at his sides. 'I don't believe it.'

'Of course you don't. Who would? But you wait and see. I'm just telling you this cosy tale because you're the one who's most involved. I'm not yakking away to all and sundry. Cuckoo. Charles. Don't tell Leni, either; no need. They'd probably say I was out of my mind anyway: it's not the sort of thing you can believe. But I know my Grottorosso. I've known him for a long, long time: he's the kind of person people call a "caricature", only because the reasonable, average, normal mind couldn't possibly comprehend the kind of creature he is. Larger than life, they say, and so he is. Large as death too. My husband once told me that when he was a kid, about six or seven, they found him stuffing petrol-soaked pellets down the throats of baby birds and setting them alight with matches: to watch them explode. Now that's a happy little pastime, don't you think? Childish curiosity? Or a wild imagination? I mean, let's face it, who could invent that kind of thing?'

'God Almighty!' said Marcus.

'He has absolutely nothing whatsoever to do with Grottorosso, honey. He's the one thing he did not create. I can see from the expression on your youthful face that you don't believe me. If you don't close your mouth you'll trap a bat.'

'No. It's not that . . . I mean. Well.'

'Yes. Well. Of course I may be totally and completely out of my mind. I have no proof, Marcus. I can't be certain . . . I have just put two and twenty together and come up with Bingo! *I* know I'm right, but what the hell. Put it to the test yourself: my theory. You say that he's invited you for drinks tomorrow, right?'

'To look over the ship.'

'Well, if that's what you do, that's great. If that's all. On the other hand,' she bit off the thread, tucked it into the back of the canvas, 'if he suggests that you might care to take over the role . . . that you'd be so great for it . . .'

'Take over the role!'

'Sure. No doubling. You're to be It. Him. L'Aiglon in person. Bet your ass.'

'But I can't act.'

'He has a nifty little speech about "clay", "master craftsmen" and "potters". He'll do it for you, have no fear. Hates actors . . . he has to be a creator. Not acting won't phase him, he'll love it. Just see. Don't take my word, I *could* be biased. Give it a whirl, why not? And what you do is up to you. Great opportunity, if you want one. But just remember one important thing, you'll never be quite the same again. You'll change out of all recognition. Look what he's done for Wolf Hagel, if you follow? Grottorosso is the famous apple in that cliché old barrel, know what I mean? The Spoiler.' She lifted the canvas and held it at arm's length. 'I'm soothed enough for this afternoon.' She rolled it into a cylinder, stuffed it into a bag of coloured wools, took off her glasses. 'I'm going to take a look at our hostess; she's somewhere down at the point there, bickering about with Tonnino. I wish she wouldn't, she ought to have stayed in her room . . . she's awfully tottery today, she could take a fall . . .'

270

'Yesterday was a hell of a day.'

'Right. She does too much.' She got up, put the bag on the table with her glasses. 'I reckon that's what happened the other day at the beach: when you found her.'

'I reckon.'

'She fell, right?'

'Right.'

She went over to the steps, paused for a moment, picked a head of honeysuckle. 'Bruna says there was mud . . . and little stones in her jacket pockets; they are quite out of shape. Can't even iron them flat. Must have been a hell of a fall?'

'It was, yes.'

She turned and looked at him for a second, twisting the flower in her hands, then she smiled suddenly a warm, generous gesture.

'That's my boy,' she said softly, and went away down the steps.

Chapter Nine

Leni stood uncertainly in the wide stone arch of the front door: Hungarian blouse, cut-off jeans, hands in pockets, bare feet curling over the edge of the marble steps, watching the dark Mercedes sweep up the curve of the drive taking Marcus to his rendezvous on the *Papageno*.

She watched all the way, until it was suddenly almost lost to view, became a vague flickering through the heavy leaves of the fig trees; and then had gone.

And silence.

Well: an almost silence. The Triton spouted water into the fish-pool at his tail, a warm eddy of wind rustled through the courtyard, jostled the spiky leaves of the oleander, rippled along the broad banners of the banana, spiralled a Catherine-wheel of dust and dead petals into a corner of the arches, and then faded away. But these were whispering sounds and they only served to emphasize her unease and disquiet; the great silence pressed all about her like fluid.

She was alone.

It was the first time, apart from the trip to Lübeck, that she had been without him and on this occasion he had chosen to leave her, quite willingly, not she him. He had made no suggestion that she should join him on the trip to the ship, even though she was not invited in the note from Grottorosso: but he could have taken her, surely? If he'd wanted to. Or suggested that she go with him? It seemed that it had not occurred to him at all.

Of course he had been extremely preoccupied dressing himself: and had paid scant attention to her veiled hints, only saying that he wouldn't be long, the house was jammed with people, so how could she possibly be lonely? So she had nodded glumly, half agreeing, and sat in silence watching him prepare. Polishing up the black boots unworn since London, combing and arranging his hair with the diligence of a girl preparing for a dance, easing himself into his best white jeans, complaining mildly that he had put on weight, tucking shirt-tails carefully round his backside with the comb so that there were no 'unsightly ridges to spoil the line'. Amusing: if she hadn't felt so wretched.

Eventually he gave himself one final look in the long bathroom mirrors, turned this way and that, declared himself satisfied, gave her a fairly absent-minded kiss, hurried down the staircase to the waiting car: long, low, sleek, with black glass in the rear windows so that when he slid into his seat she could no longer see him. Only the vague shadow of an arm waved in a half salute as they went silently up the drive to the road.

Leaving her where she presently was: hands in pockets, toes curling on the step, alone. She shrugged, crossed the sharp gravel on her heels to the fish-pond, sat heavily on the raised stone rim, wrapped her arms around her knees.

We've changed, she thought, quite changed. In a matter of only about three weeks. How strange it is. It has been so gentle that it has been almost unnoticeable: nothing terrifying; no sudden wrenches, no blinding flash and hey presto! No sudden trick to unnerve me. Worse than that really; a dawning awareness which has gradually nudged me into acceptance. We have changed and that is that. A subtle weaving of brilliant threads through the safe, comfortable, tweedy fabric of the life which they had invented for themselves from the moment that they had met in Gus Bender's Studio. It had altered the texture for good.

In a dreadful way, she thought, it was really all her fault. She should never have gone to Lübeck in the first place;

273

that's where the changing had started. Should have resisted all family blandishments, all emotion, all loyalty to Horst, and not gone, 'Never Go Back', they say. She had. Fatal error. Instead she should have joined Marcus on the holiday: tent, bedrolls, frying-pan, discomforts included. They could have hitched, drifted happily about wherever they wished, been together, stayed safety within the confines of their own planned lives, the boundaries which they knew. Instead she had gone her way, duty bound, and he had come here and wandered, as he had put it, 'into someone's garden' and been bidden to stay. And that had made the second vital moment in the change.

For her it had not been the cultural and emotional shock that it had for Marcus. She was accustomed, with one or two minor and some major differences, to the kind of life into which they had moved. Her own, after all, had not been so very different, before Leni Minx, and it had not been difficult to adjust. Too easy in fact. There had been times indeed when she had been uncomfortably aware that she had given herself away as Luise: but each time she suspected an error of that sort she made a greater one as Leni to erase it. And had survived, as far as she knew, intact. Even though quite often the strain was acute.

However, things had been different for Marcus. He had fitted into this new life, once so alien to him, as easily as a finger into a thimble; accepted the sudden flow of affluence with alacrity, eagerness even, as if he was making up for the drab years of deprivation, disillusion and what he called 'tinned spaghetti and rising damp in Dorking'. He had no compunctions about making errors, as she had, for he had nothing to hide, and he was constantly asking that his faults in such minor things as table manners, social behaviour, or even the complexities of accurate speech, should be corrected. Not from her; for she was Leni who was not supposed to know, but from Cuckoo who did; and was a willing teacher.

He clearly delighted in 'learning' and not just the social trivia of life but about books, music, painting and everything which filled the house and the garden into which he had 'wandered'. The thing which worried Leni the most was the inescapable fact that he seemed to be busy trying to assume the kind of background which she had been at great pains to reject for herself.

At night he generously shared with her whatever nuggets of wisdom and learning he had gleaned during the day: and she would appear to be dutifully grateful, careful not to correct him if he were wrong, or show him that most of the time she knew these things already. Most of the time. Not all. For they were dealing with very different cultures. English and German. A chasm lay between them. So for much of the time she was able to listen with suitable awe to things which were, indeed, absolutely new to her; for the rest she kept her tongue still and just nodded her head. All this 'learning', however, didn't prevent him from taking the greatest pleasures in the physical, sensual things of this existence, like long, lazy mornings on the terrace of 'La Civette', the pool in the afternoons, the simple elegance of the meals which Bruna prepared, the wines they drank, the picnics which she also packed for them to take up into the hills or along the coast when the splendours of the villa grew overwhelming; for even he discovered that too much could be, too much. And then there were the baths. She would always, and she couldn't think why, equate three baths a day, or anyway, two, with the ultimate in luxury and decadence. Even at Schloss Lamsfeld once a day was considered normal, if extravagant, unless one had been riding or working the fields, and she dated the corrupting, for she could consider no other word, of Marcus from the moment that he discovered unlimited hot water, bowls of wrapped soaps, and piles of crisp, fresh towels.

Thus the leisure and luxury of their days bewitched him utterly, and so too did the pleasures of the evenings:

especially the concerts, and after dinner the word games, which they sometimes played, in the wavering glow of candles on the terrace; cognac, coffee, scattered dictionaries, Cuckoo laughing at some absurdity. Archie Charlie searching for a word in the rustling pages, Marcus smug with triumph when he won; playing games which she could not properly join because her English was strictly limited to the words which she needed to express herself. Or not herself as it happened; but Leni Minx. The concerts, on the other hand, didn't worry her at all. They were very similar to the ones at Lamsfeld. One evening perhaps Schubert, on another Dvorák, at another a 'Cuckoo Mixture', as she called it herself, which ranged cheerfully from Schwarzkopf and Placido Domingo to Sophie Tucker or Elton John. She had nothing to do but listen.

However, the word games were different. These too they had played at Lamsfeld, but within the terms of mainly German reference, names with which she could be familiar. Here the scope was wider, and she was paralysed with ignorance. Who was Chaucer, Amy Johnson, Bottom, Barbara Castle or Benny Goodman? She was mostly lost: and Marcus was not always brilliant himself, but when he didn't know he sought the answers, and then the 'discussions' with Archie Charlie commenced on which he feasted like a glutton at a candystall.

And that was the rub. The sudden glorious discovery of conversation with two worldly people, or three when Minerva chose to play, moved him further away than ever: for although she tried hard, she found it impossible to join him in his quest for knowledge, for her own, even in German, was fairly limited and confined essentially to her own boundaries. He wanted to explore wider fields. She was terrified that she was becoming a bore.

As Leni Minx in Canteloupe Road she was secure: she knew exactly who she was, and the role which she had invented for herself was simple, effective, and had delighted him. He had said, not very long ago, that he wanted no changes in her, that he loved her as she was, and had no desire to wake up one morning and 'find that she had changed'. Well, it was getting harder and harder, under these conditions, to stay as Leni Minx and far too easy to drift back to her original patterns of behaviour as Luise; it seemed that she was doing it more and more often. All day at the picnic, for example, she had been Luise, and apart from a few limited moments when she had remembered her rôle, she had not played Leni at all. And yesterday at 'La Civette' she had got into a fearful muddle, behaving in a perfectly ridiculous manner. She had found it impossible to suppress the emotions of Luise.

She had not behaved as Leni at all; instead she had played a desperate game of Leni/Luise and had so confused herself that she had ended up in tears of self-pity and provoked a juvenile argument on jealousy which shamed her.

The whole tedious little moment at 'La Civette' had seriously undermined her belief in who she was supposed to be, and the strain of mixing the two together was beginning to tell. She had behaved in a thoroughly bourgeois manner: neither as Leni, who would have dealt with the whole situation in a totally different way, nor as Luise, who would at least have had more dignity about it all. And in any case, whatever her behaviour, it had not prevented him from going off to the ship. And that was another source of concern. Why go? The film was sure to be cancelled after Wolf's dreadful accident, and in any case Marcus had insisted that he would not accept such a job even if offered. So why? Curiosity? Wilfulness? Independence? Worst of all – the Film Star?

Oh Wolf! Poor Wolf lying there in his cool, antiseptic, shadowed little room. So strangely tall in the narrow bed, bandaged, mute save for grunts and sighs, brown eyes dulled with pain and fatigue, pressing her hand from time to time in gratitude for her presence. A comfort. But what had happened? An accident? When she had asked him in a whisper, he had pressed her hands twice, strongly, as if in assent. Yes: an accident.

She got up from the pool, arms wrapped around her shoulders as if to hold herself together, for she really felt that she was slowly falling to pieces, and the discovery, just a short time ago, of her passport, lying under the little false canvas bottom of the Army Surplus, had brought all these terrors and doubts to a positive head.

Marcus, busy with his toilet, had asked for a loan of her hair lacquer, and she had rummaged about in the Army Surplus to find it, and found the passport as well. The damning evidence, which she had kept securely away from him, of her identity as Luise.

'Uncle' Desmond was arriving in a day or two: they would all drive home together. What then would happen to the passport? It would have to be shown at Immigration, naturally. And if Marcus saw it, as he was almost certain to do, how then to explain that she was really someone quite else? The slim little book in the Army Surplus posed as great a threat to her happiness as anything which had happened so far . . . even the trip now to the *Papageno* about which she felt such unease.

It was all too difficult, she thought, it is getting beyond me, I can't reason or manage it any more. Staring wretchedly at the Triton spouting water, she felt as lost and bewildered as she had at the Schwarzbrücke looking up the hill to the petrified snake of the Wall writhing through the ruined Lamsfeld orchards.

The unreal had come face to face with the real.

Thus it seemed to her, standing forlorn by the pool, that the demons were upon her, the light in the courtyard had dimmed, the breeze had cooled.

Head bent, eyes rimmed with thin tears of helplessness,

arms tightly about her body, she trod across the gravel to the house, into the cool hall, the silent drawing-room, the shaded terrace. All empty. Silent, save for the soft bubbling of the frog-fountain. Down the steps on to the lawn, a scent of warm pines, honeysuckle; at the far end, a smudge of blue. Cuckoo's shirt . . . and Cuckoo crossing the grass towards a high hedge. Disappearing.

She stood for a moment, hands to face, wiped her eyes, found herself running on urgent feet down the springy turf to seek comfort.

Beyond the hedge, the vegetable gardens, and among the beans, peas and lettuce, the flowering heads of onion like lavender gong-hammers, Cuckoo on a milking stool, weeding. A wide straw hat, blue shirt, barefoot. She looked across the gong-hammers, waved her handfork.

'I was feeling rather fidgety: weeding helps me calm down. I don't know why. I mean why I was fidgety. That boy gone then? Marcus? Off to that foul ship?'

'Yes: he's gone, just now.'

'Stubborn youth. I can't imagine why. Have you got hay fever?'

'No. I just sneezed.'

'Be an angel and bring that old box over, will you. Just beside you, mind the prickles; you haven't any shoes on.'

'I like bare feet, don't you?'

'Always wear them. Love the feeling of hot dust between my toes, do you know? Very earthy, of the earth, peasanty-real. Very real.'

'Real. Yes. Could I help you?'

'Well, if you want to. Can you tell a weed from a lettuce?'

'I think so.'

'Uncertain. Well: look, this here, this red thing, Treviso. All the rest are weeds. Guard the red, rip up the rest. This is the stuff to look for, see?' She held up a bunch of clover-like leaves. 'The dreaded oxalis. Never had it here before I went and bought four bales of Russian peat and now we can't get rid of it. Tonnino has never forgiven me. Frightful stuff, spreads everywhere, impossible to eliminate, very subversive; like their Faith.' She threw a handful into the box. 'Minerva back from the hospital?'

'No. I didn't see.'

'Off tomorrow, with that unhappy boy. Much to Archie's relief. What a dreadful business it all is: such a "convenient" kind of accident, I feel. Do you know what I mean? No. Well, never mind. Just me. I'm so suspicious. That odious man has caused such unhappiness in so short a time. Archie is quite ill with fury and frustration, and then this accident happening, and Minerva suddenly so tight-lipped and unlike herself. I do wish he hadn't gone.'

'Marcus? I think that maybe he wants to see that Film Star woman.'

Cuckoo looked up in surprise. 'Marcus? That silly flirty creature? Not his type at all, surely?'

'Oh, I think so. I think very much his type. For example: at the swimming-pool.'

'Swimming-pool? What?'

'The picnic time.'

'I don't understand you, dearest girl.'

'At the picnic they were swimming, and I think she . . . what is the word?'

'I can't possibly imagine.'

'When it is *more* than just flirty . . . when it is *much* more . . .'

'You can't mean seduce, can you?' said Cuckoo vaguely.

'Seduce. Yes. She did that to him.'

Cuckoo looked at her in astonishment. 'Seduce Marcus? At the pool; the picnic? But she couldn't *possibly*. They didn't have time!'

'They did. He said to me. I knew. "A quick bang with a tart," he said.'

'Leni! Oh my dear, the things that happened at that picnic! One reels! How dreadfully tiresome for you. Were you absolutely furious with him? I do hope that you gave him hell.'

'Oh yes. I was furious.'

'Honestly! Faithless brute! I hope he was deeply ashamed?'

'Why? I am not his, you see? He does not belong to me. We are just together, we have made no vows. He is quite free.'

'They always are, men. Free. Vows or not, my dear. Oh! Vows don't matter; not in marriage. Like pie crust, you know; made to be broken.'

'And she came on that boat, you see. It brought all trouble: we were happy until it came, everything was so lovely, unreal, a dream; and then it came and it was the real world chasing our happiness away.'

'I really don't quite follow what you mean by "real" world and "unreal". There is no difference is there? Life *is* real. All of it. Death is real too, they are inseparable from each other. I think that perhaps what you mean is that we invent parts of it for ourselves, and those pieces, the invented ones, are the only parts which make life bearable; they have a scheme, a plan, because *we* make them. Real life is so hideously clumsy, unplanned, callous and brutal: is that what you mean, do you think? We have to make the invented parts to get through the real.' She grubbed up a length of creeping buttercup, stuffed it into the box. 'That's really why I rather hate this Uncle Desmond person who is coming to take you both away from me. Do you follow. Like the ship to you, he is the intruding part of real life interrupting my "invented" part. When you go away I shall have to return: and I shan't very much care for that. While you have been here I have suspended belief, as it were. Just for the time I banished all unpleasing, ugly, distressing things as far as I possibly could, so that we should have a simply lovely "invented" enchanted time, and now of course I can see it coming to an end, and I am resentful, silly, selfish, and sad. Weary too. But that is *my* invented life, Leni! Not yours. You are far too young yet to have to invent anything to make your life bearable. Look, my dear, how much you have!'

'You are so certain,' said Leni.

'Not about everything. Just that.'

'Certain and sure. Marcus said that you and Sir Charles know just who you are, that you always have done and always will; that there are no doubts.'

'Does he? Does he indeed?' said Cuckoo. 'How wondrously simple. The older we get the less certain we become; that's my experience. Hence the need to "invent", you see. To smother doubt. But at your age one is so much more confident about whom one is and where one is going and why; you haven't had the time yet, my dear, to become disillusioned. You will see. Doubts come later.'

Leni stuck her fork into the dry earth, pushed hair from her forehead. 'Mine have come already,' she said.

'Nonsense, foolish child!' Cuckoo wrenched about among the weeds, pulling at buttercup and groundsel. 'Nonsense! You just feel abandoned because that faithless betrayer has gone off to see the Film Star; which I very, very much doubt. He probably feels rather uncomfortable now it's all over . . . they usually do. Guilt. No. I think he's gone to see how the vulgar-rich live. Curious. I'd be curious myself: if I didn't already know. That's all. I think that you know, very precisely, exactly who you are.'

'Yes,' said Leni staring through the pea-sticks. 'I do.'

'Well. There you are then. We've got that on board.'

Leni pressed her hands to her eyes, when she spoke her voice was forced down through her nose.

'What dear?' said Cuckoo. 'Lovey, it *must* be hay fever.'

'I'm not who you think.'

'Not?' said Cuckoo, tugging at a root.

'No.'

'Who then? I'm dreadfully bad at guessing-games. You know I never win.'

'My name is Luise von Lamsfeld.'

It sailed into the air like a ball thrown for a dog, a kite cut loose to the breeze, a stone dropped down a well. Gone. Irretrievable.

Cuckoo looked up slowly. Pushed back the brim of her hat. 'Do I follow?'

'I don't know. But I am Luise von Lamsfeld, I have three elder brothers, I live in Schleswig Holstein, and we are quite rich. I think.'

'Is this a tease, Leni?'

'No. Not so.'

'It's quite true?'

'Yes, true.'

'There is a granny: in Hamburg?'

'No. A lie.'

'And Marcus?'

'He doesn't know. Only you.'

'And now what on earth am I to say to all this?'

'I don't know.'

Cuckoo dropped the handfork into the box, started to peel off her rubber gloves. 'Well. I declare. Do you want to say anything to me then?'

'I would like to. I don't know what to do. Will you help me?'

'I'll try. Let's get out of the sun, under the apple-tree up there.' She got up stiffly, brushed dust from her skirt, adjusted her hat. 'You're quite sure? You want to talk? I'll forget about it if you'd rather?'

'No. Please. I want to talk. Just saying what I did is good. Please?'

They walked together up long lines of raspberry canes,

Cuckoo leading. From behind she felt Leni reach out for her hand, took it, pressed it for comfort, drew her alongside, so that they walked shoulder to shoulder, crushed between fragrant leaves. Cuckoo smiled at her, blue eyes sparkling.

'I am also,' said Leni wearily, 'a countess.'

'Are you now! Whatever next? You really are an odd creature,' said Cuckoo. 'I mean, do admit!'

He sat back in the Mercedes, his legs struck straight before him for fear that he would crease the immaculate white crispness of his jeans.

I *have* put on weight, he thought. Or else Bruna has made a terrific job of shrinking them. Either way, I don't think that Count Grottorosso will complain. Give him an eye-full: why not?

'I'm off to see the Wizard, the wonderful Wizard of Oz: tum, tum. I suppose I ought to feel uptight: strap myself into my trauma-jacket. Not me. Not that sort. I came up the hard way.

Take over the role? Me? Minerva must be barking mad. You mean to say he chopped up that dozy Kraut deliberately just so that he could get me for the part instead? Wild; way out, way, way out. Kerrazy, man. I mean, she's getting on a bit, Minerva. Smashing, great. I dig her: but she's strictly No, No, Nanette-time. Not of today. No way. A bit out of touch maybe? A touch of the sun? A pastis too many? Glug, glug, glug. She can put them down. 'Just a theory', she said. 'I could be wrong, Marcus.'

Maybe you are, lady.

No, but seriously. I mean, that's what I'm going for. To find out. I mean, it's a very big deal that, very big. If true. Big, big deal. Star Time.

Looking back, I can see he was very interested at the picnic. Very. Indeedy. Flattering: now that I know the

284

reason. If I do. If it is the reason.

And so what happens if he does suggest it, then? What? Temptation. Temptation. Big, big temptation. For the good things; the sweet life, this kind. I like it. But I'm not barmy enough to think that it just comes to you handed on a plate. It never comes like that . . .

Unless he asks me.

A Movie Star.

Something Jeremy never got. Or Decca. Longed for, yearned for, cheated, lied, and lay for: the pair of them. I know. Not that dumb. I had ears. Eyes. And they never got it. Nowhere near. No way.

Supposing he asks and I say 'Yes' and have a go. And fail. What then? I'd get the loot, I suppose. If I finished the job. And after? Become like them? Sour with failure, rancid with envy: she playing someone's Mum on the telly, doing Voice-over for custard powders. 'Dreamily, creamily'. He dragging the tenth tour of 'My Fair Lady' into Nairobi. Tacksville. Want that? Your idea of a 'gig', Marcus?

Lived all my life with failure. Until old Desmond. I know all about the Near Misses, the Not Quites, the Haven't Gots. Backwards. Spent the most formative years of my life among them. Didn't I? Ask any psychiatrist. It's very harmful.

You have to fight hard not to go under.

Who was it said 'You either have it, or you've had it'? Dead right. So say no more.

So that's what you face, mate. You can face it but could you stomach it?

Oh, they tried. Yes, they did. She did anyway. Give her that. But they never actually set the stage alight. No one exactly beat down doors to see them, they never what is laughingly called 'exploded' on the screen. Or off it, come to that. Hardly ever even got up on to one.

Funny: he didn't seem to care so much. Only her. On

and on and on. Oh Christ! Remember? That time just before the Fall: before Dorking. Some party she gave: big deal. One of the 'Uncles' Toby Weissberger no less, coming down the stairs with some others. Didn't see me, I was looking for their coats in the downstairs loo. But I heard him. I remember him. Big ears, small hands.

'Decca York is the only woman I know who actually screwed her way to the middle.' He said that. I didn't exactly know what it meant. Not exactly. Not at twelve. But they all stopped laughing when they saw me. With their coats.

I really want that world now? But come on: let's face it. It was all a long time ago. Maybe my world, if I got it, wouldn't be like that. Perhaps more like up at the villa. I don't see why not. Elegance, grace, good manners, security, knowing who you are. A successful world. Why not?

Never expect failure. They don't.

'I Do Not Expect To Fail.' My new motto. Just invented it. And the alternative? Well: shuttling round the Home Counties with a truck of second-hand furniture: stripping down and dressing up for Gus Bender and his Nikon. There has to be something better than that: hasn't there? Perhaps there is. Possible. I might find out very soon. And about the Hagel business. He probably tripped over his bootlaces, if I know him. That type. Wet. And Minerva can exaggerate things, get it a bit off beam. Wild. Very American. Overstates. We'll see.

The car swung down on to the Corniche Inferieure. On his left the whole bay: small coloured triangles idly tacking about in the breathless evening air, a speedboat scoring its way across the water to the end of the Cap; and lying almost dead centre, sleek as a sunning dolphin, the *Papageno* splendid in her serentiy.

That doesn't look like failure down there, to me, he thought. Nothing tacky there. It shimmers with success, power, goodies galore.

And I'm on my way. Because he asked me. Because perhaps he'll think that I am right for his film. I've got a bloody sight more going for me than old Hagel. I know that. Not Modest. Not me.

Proof? You want proof, sir? Well: funny you should ask, but I'm not ashamed to admit that I have it all ready to hand. The proof you want, sir? Signorina Sylva Puglia, a great International Star, adored by millions, the Sex Symbol of the Decade. And who does she pick to share her favours with at the biggest picnic of the Season on the Côte d'Azur, France? Marcus Edward Pollock. No less. That's who. Me. She could have had anyone she liked. Just lift a finger and they'd all have come lurching: they were slobbering after her like a pack of randy dogs all day. But she chose me.

And he's chosen me: if Minerva isn't out of her cotton pickin' mind, and if that is so, then I must have something to offer, right? Stands to reason. And I will accept everything on offer with open hands. Why not? I don't want any more of the Take-Away-Life, thanks. I've had better. Got a taste for it now. I don't want anything cheap or tacky ever again.

And Leni? She'll learn to like being rich. It's easy. She'll catch it from me. Very contagious.

The car came to a stop outside the Hotel Welcome. At the quayside a trim launch at the foot of the steps: two smiling Italian crew members sparkling in pale blue, the Grottorosso crest, a fountain in an olive-wreath, embroidered on their chests and splendid in black and gold on the limp flag at the stern.

He stepped down into the launch; the sailors waved to a couple of girls on a balcony, cast off, spun the engine into life and headed for the middle of the bay. He stood braced in the stern beside the now streaming flag, the spray prismatic with rainbows, the sleek lines of the ship coming nearer and nearer. Above the roar of the engine one of the sailors was singing.

Nothing tacky here, he thought. Nothing. That's the Big Time ahead.

The only time that Marcus had ever been on a boat was years ago during one Half Term, when Desmond and Decca had hired a rather glossy Cabin Cruiser and they had gone from Windsor to Marlow: with a stop-off for Pimms and lunch at Skindles. It was something he had remembered all his life, until the instant that he set foot upon the scrubbed deck of the *Papageno* when it was obliterated for ever by the size and splendour of everything about him.

Nando Belluno had met him affably at the gangplank, and taken him on the tour, for, he explained, Grottorosso preferred to remain resting in his cabin. The strain of the last two days, tragic days, he murmured with a sad shake of his head, had exhausted him. So from Engine Room to Bridge they went, Marcus slightly glazed with wonder at the length of the Dining Saloon and its table to seat eighteen; the walls of the library, ridged with the spines of a thousand books in blue, green and scarlet leather; the Main Saloon whose colours stemmed entirely from the splendid T'ang camel which stood, bolted securely, under glass to a marble table in the centre; the Cinema with armchair seats covered in crimson suède, and the glittering Galley, precise and surgical as a scalpel. A vastly luxurious ship, bearing no resemblance to maritime matters whatsoever. It would have been perfectly possible to spend weeks on board, without ever setting foot on deck, and never realize that one was at sea at all. Providing the weather was dead calm or one was in harbour. It was crammed, discreetly, with every kind of artifact and comfort, cunningly designed to take one's mind off the sea, its immensity, and one's own insignificance.

Marcus privately considered that as a luxury penthouse in a Knightsbridge High-Rise it was a triumph: as a seagoing vessel on the other hand, a vague disappointment.

Under the awning at the stern he saw Sylva Puglia, somewhat alarmingly dressed in black, her hair severely braided about her head, sitting in a rattan chair reading *Paris Match*. She waved hesitantly, and as Marcus went across to her, feeling slightly uneasy, Nando Belluno muttered something about returning in a few moments, and plodded off down the deck.

'You come to see *Papageno*?' She was looking professionally sad.

'Yes. And to have a drink, with Grottorosso. You coming?'

'Me?' She laughed a cold laugh of disdain. 'I do not get invited. We meet at dinner. Is enough. A very pretty ship, isn't it?'

'Very. Wonderful.'

'But sorrowful now. You know of Wolf?'

'Yes. Minerva said.'

'So terrible. So terrible. But maybe now we all go home. Kaput. Finito.'

'I'm sorry. Bad luck.'

'For all. Most for Wolf, but for all.' She folded the magazine, looked with sudden intense interest at something on the back cover. 'You are not mad with me? For the time at the swimming-pool?'

Marcus flushed lightly, cleared his throat. 'No. Of course not. As much my fault as yours.'

'You didn't like me?'

'Well, yes, I mean . . . yes. I mean; what a thing to ask.'

'I am curious only. Poor Sylva. I feel very wicked, you know.'

'Oh? Oh well, you mustn't feel that; I mean, you know . . .'

'But I *was* wicked, you see. For ten thousand francs.'

Marcus sat on a small stool beside her. 'Ten thousand francs? What was wicked?'

'Grottorosso said he would make a bet, like at the races, you know? That I could not have you. That was wicked, no?'

Marcus sat bolt upright. She put a hand quickly on his knee.

'But I enjoyed very, very much. It was just for fun, you know, the bet.'

'When did he say that?'

'When? Oh, when he was leaving he said to me, "I think I go. Will you come with me?" and I said, "No, it is such a happy day, and so many pretty, pretty gentlemen." and he said, "I will bet you ten thousand francs there is one pretty gentleman you won't get." He pointed to you – all in yellow. Right?'

'Right,' said Marcus in a cracked voice.

'He said you were the "special" friend of the old woman who gives the picnic. Is true?'

'Godson. I'm her godson, that's all.'

'Oh? I don't know this. Anyway. It was wicked but I tried, and I liked very, very much.'

'Good. Thanks a lot, smashing of you to tell me. Did you collect?'

'Please?'

'The ten thousand francs?'

'No.' She patted her braided hair, raising a bare arm high above her head.

Marcus averted his head, glowered at the deck.

'Pouf! Ten thousand francs! What is that? He said he would take me to Cartier in Monte Carlo . . . but that was before Wolf. So . . .' She shrugged, smiled, put her hand on his shoulder. 'It is only a little joke, you know? And I won, isn't it? That is enough for Sylva; was very, very nice.'

'Good. I'm very glad, Really chuffed.'

Nando came back, a little out of breath, preventing any further discussion. 'I think that we should go: Grottorosso is waiting,' he said.

'Nando! In my pretty cabin there is water everywhere, you know this? The wash place is full, it will not go away.'

'I told you not to wash your hair in there. Speak to Peppe, not to me!'

'Peppe will not speak to me. He sticks out his tongue . . . he hates me. Poor Sylva . . .' But her voice drifted away as they went down the deck.

'Puttana!' muttered Belluno. 'Puttana! Lei é un putridúme! Excuse me. I would say to you before we speak to Grottorosso, please remember that this is a very sad ship, eh? A catastrophe! Months of work and hopes destroyed by one stupid slip, one error. It is wise not to speak of this to him, please. He is a fastidious man, and very private, he dislikes to speak of personal things or anything which is in the least ugly or unpleasing. You have seen the beauty of this ship? He created all. So you will realize the sensitivity and style of this man. Incomparable. His sense of form, of purity cannot be matched by any other Master in his field today. So speak, if you will be so kind, only of charming things, help to distract him from his sadness. It is understood?'

Marcus nodded. He was still too enraged by Sylva's confession to make any comment.

Belluno, for his part, wanted no difficult questions asked, or anyone to make the slightest error of judgement. It was perfectly possible, he thought, that the Princess had been accurate in her assessment of the unfortunate 'accident' to Hagel: but that was really not his affair.

What was his affair was presently at his side moving towards Grottorosso's steel stateroom. If the film was to be secured, at this last deplorable moment, then it was possible that an arrangement might be made with this Divine Intervention, though he very much doubted that it had anything to do with Divinity personally. And if he felt some small shadow of remorse (for he was a family man and kind at home) that he was behaving like a eunuch accompanying the newest concubine to the harem, or worse still delivering a healthy young animal to the vivisectionist, he put it from his mind: he was a Producer first and foremost, the Film must be saved above all else. Eight weeks to go before shooting started, and already his mind was eradicating remorse as the possibility of stimulating publicity phrases swung before him. 'The Look-Alike-l'Aiglons'; 'Year Search for L'Aiglon Ends on Riviera Beach' . . . or words to that effect. Things were desperate; especially financially, but if all else failed in the end, there was always the merry little spring bubbling away in Tuscany. He tapped the stateroom door.

There appeared to be no grief, and little sensitivity, in the cool, smiling, Grottorosso who came towards Marcus, trim in form-fitting grey tracksuit, white sneakers, and a platinum wristwatch the size of a muffin; a bottle of champagne already opened in one hand, the other extended in greeting.

'My dear Pollock! So good of you to come, it makes me very happy.' He poured two flutes of Roederer Cristal and indicated that Marcus should seat himself on a low steel and leather chair while he himself chose the long buttoned settee on which he lay prone, relaxed, comfortable; inducing an immediate feeling of informality and ease. He imagined.

'We have had a tragic time, as you perhaps know, so it is pleasant to have some slight diversion. I am sad that we could not lunch, as I suggested, but the days have been so occupied by this disastrous business that there was not the time. However, we shall have our drink instead, eh?' He raised the flute. 'Chin-chin! Now then,' he said, setting his glass aside, 'what do you think of my ship? She is pretty, I think?'

'Great. Like a super penthouse.'

'She is my home. I live on her all the time practically . . . go where I will. It is a very agreeable life.'

'What's the furthest you've sailed her?'

'The furthest? The longest voyage? I think, so far, Bermuda; not so far, but very pleasing.'

'Bermuda! The Atlantic, in this? Kidding?'

'This is a ship, Pollock,' said Grottorosso with a polite smile. 'Not a celluloid duck.'

'And you've got a terrific tape-deck there.'

'Ah! Music! My greatest solace. It soothes the savage breast, and eases the weary heart. I have need of it often, alas!'

Well, thought Marcus, my breast is pretty savage right now. That silly scrubber and the bet. What did he do that for? Why put her on to me? Perhaps Minerva is right. Just have to see. Settle back; I know his type, they take a long time to get to the point. Wander round with a load of oblique questions, then jump you.

'You look, what is the word?' Grottorosso searched the air cautiously with manicured fingers. 'Dashing? Is that right?'

'Don't know. Sounds all right.'

'Very slick and sleek.'

'Oh well, just tidy. An honour coming here, after all.'

'Perhaps – your hair?'

'My hair?'

'It is very . . . arranged, is it? The other day when I saw you, it was different?'

'Lacquer,' said Marcus thrusting a hand through his fixed hair and brushing it hard. 'There. All gone. It comes out easily. That better?' He combed it roughly into place with his fingers.

Grottorosso nodded contentedly. 'Much better. More virile.'

'I'll have to remember that, won't I?'

'Now you really resemble l'Aiglon. So strange, I was astonished when I saw it. I immediately thought of you to double for Hagel, as you know, but now that we have no star, we have no need for a double. It is tragic.'

'Yes, I'm sorry too. Sounded a super idea.'

'It pleased you?' There was caution in the question.

'Naturally. What else? Vienna, movies, getting somewhere. A new opening.'

'It would have been a very big assignment, hard, demanding.'

'That would have been okay. I like a challenge.'

'This would have required a great deal of physical expertise.'

'Fine. That's my job. I can do that.'

'Hagel couldn't. That is why I considered you. He looked very well for the role, handsome, strong, many things he had externally. But inside he was . . .', a shake of the platinum head, a deprecating smile, eyes glazed with the pain of recollection, 'He was like a woman. Timid, passive. Ach . . .'

'That's not much good, is it?'

'Not at all. Also his eyes were brown, not blue, his hair not right.'

'Didn't seem to have much going for him, did he, really?'

'One thing. He had an excellent screen presence, which he lacked in normal life. It is strange what the camera can do. It was not unkind to Hagel.'

'It's not unkind to me either, as it happens.' Marcus looked modestly into his half-empty wine glass.

'Not unkind? The camera? To you?'

'To me,' said Marcus. Crikey! That's gone down like a penny in the slot.

Grottorosso had risen from his settee rather quickly, refilled their glasses, spilling a little, for his hand shook slightly. Perhaps it was only the gentle movement of the anchored ship on the swell.

'You did not say to me about the camera?'

'Well, you didn't ask, did you?'

'No, that is so. I did not expect this. This is extra! Have I ever seen you perhaps?'

'I doubt it.' Marcus grinned over his glass. 'Of course you *may*. But if you ever had I think that you'd recognize me.'

'In England, is it? America?'

'In England mostly. But I'm quite popular in the States, Germany, Japan, even the Arab Emirates.'

'I had no idea,' said Grottorosso in surprise. 'Forgive me.'

That's okay, thought Marcus. But you're up the wrong tree. You think we're talking about movies. I'm talking about Gus Bender and company. Never mind.

'You have a lot of experience of this?'

'Not a lot. Enough. I'm still learning, you know.'

'Would I know any of them perhaps?'

'I don't think so, all small budget stuff. "The Gay Hussar" was one? Or "Mazeppa" another. But I don't suppose you know them, eh?'

'No . . . it is so. But you know in my productions it is not absolutely necessary to have acting experience, I prefer it when my players have none at all . . . when they come to me, shall I say, virginal, unsullied by tricks and poses, just as a piece of pure clay awaits the potter's hands. You can perhaps understand me?'

'Perfectly,' said Marcus and crossed one booted leg over the other; he's dead on cue, Minerva, I think we're off at last.

'And I am the potter. I say this in all modesty of course, it is a humble craft, but it is my delight and my joy to take raw clay and mould it into a thing of beauty, poise, strength and brilliance. The Master Craftsman and his material; simple, living, earth. Clay! Mine is the perfect balance between art and technique.'

Marcus took a sip of Cristal. 'I can't say I really *act* in the things I do. You know? Not words and so on. My job is a bit more, well, physical; know what I mean?'

'Physical? Ah! Adventures, athletic things.'

'Oh yes, *very* athletic indeed.'

'A lot of action?'

'Terrific. Never let up. But no words really.'

'Cowboy things, you mean?'

'Some. Lassoing, branding irons, bull whips, you know. But no dialogue. So really I'd be pretty much your lump of clay, wouldn't I?'

'But experienced of course?'

'Oh yes. That. Sure. I know the form, technically; great at taking direction, just do as I'm told, I never argue back.'

'Very wise,' said Grottorosso warmly, 'An essential lesson learned.'

'I started in a tough school, studio, I mean.'

'And this pleases you? To do as you are told? To obey.'

'Sure. Suits me.'

'And you would allow yourself to be, shall I say, taken in hand, trained, shaped, moulded and fired in the furnace of my creativity? I am curious to know?'

''Course. I'm a great believer in discipline. We all need it, and I reckon you can hand it out, eh? No nonsense.'

'No nonsense,' agreed Grottorosso enjoying himself more and more. 'So you are not afraid of the furnace?'

'No, lead me to it. Just tell me where it is, is all.'

'It is here!' said Grottorosso standing as straight as a staff, arms stretched wide, head thrown back. 'It is all before you: look, Pollock!'

'It is?' said Marcus gravely.

'You fail to see that it is I myself! I am the furnace *and* the potter!'

'My word!' said Marcus respectfully.

'And I am beginning to wonder to myself, daring to

consider it, is it possible? Am I mad? That after all the tragedy which has befallen us, you could be the clay?'

'I'm not entirely sure that I follow you; excuse me,' said Marcus politely.

'My clay. We have no need, Pollock, for a double as you are aware, but we have the most desperate need of a star. Of l'Aiglon. Could it be possible that it is you? Sitting there before us; could it be?'

'Me? Could it be? Goodness, I don't know.'

'I had a sudden feeling, the instant I set eyes on you at that terrible picnic, that you had many of the qualities I need. You have his looks exactly. Think, just think, of the incredible publicity this will give us! You have no need of subterfuges and disguises, you have vigour, and beneath that attractive aggression I am sure that grace lies hidden. For grace I must have also. If I can assure myself that these qualities are there, then I do believe that an incredible solution has been presented to me at this moment of disaster. Are you aware perhaps of the old English saying "When one door closes . . .".'

' "Another one opens",' said Marcus dutifully. 'Yes. I know that one.'

'Then I have a feeling that you have just made an entrance into my scheme of things.'

Marcus sat forward, as much as he could in the low chair in which he was almost slumped, chin in his hands, the glass tilting dangerously. 'I really don't think that I follow you, I don't know what your scheme is, do I?'

'If you are willing to put yourself in my hands, if you can give me your trust, your complete obedience, accept without question my decisions and my discipline, bow to my authority, become as it were, my common clay, then I am certain that I could make you my l'Aiglon!'

There was a moment's complete silence in the cabin. Marcus thought it wisest to stay still, as if the tremendous impact of what had been said was taking time to register, and that when it did, whatever he said must sound real and completely spontaneous; for in truth he was only immediately aware that Minerva had been right. The 'accident' was, most probably, deliberate. He was, and he felt it very keenly, in the hot seat. He sat staring wide-eyed at the quietly smiling face looking down at him. Dominant position: naturally.

'Goodness me,' he said eventually in a voice of wonder. 'I mean, well! You ask for a hell of a lot, don't you?'

'I offer dreams beyond dreaming.'

'Yes, I see that. And that's your scheme, is it?'

'It is my scheme.' He took up the bottle, replenished their glasses; Marcus held his as in a daze, apparently stunned by the glittering future presented to him, or the possibilities suggested, he lay back in the deep chair, staring up at the steel bulkhead and the wavering reflections of water sparkling through the porthole. How fine he looks, thought Grottorosso, confident that he had baited his hook well and that the fish was nosing around almost ready to take it. Virile, certainly, a fine head, firmer than l'Aiglon's, a better jaw and mouth, strong throat, broad chest and fine legs. He would be a worthy adversary, someone with whom to enjoy the battle of wits; and strength. A simple youth, clear-eyed, according to Puglia probably virginal, certainly not experienced, nothing coarse or knowing. But capable of being trained; splendidly endowed, she had said, and apparently quite unaware of his tremendous potential, particularly in that direction. How astonishing to find such purity, such golden elegance, such clarity in a youth today, when the majority were either doped to the eye-balls or had indulged in carnal practices from the age of ten. And what immense satisfaction it would be to teach him: to train him, to open his eyes to the opportunities which could lie ahead. At the present moment he is obviously over-awed, unsure, lacking in confidence, but within time he will be fearless, bold, standing so high and so tall that he will need my chastisement, my correcting, and my humbling. The idea itself made him feel almost faint with pleasure, so that he sprang suddenly to his feet in order to retain his strength. Marcus looked up in mild surprise.

'You have seen all my ship,' said Grottorosso with a wave of his arm, 'but not my gymnasium! And that you must see of course; it is unusual in a vessel of this size, and it is a place with which you will become very familiar if my scheme comes to pass.'

He put his arm around Marcus's shoulder, pressing tightly, fingers like iron pegs biting through the thin T-shirt, and crossed through the green marble bathroom adjoining the cabin, slid back a mirror door and stepped into the gym.

'This is an extraordinary moment for me,' he said. 'I was plunged into darkness, but now I see light, a brilliant light, a future, a hope, the possibility of realizing a dream. I am very moved.' The fingers thrust deeper into Marcus's neck muscles, who tried not to wince, gritted his teeth, grinned.

'Super gym! Golly, you really have it all made, don't you.'

'We have not the height of course . . . but I lack little.'

Modestly proportioned, the gym contained most things necessary to keeping fit. Wall-bars, vaulting-horse, mats, ropes, parallel-bars and so on. Racks of bar-bells, foils, weights, assorted balls for throwing at each other, a punch-bag. A blue rubber floor. How the hell did Hagel 'slip' on that?

'Is this where you work-out, fence, so on?'

'That is so. Every morning I do one hundred turns with the skipping-rope, you know this? Then with the bar-bells or press-ups, fifty, every morning before I take my shower. On board ship one's life can become sedentary, and that is fatal.'

'Yes. I'll bet you're strong.'

'I like to be. I am very strong, I cherish my body.'

'I can see that. I'd say you were pretty demanding.'

'One has to be demanding, as you say, to have the best, and only the best will do for me, you know. So I pay you a compliment, you see? I am certain that you have the potential to be the very best. The finest clay from a perfect seam.'

Lead him on a bit more, thought Marcus, give him a little more rope.

'It scares me rather, you know. You ask for a lot; demand the very best; I mean I'd *try*, I really would. Terrific idea. But what if I didn't come up to your standards? I mean, you know, if I failed in the end? I may be the lump of clay as you call it, and you would be the potter or whatever, but what happens if you don't like what you take out of your furnace in the end? If I didn't come up to expectations? All that work, money and effort, you know?'

Grottorosso smiled, shook his head, pulled a thick hempen rope hanging from the bulkhead towards him, swung it forcefully away across the gym. 'Ah! Well. You know that if the potter is not completely satisfied with his work, with his creation, then it is his duty to smash the pot! One must retain nothing which is imperfect.' He extended a generous hand towards Marcus's suddenly rigid body, smiling to prove his lack of fears in that direction. 'However, I am confident that we need have no thought of that, you and I. I am sure in my heart that our collaboration would be in complete harmony, we will unite to achieve something incredible and beautiful. A true work of art. A classic.'

That's a bloody confession! He's as good as said it. Chopped Hagel up! Nothing imperfect. The broken pot bit. Clear as clear. It's all been deliberately planned. He's out of his skull, doesn't know it, but he's ready for certifying the next time around; if they catch him. And the next time around it isn't going to be me, that's for sure. Standing there, hands on his hips, smiling, smiling, eyeing the goods. I wonder, just for the hell of it, how far I can take him now?

He leant against the wall-bars, hooked one hand, one heel through, knee slightly bent, thumb of his free hand thrust into his broad belt, a provocative pose he knew well, smiling, insolent, heavy-lidded.

Grottorosso came silently towards him across the blue rubber floor. 'You smile?'

'So crazy. Crazy.'

'So crazy? Why do you say that? It is wonderful, amazing perhaps, I think even a Divine Intervention: do you think it is not meant, this meeting of ours? So strange: Recollect, Pollock! I am about to start work on a great project, I am in despair, I think that we are lost, that perhaps after all we must abandon our plans. Darkness! Then I must go to a picnic, in a crowded garden, in a stranger's house, in an alien land and there, suddenly, I come face to face with my protagonist! Do you not think this amazing?'

'Amazing.'

Grottorosso stopped two paces away from the indolent body hooked to the wall-bars, his eyes moved across it thoughtfully, lips folded in a twist of smile, rocking gently on his heels. 'You are wearing all white. L'Aiglon, you know, was very often in white. He had a uniform of great beauty. The white uniform.'

'You fancy me, don't you?' said Marcus softly.

Grottorosso froze. Smile died. Eyes widened. He drew back two paces. 'You said?' Eyes slate.

'That you fancy me. I can tell right off. Had a lot of experience of people like you. I know by the way you look; from the way you touch. I get the message even though it is tangled up in your own private code. But in perfectly plain

301

English it's called "lust".' He grinned cheerfully. 'It's a bit disgusting, don't you think?'

'Are you mad?'

'Maybe a little. But don't say I've got it wrong, have I? Can't have. I've been picking up signals all evening like radar. Discipline, obedience, the Potter and Clay stuff: moulding me in the furnace of, what was it? Your creativity or something. It's all old tape; pretty obvious, isn't it? The Master and the Slave trip. And smashing the pot! I ask you! That was old Hagel, wasn't it? Didn't make the furnace, or wouldn't. Which? Doesn't matter very much anyway now, does it? He got the chop. Imperfect.'

'You rave. You are ill, drunk . . .'

'Angry. Not ill, or drunk. I reckon you fell for the blue-eyed-blond-innocent-look. Do it pretty well, I know. It's what we call in the job the "Vulnerable Look". Know what I do? Never asked, did you, and I never said really. Not movies. I pose for dirty pictures in porn magazines and for very private collections. Know what I mean? Erotic Not Explicit. That's my firm's motto.'

Grottorosso lowered his head, raised his shoulders, arms clear of his body, fists clenched, a bull ready to charge.

'I will smash you into pieces,' he said hoarsely.

Marcus unhooked himself from the wall-bars, stuck his thumbs in his pockets, stood upright, legs apart, smiling. 'No you won't,' he said evenly.

Grottorosso's face was as grey as ash. 'Checca! Whore!' he whispered. 'I despise you. You are filth.' He turned and walked quickly through the green marble bathroom to his stateroom beyond. Marcus close behind him.

'I rather despise myself if you want to know, but there's such a hell of a demand for the stuff we do. Come in all sizes, matt or glossy, black and white or colour. Colour comes more expensive. But I try to console myself that I am supplying a desperate need: form of therapy, you know? But one thing: I'm *not* a whore or whatever. Draw the line at that: you can look all you want. But no touching.'

You revolt me. Got off the ship.'

Marcus picked up his half-empty glass, finished it. 'Glad to. I've got what I came for, thanks. And you know I am only doing the decent thing by telling you all this stuff. It's better that you know now than later, isn't it? I mean, thanks for the offer and all that, very tempting, but I'd hardly really do for your saintly hero, would I? Just think of the publicity you'd get in smutty old Angleterre alone! They'd dig me up somehow; all those Sunday papers; can you imagine the headlines? And the French! How would *they* feel. Make you a laughing stock, wouldn't it? Or worse perhaps, Mr Grottorosso? You tell me. I could have held my tongue, couldn't I? Gone along with your scheme. Easy. I can take care of myself, but at lease I've been dead honest, you've got to give me that, I didn't cheat you. I'm not tacky.'

Grottorosso opened the door of the cabin. 'Get out,' he said. 'Out! Degenerato!'

Marcus stepped into the evening sun. 'For a minute,' he said, 'I was afraid you were going to say that you'd never been so insulted in all your life,' and turning on his heel walked down the deck.

Monet would have made a pretty good job of us, thought Cuckoo, just as we are now. Two ladies sitting in the dappled shade of an apple-tree, a drift of poppies, green summer grasses, a high clump of valerian: me in my old straw hat, Leni bare-legged, the sun spilling over her white blouse like a scattering of sovereigns.

And now I suppose that she's said it all, she thinks that she's said too much. One does. And bites one's tongue. But she really did have to get all that off her chest. Goodness! What a muddle we make of life; as if it wasn't muddling enough anyway without us further confusing it all. We are never satisfied. And it has all, it seems to me, been so wonderfully unoriginal. I imagine she thinks not; possibly feels that I am stunned with shock and that I sit here in silence only because I don't know what to say. And I don't. For the moment. A lot to digest, and it's such a familiar story; daughter spurning family, tradition and Mamma. Just what a thousand thousand other girls have done and will do for ever and ever. Nothing new. Poor little love sitting there, shoulders hunched in that frightful peasant-blouse, chewing the side of her thumb like a Mars bar.

'Leni,' she said sharply. 'Don't do that! You'll be down to the bone in five minutes.'

Leni closed her hands into fists and sat on them. 'I've said such a very lot of things. You are angry, isn't it?'

'Not in the least. Why ever would I be angry, for heaven's sake?'

'Because I have been so deceitful.'

'Not to me,' said Cuckoo. 'You haven't deceived me: all I know and love is Leni Minx.'

Oh! but I have deceived you, thought Leni, about Mr Bender and the Studio. That's deception. She had decided, almost as she got to that point in her story, that she couldn't quite bring herself to admit to the Studio; her part in it, or Marcus's. As far as Cuckoo knew they had met while he was delivering furniture, true enough, to a place where she worked. For some reason Luise had instinctively imposed her own standards over Leni once again. She looked across at Cuckoo lying back on her elbows in the grass, hat at the back of her head, staring up into the leaves of the apple tree. She's not an old woman. Not motherly. Someone I know and love and trust. A contemporary. I haven't shocked her? Surely not.

'What you have to do, right off, my dear, is tell him: as soon as possible,' said Cuckoo.

'I knew that you would say this,' said Leni dejectedly,

and started to chew her thumb again.

'But I have to say it! I mean, you can't go on pretending to be one person and fighting the instincts of another. If you see what I mean. You'll just have to be *one*. Otherwise it'll exhaust you and confuse the poor boy most terribly.'

'I don't know which one to be, Cuckoo! He doesn't want me to be someone else. He said,so. He likes me as I am, as Leni Minx.'

Cuckoo sat up, resting on the palms of her hands. 'But you aren't someone else, I mean you won't be, will you? Just because you have the word Gräfin on your passport and a different name? He isn't in love with your name, he's in love with who you are, and who you are is who you always have been, so you say. I mean, do admit, you tell me you are a whatchermacallit, a hermit crab. All you've done is change shells. *I'm* totally bewildered now.'

'No. It's true. That's what I said.'

'Well, that's all you need fuss about. Tell him. He'll probably have a boring joke at your expense . . . but really, being a Countess is not much, you know. Who cares? It meant more in my day . . . but now! Heavens. I know a Duchess who runs a tea-room and a Marchioness who weaves ghastly shawls and rugs on a loom in a windmill in Kent. The title-thing is absolutely second-rate, unimportant now. There are so many perfectly impossible ones flying about – film people, grocers, property dealers – that one is almost embarrassed by having an inherited one for oneself. I'm quite amazed that when you ran away you didn't join some frightful gang, you know? A Baader-Meinhof thing, the Red Brigade or Army or whatever it calls itself. So wonderfully old-fashioned to trot off and sing in a bar, do admit! Like joining a circus.'

'I'm not a militant. I wouldn't want to destroy anyone, or any thing. Anyway it's only the bourgeois girls who do that. Daughters of the people who suddenly got so rich in our country after the war; even during it, you know?

305

Merchants, bankers, builders, industrialists . . . rich, greedy, so vulgar that their children even are revolted. But I didn't have that background: I don't despise my brothers for loving their land. I just didn't want to be a cabbage on it myself.'

Cuckoo pulled off her hat, ruffled her hair. 'You know something frightful? Right at this moment I'd give my eye-teeth for a couple of puffs at a "reefer".'

'I don't know this.'

'A ciggie. Pot. You call them "joints", and I know that you've got some, unless you've been burning your mattress.'

'Oh! You could smell . . .'

'Rather delicious. Memories of autumnal afternoons, blackbirds chiselling in the Michaelmas daisies.'

'Well, I have,' said Leni and from the back pocket of her jeans pulled a scratched Benson and Hedges tin. Inside three thin, and not very well rolled, 'joints'.

'My dear! What joy!'

'Marcus was furious I brought them. I hid them in my little bag. I don't smoke so much. One sometimes, for happiness.'

'I long for one. Let's find happiness together,' said Cuckoo.

Not really Monet after all, she thought. Lautrec? Splendid title for the catalogues. 'Two Ladies in Poppies, Smoking Pot'.

'Did I give myself away, to you?' said Leni lying back in the grass, one hand over her eyes.

'How could you give yourself away to me? I didn't know who you were except for your name, and that you'd been to Hamburg to see your grandmother. I didn't think that you were totally uneducated. At the picnic you were marvellous. Confident. I suppose I thought that just a *tiny* bit odd. So socially aware.'

'It's been worrying here, to not make mistakes. In

England it was not worrying. But here . . .'

'Well, you can relax. There is nothing to fear.'

'Except about Marcus. He likes this life too much. I don't think he really wants to go back to what it was like before. Where we live: how we live. I don't know.'

Cuckoo leant her back against the scaly tree, looked up into the leaves. 'All this will fade as quickly as his suntan. You'll see. In a week's time he'll be busy polishing up his Sheraton and Chippendale, or whatever do does in his shop.'

'Desmond's shop. Shops.'

'Desmond. Beastly old Desmond, coming to take you away.'

Leni rolled over on her stomach, pulled a long stalk of grass between her fingers. 'Perhaps if I could marry Marcus it would be better. Because than I would just be Mrs Pollock, and I would not feel so German. I hate to be German.'

'How absurd,' said Cuckoo. 'Why?'

'Because everyone hates us.'

'Do they? I don't. I don't really hate anyone. Grottorosso perhaps. Him.'

'Because of six million Jews, that terrible formula.'

'Ah! that. And five million others. Not *just* the Jews. But that's nothing to do with you, is it? You weren't even born then, Not thought of.'

'Even Bruna hates me.'

'Nonsense. Absolute bunk. Bruna! My treasure?'

'Yes. Not nonsense. Once when we went up to the hills for a picnic she told us such a pretty place; very calm, she said, and she showed Marcus on the map. A fine view, so peaceful. There was a little stone thing there. On it were four names and it said, "Shot By The Barbarous Enemy, June 1944". And when we got back here she said did we see it? and Marcus said yes, and she said that they had had to change the word "Germans" to "Enemy" because it

307

was peacetime now, but all French people would remember.'

'Bruna had brothers in the Resistance; it is difficult, I admit. And the French have been occupied three times in about a hundred years, it is impossible to forget. 1940 is branded deeply on a great many hearts. It's difficult for us to realize. But it is not your fault and not your responsibility, you have to grow beyond that. Learn *from* the past, live *for* the future.'

'I suppose. But I will find it easier in England. But maybe he will not ask me to marry. I don't know. He is happy just like we are.'

'And you love him very much?'

'So much. So much. So it must be enough for me.'

Cuckoo pressed her 'joint' into the trunk of the tree, crushing it flat.

'It was not so good?' said Leni anxiously.

'Well. Not terribly. I mean I'm not radiant with joy all of a sudden.'

'Maybe it was cheap stuff. And perhaps old. Is possible?'

'Not an expert.' She pulled on her hat. 'He was only going for a drink, wasn't he?'

'He said. Maybe one hour.'

'Should be back soon then, it's nearly seven.'

'At night sometimes, you know, I wake up just to watch him sleeping; he doesn't know and I can look at him as long as I like.'

'In the dark? Leni!'

'Well, I "feel" him there. Hear him breathing. He speaks sometimes, you know? While he is quite asleep.'

'Heavy sauces and cheese at dinner. I'm afraid. So unwise, but Bruna will do it.'

'Maybe. Dreaming.' Leni squashed out her own 'joint' on the back of the cigarette tin, blew the ash away, slid the tin into her pocket. 'What is a shrimping net?' she said.

Cuckoo raised her head suddenly, looked up across the rows of tidy vegetables and fruit lying below; Tonnino had started the evening watering, spraying the hose high in crystal arcs.

'For catching shrimps. In the sea. Little grey things . . . you know.'

'Oh yes. I know. Once he said, in a very clear voice, "Cuckoo! There is no shrimping net. Not without the net!" ' She looked down at the spraying water, the dripping leaves. 'Isn't that a funny thing to dream? And you were in it.'

'Most odd: to be in it.' She got to her feet. 'Tonnino puts me to shame. I have done nothing.'

'My fault. And I have been very boring, I think only of me.'

'Rubbish! Come along, we'd better collect the forks and then go up to change. I'm so *glad* you told me everything. It's far easier once one shares a problem, don't you find? It makes things less of a burden, one doesn't have to carry it all on one's own, that's hideous. So you just pick the right moment and tell him the other part of your life.'

'My two souls,' said Leni. 'Goethe says: "Zwei Seelen wohnen, ach! in meiner Brust".'

'Does he?' said Cuckoo taking her hand and starting down the grassy slope to the vegetables.

'It means, "Alas! I have two souls in my breast".'

'And very lucky you are, dear; some people don't even have one,' said Cuckoo and pushed through the raspberries.

Minerva saw him at the traffic lights at Pont St Jean. Wound down the taxi window, stuck out her head.

'Hi! Going there, or coming from?'

'From.'

'Want a ride?'

They drove to Avenue de Verdun in silence; she put her hand on his knee. 'Want a drink? I do.'

'Yes. Great.'

'If you know somewhere, tell the driver.'

The terrace of 'La Civette' was packed, but they found a small table crushed up at the back, ordered two beers and two pastis.

'It saves time,' said Minerva and lit a cigarette.

They didn't speak until the drinks arrived, sat looking beyond the chattering crowd to the thin strip of sunlit sea far beyond. There was no breeze; the air was heavy with tobacco smoke, coffee, Ambre Solaire, and the despair of Jacques Brel.

'I have just the vaguest feeling that you are not going to give the movies a whirl; am I right?'

'Absolutely,' said Marcus and, after a long swig of his beer, he told her.

She sat in silence, looking ahead, not once interrupting, registering nothing save for an occasional arching of thinly pencilled eyebrows. When he finished, she stubbed out the cigarette, unclipped her earrings, and laid them on the table.

'Either these baubles are too heavy, or I'm getting terribly, terribly old. I think *old*. A day like today slays me. So my hunch was right?'

'Yah. Right. He as good as said so. Broken bloody pot. Imperfect! I really saw red. He didn't even seem to realize what he'd said. Mind you, I was leading him on.'

'So it would seem. Well, Wolf says he can't be sure of anything. Which is dandy. He says he was fine in the morning when he woke, had coffee and fruit juice in Grottorosso's cabin – you might mark *that* incident – and then they went to the gym. And just after they started whatever they were doing he began to feel dizzy, giddy. He remembers nothing more but fright, pain and that bastard's face. Now what do we make of that? Did he dope him too! That's too much.'

'I wouldn't put anything past him.'

She cupped her face in her hands, turned towards him
with a thin smile. 'Leading him on? The photographs, the
porn stuff. True?'

'Almost true. I tarted it up, gave him the impression it
was centrefold stuff, you know, being very butch with a
full erection in a tartan armchair. I made it even worse
really; hinted at whips and chains and bondage. That really
gave him the big heave. The bit about being a star of the
porn mags was all rubbish.'

'What's the true part? You rather not say?'

'No. I don't care., I do pose, not that sort of stuff, it's
just, oh, I don't know, it's sort of "teasing" stuff,
harmless really. Honest.'

'Would you call it Discreet Stimulation?'

'I might. Or Geriatrics Delight more like. Are you
shocked?'

'Honey, if I was shockable I'd have been in cryonic
suspension forty years ago. I'm just stunned that you
should think of such a brilliant way to strike. It's wild.
How did you know?'

'We call them "crotch watchers" in the business. They
all look very gentlemanly, very discreet, serious, correct.
Just that they drop their eyes from time to time . . . you'd
never suspect them, so respectable. Hell! We've got a
couple of Bishops on the lists, not to mention some Very
Revs. and a big butch General. You'd be amazed.'

'I wouldn't,' she said. 'And Grottorosso figures as a
"crotch watcher"? Well, well. I mean, not that I didn't
know. I just didn't know that you did. If you follow me.'

'Took me five minutes: you can spot one a couple of
fields away. Mind you, it's not my job. Not my "calling".
Just that if I need a bit extra I go up to the Studio, strip
off, wag it about a bit, and pocket the loot. In cash. No
Full Frontals. Never starkers. Our Mr Bender would have

a fit; anyway he says "a draped bum is far more suggestive than a bare one". And he should know, he's been flogging them for years. All very discreet, good clientele, well established. A kind of cock-teasers' Fortnum and Mason.'

'We live and learn,' said Minerva. 'I reckon that between the two of us we've scuttled the good ship l'Aiglon, don't you?'

'Yah.' Marcus made circles on the table-top with his beer glass. 'I don't even know why I did it. I didn't like Hagel that much; minny kind of chap. But I don't know, when he said about the broken pot and the furnace and all that crap, and then when that stupid scrubber Sylva-whatever hit me with the bet-bit, well . . . I just folded. I mean, betting that tart she'd never screw me! I mean, what kind of tick is he?'

'Sick,' said Minerva. 'He'd get it out of her blow for blow, hair for hair, I've seen him do it before. Then he goes over it again and again, recreating it all to himself in the darkness of his mind. Bet your ass. It's so like him. It's just the kind of proxy-screw he loves. If only you knew, honey?'

'Hell take it! I *do* know!'

'So you do.' Minerva laughed and put a hand on his. 'Don't look so angry, and don't look so disillusioned. I think that you did what you did, in whatever manner you did it, as a way of defending principles. Would you agree? Or is that word one with which your generation is not over familiar?'

'Where I came from,' said Marcus, 'they were things you couldn't afford to have.'

'I know. They have become stunningly expensive.'

'I've heard more about them here, since I came. Isn't that funny?'

'With Cuckoo and Charles? No. I'd say that that was right. I sometimes think that they invented them, but I

312

can't be sure. At least they keep them polished brightly, and you've noticed. *That's* good. That's just great. I'm so old that I'm time-frozen, I know that. I look, and I sound, like something in the "Late, Late, Late Show". The forties were my happiest days; everything that came after them frightened me witless. So I rooted there; but even then principles were dying . . . but it was part of our tradition, our generation's, to fight for them even if we weren't all that certain what the hell they were, but we fought. The Cuckoos, the Charlies and the me's: it's an idiot's war, we can't win today. But I have a feeling that you've been doing just that yourself, this evening on the *Papageno*, and I think that's just great, terrific! It gives me a kick, I drink to you, Mr Pollock, sir! Whatever means you used.'

She raised the almost empty glass and drained it. 'Now,' she said, pushing the earrings into her large Vuitton bag. 'We must go. But just remember, illusions are for losing, Marcus. And when we get back to the villa, silence, okay? Nothing to Cuckoo or Charles; it's not their affair, ours. Let's not spread the muck. Let it lie, agree?'

'Agree. There's nothing I want to talk about.'

She collected the bag, stuck it under her arm. 'Our secret then, ummm?'

'Fine. Ours. I'm good at secrets.'

She smiled and bowed her head slightly. 'I know you are,' she said, and signalled for the waiter.

Chapter Ten

Marcus lay back comfortably in a wide buttoned-chintz armchair, Leni on his knees, her arms about his neck, looking through the pine to the lights of Villefranche away to the right, rippling in waving bars across the dark water of the bay.

Thunder rumbled and grumbled, rain platter-plittered through heavy leaves, the frail sound of an accordion and a lost melody drifted wistfully through the night. She pressed her lips into the hollow of his neck; he held her closer.

'It's going away. You hear? The storm.'

She nodded, kissed him.

A sudden, rolling crash of thunder, soft splashing, whispering; the accordion fading, loitering, under the mutter and murmuring; and then only the rain rustling, and the darkness.

'All over,' he said. 'All gone.' Switched off the cassette-player at his side. Leni brushed her spiky hair against his cheek.

'I love it,' she said. 'It is so beautiful. It will always remind me of now, of here.'

'Want any more? Play something else?'

'No. No, leave it there, leave it with "Equinoxe", don't spoil it, the storm has gone; like ours. It's funny, isn't it?'

'Like ours? Did we have one?'

'Well. Not a storm. Thunder somewhere. My fault. But it's gone now, Like on the tape.'

'I didn't think so.'

'Oh well, being stupid about the Film Star, and you going to the boat, and everything. I was being very boring.

Borr-ing, as Cuckoo would say. She nearly did.'

'Say so? When?'

'When you were on the boat. We had a talk.' She got off his lap, walked to the windows, stood with her hands on the balcony rail.

'What about?' He sprang the cassette of 'Equinoxe' from the machine, put it in its box. 'Want to hear a bit of "Evita"? She's given us that as well.'

Leni shook her head. 'No thank you. I can't hear the words anyway.'

Before she left for Rome, Minerva had dumped, as she called it, all her 'toys' which she had brought along to help pass the time on the *Papageno*. A stack of paperbacks of various persuasions, the cassette-player and a rack of tapes. 'Scrabble', three straw hats, a viciously ugly Greek vase from Piraeus, a donkey-cart from Taormina, a shell-box from Elba. 'I'm God's gift to the tourist touts: I don't need them now and I didn't when I bought them. *Why* do I do it? But keep the 'player, it might give you some fun.' And she had left on the afternoon flight for Rome with Hagel and a pale nurse, asking that no one should go with her. 'I can't bear any kind of farewell, even if it's only for a forty minute flight to Rome, so just let me go on my own. I'm very capable; but if you came I'd fall apart, lose the tickets and weep floods. Stay here and look at that clear, beautiful, empty bay below. Don't you love it!'

Early that morning, before anyone but Bruna was awake, the *Papageno* had raised anchor and slipped away at first light.

'Where did it go?' cried Minerva.

Bruna shrugged, threw open the shutters of her room. 'I don't know where it went, but it turned to the left at the end of the Cap.'

'Rome!' said Minerva, climbing out of bed and hurrying to the windows to see that, indeed, the ship had gone, and the bay lay still and serene in the early sun.

Looking down from her balcony in the dark, Leni experienced the same feeling of calm and relief at its absence: the only thing now which hung over her head was the passport, which might, indeed, provoke a *real* storm, and the fact that tomorrow marked the arrival of 'Uncle' Desmond; time was limited.

'Why did Cuckoo nearly say you were "borr-ing" then? Tell.' He came across to the windows, leant against the folded shutters.

'Oh, you know how stupid I am? I was being sad being alone, the first time, you see, and I got depressed and cried and went to Cuckoo and, well, we talked about things.'

'Why did you cry? What for? And talked about what things?'

'Nothing really. Things. I am silly, you know, I am just a joke truly.'

'A German joke,' said Marcus, 'is no laughing matter. What's it all about?'

Leni pushed a hand through her hair, the airplane slide clattered to the tiled floor. 'Look what I've done! Perhaps broken . . .' She stooped, picked it up, dusted it, put it in her shirt pocket. 'Cuckoo said to pick a good time, is it now?'

'Is what now?'

'This is a good time?'

'What to do?'

'Show you something.' She pulled the passport from the same pocket, offered it to him with a far from certain hand.

Marcus took it into the room, looked at it in the light of the one small bedside lamp. 'Your passport? What for?'

'Open it,' she said from the balcony.

He did, flipping through the pages. 'It's all blank. Visa, Visa, Visa, Visa . . . Good God!' He suddenly spread it wide. 'Who's this?'

'Me,' she said in a very quiet voice.

316

'With all that dreadful hair? Terrible long, fair, hair over your shoulders? You?'

'Yes. I cut it.'

'God-awful.'

'I'm sorry. It was two years ago perhaps.'

'It's like a mug-shot.'

'I don't know what is.'

'And what's all this rigmarole Gräfin Luise and all the rest?'

'My name.'

'Your name? Gräfin? What about Leni then?'

'It's not there. You see, it's my, well, my stage name only.'

He jabbed a finger at the opened pages. 'And all this stuff is who you are? Gräfin, Luise whatever?'

'Not whatever. Von Lamsfeld.'

'Well. Whatever; it's a hell of a mouthful. What's "Gräfin" for short? Graffi?'

'No. It's not. You can't make it short; it is not my name.'

'What the hell is it then?' He closed the passport, dropped it on the seat of the chair. 'I think you looked awful, with that hair.'

'It's my title. I am a Countess.'

'Hoity toity!' he said, collecting the cassette-player and going towards the bathroom. 'No good trying to impress me: I know too much about you, my girl.' He turned on the taps, poured bath oil, pulled off his shirt.

'It's who I am.'

'You'd hardly guess it from your behaviour; but you might from your cooking.'

'It's not funny.'

'I know.' He took off his jeans, folded them. 'I told you, German jokes aren't.'

'It's not a joke. And you don't care?' She came into the room, picked up the passport, put it back in her pocket.

'I don't see why I should, do you? I mean do *you* care? Is this why you were all miserable, and bored the backside off Cuckoo?'

'Because I hadn't told you, and you'd have to see in the car with Desmond.'

'Big deal. I really can't see what you're in such a tizzy for. My dad's name is Jim, Arthur, Pollock; only he calls himself "Jeremy Steerforth", and my mum is Jessy, Edna, but she called herself "Decca York". It didn't make a blind bit of difference; those were *their* stage names, but underneath they were still just Jim and Jessy. It didn't alter anything: that was the tragedy. I don't see what difference a name makes at all. I like you as Leni; that's how I met you, and I like who you *are* as Leni. If you think I'm about to start calling you Luise or his dotty Gräfin-whatever, you have another think coming. I don't like change. It muddles me.'

'I don't want you to.'

'Good. Because I won't anyway.' He picked up his towel and draped it round his shoulders. 'See?'

She nodded. He crossed to her on bare feet, took her chin between his thumb and forefinger, tilted her head gently backwards, bent his head and pressed his lips to hers.

'There,' he said. 'Very nice and sweet. Dayleecious. Are you a rich Countess, or whatever? Is that going to be a drag?

'No. I'm poor. I ran away, you see.'

'Yah. I ran away too. Tell you all about it later if you like. I'm going to have my bath, it'll be overflowing. And I'm going to be really corrupt and listen to Ella Fitzgerald while I do.' He kissed her again, and went into the bathroom leaving her standing in the middle of the floor with a beating heart. Suddenly he put his head round the door, steam drifted. 'Leni,' he said. 'If I find you wearing a tiara in bed when I come back, I'll chuck you, and it, over the balcony. So watch it!'

He had got pins and needles in his left arm some time ago.
Gently he eased it from beneath her sleeping body: she
murmured something, sighed deeply, rolled on to her side
as he went from her bed and crossed to the balcony,
fumbling for cigarettes and lighter on the dresser. Taking a
cushion from the chintz chair, he put it on the balcony
floor, sat down, his back against the folded shutters,
rubbed his arm to restore circulation.

Isn't it funny how little we really know about each
other? How much we manage to conceal. Even though we
screw like ferrets, share the same bath water, eat the same
meals, lie together in the same bed; we never *quite* tell it
all. Strangers really. For most of our time. Keeping secret
little pockets of individuality to ourselves. Not fully
sharing. Not giving ourselves entirely away. Never open;
really open. Holding on to fragments of 'self', the private
'us'.

I wonder why?

A form of self-preservation, I suppose. Concealing the
areas in which we can be hurt. Like she did last evening
after I came back from 'La Civette'. She very nearly
succeeded, but not quite.

'You were such a long time,' she had said. 'You told
me just a drink, maybe for an hour?'

'I wasn't much longer. I had a drink on the ship, then
met Minerva coming home.'

She waved an anxious hand. 'I know. I know. It's all
right. I was just worried.'

'Why? Think we'd sailed off and left you all forlorn?'

'Something like that.'

'I mean, what was I supposed to do? Send a pigeon or
something? You're going to be a nag.'

'You mustn't be angry. I was, just, well, you know . . . if
you love someone.'

'I do love someone. Now shut up. Sorry I was late.'

'And the ship? Was it fine? You are glad you went?'

'It was very fine. Yes, glad, it's terrific.'

'And they were all there? Lilli Scarlatti, the man with the glasses?'

'Belluno. Yes, he took me round.'

'And the Film Star one?' Got to her at last.

'She wasn't there.' Lie. Keep things tidy.

'Oh. I thought she would . . .'

'Gone to the hairdressers. All that lovely red hair.'

A long pause. Then.

'At six o'clock in the evening?'

'This is France, Leni. Not Shepherd's Bush.' Slipped round that one nicely.

'Well, I'm happy it was so lovely.'

'I didn't say lovely. It was fine. Glamorous. And I didn't screw Sylva Puglia.' True.

'I don't know why you think I am so worried that you did.'

'Of course not? You look as calm as a sitting hen.'

'It's because it is so hot. Thunder somewhere maybe. A storm coming.'

'Clear as clear. And the film is off, as far as I know. We didn't mention it.' How the lies trip off the tip of the tongue. But 'helpful' lies. Don't do any harm; but it didn't really make much difference to her, I knew that there was more than the film and Sylva Puglia on her mind: and of course it's all come out tonight. But only now. The passport. As if a name mattered.

I suppose she really thought she'd never have to tell me about the ruddy Schloss or whatever, or the mother and the hairy brothers. She'd just keep that all to herself. Her little fantasy. Didn't reckon on cruel governments and passports. She'd have got herself into a dreadful muddle in time: and me. And as if I cared anyway. I love her; she must know that. I don't give a tinker's gob what her name is. He lit a cigarette, cupped the lighter flame in his hand lest he waken her. As long – he blew a stream of smoke high into the still night air – as long as she doesn't revert. Change back into the Prussian po-faced creature I saw. All that long hair and the neat row of nasty little pearls round her neck. Like those spotty English Debs getting engaged in *Country Life.*

'My dear!' Decca used to say. 'Take a *look* at the retouching, for gawd's sake! And those awful long English teeth, throats like corduroy. They always marry Guards Officers from Windlesham.'

Decca.

Didn't say much about Decca, did I? Or Jeremy. Just enough to make her feel happy and 'quits'. Didn't go into the turgid bits, the Chekhov elements, LSD, shooting the dog, the frenzies, all the rest of it. Just enough to make her feel we were sort of 'twins'.

'We both ran away then?' she had said.

We both ran away. So we need each other. I wonder why it took her so long to tell me? Or why it took me so long to tell her? Guarding our lives? Secrecy. Why? Perhaps she thought I'd be furious and clear off, slamming the door. Perhaps she thought I was a Communist, or a Trendy-Lefty. You never know. I'm not. But I don't ever remember that we've discussed politics. Perhaps she thinks I am? I'll have to tell her.

Telling. Telling all.

Funny how she couldn't bring herself to tell Cuckoo about Gus Bender and the Studio. What we did there. I wouldn't either. Now why? It's not a question of trying to deceive, not that. I just couldn't say it aloud to Cuckoo. I'm not ashamed of it; I talked to Minerva happily enough; no qualms. But somehow she isn't quite as, what? Vulnerable? Why do I feel that? Why not just come out with it and say? She'd very likely laugh her head off. Terribly amusing: do admit?

On the other hand it might hurt her, disappoint her. I don't know why I feel that, I just do and I wouldn't want to hurt her by one fraction of a fraction. Never that. I wouldn't want her to look at me with different eyes. See a shadow there. Plenty of shadows lurking in those strange blue eyes; but not when she looks at me. Never then. As clear, as calm, as deep as a summer lake. Only with me. If anyone was really looking they'd think it was a dead giveaway. Archie Charlie this evening walking down to the point after dinner. Was he saying so?

'It's very pleasant, isn't it? Looking across the bay without all those wretched fairy lights on that damned ship. Very pleasant.' Archie Charlie, one hand in his pocket, in the other a glass of brandy. The air, warm and sweet, smelled of oleanders and broom. 'I don't know if you like the stuff you're drinking. Prefer a brandy?'

'No,' said Marcus. 'No, this is super. Williams?'

'Made from pears. Get a fearful kick if you take too much. Laid me out once in Switzerland, in my salad days.' He looked back towards the sea. 'Yes. Much nicer without it. A thoroughly disturbing influence, I'd say. Cuckoo was really dreadfully fussed all the time it was there. I have a shrewd feeling that she was worried that you might get involved somehow.'

'Involved?'

'The Italian fellow. Grottorosso. Rather impressed by your looks at the picnic, I seem to remember.'

'Oh that. Yes. The l'Aiglon look. All fizzled out after the accident.'

'Ah, yes. The young German chap? I really didn't register him.'

'That was the whole trouble. No one did.'

'I'm usually pretty good at that sort of thing. Noticing. The little things. Do you know? The little things that other people overlook. My job of course, sifting out the fragments; as an historian. Putting what may seem to be

322

irrelevant little pieces together to form a whole. Very satisfying; sometimes. I don't miss very much.'

'The German boy?'

'Well, I suppose I hardly met him. Such a day of crowds.'

They had reached the end of the lawns at the point by the crumbling urn. Archie Charlie stood for a moment, his hands resting on the stone wall looking out across the sea, to the distant lights of Cap d'Antibes sparkling like diamonds on tremblers.

'I really don't know how to thank you for what you did that first evening,' he said suddenly. 'Really most deeply grateful. I hope that you know that?'

'Yes, I do. Thank you. I really wasn't anything. She was in no danger. Just a slip, that's all.'

'I am very much in your debt. I know that.'

'And I'm in yours. All this time here, your hospitality . . .'

'Well. One hopes that you have been happy.' He straightened up and turning his back on the sea started to walk slowly up the lawns to the house.

'Tremendously happy, thank you. And our transport arrives tomorrow. In Nice.'

'Transport?'

'My uncle. Arrives tomorrow.'

'Ah yes, of course. End of the holidays, what? I rather fear you have been a bit stuck with the Dodos here. Not, what's the word I mean? Swinging.'

'Dodos are extinct, aren't they? No one is here.'

'Well, we're *almost* extinct. Some people are frightfully chuffed; can't wait. The frivolous, aristocratic parasites, off with their heads. I am certain that you must be very familiar with the rhetoric.'

'I don't know much about all that. Not my song. But I do know one thing for sure, you're the only real grownups I have ever met in my life.'

Archie Charlie laughed: a soft sound like a deer

323

coughing. 'Not absolutely sure how to take that.'

'You aren't old, or young. Just there. In the middle. Firm. Sure. Precise. Knowing. Laid back, grown up.'

'I really don't think it is quite as simple as that: you make it sound very pleasant. But I'm not certain you are right. Wish it was.'

'I have never been as happy anywhere in my life as I have been in this house.'

'Thank you.'

'And I have never learned so much.'

Archie Charlie turned, a half smile. 'Learned! What on earth have you learned here?'

'It would sound pretty silly if I tried to tell you. It was rather as if I had joined a relay race, do you follow? And that you had offered me a baton to run with . . . and I'm running.'

'You did not learn from "lectures", I trust.'

'No. From example.'

Archie Charlie coughed. Two soft barks.

'Have we really got anything left that is of use to you today? I really can't believe so. We are members of a dying tribe. There is no place for us in the new society, like the Amazon Indians. I am an historian, so I know the pattern of history, and the shape it takes, rather like a great, slow, deep-cutting river, wearing its course down through the stratum of time. We, and the things which we stand for, are now on the river's edge, on the bank, waiting to be swept up and carried away until not a speck remains. I don't honestly think that Cuckoo and I will mind too much when the moment comes. We are old now, we are also childless, we have had a pleasant life: not excessive, not too little, and it has lasted a fairly long time, and after we go there won't be a trace left of who we were, or what was. That, perhaps, is the only wistful thing about it all.' The soft laugh again, sniffing his brandy glass. 'On the other hand, I don't suppose that there will be anyone about who

324

cares much. This'll be blocks of flats by then. Sodium lamps instead of parasol pines, tennis courts where Cuckoo tends her broccoli and beans, car parks where the Triton blows his shell. But there you are. It's the historical pattern, time manoeuvring itself, bringing the bottom to the top and the top down to the bottom. The river surges up every so often, bites into its course, sets off again, getting narrower and meaner. But inexorable.' He smiled. 'However, if you think that you have learned anything here, I'm happy. If you feel, as you say, that you have been offered a baton and taken up the race, then I am doubly pleased. But I must just warn you that you are running with valueless currency. You have to know that. It won't buy you half a loaf in the brave new ideological world you are inheriting. Mark my words.'

'I shan't leave the race.'

'That's your affair. Good luck. And, by the way, none of this on the terrace. Cuckoo would upbraid me for being negative again, which, I suppose, I am.' He turned and put his hand lightly on Marcus's arm. 'When you leave, whenever that may be, be gentle at the parting. She's going to miss you exceedingly, I fear.' With a fleeting smile, swift as a blink, he went on towards the steps.

Cuckoo, seeing them approach, raised one arm, bracelets sparkled. 'You've been ages! We are quite bereft. Leni thinks a little music perhaps? A good idea? So still . . .'

'As you like,' said Archie Charlie. 'What shall it be?'

'No Mozart this evening.' she said. 'So many fiddles; and I really never could abide a fiddler. Play the Franck in D Minor, that's my mood: romantic, haunting.' The lips were smiling; the eyes were filled with shadow.

His cigarette had grown a caterpillar of grey ash which he let spill on to the red tiles beside him: stubbed the butt against the shutters, pressed it into the tangle of bougain-villaea framing the windows.

No; that's what it was. He was 'saying it' all right. No doubt about that. Looking back on it now it's as clear as clear. I was a little bewildered down there with him, but I can see it all perfectly now. 'The little things which other people overlook.' Almost an implied threat, you might say. Keep off, young man. I know. You fancy my wife.

Perfectly potty.

You can't stop people looking at each other, or *how* they look at each other, can you? Any rules against that? I don't know exactly how I look at her: with pleasure, that is certain . . . and happiness. Is that bad?

I suppose that I've got to admit that she looks at me in a different way. I've seen it sometimes when I have turned suddenly and caught her unaware. It's terrific. Clear, wide, very calm. Brimming. Makes me want to laugh aloud with delight; sometimes I *have* laughed. And she joins me, and we've said nothing. But I'd just like to take her in my arms and swing her round and round, like we did as children . . . just to hug her to me, all laughing. To hold her.

That's all. Nothing wrong in that; is there?

He hunched forward looking through the balcony railings. Across the dark water the sapphire light of an ambulance winked urgently along the coast road to Nice. Turned at the point, was lost.

Except it seems to worry him. Archie Charlie. All that heavy-breathing stuff about age, Dodos . . . making everything sound ugly. I mean, that's desolate! That's really negative: and then saying that the 'baton' was valueless currency. He didn't know I meant that I'd taken it from Cuckoo. Not him . . . and that it isn't valueless; I know it, and so does she and the hell with him; I'm running, I'll stick the race.

'Be gentle at the parting,' he said. Come on now! What does he think I'll do, for Pete's sake? Run amok, have hysterics, clobber the staff. What?

I'll be gentle. I know that far better than he does . . . and I know that it's time to go now. Time to leave: you get a sort of feeling; it all starts spilling out a little faster every day. Feel the emptiness coming up behind you. You've got to go.

He got up, pulled the shutters close, felt his way across to his bed, cracked his foot against cool brass, eased himself on to crumpled sheets, reached out a hand and touched Leni's shoulder. She murmured, turned towards him, sighed. Was still; soft breathing. He looked up into the dark. Time to go. And tomorrow old Desmond again. Nice to see him. I feel quite glad; no, *really* glad. Lot to tell him. He'll have a lot to tell me. Wonder what the 'surprise I'm bringing with me' can be? Never can tell with Des. A pound of Walls' sausages, maybe the Range Rover he wanted; grown a moustache? It could be anything.

It was very tall, extremely elegant in pleated honey silk, over forty, with legs as long and slender as the prongs of a tuning fork. She moved slowly towards them across the Negresco terrace with over-studied cool; hand lightly on hip, the other resting at her throat amidst a tumble of gold chains, arm a-glitter with chain bracelets, twenty rings to her fingers.

Desmond rose, pulled out a chair. 'Bea Huntlee,' he said. 'Of Huntlee and Palmers, you know?'

'Not the Reading Huntleys: I'm not biscuits,' she said, sitting with extreme grace. 'Portobello. Interior Decorators. Inching, with *wild* abandon, towards Sloane Street. And you,' she said turning slowly to Marcus and fixing him with enormous brown eyes 'are divine!' He blushed, dropped an olive. 'We've never met? And I've worked with Desmond, in the trade as it were, for donkey's years, but better late than never.' She peered across the table, moved aside a bottle of Perrier. And who is that hiding its light under a bushel of Hungarian cross-stitch?'

'It's mine,' said Marcus, recovering. 'Leni Minx.'

'We've met!' said Bea with conviction. 'Certain of it. Bell rings.'

'I don't think so,' said Leni, her voice fuzzed with awe. 'I come from Germany.'

'Well, so what? I'm neither allergic nor nationalistic, and I've an amazing memory for faces. I *know* we've met, or I've seen you, and I do wish that you'd stop crouching there in your chair as if the gates of hell were about to open just behind me. I'm really amazingly simple: the maquillage is a "front" to hide my natural terror. Face comes out of a bottle: several: eyelashes are fur, the hair is a switch, and dyed at that. It's not black at all. Mouse. Feel better? I'm a *total* fake, which is why you have had to wait such hours for my over-rehearsed entrance, and why I move very carefully, as if I might put my back out. It's not the back: I just could fall apart at the seams with fright.' Suddenly she leant towards Leni, lowered her voice. 'And Miss Minx, if you are dazzled by the vulgar display of gold which you see before you, so you should be. It's worth a small fortune; which is why I can't insure it, and why I have to wear it all. All at once. It weighs a ton and ruins the dress. Givenchy would strike me dead. But what . . .' she said with a sigh, 'is a tart to do?'

Leni laughed suddenly. Which relieved Desmond greatly. He knew Bea's performance off by heart; he also knew the effect that it could have on some people, especially women, who resented it or were irritated by it, overlooking, as they did, the fact that the directness and boldness of her attack concealed a quaking heart and a deep sense of inadequacy. Although Beatrice Huntlee had made a wild success of all her business ventures her emotional life was a series of charred ruins dotted along the rocky path of her life. The sort of disaster score she held made a woman extremely unhappy and uncertain, Desmond knew. And he forgave her all the bombast because he enjoyed, enormously, her company, her wisdom, and her shrewdness.

'Of course she's running herself into the ground with sledge hammers,' he said mildly. 'What you may not know is that she is a fantastic cook, can scrub a floor with the best of them, change a tyre, and drive like a feller. We had a fantastic trip down,' he said, turning to Marcus, 'fantastic. She did the first leg, I did the second, and so on. Avignon last night for dinner, not bad. Nice today for lunch.'

Bea chose a thin cigar from a box and lit it. 'And the car was but *loaded*. I was certain the springs would go on the Abbeville-Paris bit, the pavé. Crammed with tinsel junk for a client of mine who had built herself a perfectly ghastly palazzo near Mougins; wrought-iron, plate glass, and wheelbarrows full of petunias. Know the kind? I've brought down a stack of amazing kitsch she wanted; frilly glass and terracotta shepherdesses. That's why we're here. Des thought it would be fun.'

'I said, dump it all in the car, cheaper than Pickfords, drive it down ourselves, couple of days on the Coast, some good grub, good wine, pick up the children and get back.' Desmond finished his vodka, picked out the lemon ring and ate it.

'The children,' said Marcus. 'That's us, I gather?'

'That's you,' said Desmond with a grin. 'And it's about time you got back to work, don't you think? Three weeks in the flesh pots, I gather from your cards.'

'Yes,' said Marcus. 'It's time.'

'Finished my drink,' Desmond, getting to his feet. 'Let's go to the bar, Marcus, a couple of things I'd like to talk about before dinner. You'll forgive us?' he said to Bea and Leni. 'Not confidential, just boring. I'll send you replenishments?' But they declined, and he led Marcus into the high-domed lobby.

'Overpowering?' said Marcus.

'Not really.' Desmond straightened his tie, shot his cuffs. 'Known her for aeons, though you must have met? She said not anyway. I've done a lot of work with her firm. She's got extraordinary taste and imagination, but not in her choice of gentlemen. Alone now; the Palmer part of the business hopped it with the till one day. She's making a small fortune buying hopeless houses in Battersea and Kentish Town, painting everything white and trailing something green over them. I mean, that's what *she* says. It's tougher than that. She's got a weird clientele. Racing drivers, film stars, Arabs, TV personalities, whatever they may be, and Pop Singers with sauna baths on Kingston Hill..'

'Married?' said Marcus.

'Was. Came unstuck. He shacked up with the best man. Embarrassing. But she bears no grudge. Said the best man was the prettiest of the pair anyway. Great girl.'

They turned into the bar.

'Serious?' asked Marcus. 'I mean you?'

Desmond ran a finger worriedly round the collar of his shirt. 'Well: as a matter of fact, may sound a bit loopy to you, but yes. That's the surprise I mentioned in my card, remember? I sort of, whatdoyercallit . . . pressed my suit and she accepted. Fact is, I've banged on for a hell of a long time on my own. It's a pretty lonely life; I'd quite like to hang up my hat so to speak. She's willing. Got a bit of a shock when I first sugggested it but she's come round now. It's all on: Registrar's Office: nothing silly at our ages. Wanted you to know first though. You don't think I'm daft, do you? Lost a slate?'

'I think it's super. Terrific. Great, Des, really.'

Desmond smiled nervously. Picked up his empty glass.

'Good. That's a relief. As a matter of fact I think it's pretty terrific myself. Same again?'

On the terrace Bea refilled her glass with Perrier, chose a

pistachio nut.

'Does it all come out of a bottle?' said Leni suddenly.

Bea turned towards her very slowly. 'What come out of a bottle?'

'Your face.'

'All. Layer by layer.'

'It's hard to do?'

'Deathly.'

'It's so beautiful.'

'Thank you. I'm as blind as a bat. Ever tried to stick on your eyelashes wearing bifocals? Amazing caper.'

'No. But could you show me how. To do your face?'

'I actually "do" houses, dear; not people.'

'It's so fantastic . . . could you?'

'So are the bones in your face. Fantastic.'

'So what could I do to look as you?'

'Patience. And follow the instructions on the labels.'

'I can never go shopping. Marcus hates to.'

'And Desmond. The one maddening fault.'

'Perhaps we could go together? There are two days, isn't it?'

Mongins, tomorrow. We could the day after, Thursday. I know that Des wants to start back at dawn, dawn my dear, on Friday. Catch the Saturday boat at Calais.'

Leni clapped her hands with pleasure. 'Could we? And my hair . . .' She pulled it distractedly. 'So dry, all sand and sea and salt.'

'And too long.'

'Too long? It's short!'

'Not short enough: crop it, like a choir boy's, with a side parting. It's total disaster as it is. You look like Grock.'

'Oh.'

'And that piece of butter muslin to which you seem so deeply attached.'

Leni stroked a little puff sleeve, anxiously. 'My blouse. It is Hungarian. Hand-made.'

'Precisely what it looks like.'

'And you don't like?'

'Deadly. We can do better than that, and with your bones, and those eyes. I mean, no one is actually forcing you to dress at Oxfam, are they?'

There was not the least shred of malice in Bea Huntlee's voice or in her manner, which was instantly apparent to Leni, whose antennae swept anxiously about seeking any form of disparagement of discouragement. As she had resolutely decided that from now on, whatever happened, Leni Minx was who she was going to be, without the least shadow of a doubt, and that Luise was to be utterly banished, she had made up her mind to complete the portrait which she had started, and almost abandoned during these last three weeks, so that it could be fixed for good and framed. She would need help. In the distant past, a past she remembered only in faint glimmers now, Mr Seeger had 'invented' her; from rabbit jacket to white Nō make-up. She would require advice again, and Bea Huntlee, with her extravagance and experience must surely be the person. In fairness, the awful blouse was a quick buy for a hitch-hiking trip, the sun had coloured and polished her face so that it looked like a schoolboy's apple, and her hair had grown ragged and unkempt. But no one had seemed to mind at the villa, and during the picnic, having made a special effort, she had felt perfectly acceptable. Now that she was to be Leni Minx for ever she wanted a fixed style. She knew what, but not precisely how. She wanted the shell she was about to inherit to contain her perfectly: and identifiably.

'I know that you only "do" houses. But I would be so happy if you could do it to me. Is it so different?'

Bea half closed her eyes, her head on one side. Regarded the scrubbed, shining, determined face before her. 'No,' she said at last. 'No. As long as the structure is sound. You mean a complete transformation job?'

'I know what I *want*,' said Leni. 'If you would tell me how to do it.'

'Thursday then,' said Bea. 'Give me time to polish up my fairy wand.'

In the bar, Marcus sat making vague geometric shapes on the table with ten peanuts.

'What do you think then?' asked Desmond. 'An idea?'

'I'm a bit winded. It's a terrific idea.'

Fact is, I'm having to do too much. And now I've got to consider Bea. I want to be with her, promised her that, ease out of things gently. Start a life together, make it work. Really work for us. So much travel gets me down now. And I *can* delegate; never been one of those idiots who won't delegate; essential to the well-being of the Firm. Spread the responsibility. Of course I'd still be Boss. Very much so. But if you thought you could do it, and I think that you could, it would give you an incentive and a future, take a weight off my shoulders – I'm sixty-five this year, you know, grisly thought – and add to your budget a good deal. And who knows? In time, if you wanted to, you could take the whole shebang over more or less and let me clear off with Bea and my fishing rods. That's what I'd really like. What say?'

Marcus looked up slowly. 'Remember that day, all that time ago, in the Café Positano, egg-and-bacon sandwiches: you gave me pocket money? To buy toothpaste, and soap, you said? Remember?'

Desmond nodded, lips pursed. 'Well then?'

'That's what I say now. What I said then. Thanks. Thanks. Des.'

'That'll do. Good. I'm glad.'

'And, by the way, won't go into it now, but Gus Bender's out. Finished.'

'He is?'

'No. *I* am. Never again, that was a long time ago. When I was a kid.'

'Glad to hear it. You really wouldn't have the time anyway, not now. And it wouldn't be – fitting. Tell me all about it later. Can't leave the doxies sitting out there much longer, just wanted to get your reaction before I went any further. Shall I tell them at dinner? You wouldn't mind? How about Leni?'

'She'll flip.'

'Still happy, you two? Holidays can bugger up a relationship, I know.'

'No. A lot to tell you one day. But we're through the maze. She's mine all right.'

'Well, that's nice. Now then . . .' He looked at his watch, called for the barman, sorted out his money. 'Booked a table at Le Casbah, marvellous couscous. We ought to be off in a moment. You like couscous?'

'Never had it.'

'Must try everything; once.'

'And we leave Friday morning?'

'I'd like to, Saturday boat. Sunday to sort things out, Monday a big sale up in Harrogate. Art Deco stuff, might be junk, but can't afford to risk it.'

'So it'll be dinner Thursday night at the villa. She's very anxious, Cuckoo, longs to meet you, and if you're in Mougins all day tomorrow . . .'

'Well, it's very kind,' Desmond had put the invitation which Cuckoo sent by Marcus into his wallet. 'All right if you accept for me? I don't have to write, do I?'

'No. No, I'll say. Thursday evening? She said come about six-thirty. Swim first if you like, but I know you.'

'No swimming thanks. Six-thirty is fine. We ought to make it an earlyish night . . . sparrow-fart on Friday; like to get to Barbizon that night.'

'Christ!' said Marcus almost to himself. 'Christ! It's all suddenly coming to an end, just like this.'

Cuckoo's room was, apparently, empty. Bruna closed the

334

door quietly, carried a flat basket of ironing to the chest by the windows.

'Bruna?' Cuckoo from the day-room.

'Yes. Me. Your ironing and the menus.'

'I'm in here. Putting my feet up. Terribly hot. Like July.' She lay, amidst a flurry of lace and broderie Anglaise, on a chaise-longue, a small table beside her; one rose in a fluted vase and a silently ticking travelling clock.

'The menus,' said Bruna, handing them to her.

'You are kind. You write so prettily. And that lovely violet ink.' She looked at the small cards. ' "Filet de Daurade Royale froid, avec un sabayon de langoustine". It sounds good, doesn't it. But Thursday. I mean the daurade? Really fresh?'

'From the sea as I looked,' said Bruna and went into the bedroom to put the ironing away.

'And "Noisette d'agneau à l'estragon". Well. That's all right. And so on – and the date at the bottom. Perfect.'

'Why a menu for six people I can't imagine,' called Bruna. 'We never do. Only for twelve or over.'

'Souvenirs. That's what. For the children. It's Last Night.'

Bruna was pulling drawers. 'The house is suddenly like a tomb: thank God. No one breathing. Such peace. Oh là là!'

Cuckoo covered her eyes with her hand swiftly. Let it drop. 'What about Fanny and Maria, did you mention what we spoke about?'

'Leaving next Saturday. A fortnight's wages; it's all "liquid" anyway. Maria talks through a hole in her head but my God! She can iron like the seraphim. You'll miss that.'

'I thought we might ask her to stay on.'

'For the ironing? I'm not so bad, am I?'

'No, not for that. Just to help out.'

'I don't need helping out, not when the house is empty.'

'You may,' said Cuckoo evenly.

Bruna, hand to a cupboard door, closing it, froze. Shut her eyes. 'As you like,' she called, shut the cupboard door.

'You've been wonderfully kind and good, Bruna dear. Worked so hard. The picnic, the young people, Princess Minerva . . . and so much more. I do thank you.'

'No need. Duty is duty. I'm not senile. Yet. If it made you happy . . .' she slammed a drawer shut to stop her hand shaking.

'It made me wonderfully happy. Except for one tiny thing.'

Bruna stood perfectly still in the centre of the bedroom, looked up at the ceiling. Cuckoo was silent.

'Which was what?' said Bruna, picking up the empty basket.

'Oh, a silly thing. But apparently it hurt terribly.'

Bruna came to the day-room, a frown of concern on her face. 'I did this?'

'Yes. You.'

'To you? Never!'

'No. Not to me.'

'You'd better say. I don't understand when you speak in riddles.'

'The time the young people went up to the hills for a picnic. It was then.'

'They went to the hills often. Many times. I cut the sandwiches, I should know.'

'Once there was a memorial; to the Resistance.'

Bruna tapped the basket against her knee. 'There are many in the hills. Everywhere.'

'I think that this one was chosen particularly. By you.'

'Chosen?'

'Well . . . you suggested the place to them. Marked it carefully on his map. You knew it was there, you knew she was German. Do you see?'

'You think this was deliberate? They said that to you?'
Her indignation was strong but uneasy, she looked beyond
Cuckoo to the sea.

'They didn't *say* at all. Just that it was there and that it
had made her deeply unhappy. She thinks that you hate
her because she is German.'

'So?' Bruna stared steadily at the sea.

'You don't do you? Surely not?'

'No.' She lowered her eyes, buttoned and unbuttoned
the neck of her pinafore. 'No. I don't hate. Not now. After
forty years. Not *hate*. Not *hate*. She's a child. But I don't
see any harm in reminding her what they did. They forget.'

'But she had nothing to remember! She wasn't even
born! She knows exactly what they did . . . all. She is
bitterly, bitterly aware of what was done. They are a new
generation, Bruna, they asked questions and were appalled
by the answers. She can't be held responsible for the errors
of her parents: she had to have the chance to carry her life
without guilt. Don't you see?'

Bruna tucked the basket under her arm. 'She carries the
seed. They all do. They won't change.'

'They won't change if we don't help them to.'

'They should bear the guilt. Why not? We bear the grief
of the deaths they caused, don't we? Has she ever noticed
how many women are still in mourning in this country?
Forty and even sixty years later.'

'But she's a child. She's twenty. The same age as you
were then, exactly, with the same hopes, the same dreams,
the same despairs. There is no point, or justice, in
reminding her of something which she didn't do. And for
which, anyway, she wasn't responsible. I mean, you must
see that, dearest Bruna?'

'I suppose . . .' She shrugged, rubbed the side of her
face.

'I know you don't *hate*, you couldn't. Be an angel, will
you, and tell her this? Before she goes tomorrow?'

337

Bruna looked at Cuckoo in disbelief. 'To apologize? Is that it?'

'It would be kind. She's sure you hate her. Could you just say that it was unintentional? Before they leave. For my sake?'

Bruna looked at a thin hand plucking vaguely at a ribbon, the menu which had scattered to the floor, the thin net of perspiration running along the fading hairline.

'May I sit?' she said.

'Bruna dear! Of course, sit, sit. You look so severe standing there; like a hat stand.'

Bruna sat slowly, upright, hands folded together, basket leaning against the chair at her side. 'The boy pulled you out. Didn't he?'

Cuckoo turned away quickly, hands to her face, looked through the open windows to the sea; flinched, turned her head and stared up into the branches of the parasol pine. From light years ago, Archie's voice: 'A damned fine totem pole at the edge of the lawn.' Scrumptious! My scrumptious. How idiotic. To go shrimping. Without the net.

'Are you bargaining?' she said quietly.

Bruna's hands closed into fists. 'Yes. If you like.'

'I don't.'

'But he did?'

'Yes. He did.'

'It was not a slip, a little fall?'

'No. Not. Deliberate. I tried.'

Bruna gave a cry of smothered pain, her hands to her mouth. 'Ma belle! Oh, ma belle!'

'You asked,' said Cuckoo wearily.

'But why? Tell me why, I who love you so.'

'I'm unwell.'

'How? You know?'

'Only too well.' Cuckoo suddenly laughed. 'What

338

nonsense. *Too* well. *Un*well. Such a difference.'

'It is grave?'

'Irreversible.'

'Pain?' Poker stiff now, eyes clear, hands folded.

'No. No pain. Isn't that good? I don't think there will be. Which is a blessing. Just a slow, what can I say? A slow wearying, fading. It's leukaemia. Simple as that.'

'But what will you do?'

'Do?' Cuckoo shook her head wistfully at the absurdity of it. 'Die,' she said. 'That's what I'll do.'

'And Sircharles?' She pronounced the words as one.

'Doesn't know. Yet. But is guessing; he suspects something, I think; old age, I rather imagine . . . senility. Which is maddening because he'll fuss me. No one knows except you: and the specialist.'

'There is no doubt?'

'None. That's why I went to London. Not for Harriet's wedding bash. No. It's certain.'

'Well.' Bruna brusquely arranged the stiff blue pinafore over her knees. 'I'm glad I know. I knew anyway; the moment the boy brought you here, that evening. I'm not a fool. Now that we know where we are we can get on with things, can't we?'

'Nanny Peverill! Remember her? Such a long time ago; such a comfort. You sound just like her. Very un-Italian. No sobs and wails.'

'Very un-English to do what you did' To walk into the sea. No courage.'

'Perfectly right. None. I apologize. I'd reached the finish, I thought. Then he grabbed me, held me up. He was so amazingly strong, alive, young, I could feel the force pouring through me.' She flicked a ribbon over her shoulder. 'My first transfusion. And when they both arrived the house suddenly became alive again; this Pompeii of a place. There was a wondrous surge of youth and life. We haven't had that here for years, apart from

339

the picnics. It would have been idiotic to let all that go, do admit?'

For a moment Bruna's eyes were strangely bright, her lips firm. Then she buried her face in her hands. No sound; her knuckles white.

'Dearest Bruna! Don't!' Cuckoo got up and went to her. A light hand on the shaking shoulders. 'My dear! I'm not going to keel over tomorrow, or drag myself from room to room like "Camille". It's progressive. We'll have to see how it goes, and you've brought it all on your own head, my dearest, all your fault. Tricking me into saying it like that. Utterly foul and underhand. But I'm very grateful that you have. Whooooo!' She spread her arms wide. 'Oh! The relief! To have *told* you, to share! Now then. I have kept my side of your disgraceful bargain and you must promise me to keep yours, you will?'

Bruna pulled up a strand of her hair which had slipped from its fastening. 'Before God. This evening. When she gets back from town; she's gone shopping.'

'The boy too?'

'No, he didn't. He's down at the pool or somewhere: I don't know.'

'There is one other thing, very important, I want to say to you. When the time comes, don't let Archie fuss me into some ghastly clinic. I don't know how you are going to stop him, but you must. I won't prolong anything which I find to be unbearable, ugly, distressing or undignified. I'll make sure of that; and when that moment comes I want to to be alone with you, here, in this room, at this window, looking at this sky. Just us? Do you understand me?'

Bruna didn't trust her voice, so she nodded. After a time she cleared her throat. 'Ah, ma belle! I wish, oh! how I wish . . .'

Cuckoo stopped her with a swift raising of an arm from a billow of ruffles. 'Bruna dear! If wishes were horses beggars could ride,' she said.

He was sitting at the far end of the pool, a book propped up against his knees, among the tumbled blocks and capitals. She stood under the Albertine arch, a half hoop of dead blossoms rather like, she thought, dirty handkerchiefs. Starting down the steps, calling to him as she went, seeing him look up and lift a hand in welcome, she took a deep breath. Strange how one really *does* do that before something unpleasant: like cleaning up dogs' messes, washing a hundred pots and pans; telling a lie . . .

'Alone we are! Deserted? How odd!'

'Well, Leni's gone to have her hair done. Or something. terribly secret. She's in a great state, hatched some plot with Uncle Desmond's doxy.'

'Doxy? Surely not?' She laughed and sat on a block beside him.

'Something like. Probably going to dye it green, I wouldn't wonder.'

'What are you reading? You are almost at the end.'

'*Persuasion.* I promised Archie Charlie to get it finished before I left. But there won't be time for "questions and answers". And I liked that.' He closed the book, laid it aside. 'Also I wanted to just be here, alone. I love this place.'

'I'm interrupting!'

'Oh God! No! Never. It's just last-day nostalgia. You know. Trying to burn it into my brain so I'll always remember, every stone, crack in the stone, every bud on the Morning Glories, all of it. These tumbled columns. Mars over there, the pillars, it's all a bit like Pompeii, isn't it?'

Oh, how marvellous, she thought, an oar thrown to help me steer my course.

'Pompeii! I was just talking to Bruna about that: how odd. You've never been there though?'

'No. Never. Pictures. A movie. Read about it.'

'I always think that this house is a bit like Pompeii,' she said. 'Can you possibly imagine what I mean?'

'No. Frankly. Pompeii is dead, isn't it? Ruins?'

'Wasn't; it was once tremendously alive, gay, rather wicked, bursting with life: all sitting under that awful looming Vesuvius, everyone quite unaware. Terribly like this place; strange analogy but I think it fits. It was marvellously jolly and bustling here once. Years ago. Archie and I were the golden beauties, he was wildly handsome, can you believe? The house was crammed with youth. Although some of our friends *were* just a little older than we were: a fatal mistake. They die off so much sooner. But they were rather exceptional creatures, which made life very particular and invigorating.' She looked at him with an apologetic smile. 'Names I fear you may not think were real. Jean Cocteau? Zelda and Scott Fitzgerald? Gerald and Sara Murphy, they lived at Cap d'Antibes and practically *invented* the Riviera; then Cole Porter who had a rather tiresome wife, and Minerva of course, Etienne de Beaumont and oh! crowds of others. We read and played music, painted, and argued and danced, and drank a very great deal. It was all tremendously fast. I mean *hurrying*. As if we all knew that it was going to end suddenly and that we had to gobble up every single lovely crumb before they took away the feast. Which of course they did: in 1939, and never brought it back. Nothing was ever the same again.'

She looked across towards the Albertine arch, the still pines shadow-barring the long lawns. 'Oh! The voices in this garden. The war split us up. Archie marched off to Cairo to be brilliant in the Secret Service, I tore off to England and fitted gas-masks and learned about splints and hot sweet tea for shock and all that – and had the most marvellous time with my Officers. The Americans were so attractive! Those marvellous trousers we used to call "pinks". Such a terrific time. Bomb parties at the

Dorchester with monstrous Emerald Cunard who always collected fascinating people round her . . . parties all the time and lots and lots of people to invite to them. Of course,' she traced the outline of her bare foot on the hot stone, 'many of the people didn't always come back. Especially the ones in the RAF; it wasn't all joy. Of course not. But one was young, one seemed to heal then. It's harder now. And it's all gone. Archie and I, and beloved Minna; that's about all of our set who remain.'

She knew she was talking far too much and too fast, but he hadn't interrupted her, smiling in quiet disbelief almost.

'Oh, I know you don't believe me,' she said cheerfully. 'It's all so improbable now; life then was so different. I'm only telling you all this utter trivia because when you said "Pompeii" I was reminded.'

'And how is it like Pompeii? I mean perhaps it was, I see that. But now? Surely not? Where was the volcano? You mean it was the war?'

'Oh no! Not the war. Age. After the war we struggled on for a bit. Archie and I came down here to live when his father died. It was quite fun. The older chums had peeled off, died. Our contemporaries were fairly amusing. But it wasn't the same. And then quite suddenly, almost before one was really aware of it, we were middle-aged: and then we were old. The ashes had started to fall. It was a very quiet volcano, but equally devastating.'

He looked across the turquoise water. 'I really meant that all this, the pool, looked like Pompeii . . . not the villa.'

'This wasn't here in the early days . . . we used to bathe down at the flat rock.' She stopped. He had turned and was looking at her steadily. 'Where we "met". The old picnic place. This is all post-war. We weren't really very grand in those lovely years: our pleasures were much simpler. A hamper of delicious wine, a portable gramophone. "conversations" above all. Picnics in the

343

hills. But now: well, all the real friends are dead, the contemporaries dreary, you saw most of them at the picnic. Dusty, ageing, rutted. Stuck. And "family", my family, is deathly. And anyway they all prefer Cornwall or Scotland. Can you believe it?'

'Hard to.'

He's going to ask me why. I know that. This is his last chance. He's trying to phrase the question. Hurry on, deflect him if you can. Mad to come down here. Mad. But I couldn't not. Couldn't not.

'So now, you see, it's Villa Pompeii. It all looks divine in the sun, so does the real place; lizards run about, the flowers and trees flourish again, the fountains run. But in the shadows, if you listen, you can hear the lurking sounds of weeping . . .'

He looked at her from lowered lids. 'No laughter? Don't you hear laughter as well?'

'Not much. The laughter was so much earlier, the ash smothered it.'

'But *we've* laughed?' Almost a murmur.

'Oh yes! Of course! That's what's been so marvellous, why I've been so happy again. And my beloved Minna was here as well, and she always makes me full of joy: we don't see each other often, but she is always the same. The sort of American they used to be. Strong, brave, funny, alive, tough and principled. She hated the changes which came, so she just stayed where she was, in the forties. Deep Frozen. Very wise. She's managed to avoid most of the distresses that way. "With Blondie and Dagwood in the White House, there's no place for me in America," she said. So she'll stick it out in Tuscany. And I'll stick it out here . . . with Archie entombed almost permanently in his Museum place, dear Bruna banging on about how she hates the Huns; she's so *boring* about that. I can't play Bridge so I'll get on with weeding my onions, you see?'

'Very suburban.'

'Utterly. I loathe it. Just before, well, just before we "met" I'd been in London. It was such fun! I adored it all; parties, invitations, so much to do. It was the most awful anti-climax coming back here. I mean, you do see?'

'Well, I couldn't see for *me*, if you follow? But I suppose I see for you. I didn't know that you hated it so here. I didn't know that. Even feel it.' He couldn't look at her.

She shrugged, shook her head, fixed the velvet bow in her hair. 'Oh, I don't absolutely hate it. Not so vehement. I just get desperately depressed sometimes. I feel buried. Do you know?'

'Yes. Is that why . . .?' He picked up Jane Austen, wiped imaginary dust from the cover.

Here it comes, she thought, help him with it, God knows you've been showering him with false clues.

'Is that why what?'

He looked up uncomfortably. 'I shouldn't ask. The shrimping thing? You said. Do you remember? Without the net? Is that why?'

'I'm afraid so. Wasn't it frightful? Just became completely dotty with depression. I think I told you at the time. A little mental aberration. That's really all . . . but I'll never attempt that again. Such an idiotic thing to try and do.'

He was looking at his knees, pulling a thread from the seam of his jeans. 'I thought it was . . . something more.'

'No,' she said briskly. 'Nothing more. Sheer, stinking self-pity. That's all. And when you all leave, which will be beastly, I think I will too. Off on a little trip, just on my own. There are lots of places I haven't been to. I *must* be a bit more enterprising, don't you think? Adventurous? San Francisco, Peking, Oslo . . .'

'If it would be fun.'

'I think perhaps. But we are still conspirators, remember, you'll never, never say, will you, about not slipping? It would be so dreadfully hurtful to everyone.'

'Absolutely.'

She got to her feet, tucked up the cuffs of her shirt. 'Now then: after that dire confession, of which I am thoroughly ashamed, I must go and get on with things. I do rather long to meet Uncle Desmond tonight, we must turn him loose in Archie's Museum place, mustn't we? All those bits and pieces; he'll be fascinated. You've got an early start in the morning?'

'Car's coming at seven. I've packed nearly everything. Leni wants me out of the room when she gets back. I don't know why. This dotty hair business or whatever.'

'Well, look here: I suggest this.' She had moved to the edge of the pool and stood looking up to the top of the steps, shielding her eyes. 'I'll stay abed in the morning. Far too early for me and I'm like Minna: I simply loathe farewells. So we'll just go off as we usually do, at the end of every evening, don't you agree? I mean, do admit, "Goodnight" is far less final than "Goodbye".'

'I'll tell Leni.'

'Yes, do. Much, much wiser.' She had started towards the steps. 'Tea, in fifteen minutes.'

That was what you might call a little piece of 'invented' life to help get one through the real. The real life is so terribly arranged. So callous and brutal. Leni should have been here to see how well I did it. On the other hand, perhaps not. She pulled herself discreetly up the steps, one hand on the iron rail, the other in the pocket of her skirt. Halfway up she stopped and looked back. He was watching.

'This boring old Albertine. All dead. One blossom left. So untidy. Coming up?'

He raised the book above his head. 'Four pages to finish. I might as well.'

'I'd finish them if I were you. You never know. There might be a surprise at the end. Who can tell?' She turned and walked away down the lawn, tried to whistle, but her lips were dry.

For a moment he sat with the book balanced on his knees. I know how it ends. No point in going on, I know: she made a super effort, but I know. Lied, all the way. Lies. I could tell. Could tell. No light in her eyes, no light. Dark, dark, dark. What she was telling me, is that after tonight I shall never see her again.

On the terrace the Laurent Perrier chilled in its bucket, the frog-fountain bubbled, a tumble of white roses spilled falling petals silently among the nuts and olives.

'God! I'm mad for it all. Every tiny thing. Each place you look you find something simply exquisite. It is the MOST divine house.'

Bea Huntlee followed Cuckoo to the chairs by the fountain. 'If you only knew how magical it is to see just *one* lovely thing; after months and months of burgundy axminster, quilted vinyl bars, Lowry reproductions, and acres and acres of stripped pine you'd know how I feel this evening,' she said.

'Where are these enormities to be found?' said Cuckoo, sitting in one of the cane chairs and indicating that Bea should join her, for she had taken an instant liking to the tall, weary woman at her side.

'In practically all my clients' pads,' said Bea. 'Some want a bit more "glit", or glass, but by and large it's beige for the beigeous. Or Burgundy. God!'

'You must know more about bad taste,' said Cuckoo, 'than anyone else.'

'My stock in trade,' said Bea. 'That's how I make my loot. Kitsch and glit.'

Archie had opened the wine, filling the glasses with care.

Marcus took two, carried them to the end of the terrace for Cuckoo and Bea and Archie gave one to Desmond.

'I hope it's cold enough? Do hate warm champagne.' He raised his glass. 'Your health.'

Desmond sipped his wine, looked about the terrace with content. 'All very pleasant. You've been a very lucky fellow,' he said to Marcus. 'I'd say this was paradise, frankly. It'll be a wrench to leave, won't it?'

'A wrench,' said Marcus, and took an almond quickly.

'Where's Leni then?' said Desmond. 'You mislaid her somewhere this afternoon, Bea?'

'No. She's in the house,' said Archie. 'The last time I saw her she was tearing up the stairs with her head in a plastic bag from Galléries Lafayette.'

'Good God!' said Bea' 'She hasn't smothered, has she? That wasn't the idea at all, we've spent practically all afternoon wandering about endlessly, looking for a present which she insisted that she simply had to give tonight.'

'A present?' said Cuckoo.

'Do you have a tame bear in the house by any chance?'

'No.'

'This is for someone, or something, called "Bruin".'

'Bruna!' cried Cuckoo with a clap of hands. 'My treasure! How divine! Leni did this?'

'My dear, it took hours. Hours. We finally ended up with something of such amazing horror that if your treasure isn't blind she will be by the second she claps sight on it.'

'What can it be?' said Marcus taking a glass of wine.

Bea shook a scatter of charms and fobs over her fist. 'A ten inch block of clear plastic, stuffed with dead seahorses, sequins, and shells. That's what it is. She says it'll be very useful to whoever-it-is.'

'Why?' said Cuckoo.

'Because it has a dolly little barometer on it as well. And

348

apparently the recipient will now be able to tell precisely when, or when not, to put out her washing. Logical?' Bea sipped her wine.

'That's Leni,' said Marcus. 'Logical.'

'And stubborn,' said Bea reaching for a thin cigar.

'As an ox.'

'And she knows, I may add, just exactly what she wants.'

'But, I mean, did she have enough money? I didn't have a great deal left to spread around.'

Bea dropped a spent match into an ashtray. 'My dear Marcus: she had an Army Surplus bag which literally bulged with crumpled Deutschmark notes. Throwing them around like rice at a wedding. She wasn't mean.'

'Leni? Where the heck did all *that* come from?'

'She rob a bank recently? We spent what seemed like a year in Crédit Lyonnais changing the damned stuff. She's stubborn all right.' She was about to take her glass when she stopped. 'Listen!' she said, a finger high in warning. 'Hark! Is that singing I hear? Or frogs?'

There was a silence on the terrace. From far away, as if from some open window in the house above them, a small voice drifted into the still air.

'Singing!' said Desmond. 'Oh! I know that song! What's its name? From years ago?'

'Well listen,' said Bea. 'Don't chunter on.'

'Got it,' said Cuckoo after a few moments. 'I know. Of course! It's that song you and she sang together that first evening, remember, Archie dear? Lilian Harvey?'

' "Congress Dances"! That's it!' said Desmond. Goodness me, yes. That takes me back; donkey's years. Lilian Harvey! Went to see it five times, absolutely besotted by her. Glorious creature. "Just Once for All Time". That's it!'

The singing had stopped. Archie sat down slowly on the terrace steps. 'We sang a little duet, didn't we? She in

German, me in English . . .' He started to hum softly. 'Dee de de dum dum, Dee de de dum dum, dum dum, dum dum . . . I think it goes:

> "Just once for all time
> Does good luck greet you
> And lead you on
> To paradise . . ." '

Desmond grinned at Marcus. '*Exactly* what I said just now, didn't I? Same thing? Paradise, eh? Luck greeted you all right.'

Marcus looked directly across at Cuckoo. She was smiling, eyes wide, very clear.

'Just once. For all time,' she said, and looked away.

Bea fiddled among her several chains, found a small gold pocket watch and snapped it open. 'Marcus dear? Seven-fifteen exactly.'

'So?'

'So it's time you went to collect Leni. She said to. I was charged precisely. Seven-fifteen, not a second later.'

He placed his glass on the round table. 'Now, why have I got to go and collect her? She knows the place like the back of her hand.'

'I'm failing in my duty,' said Bea. 'We both are . . .'

He went out into the cool, shadowy hall, put one foot on the bottom step of the staircase. And stopped.

She was standing at the top: on the edge of darkness. Hair burnished, flat to her head, cropped close like a boy's, a severe side-parting, the airplane slide.

Immaculate. A simple short black dress, tight as a skin, long sleeves, the silver shoes, her grave oval face, white as white, not harshly so, blended, smooth, shaded, like a flower on the pale stem of her neck; green eyes sparkling, lustrous, a hint of mockery, one arm stretched towards him, fingers spread in supplication.

350

He looked up at her in amazement.

'You see?' she said quietly. 'You were wrong. A name does make a difference.'

He opened his arms wide to her.

'Fantastic!' he said.